THE SPANISH

Claire Gruzelier

Contents

Chapter One

A cold January wind wailed around the shadowy house. Beatrice huddled on the top step of the unlit staircase, chewing her bottom lip and darting uneasy glances down the hall at the half-open bedroom door.

She'd tried contacting Mum at the shop but the phone just rang and rang, then switched to voice recording. Must've left work already. But her mobile was off, so she was probably driving. No use calling Dad. He was down in London for the day. What should she do?

Suddenly she heard a key scrape in the lock. Jumping up, she peered over the banister into the gloom below. A wild gust of wind flung the front door wide open, slamming it against the wall with a crash, and in staggered a windblown figure wearing an old lilac waterproof and carrying a huge cardboard box.

"Mum! You're back," she cried. Everything'd be all right now.

Mum glanced up as Beatrice sped downstairs, her long, blond hair fanning out round her shoulders in the up draught.

"Here, Bea, give us a hand with this lot, will you?" she urged, balancing the box against the door jamb and thrusting a clutch of plastic bags into her arms. "It's the last odds and ends from Aunt Rosita's flat. I called in to pick them up on the way home."

"Mum –" began Bea urgently.

But Mum was busy heaving up the cardboard box and struggling with her back against the door to shut out the blustering gale.

"I feel like I've been blown to bits," she exclaimed, shaking the tangled, dark hair off her face. "Shall we turn on a light in here?" with a flick of the hall switch. "Boys back yet?"

Bea shook her head. "No. But, Mum –"

"Yes, dear, in a minute," interrupted Mum over the top of the cardboard box. "This carton's so heavy it's almost pulling my arms off."

She threw a glance round the narrow hall, but seeing it cluttered with the usual jumble of outdoor coats and muddy trainers, whisked straight along the passage into the kitchen. Dumping the box on the scuffed vinyl beside the vegetable rack, she turned to Bea, who'd run after her, announcing as she pulled off her jacket and tossed it over a chair, "I'm simply dying for a cup of tea. Shall we put the kettle on?" She headed for the sink, adding over her shoulder, "Perhaps you could run upstairs, Bea, and ask Jamie if he'd like a mug too. How's he feeling?"

"Mum, that's just what I've been trying to tell you," burst out Bea, dropping the plastic bags among the unwashed dishes littering the worktop. "I think his flu's got worse."

Mum wheeled round in surprise.

"Why? What's happened?"

"Well, when I came home from orchestra practice this afternoon, I stuck my head round the door to see how he was, but he seemed to be asleep. So I tiptoed out again so as not to wake him up. Just now I was starting on some History homework in my bedroom, when suddenly I heard these noises…"

"Noises?" prompted Mum, motioning her to keep up as she started back into the hall.

"Yes… like somebody shouting."

"Shouting?" Mum paused with one hand on the newel post.

"Yes. Through the wall, you know." Bea bustled her on upstairs. "So I ran in to see what the matter was – and there was Jamie sitting bolt upright in bed, all strange and wild-eyed. I asked if there was something wrong, but he just grabbed my arm and stared at me as if he didn't know who I was and mumbled something about Adam and scorpions crawling up their sleeping bags. It was really weird…"

By this time they'd reached Jamie's room at the far end of the passage. They listened for a moment, but no sound came from inside, so Mum pushed the door open. They both recoiled before the sour stench of sweat and disease.

The small room was dimly lit by the yellowish glow of the bedside lamp, from which sprang strange, elongated shadows of dusty model aeroplanes and origami birds dangling on thin wires from the ceiling. The wind moaned in the bare branches of the sycamore tree outside, rattling the window frames as though questing for entry. From the scowling face of a white Indonesian soul-mask on the wall above Jamie's desk, the empty eye sockets gaped like a death's head.

Bea hesitated in the doorway as Mum picked her way through the loose papers and dog-eared folders strewn across the floor. Side-stepping Jamie's battered guitar case, rank-smelling old overcoat and a rucksack of dirty washing, she stooped to pull away the dangling earphones.

"He hasn't touched the juice and sandwiches I brought up this morning," she noted with a quick glance at the bedside table.

She bent over the bed where Jamie lay sprawled, thin and lank, among the tumbled bedclothes. Bea crept closer, peering over Mum's shoulder at her older brother tossing restlessly to and fro in a faded old T-shirt and sweat-sodden shorts. He seemed to be fighting off the tangle of sheets, uttering low groans from between parched lips. His chest heaved with the rasp of spasmodic breathing.

Mum stared white-faced up at Bea, who hovered beside her mutely twisting and untwisting her fingers.

"But, Bea, he didn't sound ill when I rang at lunchtime. He was sitting up listening to music. Claimed he was feeling better…"

Her voice trailed away. She touched his throbbing temples and instantly started back.

"Why he's burning hot – like fire!"

Jamie opened his eyes and gazed blankly at them from far within their hollow grey depths. The pupils were stark and dilated.

"Jamie! Can you hear me?" cried Mum, sinking down on the bed. She reached out one hand to smooth back the snarls of long, fair hair clinging to his damp forehead, carefully avoiding the spiky metal bolts that seamed his brow and earlobe.

"You see, Mum," whispered Bea from a dry throat, "I told you he didn't recognise me. What's wrong with him? Why does he keep on moaning and mumbling like that?"

"Looks a lot worse than a case of flu to me," Mum murmured, raking his face with anxious eyes. "Thank goodness he had the sense to catch a train home from Exeter yesterday…" She turned to Bea. "I don't like this. He seems delirious. I'm calling an ambulance right away."

*

The wind had died down and the stormy sky was spitting rain by the time the twins arrived home. Bea, who'd been stationed by Mum at the window to watch out for them, sprang to the front door.

"Hey, what's goin' on here, Bea?" demanded Marcus, gaping at the ambulance with flashing blue lights parked in the driveway behind their old family estate. He slung down his school bag in the porch and stood scratching his curly brown head, school tie hanging crooked as usual. "An' why's that ole busybody gogglin' at us like that?"

Bea glanced in the direction of his pointing finger. The raised lace curtain at next door's bay window suddenly dropped level. Old Mrs Tibbs having an absolute field day.

Meanwhile Marcus had almost collided with a business-like paramedic who was manoeuvring the foot of a stretcher round the bend in the stairs. From the living room doorway Geoff stared at the inert figure strapped under a pale green blanket as it passed straight under his nose.

"That was Jamie, wasn't it?" he observed coolly. "Where're they taking him, Bea?"

"To hospital," she replied. "Where d'you think?"

"To hospital?" Geoff raised his eyebrows. "What for?"

"To run some tests."

"Why, what's wrong with him?" asked Marc.

"They don't know, stupid. That's why they're taking him to hospital."

"Where's Mum?" persisted Geoff.

"Going with him in the ambulance. She's just packing some things to take along."

"Hey, c'n I go too?" broke in Marc. "I've always wanted to ride in an ambulance with the siren screamin'.'"

"No, you can't." Honestly, you'd think even twelve-year-olds could show a bit more sense! "You're staying here with me. Mum's managed to contact Dad. He's on his way home from the station now."

"Is Jamie gonna die?" blurted out Marc. "He looked yellow as mouldy cheese."

"Of course not," she snapped back. "Don't be silly."

"Jus' checkin'," Marc reassured her with an amiable grin. "Keep your hair on, Bea."

"If he did," speculated Geoff, "I could keep his old microscope, couldn't I? I know it's not as good as the one I got for Christmas, but I wouldn't mind it anyway – for second best –"

"Yeah, an' I c'd have that ace book Great Aunt Rosita gave him once about the solar system," added Marcus. "He never reads it now. An' I c'd have his old football boots too."

"He's not going to die – I've told you," repeated Bea crossly. "Now here comes Mum. Don't you dare say any of this to her…"

The boys lost interest in her the moment they set eyes on Mum, labouring downstairs with a bulky overnight bag.

"I've packed his toothbrush and comb," she was muttering to herself with a furrowed brow. "Will he need more than two pairs of pyjamas?"

Geoff pounced on her at once.

"Hey, Mum. Marc says he's going to have Jamie's old football boots if he dies, but I reckon I ought to. After all, he as good as promised them to me when he went to uni in the first place –"

"That's not fair," burst out Marc. "You got that ole camera of his when Mum and Dad bought him a new one for his overseas trip. An' I on'y want Great Aunt Rosita's book. That microscope's worth lots more. I should have the boots as well."

Bea darted forward. Selfish little pigs! Couldn't they see how upset poor Mum was, without adding to it all by squabbling?

"Boys. Boys!" cried Mum, dropping the overnight bag and raising both hands in protest. "Whatever gave you the idea that Jamie's going to die? Once he gets to hospital, he'll be right as rain."

Clearly she was saying this more to reassure herself than them.

"Now, Bea," Mum turned to her in the doorway, "better start dinner now or the boys'll tear the place apart. There's a packet of mince in the fridge and a tin of tomatoes in the pantry –"

"Yes, Mum," broke in Bea. After all, she was eighteen and knew where everything was. "Don't fuss."

"Oh, where's your father?" Mum sighed, gazing anxiously round. "I thought he'd be here by now. Tell him I'll ring as soon as I know anything definite –"

At that moment there was a rattle at the back door and a tall figure appeared, shedding his rucksack and unbuckling his cycle helmet as he strode up the hall.

"Graham! At last."

Mum started towards him, her face radiating relief. Bea knew how she felt. Good, old, dependable Dad! Now he was home, everything suddenly seemed a lot less scary.

Dad nodded to the ambulance driver, who said they were ready to leave. Bending down, he picked up the overnight bag, then accompanied her and Mum down the front path, promising to remember that the boys' swimming kit was in the airing cupboard and that Marc had to finish his Physics assignment tonight without fail. He helped Mum into the back of the ambulance and, as he handed her the bag, Bea saw him squeeze her fingers as he urged her not to worry about things at home.

"No, I'm not worried now you're here," replied Mum tremulously.

"Let me know when you need a lift back."

"I'll ring you from the hospital. But it mightn't be till late."

"Doesn't matter. I'll be up."

She paused for a moment.

"Oh Graham, Jamie –"

"He'll be fine once he gets to hospital, Marisa. Now go!" With a smile of encouragement, he shut the ambulance door firmly behind her.

Bea felt safe when she saw Mum and Dad together: they rarely argued, even when they disagreed.

The twins had already run off shouting, probably to raid the fridge, and she and Dad made a dash for the house as the rain began to patter down. Dad stooped to pull off his cycle clips as they stood in the shelter of the porch watching Bob, the retired policeman from across the road, officiously clearing aside the assembled neighbours so the ambulance could reverse out of the driveway.

"D'you think Mum'll be back tonight?" she asked in a small voice.

"Yes. But you'll probably be asleep by then."

"Oh Dad, what d'you think's wrong with Jamie?"

Dad's deep voice was calm, as he reached an arm round her shoulders and gave her a comforting hug. "If I knew that, I'd be a medic not an aerospace engineer, wouldn't I? Now come inside and shut the door or we'll end up with Bob over here, enquiring into all the ins and outs of the matter. I could see he was working up to it while we were standing out by the ambulance. Your mother'll tell us the news when she rings later."

Bea shut the door, but as she turned to follow him into the kitchen, she felt a cold shiver flutter up her spine. What was going to happen to Jamie?

Chapter Two

Thank heavens I usually walk home from work, thought Elinor Mitford, as she sat biting her lip in an almost stationary queue of rush-hour traffic stretching as far back along the Newmarket Road as she could see in her rear-view mirror. Through the blackness of the night and the pelting downpour, which was finally easing to a half-hearted drizzle, reflections of bright streetlights shimmered in puddles along the roadside.

"…And now for the six o'clock news," advised the Radio Three announcer cheerfully.

That late already? Drumming her fingers on the steering wheel, she peered forward through the rain-blurred glass. How much further to this damned junction? In front of her eyes the windscreen wipers swished back and forth, sweeping the raindrops clear in two distinct fans.

More earthquakes in South America. A plane gone missing over the Bay of Bengal. Just one disaster after another… Not such a great idea to make this detour on the way home tonight…

Her mind drifted idly back over the last half hour, spent with her older sister at Fen Ditton. Cathy was busy clearing up after a children's party when she called in to drop off her niece's sixth birthday present – a pair of gilded hair clips from the gift shop of the London museum where she'd been doing research that day. How Amy's little face lit up at the sight of their tiny, fan-shaped ornaments, sparkling with emerald and amethyst glass jewels!

Cathy was so lucky. A supportive husband with a partnership in a thriving law firm, a home of her own and two happy, healthy children, whose noisy chatter filled their tastefully refurbished Victorian cottage with life. She even managed to balance her academic interest in eighteenth century engravings with a part-time job as accounts manager at Amy's primary school. Contrast that with her own empty existence. Unspeakably depressing...

The white transit van in front began to edge forward. Elinor automatically eased out the clutch and her trim, blue Audi inched another couple of feet closer to the traffic lights.

Up ahead a distant siren suddenly blared out through the darkness. A momentary flurry as the slow-crawling stream of cars parted, scrambling hastily up onto the road verges, then ground to a standstill. Into view flashed the dazzling blue lights of an emergency vehicle, nosing its way impatiently through the gridlocked traffic.

At last the ambulance turned right and, reaching clearer ground past the lights, accelerated with a roar and tore off shrieking in the direction of the hospital. Now it'd vanished – carrying inside it someone she'd never see, never know, the victim of some car crash or heart attack perhaps, someone quite unconscious that the paths of their lives had almost crossed that dark, January evening…

"… And now, with Mozart's keyboard concerto No. 14 in E flat major, the European Haydn Ensemble, fresh from their recent engagement at the Opera House down under in sunny Sydney…"

Sunny Sydney. A sudden gush of memories flooded over her like a dam burst. The low throb-throb of deep-toned engines and the salty tang of sea water laced with acrid whiffs of diesel aboard the harbour ferry. Wriggling her bare toes in the fine, warm sand at Manly Beach. The early morning smell of fresh toast wafting down the hallway of their flat. She flinched as a stab of pain shot through her.

Oh why had she ever believed that her research degree mattered more than Paul? Tonight she could've been riding one of those big blue and white buses through the tree-lined streets of Elizabeth Bay back to their airy apartment with its glorious harbour views. A little later, in the cool of the evening, Paul would've arrived home – broad-shouldered, good-humoured and refreshingly down-to-earth – from his busy day at a high-rise architect's office in the central business district. They'd probably have eaten dinner on the terrace wreathed with scarlet bougainvillea, as the sun sank in a blaze of purple and gold behind the bluff...

Elinor sighed.

So she might've been living a long way from home. But it wasn't a sentence of permanent exile from Europe: you could fly back from Australia in a day. And thanks to the internet, she would hardly have been intellectually marooned out there. A way of finishing her thesis could surely have been found. She should never have listened to Dad, who'd terrified her into bolting home with his gloomy predictions of academic frustration and a shortage of museum-related employment...

Then again, after Cathy phoned to tell her how ill Mum was, what else could she do? How cut off she'd suddenly felt from her family. Was it any wonder she'd panicked and jumped onto the first plane home?

But the look on Paul's face – he was incapable of deceit. *So your family are more important to you than me*, it said. *So your career matters more than our life together...*

Once past the junction, the traffic began to flow more freely.

The sight of Mum wasting away before their helpless eyes: at first lying frail and silver-haired on the damask chaise longue by her bedroom window, wrapped in a thin shawl; then too tired even to get out of bed in the morning, until finally the room was empty except for herself, burying her sobs in that lacy cobweb of a shawl, the last gift she'd ever given her mother...

And seeing Dad, brought up in the old public-school tradition of stiff upper lips, broken down with sobs in his study on the morning of the funeral. How could she leave him alone in that big house full of memories? Cathy's hands were tied, with Richard and the children. Nick was a dear brother, but he was just a man. So she'd dragged her feet over returning to Sydney. The emails dropped from one a day to one a week. Finally a note arrived from Paul saying he'd met an Australian girl called Beth and they were planning to get married. He hoped she'd understand...

Elinor shivered. She understood only too well. Then she'd been at the crossroads of her future – but eighteen months on, it was all too late. She'd turned twenty-seven. She was nearly thirty. Life had passed her by. Her Cambridge school mates were scattered across the globe. Her Courtauld Institute friends had accepted lectureships at Seville University or research posts at the Museum of Fine Arts in Boston. Only she remained behind.

She finally turned off the busy Tillington Road into a quiet lane behind the terrace of tall Georgian houses and manoeuvred the Audi's snub nose into one of a long line of orderly garages.

So here she was: the late-born and unexpected addition to the family, who'd boldly headed for the bright lights of London to study for an intellectually suspect degree, who'd declared, and even half-fulfilled, her ambitions for overseas travel by almost emigrating to the other side of the world, now trapped like a bird in a hunter's net in the stifling, antiquated offices of the Lydgate Museum not a quarter of an hour's walk from her childhood home. Ironic really.

She switched off the Mozart in mid-note and climbed wearily out of the car.

*

The dismal downpour began again as she was hauling the garage door shut. So she sprinted up the water-logged garden underneath her big, black umbrella and clattered down the back steps into the basement lobby. Thrusting her wet umbrella into the cast-iron stand, she hung up her black woollen coat and beret neatly on the brass wall hook beside her father's tweed walking jacket and exchanged her outdoor shoes for an old pair of frayed satin slippers that had once belonged to her mother.

As she turned to the wall mirror opposite the kitchen door to tidy her hair, her glasses instantly steamed up in the cocooning warmth of the house. Just like the old days, when she used to run in from school on wet winter evenings. She'd push open the frosted glass door into the glowing kitchen, rubbing off the condensation with her fingers, to be greeted by the smell of lamb and rosemary casserole simmering on the hob and Mum's voice calling out,

"How about a mug of hot cocoa and a toasted tea cake?" or "Fancy a cup of tea and a buttered muffin?"

She smiled to herself.

But now, no matter how hard she stared into that mirror, she saw no welcoming light in the kitchen. Home wasn't home without Mum. Her shoulders drooped.

Still, Tuesday night was dance class. She checked her watch as she pushed open the kitchen door. Twenty to seven. Just time enough to sort Dad's dinner and make it to the leisure centre –

"Is that you, Elinor?" interrupted a querulous voice from the neighbouring room.

"Yes, Dad," she called back, snapping on the light switch.

"Mrs. Bridger's tidied my desk again and I can't find my copy of Haskell and Penny…"

Couldn't even wait to set eyes on her before he started complaining about the cleaning lady.

"I'm sure I saw it on the table in the drawing room this morning," she shouted back, pulling open the door of the refrigerator in search of yesterday's leftovers.

"What's that?" demanded Dad's voice.

Elinor clicked her tongue. Setting down the saucepan she'd pulled out of a drawer and composing her face into a mask of patience, she thrust her head around the door.

Although Belmont Terrace faced onto the busy Tillington Road, the breakfast room was sheltered from the noise of passing traffic by a row of thick evergreens. The long, gold velvet drapes were closely drawn to shut out prying draughts and the only sounds within were the measured tick of a stately grandfather clock and the subdued crackle of a well-bred fire on the hearth. Bright lights glinted along chains of crystal droplets dangling from the central chandelier and out of the portrait above the mantelpiece the disapproving dark eyes of a long-dead ancestor in close cap and pointed Jacobean lace ruff stared reproachfully at her abrupt entrance.

Her father occupied his usual winged armchair beside the fire. A spare, elderly man with a high forehead, fierce eyebrows and a hooked nose that lent him the appearance of a scholastic bird of prey, he sat hunched over the newspaper in waistcoat and shirt sleeves. But as Elinor looked in, he glanced up over the tops of his spectacles.

"So here you are at last, my dear," he greeted her in tones of habitual martyrdom. "Do come in and shut the door. You're letting in a draught."

Reluctantly Elinor stepped into the room, pulling the door to behind her. Her footsteps sank into the soft pile of an antique Savonnerie carpet, laid over the polished parquet floor.

"I was beginning to worry that you might've had an accident," her father went on. "I rang several times, but your mobile was switched off."

Because she knew better than to leave it switched on, of course. Now Dad was semi-retired, he had all the time in the world to pester her with trifles.

"It was the traffic," she began. "I left London on the earliest train I could, to be back in time for my dance class."

"Surely you're not planning to go out again tonight?" exclaimed her father, glancing towards the window. "It's raining –"

"Now, Dad, I'm definitely going to class tonight," she announced, to forestall any further objections.

"I can't imagine why you want to learn flamenco in the first place," he replied with a peevish rustle of newspaper. "Besides, dancing's for the young."

Did he shoot these savage little barbs at her on purpose? Or had the cut and thrust of countless academic feuds blunted his perception of the suffering of others?

She struggled to swallow her resentment.

"OK, but almost everyone in the class is older than me, you know."

"'Than I', Elinor," he corrected briskly. He was a past master at shifting his ground whenever she managed to parry a thrust. "And I do wish you'd refrain from using vulgar expressions like 'OK'… Well, do just as you like – you always have. Here am I waiting hours for you to arrive home. And now dinner's going to be late – again. But of course I'm only your father…"

He could perfectly well have fixed the meal himself. In the old days he was forever cooking tasty snacks to tempt her mother's failing appetite. But when he adopted this tone, argument was useless. Elinor retreated to the kitchen.

Dad soon followed. While she was hastily rinsing the rice and setting it on the range to boil, he seated himself at the pine table in front of their massive Victorian dresser with its shelves of old, willow-patterned china and asked after Aurélie at the Fan Museum in Greenwich: how had she enjoyed her winter holiday in Morocco? Did she prefer her current post to her old one at the Victoria and Albert…?

Elinor responded automatically, her mind fixed on assembling a bowl of lettuce and tomatoes.

"So you're in too much of a hurry to prepare the salad properly tonight?" he enquired plaintively. "Remember how your mother always served salad in separate little dishes. I don't like everything tossed up in a mess together."

Elinor folded her lips on a hasty retort and reached down the small, cut-glass dishes.

Mum had always known how to keep Dad happy: slippers set to warm beside a cosy fire, evening paper folded on his seat, everything in order, awaiting his return from college… But now her guiding hand on the household tiller was gone, they both felt miserable and adrift. However hard she tried, she could never care so much about his comfort as Mum had and sometimes it frightened her when she caught herself actually hating him…

Hastily she threw the tea towel over her shoulder and returned to the breakfast room. Dad trailed after her and resumed his place by the fire. He watched her open the doors of the gleaming rosewood sideboard.

"So we're not eating in the dining room tonight then?" he observed mournfully.

"No, Dad," replied Elinor, setting out a single table mat and coaster. For as long as she could remember, her father's place had been laid on this reproduction of an eighteenth-century engraving of an old London theatre. "I thought it wasn't worth going to all that trouble for just one person."

"You're planning to eat before you leave, aren't you?" he asked in alarm. "When women grow thin and haggard, the effect is terribly ageing."

Why was he always harping on about her age?

Elinor swallowed hard, but her hands trembled slightly as she set out the sterling silver cutlery.

"It's all right, Dad – really," she assured him through gritted teeth. "I'll snatch a quick sandwich in the kitchen before I leave. Besides, I had tea at Cathy's on the way home –"

Cardinal mistake! If only she could bite back those words. But it was too late.

"So you've been visiting your sister?" he asked in injured tones.

Nothing for it but to nod and wait for the flood of reproaches. He always hated feeling left out, like a child who hadn't been invited to the party.

"I don't see why you drove all the way over there when you knew I'd be waiting for you at home."

"I wanted to give Amy her birthday present. When I arrived, the children'd all just left and Cathy was exhausted. So we sat down together with a cup of tea and a slice of birthday cake before I helped her clear up."

"Birthday cake! Elinor, you can't live on sandwiches and slices of birthday cake."

"It's only once, Dad," Elinor reassured him briskly, polishing the long-stemmed, crystal wine goblet with the tea towel over her shoulder and fetching the silver salt and pepper cruet.

"That's what you always say," retorted Dad, obviously nettled. "Now this young man you went home with last night – I suppose he's a respectable sort of person, is he? You know I make it a rule never to pry into my children's private affairs and I was a model of discretion when Catherine insisted on marrying that boy, but –"

"Dad," she protested, "Richard was almost thirty. And it's nearly ten years ago now."

"Is it really? Seems like only yesterday. I remember us all gathered in the chapel and your dear mother in that very fetching hat with pink roses around the brim…" His eyes narrowed in suspicion. "But I won't be put off like this, Elinor. I'm only concerned about your well-being. Who exactly is this Edwin Chadwick? Does he have respectable academic credentials?"

As if the only qualification necessary for a successful relationship was "respectable academic credentials"!

"Of course, Dad," she answered aloud. "He's published a number of papers and a recent book on numismatics. Took his undergraduate degree at Oriel."

Dad seemed not to notice the hint of sarcasm in her tone.

"Oriel?" he exclaimed in horror. "You don't want to get involved with an Oxford man, Elinor. Their opinions are highly intellectually suspect."

"But I'm not involved with him," cried Elinor, wheeling round to face him. "I drove Edwin home from the museum reception last night because he doesn't own a car and would've had to pay for a taxi all the way out to Melbourn. It was an act of kindness."

"That's what you say now. And to do you justice, Elinor, I'm sure you believe it. But I know how these things happen –"

"Dad, Edwin Chadwick's in his mid-forties. He looks like one of the Seven Dwarves, he lives with his mother who's eighty-two and his house is over-run with wildlife."

"So you went into the house?" shot back her father.

"He invited me in for coffee. I should never've accepted. I could hardly drink it, I was so distracted by his cages full of birds. They were everywhere: in the dining room, the sitting room, the kitchen; all flapping and cheeping and rustling and pecking. It was utterly horrible!"

The mere memory made her shudder.

Dad instantly changed his tactics.

"Well, well, never mind that now," he coaxed. "Calm down, Elinor, or you'll make yourself ill. Now why don't you take a glass of wine and some soup with me, there's a good girl."

"But I don't want any wine or I won't be able to drive to my flamenco class," she burst out miserably.

"At least eat a bowl of soup. I'll lay a place for you while you're serving up – I can smell the most delicious aroma from the kitchen. What is it tonight, my dear?"

"Leek and potato."

Now he pointed it out, the smell of the soup bubbling on the stove was warm and inviting. And the night outside was cold and wet. Perhaps it'd be easier to stay home after all…

"Oh all right. I'll just have some soup – and then I'll go," she conceded.

"What a splendid idea, Elinor," agreed her father pleasantly.

When she returned with the steaming porcelain bowls on a tray, she saw that he'd already set another place at table. He pulled out her chair with old-fashioned courtesy.

"Now, Dad, I'm only having soup."

"Of course, my dear. Just as you say. Now let me pass you the bread rolls. Would you like some butter? Isn't nice, hot soup like this just the thing for a cold, wet January night? Such a pity you're going out again, you know. I'd been thinking… But never mind. I mustn't be selfish."

Elinor heaved a sigh. "Well, Dad, what is it?"

"It occurred to me that after dinner you might be so good as to cast an eye over the draft of my latest chapter. It concerns the tourist trade and its effect on the economy of Georgian London. I really believe I've hit on something and you know how I value your opinion. Why don't you stay home tonight, Elinor?"

"Well…" Elinor faltered and then stopped. Beaten, as usual.

"That's my good girl," exclaimed her father. "Now why not take a glass of wine from the college cellar? This vintage is one of the best of recent times and I wouldn't like you to miss the subtle way it complements the flavour of the soup."

He poured the gleaming, ruby-red wine with a gurgle into her waiting glass. Elinor sank into her chair with a gesture of quiet despair.

She loved Dad, but he was driving her out of her mind. She felt like one of Edwin Chadwick's birds, trapped in its cage. The fact that her cage was tastefully gilded and furnished with objects of priceless antiquity made no practical difference to the grim reality of her imprisonment. Under the guise of concern for her welfare, subtly seasoned with emotional blackmail and the faintest hint of bullying, her father was gradually but relentlessly smothering the life out of her…

But what to do about it?

Chapter Three

Jamie's going to die. Jamie's going to die – and there's nothing we can do about it.

This terrible realisation struck Beatrice as she huddled close to her mother on a bench outside the intensive care unit. Even Mum believed it. Bea could read it in her stricken face.

"The flesh's simply fallen off him," murmured Mum piteously, her head bowed and her gaze fixed unseeingly on the grey vinyl floor tiles. "He was thin enough before, but now he's just a skeleton. And his skin looks just like – like yellow parchment. And the way he stares at me! He doesn't know where he is or even who I am. Oh Bea!"

She raised her head. Her dark eyes were swimming with tears. Bea felt her own throat tighten and reached out a sympathetic hand to grasp Mum's.

"But – but he's been here for two days now," she faltered. "Can't the doctors do something?"

"They've been trying. They've run all kinds of tests, but I still don't think they've got the first idea what's the matter with him. I'm beginning to believe they never will…"

Bea squeezed Mum's cold fingers. Mum was staring beyond her, not at the blank white walls opposite, but far back into a happier past.

"Do you remember how patient he used to be when he was a little boy?" she whispered huskily. "Sitting crouched over his desk for hours on end, gluing together all the little components of those model planes? And how fussy he was about painting them the right colours – down to the tiniest wing struts?"

Bea nodded wordlessly, a great lump swelling in her throat.

"And those beautiful blue and white china canvases in his A-Level Art show," Mum went on with a ghost of her old smile. "You could see every leaf on the willow trees and every wave in the water, couldn't you? And remember how much we laughed when he acted Andrew Aguecheek in the sixth form play? My little boy. Crying when he thought he'd lost his old patchwork bunny… So much promise all just running to waste. I thought I'd outgrown God years ago, but really now, Bea, I think there's nothing left to do but pray…"

She hid her face in her hands and burst into tears.

Bea trembled. Mum hardly ever cried. With a choking sob she flung her arms around her shoulders and they both wept together on the bench, clinging to each other like doves cowering before an icy storm blast.

At that moment a nearby door opened and a grave-faced medic in a black beard and blue scrubs appeared on the threshold.

"Mrs Willett, will you come with me?" he urged in a deep voice.

Bea's heart lurched with terror. She felt as though she was suffocating. Mum started up in blind terror, shedding her clutching hands, and instantly vanished along with the doctor.

Bea was left alone, staring straight ahead of her.

It was like a nightmare. The whole world was sliding out of control…

*

"Now you leave this to me," warned Mum that evening in the kitchen before Dad arrived home from work.

Bea glanced up from the sink and nodded, bent on doing whatever she asked. Poor Mum was so pale and tired. She looked absolutely worn out after spending so many days at Jamie's bedside – and so many sleepless nights.

"Why?" piped up Geoff's voice from the other side of the open kitchen hatch, where he was busy doing homework on the computer in the dining room. "What does it matter, now the doctors've found out what's wrong with him?"

"Because I need to break this to your father myself," asserted Mum. "Now promise me, the pair of you."

She sounded so solemn that Bea duly promised, though she couldn't see why Mum was making such a fuss. Geoff was furiously tapping away on the computer keyboard next door and only grunted in response.

"I should never've said anything," whispered Mum, rattling a pot out of the kitchen cupboard for the carrots Bea had already peeled and rinsed. "I didn't realise he was listening on the other side of the wall. You go and set the table, Bea dear. I need to think how to put this…"

Bea cast a sideways glance at her mother's fretful brow as she left the kitchen. Sometimes grown-ups mystified her. Wouldn't Dad be over the moon about Jamie being out of danger? And why hadn't Mum already rung and told him the good news?

The dining room table was a mess, as usual. She tossed Geoff's school bag into a corner, then swept up the scattering of post, magazines and advertising leaflets and bundled them on top of Dad's upright piano. From the bottom drawer of the sideboard she pulled out a clean cloth, carefully edging past her harp, which stood stiffly beneath its dust cover near the window like a veiled prima donna. As she clinked through the cutlery caddy, her gaze rested a moment on Geoff's happily absorbed profile.

What were the chances of Mr Tactless keeping his mouth shut as Mum'd asked? Zero. If she were Mum, she'd get whatever she was planning to say over with as soon as Dad set foot in the house. The hands of the carriage clock on the mantelpiece were nearing five past seven. He'd be home any minute now...

Footsteps clattered in the back porch and the kitchen door creaked loudly.

"I can smell fish pie," exclaimed Dad as he entered along with an icy draught that gusted through the house like a whirlwind. "What news from hospital tonight?"

There was a short pause followed by a murmured exchange in the kitchen. Bea went on laying out knives and forks, straining to overhear what was being said.

"Malaria," burst out Dad's voice. "But how in God's name can he possibly have contracted malaria?"

Geoff turned his head from the computer screen.

"It's quite simple, Dad," he called out helpfully. "Jamie got bitten by a mosquito – probably one of the species plasmodium ovale, vivax or malariae. It's unlikely to've been plasmodium falciparum."

"Well that's a relief," retorted Dad with heavy sarcasm and then, thrusting his cycle-helmeted head through the open hatch, "So why not falciparum?"

"Because then he'd've been dead days ago," answered Geoff with relish. "It's often fatal within a few hours of the first symptoms appearing, since it infects all ages of red blood cells. The other strains attack only young or old ones."

"Yes, well – why don't you go and wash your hands for supper, dear?" suggested Mum from behind.

But it was never easy to distract Geoff from his self-imposed crusade for adult education. By now Bea had finished setting the table, but she leaned back against the dresser, interested to see what would happen next.

"Look here, Dad," Geoff enthused, pointing at the computer screen in front of him. "I've found this really cool site about Parasitology. Malaria can attack your brain and spleen and cause liver and kidney failure. You may suffer recurring outbreaks for years afterwards. And did you realise that it's the female anopheles mosquito that transmits malaria, not the male, who feeds on nectar – ?"

"Look, all this is fascinating," broke in Dad, unbuckling his cycle helmet with a frown, "but I already know malaria's transmitted by mosquitoes. What surprises me is that, as far as I'm aware, there aren't any malarial mosquitoes – either male or female – roaming around England in January. Though of course you, with your wider knowledge of the insect world, may be able to correct me on this point, as on so many others."

The jibe flew straight over Geoff's head – as usual.

"No, Dad, you're quite right," he agreed instead with warm approval.

"Glad I'm still not too old to be right about something," grumbled Dad in an undertone.

"So from this we can deduce that Jamie didn't contract malaria in England, can't we?"

There was a short silence as Dad withdrew his head to consider the implications of this statement. Next thing they knew, he'd materialised in the dining room doorway, pulling off his rucksack.

"But Jamie hasn't been out of the country for months," he declared. "As far as I'm aware, ever since last September he's been either at home or down at college in Exeter." His expression clearly showed that he felt this argument was watertight.

"Yes, but he was in the tropics last summer." Geoff's voice rang with triumph. "I've been reading all about it – it's just mega. The incubation period for malaria is usually one or two weeks, but it can last for up to ten months."

"But he's hardly likely to have caught it while he was in South-East Asia with Adam," objected Dad. "They both had a course of anti-malarial shots before they left the country. In view of the mountain of mosquito nets, insect repellents and bottles of pills your mum loaded Jamie down with, I can't believe he could've caught anything more serious than a cold. What do you know about this, Marisa?"

And he suddenly wheeled round to face Mum, who'd entered with a jug of water for the table. She stood smoothing out imaginary creases in the red and white checked cloth in an effort to avoid meeting his eye.

"Well go on," he urged. "It's no use trying to shield him. Out with it! Left them all at home, didn't he?"

Mum was finally forced to look up. She shook her head vigorously.

"Oh no," she informed him with perfect candour. "He had everything with him. I packed the pills myself, didn't I, Bea? And he went on taking them for several weeks. But…" Her voice faltered as she tried, and clearly failed, to think of a diplomatic way of phrasing this. "…Well, he confessed to me this evening that the pills were making him feel nauseous. And he didn't think he was getting any mosquito bites… so… he… stopped taking them."

There was an uncomfortable silence. Then,

"Of all the bloody idiots," spluttered Dad, flinging his rucksack on the floor with such a crash that Geoff jumped in his seat. "Should've known it'd be his own stupid fault. He's always been short on common sense – but this beats all. Out in the tropics and he stops taking his malaria tablets!"

Mum laid a pacifying hand on his arm.

"Dear, I know he's behaved foolishly," she soothed, "but you can't put old heads on young shoulders. At least now the doctors've worked out what's wrong, they can cure it."

"Now look here, Marisa," exploded Dad, shaking off her hand so fiercely that even unobservant Geoff slid from his seat and, with a muttered excuse about washing his hands for dinner, vanished from the room. "I'm telling you, this's the last straw. I've had enough of Jamie's stupidity and fecklessness."

"It's just a phase. He'll grow out of it," asserted Mum.

"Just a phase, is it?" snapped back Dad. "And how about when he was five and refused to go to school at all? You said he'd grow out of that."

"And so he did."

"Not so's you'd've noticed," retorted Dad grimly. "And when he grew his hair down past his shoulder blades like a girl, you said that was just a phase too. But his hair's still down past his shoulder blades and it keeps on changing colour. And now he's got a nose stud, eyebrow studs and half a dozen earrings as well – all in the same ear! He just plunges from one phase straight into an even worse one. He won't get out of bed before eleven unless you claim the house's on fire and he doesn't seem to me to be putting much effort into his studies either. We both work hard to keep a roof over everyone's heads and food in everyone's mouths and we're paying out huge sums to fund him through university – apparently just so he can lounge around doing sod-all."

Bea eyed the mottled flush of Dad's cheeks and the thick veins standing out on his forehead like knotted cords. If there was one subject that sent him into a tailspin, this was it. Better leave Mum to handle it. She slipped out of the room to check on the carrots. Through the kitchen hatch she could hear Mum pointing out that Jamie'd worked hard enough programming at 3-D Imaging during his last two summer holidays.

"Only because that Smart woman ordered him to get on with it," barked Dad.

"And he earned good money too."

"Yes," thundered Dad, "and blew the whole damned lot on that fool trip to South-East Asia. And now he'll be lying around the house recuperating for months if I know him, so he doesn't have to go back to Exeter and do a decent day's work. Let's face it, Marisa, the trouble with Jamie is that he's got no idea what he wants to do with himself, so he just keeps on making excuses to do nothing at all. When I was his age, I'd already finished my degree and started full-time work."

"Because that's what people like us did then. Besides, Jamie chose that computer science course because he thought you'd approve of it as being economically viable."

"Only because he'd insisted on taking such a nondescript bunch of A-Levels that he wasn't fit for anything economically unviable! I ask you: Theatre Studies, Computer Studies, Art and – what was the other one again?"

"History. Well, you're the one who insists that children need to follow their own bent –"

"Yes, but at least the rest of them have some bent to follow. I don't mind running around the streets of Chesterton in the dead of night observing the phases of the moon with Marc, or brushing my teeth under the bath tap because the hand basin is full of Geoff's newts, or ferrying Bea's gigantic harp round to orchestral concerts at the back of beyond. All this doesn't bother me. What does bother me is having a son of twenty-two who hasn't the faintest idea what he wants from life – who has no obvious talent whatsoever."

"Now you're being too hard on him, Graham, you know you are. He has plenty of talent."

"All right. But he doesn't use any of it. I'm telling you: if he doesn't start pulling his finger out soon, I'll stop his bloody allowance altogether. Then he can go out and stack supermarket shelves and see how he likes earning his living like other people!"

Mum agreed that he was right of course and ended by promising that when Jamie recovered, she'd have a serious talk to him about the future.

Dad finally left to collect Marcus from astronomy club, still muttering and grumbling to himself, although looking mildly ashamed of his outburst. Mum returned to the kitchen. She sighed deeply as she pulled open the oven door to check the fish pie.

"How am I ever going to broach this subject with Jamie?" she murmured.

Bea, who was draining the carrots, felt glad that she wasn't quite grown up yet.

Chapter Four

Patter. Trickle. SPLOSH! … Patter. Trickle. SPLOSH! …

Jamie watched the monotonous raindrops chase one another down the window glass and vanish the moment they struck the wooden frame.

Hour after hour he lay motionless on the frayed living room couch, huddled under an old woollen blanket. So he was home from hospital. Who cared? Why had the doctors dragged him back into the ugly light of day where the whole world was dull and grey and boring, like this endless winter rain? Nothing to see except the dank branches of the leafless plane tree in the street outside. Nothing to do but watch the raindrops chase one another down the window glass…

Patter. Trickle. SPLOSH! … Patter. Trickle. SPLOSH! …

"I hate seeing you like this," murmured an anxious voice from behind.

Jamie didn't bother turning his head. It was just Mum. Didn't want to talk to her. Didn't want to talk to anyone. He went on staring blankly at the windowpane.

After a moment he heard her approach and felt her bend over him, smoothing the lank hair off his forehead with a tender hand and enveloping him in the comfortable smell of flour and milk and warm baking that he always associated with childhood.

"Like a hot fruit scone fresh from the oven, spread with butter and strawberry jam?" she asked in a transparent effort to tempt his appetite. "I've just baked a batch for tea and they won't last long after Dad and the boys arrive back from the air show."

Jamie shook his head wearily.

"Then tell me what you feel like eating and I'll fix it for you," she persisted. "What about a mug of creamy hot chocolate or a toasted cheese and tomato sandwich?"

Jamie shrugged without the slightest flicker of interest.

"You've hardly done more than pick at your food ever since you came home from hospital," she observed in a tone of reproach. "It's so unlike you."

"Mum, I told you before: I'm just not hungry," he snapped.

Before the words were even out of his mouth, he felt ashamed of this childish flash of temper. But it was her fault for provoking him.

Why'd she keep on nagging him the whole time? Why couldn't she just leave him alone?

There was a short pause and then she sat down on the end of the sofa. Her manner indicated that she'd decided enough was enough. He picked at a loop of wool in the blanket and refused point blank to meet her eye.

"Now Jamie, you must eat something," she began in a serious voice.

"Why?"

"Because if you go on like this, you're never going to build up your strength. You've got to try to get well."

"Don't care whether I get well or not."

"Of course you want to get well."

"No, *you* want me to get well," he retorted. "There's a difference."

She was silent for a moment. Then,

"Why shouldn't you want to get well?" she exclaimed. "You're young – you've got your whole life ahead of you. What about your degree?"

"It's boring and useless. And I hate the people who study Computer Science. They wear such freaky clothes."

"But you chose it," she protested.

"Yeah. To get you and Dad off my back. Means nothing to me."

"Then why didn't you apply for something you really wanted to study? I always thought you might audition for drama school like Adam."

"No money in acting," he replied. "It's a game for suckers."

"Well, what about this summer project you and Adam were planning? I thought you were going abroad with a play."

"That's just something to do in the holidays – for fun. Besides, it's a total non-starter anyway. We're never gonna be able to fund it."

"So what do you actually *want* to do with your life, Jamie?" she burst out. "I've suggested everything I can think of. Surely you must have some ideas of your own?"

"You know what my idea was." He turned accusing eyes upon her.

"I know what your idea was when you came back from Indonesia. It was totally impractical. You can't spend your life helping Faye and me run a fair-trade craft shop."

"Why not? I like ethnic art. And I like painting things to sell too. That Indian woman who bought the wooden flowers I carved said she thought I had real talent."

"Yes, but it's just a hobby – not something you can turn into a full-time occupation."

"You have."

"That's different. While I was tied down looking after all of you, I didn't have the energy for a career in stage design anymore. So I had to find something local and part-time… But a clever young man like you can't spend your whole life serving behind a shop counter."

Flattery. Wasn't gonna fall for that.

"What's the difference between that and sitting all day in front of a computer screen programming?" he countered.

"Why be so negative? There're lots of exciting opportunities in computer technology nowadays. Now look, it's being ill that's making you feel so moody and depressed. You need something to do…"

She suggested several undemanding activities like listening to music or watching TV. Jamie irritably rejected them all.

At last she hit upon what she clearly thought was a brilliant suggestion.

"I know," she exclaimed. "I've been meaning to sort out the odds and ends I brought home from Aunt Rosita's attic the night you were rushed to hospital. I remember dumping a big cardboard box somewhere in the kitchen. How about if I hunt it out and bring it in here for us to look through together?"

Jamie couldn't summon up the energy to say no. Before he realised it, she'd whisked off in the direction of the kitchen, presumably to fetch the box.

Of all the bloody stupid suggestions! As if he'd have the least interest in trawling through a load of old garbage belonging to his ancient, dead great aunt. He returned to staring out of the window at the drizzling rain, obstinately closing his ears to the muffled noises coming from the kitchen.

Patter. Trickle. SPLOSH! … Patter. Trickle. SPLOSH! …

His mind drifted back to the days of driving down to London to visit Great Aunt Rosita when he was a little boy. How the sight of her used to fascinate him! She was so ancient and wrinkled, sitting so straight on her chair and always dressed in black, like a monument of sorrow. Once he'd asked Mum why she always dressed like that and she said it was the old way when somebody'd died. First, the man she was going to marry – and then everybody else: his great-grandmother, his great-grandfather, all his great-aunts and uncles and cousins…

She and his grandmother lived together in an eerie, old house in Hampstead, where the dim rooms were full of dark mahogany furniture with legs carved like vine tendrils. And the only sound in the gloom was the grandfather clock ticking away the hours till his grandmother died and Great Aunt Rosita was left quite alone.

Even when she'd moved to Cambridge to be nearer to Mum, the new flat still smelled like the old house: of mothballs and wax polish and musty pot-pourri. Mum and Dad used to take him and Bea there to visit her on Sundays, not because they really wanted to go, but because Mum said they ought. He'd always been rather scared of Great Aunt Rosita with her festoons of jet beads and her black eyes hollow with tragedy, so after he grew into a teenager, he tried to make excuses for not going as often as he could…

When Mum finally returned, she was carrying a large cardboard box.

"Here we are," she announced, setting it down on the worn autumn leaf rug beside the sofa. "Finally managed to unearth it from beneath the clutter. Why does everything in this house always seem to vanish under piles of newspaper and sheet music?"

Jamie just rolled his eyes. He surveyed the box without enthusiasm as Mum knelt on the rug and unfolded the top flaps. Then he turned his face away, so he didn't have to witness the spectacle of her naïve delight as she exclaimed aloud over each worthless object she pulled out, like a child unpacking a Christmas stocking. Poor old Mum. Trying too hard, as usual…

How sad to be reduced to hopes of finding an unexpected store of share certificates that might give him and Adam the funds to attend their play festival in Spain. How pitifully delighted she was on chancing across some old photographs of herself as a child dressed up in her grandmother's black lace mantilla, and of her mother and Great Aunt Rosita sporting outrageous hats at a cousin's long ago engagement party…

"Don't they look funny now, Jamie?" she appealed, handing him up the pictures to examine.

"Hilarious."

He brushed them pettishly away.

"Oh don't be such a grouch." She glanced up with a thoughtful light in her eye. "It's not a failed romance that's at the bottom of all this moping and misery, is it?" she hazarded, gathering the despised photographs back into her lap. "I thought there was a girl at Christmas…"

"She hasn't rung or even texted since I came home."

"I see. Well, there're plenty more fish in the sea. Isn't it Adam's sister's birthday in a week or two? If you set your mind to getting better, you might meet the girl of your dreams at the party."

"No chance."

"Oh come on! You've got to look on the bright side."

The glibness of her words rang hollowly in both their ears.

Mum tried to conceal her discouragement by continuing to rummage through the box. This time she drew out several handfuls of letters, brown around the edges and fragile with age.

"There're so many of these," she mused, stacking them against a chair leg. "I can't think what to do with them all. Seems a shame to throw them away when I'm sure they could tell us a lot about our family history. Perhaps you could sort through them while you're convalescing."

"I'm not interested in dead people."

"But my grandmother claimed we came from a long line of Spanish aristocrats descended from Almagro, who sailed to conquer Peru –"

"Mum," broke in Jamie, who'd had enough, "let's face the truth. Great Aunt Rosita could never bear to throw anything away and this is the result. It's just a heap of old junk."

"I suppose all she had were her memories," murmured his mother with a sigh. And then, as she peered into the depths of the cardboard carton again, "Oh look! That's a strange-shaped box, isn't it? – the red one here. Looks quite old too – so stained and faded. You know, I think I remember seeing it before…"

She picked up the box and was about to pull off the lid when the phone suddenly shrilled in the hall. Since the pair of them were alone in the house that Sunday afternoon, no one else would answer the call. So she scrambled hastily to her feet exclaiming, "Here, hold this lot for a minute. Could be Dad…"

Before Jamie could protest, she'd tipped the entire contents of her lap on top of him and darted towards the door.

He found himself showered with odds and ends, which he was about to toss petulantly off onto the growing piles of debris that lay scattered all over the rug. But the elongated case which'd caught his mother's eye happened to bounce against the sofa back and, as he automatically reached out to catch it, the broken lid tumbled off and something dropped out. Jamie hardly registered the slip of paper fluttering out of the box and burying itself among the folds of the patchwork blanket spread over his legs. The thing that caught his eye was the object itself.

What could it be? Long and thin. Like a bunch of sticks tied together with mauve ribbon and faintly perfumed with lavender. He picked it up and examined it curiously. The outer sticks seemed to be carved of cream-coloured bone or ivory and painted with bright gold and blue butterflies and tiny scarlet strawberries… and – was that a pair of castanets? Must be some keepsake of Great Aunt Rosita's prehistoric youth… But look! As he untied the ribbon, the sticks fell open into a semi-circle of pleated paper. It was a fan.

The leaf was crowded with murky pictures of people and buildings, but from its centre stared forth the smooth, pale mask of a sexless face. A long, narrow nose with pinched nostrils, lips primly pursed and eyeholes beneath thin, arched brows that'd been cut right through the paper…

Oh sod it! As he was unfurling it, the fan'd split down one of its white-worn folds. Wasn't his fault – the paper was so old and brittle, it'd just torn in his hands…

"Why it's the old Spanish fan," exclaimed his mother, returning to the room as he stared at in dismay. "I remember Mum and Aunt Rosita showing it to me when I was a little girl and proudly telling me how it'd always been passed down in the family from eldest daughter to eldest daughter…"

Hell! thought Jamie in panic. Some sort of family heirloom and he'd just broken it. He guiltily snapped it shut to hide the careless tear.

"…But then of course Aunt Rosita didn't have a daughter," his mother rambled on, reaching out her hand for the fan, which Jamie was reluctantly forced to surrender. "She told me she was going to give it to Bea. In fact I thought she already had." She made a move to unfurl it.

"Careful, Mum," warned Jamie.

But it was too late.

"Oh it's torn," she cried. "Well – it's so old, I suppose it's not surprising. Pity it's so dirty. It's not really very pretty anymore."

Jamie glanced up in surprise as he reclaimed the fan.

"But what about these little painted insects on the handles?" he protested. "They're so finely carved." And he stroked the indentations with gentle fingers.

"Suppose so," admitted his mother, bending to study it more closely. "Such a shame it's not nicer looking. If the leaf was prettily painted, Bea might've liked to hang it on her bedroom wall. But especially with that tear in it, I'm not sure she'll even want it now."

Not want it? How could she not want it?

"But look at the sticks," he pointed out, "– here underneath that mask face – there're some musical instruments, I think… though I can't quite make out what they are."

"Oh yes, I see now… Aunt Rosita used to treasure this fan. And you know, there's a story behind it too. Now what exactly was it again? She told me once…"

"Go on, Mum, think," urged Jamie.

She strained to remember. "It was a gift to one of your great-great-ever-so-many-great-uncles from a famous lady of the stage."

"Thought it was just women who used fans."

"Not at all. Everyone did in Spain. Because of the heat."

"So what was his name?"

"No idea. That's just what Aunt Rosita told me."

"Well, how about the lady then?"

"Some long dead Spanish tragedienne, I guess. Apparently it was all terribly romantic: the great-great-great-uncle was madly in love with her, but she married an English nobleman instead and became a titled lady."

"Oh, an ordinary old love story," exclaimed Jamie, dropping his eyes onto the fan. "Boring."

"Love stories are never ordinary," reproved his mother.

At that moment the front door burst open and a din of feet and voices erupted into the hallway. Dad and the twins home from the Duxford air show.

Mum was bustling off to greet them when Jamie, who'd been idly caressing the delicate painted flowers and bright red cherries on the fan handle with the tips of his long, thin fingers, asked who'd been on the phone. She glanced round.

"Oh I meant to tell you. It was Adam. He's been up in Cambridge for the weekend and he was ringing to ask if you were planning to come to Camilla's birthday party. Said he'd been trying to contact you for days. I told him how ill you'd been and he asked if he could drop by before he goes back to London tonight. So I invited him over for dinner."

"Mum? MU-UM!" came a loud yell and Marc poked an enquiring head around the door. "There you are. I'm starvin'. Anythin' to eat in this house?"

"What about a buttered scone?" she asked, shaking her head at his boisterousness. She turned back to Jamie. "Sure you won't change your mind?"

Jamie thought for a moment.

"P'raps I might be feeling a bit hungry after all," he admitted slowly.

Mum nodded without apparent reaction and followed Marc out of the room.

Jamie sank back against the sofa cushions, gazing at the torn face on the fan, which he'd carefully spread open in front of him. The blank eyeholes stared back at him, impassively guarding their own secrets.

Chapter Five

Jamie was still lounging on the sofa later that evening, staring at one of Great Aunt Rosita's old letters, when there came a sudden, loud RAT-TAT-TAT on the windowpane. He started violently. Glancing up with a frown into the darkness between the undrawn curtains, his heart skipped a beat. A ferocious, bearded face with a wide, gaping mouth, bulging eyes and savagely distorted features was pressing its nose whitely against the glass. What the hell was it? He almost cried out as the fiendish head wagged at him and grinned horribly, like a painted dragon mask from a Chinese New Year parade.

But something made him hesitate. He suddenly noticed the creature's thick brown hair and the next moment the frightful apparition had resolved itself into the bold features of dark-eyed Adam Quinn.

Adam had been Jamie's closest friend since their first day at Marston Road Primary until his parents were divorced and he moved to Kent with his mother and her new partner at the start of the sixth form. But the two had always kept in touch and Jamie sometimes made weekend visits to London, where Adam was now at drama school, to go to shows or parties with him and his fellow actors.

Realising it was just Adam pulling stupid faces on the other side of the glass, Jamie made a rude gesture and a moment later heard a loud ring on the doorbell.

"Boys, will one of you answer that, please?" called Mum's voice from upstairs.

"You get it," yelled one of the twins from the kitchen.

"I'm busy," shouted back the other from the dining room. "You get it."

"You're closer…"

The bell rang again.

"Boys," called Mum again, "will one of you hurry up and answer that door!"

Jamie was on the point of scrambling up to let Adam in when the dining room door slammed and someone stamped bad-temperedly down the hall, grumbling as he went. The front door was flung open and he heard Adam's voice offering a cheerful greeting to one of the twins.

"Thanks, um – Marc?" Adam went on, hazarding a guess at his identity.

"I'm Geoff, not Marc," was the huffy retort from Geoff, who hated being interrupted when he was working. "Can't you tell the difference by now?"

Apparently despising all further exchange of social courtesies with such a moron, he vanished straight back to the computer.

Adam made his appearance in the living room doorway, still glancing behind him with raised eyebrows.

"Can never tell those two apart," he confessed in a rueful voice. "Especially when I haven't seen'em for a while…"

He suddenly stopped dead in his tracks, eyes wide and jaw dropping in exaggerated dismay.

"What's wrong?" demanded Jamie, who'd abruptly tossed the patchwork blanket into the nearest armchair and was now sitting upright on the sofa in an effort to look as little like an invalid as possible.

"Jamie-boy, what's happened?" exclaimed Adam in genuine concern. "Your mum said you'd been ill, but I wasn't expecting this. You look totally wasted."

"Thanks for the confidence boost," retorted Jamie. Then, on a more sober note, "Actually I still feel pretty rough, but I could do without you making a huge fuss about it too. We've already had Mrs. Tibbs from next door over here in a state after Marc told her on his way to school that I'd suffered a brain haemorrhage and was gonna be a vegetable for the rest of my life."

Adam snorted with laughter. "He'll go too far one day with those practical jokes of his."

"Well, she's known him long enough to think twice before believing a word he says. But Mum went off the deep end."

Adam pulled a face of mock concern as he glanced round the room, which was still strewn with the jumbled contents of the cardboard box. "So what's all this clobber then?"

"Stuff from my great aunt's flat. She died a few weeks ago and Mum's had to clear out her place to be sold."

"That anything interesting?" went on Adam, pointing straight at him.

Jamie glanced down. He was still holding the letter he'd been puzzling over before being distracted by Adam's antics at the window.

"Dunno," he admitted. "Can't read it, can I? It's in Spanish."

"Hey, I learnt Spanish for a couple of years, remember. Here. Give it to me." Adam held out his hand for the letter.

He studied the paper for a moment or two in silence, stroking his short, dark beard, then tossed it back to Jamie with a careless shrug.

"Can't make out a word. Handwriting's too looped and fancy."

Adam wasn't the type to persevere when the going got tough, as Jamie well knew.

"You gonna sit down?" he asked.

"Where?"

Adam gestured towards the clutter that occupied the sofa as well as both worn armchairs.

"Oh just dump it all on the floor," advised Jamie.

Adam picked up the patchwork blanket full of letters and lowered it gingerly onto the carpet. He was about to drop into the armchair beside Jamie when his sharp eyes spotted the unusual object cradled neatly in the gap between the sofa cushion and the arm rest. He leant over and grabbed it.

"What's this?" he asked, turning it over in his fingers.

"A fan."

"Yeah I know that, dickhead. But what's it doing here?"

"Found it among the pile of junk that Mum's been sorting through."

"Let's take a look at it then."

"I don't think –" began Jamie, starting forward.

But with one vigorous flick of his wrist Adam had already jerked the fan open. There was a jarring rip as the paper leaf tore right through the centre of the mask face and the fan collapsed into two separate halves.

"– I'd do that," finished Jamie lamely.

Horror sprang into Adam's face.

"Hell! I'm really sorry. Looks pretty old too. Not valuable, is it?"

"Don't worry," Jamie reassured him quickly. "It's already torn once this afternoon. I'd throw it away myself – except it's got quite funky decorations on the framework. See the fruit and flowers and musical notes."

"And castles – or towers, or something," added Adam, peering at it more closely. "Pity it's had it. Might've made a good stage prop if we'd slapped a coat of red paint on either side and stuck on a frill of black lace. Fancy me as Carmen?" jumping up from the chair to strike a romantic pose at the foot of the sofa and leering suggestively over the tattered fragments of the fan, "I throw down thees r-r-red r-r-rose at your feet, Don José. Peeck it up and you weel fall in love!"

"Ravishing," replied Jamie, unimpressed. "You've got just the beard for the female lead. Here, hand it over before you do any more damage. Really it's Bea's."

Adam stared at the fan and clapped a guilty hand to his mouth.

"Oh shit! She'll go ballistic."

"Are you kidding? You could smash her flute and cut her harp strings one by one and she'd take it all without a murmur, the size of crush she has on you. We just gotta find the right way of breaking the bad news to her when she gets back from her concert."

Adam was protesting modestly when the door opened and Bea appeared, calling back over her shoulder in the direction of the kitchen,

"Whereabouts in the living room, Mum?" She stopped short in well-counterfeited surprise. "Oh – Adam! Didn't know you were here."

"Liar," contradicted Jamie. "Where else would he be? But come right in, Bea, and take a good gawp at him anyway."

"Can't think what you're talking about," retorted Bea, colouring in annoyance. "It's probably the malaria. Geoff says it can affect the brain cells. You'll have to be careful, Jamie – you haven't got too many to spare…" Then, seeing Adam edge away in an awkward attempt to keep something concealed behind his back, "Is that the Spanish fan?" she demanded eagerly. "Mum said Great Aunt Rosita wanted me to have it. She was telling me all about finding it this afternoon. May I see?"

Jamie and Adam exchanged uneasy glances.

"Oh it's just a dirty old thing," Jamie intervened quickly. "Why bother with a fan when you've got Adam here to feast your eyes on? Whatever can be making the tips of your ears turn so red, Bea?"

Infuriated by his teasing, Bea held out her hand and exclaimed petulantly,

"You're a slimy toad, Jamie. I know one of you's got it. Give it to me."

At this point Adam realised the game was up. He stepped forward with the fan in his hand and a well-assumed expression of humble penitence on his face.

"Here it is, Bea. I've got it. And I also have a confession to make before you look at it. I was fooling around just now and it accidentally tore straight down the middle. I'm really sorry. If you like, I'll buy you another one to make up for it. You could come down to London one weekend and choose something really pretty in place of that ugly old one," trying hard to atone for the disappointment in her eyes as she opened the torn remnants of her fan. "I'd even take you out for dinner as well… Or I know – " with sudden inspiration "– how about when Jamie and I go to Spain in the summer, I could bring you back a fan from there instead?"

Bea was clearly savouring her advantage, bent on keeping those pleading, dark eyes fixed exclusively on herself.

"Oh Adam," she murmured, fluttering her eyelashes. "How sweet of you!"

Jamie breathed a sigh of relief. From the evidence of her expression, her mind was busy weighing up the immediate pleasures of a weekend in London against the more distant prospect of acquiring a glamorous Spanish fan in the summer. But at any rate Adam's resourcefulness had saved the day.

"Why don't you think about it over dinner and tell me before I leave tonight?" coaxed Adam with a winning smile. "How was the concert by the way? You gonna play me something later on…?"

Jamie watched his friend expertly smoothing away the unpleasant incident with practised gallantry. Adam was a born babe magnet. From their earliest school days, he'd only had to glance at a girl for her to fall over herself fighting to play chase in the playground or partner him in country dancing. Even before sitting his first public examinations at sixteen, he'd looked mature enough to be in his early twenties and these days, with the addition of the beard, he could easily've passed for thirty. Jamie felt like a gawky teenager beside him.

The old fan lay forgotten on the sofa while Adam and Bea stood chatting together, until Mum popped her head round the door and asked her to call Marc down for dinner. Bea breezed out of the room with a flirtatious giggle, clearly looking forward to the approaching meal. As soon as she disappeared, Adam dropped his mask of flattering charm.

"Close shave," he breathed. "Really thought she was gonna burst into tears for a moment there when she opened that fan and it just fell apart in her hands."

"You didn't have to go quite so over the top," remarked Jamie coolly. "She's such a little gold-digger, she'll be bound to pick out some huge, expensive fan instead of this little, old one. How'll you ever afford it? – not to mention where she'll insist on being taken to eat."

"It's all right. Know a nice little place I can easily talk her into. And after all, how much can a fan cost? They're just stage props."

"Yeah, but this one's been in the family for years," pointed out Jamie, picking up the old fan and turning it over in his hands. He glanced up at Adam. "I feel a twinge of guilt. More than one, in fact. If it's an antique, it could've been worth serious money."

"That's why I thought I'd better pull out all the stops to make it up to her."

"D'you reckon it could be repaired? S'pose there must be some way of sticking broken fans back together again. People at costume museums'd probably know what to do."

"Yeah, but I've never heard of a costume museum in Cambridge. You'd have to take it to London."

They both stared at the ruined fan as it lay in Jamie's open palm.

Suddenly Adam exclaimed, "Hey, you're pretty good with your hands. Why not have a go at fixing it yourself?"

Jamie hesitated.

"But I don't know anything about fixing fans."

"Can't be that difficult. Why don't you google it?"

Sounded easy enough when Adam suggested it. But as Jamie thought things over later that night when his friend had left for the station, he couldn't help feeling a slight prickle of irritation. Adam always had big ideas and then left him with the tricky job of trying to carry them out. It was all very well to suggest he repair the fan himself, but you couldn't just follow instructions downloaded from the internet when it came to antiques. You had to talk to experts at museums and stuff like that. So where could he find someone who knew about old fans?

Chapter Six

Had to get out of the house.

If Mum knew what he was gonna do, she'd've stopped him of course. But now he was feeling a lot better, she was out at work during the day, leaving him alone at home. He was meant to be resting quietly on the sofa, listening to music on his phone or watching movies on TV. But he'd made no actual promise to stay put and he was gonna suffocate if he lay about any longer, shut up inside four walls with nothing to do.

So that afternoon he pulled on his old overcoat and canvas rucksack and caught a bus up to town. He drifted aimlessly for some time around the rainy streets of central Cambridge, buffeted this way and that like a fallen leaf in a swift-eddying river current by heedless crowds shopping for potatoes, leaf tea and bunches of green daffodil spears under the blue and white striped canopies of the open-air market stalls.

As he loitered past Lion Yard shopping centre, it suddenly struck him that the public library was likely to contain career guidance material. At least he ought to look as though he was making some effort to find a job for next year. And they might also stock books about fan repair. In a short-lived burst of enthusiasm last week he'd tried searching the internet for advice but failed to turn up any useful information and had forgotten all about it since.

Having nothing else to do, he threaded his way through crowds of elderly women pulling tartan trundlers and students hurrying late to lectures with damp cheeks and furrowed foreheads until he reached the lift to the main floor of the library.

As he stood waiting, a piercing shriek of glee rang out behind and glancing down, he caught sight of a toddler in a bright yellow snow suit and red woolly hat, who scampered up and jabbed repeatedly on the call button.

The lift took a while to respond, so the toddler's mother had time to catch up, pushing a buggy heavily laden with shopping bags. She was an oldish woman – mid-thirties at least – wearing a flowing blue skirt and baggy lilac jumper. A long dark plait threaded with silver hung down the back of her sensible, navy rain jacket.

There was a whirr as the lift reached the ground floor and the doors slid open.

The woman politely motioned him ahead of herself and the toddler, who then drove the buggy so forcefully inside that it rebounded off the back wall of the lift with a clatter. Jamie found himself pinned into one corner with the wheels jammed against his ankles and a wet plastic rain hood poking into his ribs. With a conciliatory smile, the woman quickly pulled the buggy aside and asked which floor he wanted.

Before he could reply, the toddler had taken matters into his own pudgy little hands and sent the lift first plummeting towards the basement and then hurtling up to the second floor of the carpark.

"I'm so sorry," apologised the woman as the doors clanged open for the third time on the plate glass foyer of the lending library.

At this point Jamie, hell-bent on escape at any price, made a lunge for freedom. But the toddler, keen to help push the buggy out of the lift, reached up and seized its handle. His mother tried to stop him, but it was too late. He'd already rammed the sharp edge of the plastic footrest straight into Jamie's shin.

Jamie recoiled with a yell and a suppressed oath.

"Ouch," exclaimed the woman, dragging the heavily laden pushchair away. "I'm so sorry. Josh, you must take care not to bump the buggy into other people's legs." She turned back to Jamie, who was rubbing his bruised shin and eyeing the hit-squad trainee of a toddler warily, and asked if he was all right.

Jamie grunted a non-committal reply and gazed vaguely around, seeking refuge from further assault. The woman clearly felt obliged to be helpful.

"The computer catalogue's just over there," she pointed out in a kindly manner. "Are you looking for something in particular? We come here quite often, so I might be able to point you in the right direction."

"It's OK," Jamie mumbled, retreating several paces in the hope of avoiding fatal injury. "Good luck with him," he added, nodding towards the toddler, who'd just barged straight into the ladies' toilets past a tiny Indian girl with wide open eyes.

He soon forgot all about the chance encounter as he wandered along rows of books encouraging him to apply for dull-sounding jobs like accountancy, civil engineering and management consultancy. Couldn't see himself as a solicitor, or an insurance salesman, or an electrician for that matter, and what on earth did an advertising executive do? Boredom rapidly set in, so he turned away. P'raps he'd go and take a look at what they had on fans instead.

It wasn't a subject to which the public lending library devoted much shelf space. At first, crouching impatiently on the worn, blue carpet tiles with his head on one side scanning the book titles, Jamie thought the accession number he'd been referred to by the electronic catalogue was empty. In fact he was on the point of giving up altogether when something caught his eye.

Folding Fans from the Lydgate Museum by Elinor

Mitford

he read in elegant, flowing script on the cerise spine of a volume half-jutting out of the very bottom shelf at his feet.

He frowned. Couldn't remember seeing any fans at the Lydgate on school trips years ago. Curious, he pulled the book from its place and squatted back on his haunches to examine the cover.

It pictured a half-fan spread on red lacquered and gilded sticks. The pink and white flower sprays framing a Chinese garden were as delicate as porcelain painting. But what was going on in this garden? Jamie stared harder. Why – it was breath-taking! Like gazing through an open window straight into the lives of people in a totally different time and place.

There stood a low, white tea table with a stringed instrument lying on it – like a lute or mandolin. In one of the two blue chairs was curled an elegant lady with elaborately dressed hair, wearing a lilac jacket with blue undersleeves. Jamie saw her pointed chin resting lightly on one hand and her pale face turned towards a little boy in yellow trousers and a red jacket, who stood on the second chair energetically waving something as if to attract her attention. A toy perhaps? Or no – actually it looked like a tiny hand screen. In the background a white house with a red roof nestled beside a rocky cliff face and above hung feathery green willow boughs and a thin-twigged tree, starred with clusters of blue blossom and berries like glinting sapphires. Among the branches perched a slender-legged bird flaunting a long turquoise tail and a crimson crest, observing the scene with one keen, jet-black eye.

Every detail was drawn with absolute clarity: the pegs of the musical instrument, the mother's indulgent smile, even the nails in the wooden table and the butterflies flitting among the foliage with their wispy legs and curled antennae. Who were these people? What were they doing in this fragile paradise? And what was on the rest of the fan leaf – the part he couldn't see?

He turned the book over, but the picture didn't continue on the back. Frustration, sharp as a jab in the ribs, squeezed his heart until he felt himself gasping for breath…

The next moment he'd staggered to his feet in a daze. His top lip felt damp and a hot sweat was breaking out all over his body. The low ceiling pressed down upon him and the harsh fluorescent lighting made the lurid colours of the book jackets glow with artificial brightness until the room was dancing dizzily before his eyes. His knees began to sag and he could feel himself falling…

"Are you all right?" cried a woman's distant voice, jerking him back from black unconsciousness.

Jamie dimly recalled hearing the same voice ask him the same question before. But when? A reassuring arm encircled his back, capably steering him in the direction of a nearby chair, into which he dropped without ceremony, head sunk forward over his knees.

As the mists cleared before his vision, he found himself staring up into a pair of concerned dark eyes. They belonged to a woman – a woman he recognised. The mother of Josh, the kamikaze toddler.

Jamie, who hated any public show of physical weakness, jerked upright, hot with embarrassment.

"Are you all right?" the woman repeated, tactfully withdrawing her arm to allow him breathing space. "I thought you were going to faint."

Jamie mumbled some barely audible reply.

"I was sitting just over there," she explained, gesturing towards the children's book corner where Josh sat perched in the cab of the little blue and yellow train stacked with children's books, busily spinning the driver's wheel and uttering loud chuffing noises. "All of a sudden I saw you turn white as a sheet and start to sway. Feeling better now?"

"Yes – er… thanks. Just needed to sit down for a minute."

Must've overdone things a bit.

"You still look terribly pale," she added, surveying his face anxiously. "Shall I ask one of the library staff for a glass of water?"

"No, no, I'll be fine. It's nothing – really," he murmured. If Mum found out about this, he'd never hear the end of it. "I'm just about to head home anyway. It's not far."

"Well, if you're sure…"

She sounded doubtful.

"Yeah. Hey – thanks," he reassured her, straightening up in an effort to convince her he was fit to be left on his own.

She rose hesitantly, then seemed to remember something.

"The book you were holding. It dropped onto the floor somewhere. Hang on a minute. I'll find it for you."

And before he could stop her, she'd knelt down and begun rummaging underneath the shelves. As she picked up the book and handed it to him, her gaze fell on its cover.

"Oh," she exclaimed. "You're interested in fans?"

Jamie threw her a questioning glance.

"It's just that you don't look like the average fan fancier," she went on. "My sister's really keen on them too. In fact that's her book you've got there."

Jamie stared at her blankly.

"My name's Catherine Prescott," she went on quickly, checking again to make sure Josh was still happily driving the train. "My sister Ellie's the curator of fans at the Lydgate Museum and she knows an awful lot about them. Now isn't that a coincidence?"

Jamie nodded. Imagine knowing an "awful lot" about anything as obscure as fans.

"Help. Where's he off to now?" cried Catherine suddenly.

Jamie turned and caught sight of Josh, who'd scrambled down from the train engine and was now making a beeline for the lift with a book he'd grabbed out of one of the bright red carriages.

"He'll set off the alarm again. Mind keeping an eye on the buggy for me?" And Catherine sprinted after Josh, finally catching up with him near the issues desk. For someone so old she could put on a reasonable spurt of speed, Jamie noticed.

By the time she returned with the toddler loudly protesting under one arm, Jamie had pulled himself together. The last thing he wanted was any more well-meant enquiries about his health.

Realising this, but clearly planning to keep a watchful eye on him for a little longer, Catherine made another reference to the book he was holding. They fell into conversation as they joined the straggling queue at the issues desk with the pushchair, the books and the toddler, who was keen to show off his week's reading to the tolerant admiration of the elderly librarian.

Gradually won over by Catherine's business-like frankness, Jamie, who was normally suspicious of strangers, even went so far as to mutter a few words about Great Aunt Rosita's damaged fan.

"A Spanish mask fan. Sounds most unusual," mused Catherine, as she strapped a protesting Josh firmly into his pushchair before venturing out into the gloom that already shrouded the bustling, glass-roofed shopping mall. "I'm sure Ellie'd love to see it. And she might be able to tell you something about its history too. She studied hundreds of fans while she was researching her doctoral thesis. It was based around the collection in the Hermitage Museum in Russia, but she made a trip to America and several other places too."

Some people had all the luck, thought Jamie.

"Now look," began Catherine, apparently reaching a snap decision as they walked along side by side in the direction of the bus stops, "I don't want to be pushy, but would you really like to know more about that fan of yours?"

Jamie nodded slowly. He was beginning to find her brisk, managing air rather tiring.

Catherine looked pleased.

"If you like," she offered, "I could speak to Ellie tonight when she and Dad come over for dinner and arrange for you to show it to her. They've an excellent conservation department at the Lydgate and I'm sure Ellie could give you some tips on how to mend your fan. She does repairs herself too…"

Jamie ended by giving Catherine his mobile number, which she noted down on the bottom of her shopping list in small, neat handwriting. When he finally left her, she was busy steering Josh's buggy aboard a bus bound for Fen Ditton to pick up her daughter from after-school club. Darkness was closing in as he turned his flagging steps towards his own stop.

As far as he was concerned, that was the end of the business. Even if Catherine remembered to mention the subject at dinner tonight, her sister sounded like a pretty busy person…

*

By the time his own bus arrived, the drizzle had begun again and he stood dazed and drooping with exhaustion.

In the queue he'd found himself beside a swollen mound of a woman with a frizzy orange perm and a cascade of double chins. She enquired in detail about his pallor, went on to address him as "ducks" and then treated him to a full history of her own ailments despite his monosyllabic indifference. All he could think about, as her fretful voice droned on and on in his ears, was of crawling home and lying down in peaceful, unbroken silence.

When it was his turn to board the bus, he waved the fat woman on ahead of him, not wholly motivated by chivalry. She waddled up the aisle while he dropped gratefully into the first free seat he glimpsed, enveloped by the smell of wet footprints, dripping umbrellas and damp overcoats steaming in the warmth of the heating.

A moment later he realised the fat woman was turning to check what had become of him. She even seemed to be debating whether she could squeeze her vast bulk into the spare seat beside him. How to avoid being talked to death all the way home?

He swiftly swung his battered rucksack up onto his knee and pulled open the broken fastenings. Dragging out the first object that came to hand, which happened to be the book he'd taken out of the library, he promptly buried his nose in a random page. After a long moment of hesitation, the woman was hailed by an acquaintance and finally rolled away down the bus.

Jamie breathed a sigh of relief and turned the book right way up. Hadn't a clue why he'd borrowed this. Would've been better off bringing home some career guidance brochures. But he might as well see if it contained any advice on fan repair.

At that moment the bus jolted into motion and threw Jamie head-first into the open picture in front of him. As he drew back from the bright golden blur on the page, he found himself face to face with a white hare, poised erect on its hind legs in a clump of spinach-green leaves and gazing upwards at a round, silver moon riding high among the clouds. The caption told him that the fan came from nineteenth century Japan.

As the bus bumped and swayed along, Jamie began leafing through other illustrations.

A cream fan from England scattered with finely detailed and labelled specimens of botanical plants. A French court fan depicting a comfortable boudoir with a dressing table and a dog in a basket, occupied by fashionable ladies in tall, powdered wigs, who were embroidering and playing the spinet among garlands of flowers and sequined spangles. A Chinese fan embellished with a pair of gaudy pheasants, its ivory sticks embossed with green and blue pagodas. A flower fan composed entirely of an assortment of bright-hued feathers…

Greedily he devoured page after page. It was a dazzling revelation, like someone switching on a light in a dark room around which he'd been blindly groping for years. Never before had he realised there existed in this mundane world such glorious and delicate objects, crafted from silk, satin, lace, chicken skin, sandalwood, carved ivory, flamboyant peacock and ostrich feathers and decorated in such an astonishing variety of –

CRASH! The bus braked and he lurched forward against the seat in front. Abruptly roused from this paradise of fans, he peered through the windowpane, misty with condensation. Everything was dark outside, but those lighted windows must belong to the Chesterton Road shops. Missed his stop! Tossing the book hastily into his rucksack and scrambling to his feet, he stumbled off the bus.

Outside it was still raining miserably. He turned up his coat collar and set off to trudge back along the busy main road, dodging spray from passing car tyres and puddles pockmarked with fast-falling raindrops, lit by the watery beams of oncoming headlights.

But his mood of listless exhaustion had vanished. Glowing visions of many-coloured fan leaves jostled before his eyes and he owed them all to Elinor Mitford. He could hardly believe that this lady of unfolding rainbows lived right here in Cambridge and at this very moment was perhaps not far away beneath this same weeping, wintry sky. She must inhabit the most glamorous world imaginable…

Chapter Seven

"…Thus, in view of extensive Chinese interest in western Asia during the first half of the fifteenth century, it's very surprising that, among the approximately six hundred porcelains of the Yuan and Ming dynasty which we possess, so few pieces have to date been discovered in Syria…"

"Indeed," agreed Elinor, her eyes following the mesmeric motion of the bushy walrus moustache as it rhythmically rose and fell above gusts of mephitic breath from the hot, black cavern of his mouth. She edged a little closer to her open office door. "But really I –"

"Quite so," intoned her learned colleague from the Department of Oriental Antiquities, effectively cutting off her retreat by interposing his expansive red and yellow floral waistcoat between her and the threshold. "Yet have you considered how easily the apparent discrepancy can be explained by the contemporary situation in Syria?"

Did he mean the recent civil war? Jerking her gaze back onto his heavy jowls as she struggled to maintain an air of polite interest, Elinor meekly confessed that she hadn't.

"I thought as much," he declared in measured triumph. "You must realise that after Timur's campaign of destruction in the year 1400 and the sack of Damascus, along with that of other major Syrian cities, Mamluk trade suffered a serious reverse and in fact failed to recover its momentum until at least the end of the century…"

Ah! 'Contemporary' clearly meant over six hundred years ago…

Escape from Gerald Hardcastle in full flow wasn't easy. He was notorious for his habit of lecturing everyone, especially his long-suffering colleagues, in the sonorous drone of an old-fashioned vicar delivering a lengthy Sunday sermon. Elinor always tried to bear with him since he had a disabled wife at home who sank her frustration in cigarettes, alcohol and caustic self-martyrdom. But that afternoon there were a dozen jobs calling for her attention…

In the end she steeled herself to blurt out that someone was coming to see her at two. Then, diving into her office, she hastily shut the door to prevent him following her, which had happened several times before. She leant her back against the closed door, suffering acute pangs of conscience. But he simply must realise that she had work to do.

She sat down at her desk and picked a pencil out of the fan-papered cylinder in front of her, intending to occupy the few moments left before two o'clock in jotting down one or two reminders on her notepad.

She wasn't expecting to gain much from this interview. In fact she'd only agreed to it as a favour to her sister. Cathy could be so – so managerial sometimes.

Apparently she'd bumped into some student in town who claimed to have an old Spanish mask fan in need of repair. Sounded like just another shady character on the make. After all, what other interest would a normal teenage boy have in an antique fan? Quite possibly he, or whoever he was working for, had filched it from an uncatalogued collection somewhere and might try to palm it off on the museum as his own property. The chances of a real eighteenth century mask fan surfacing unexpectedly like this were very remote.

And even if the fan was genuine, ten to one it would probably have been so maltreated that restoration was almost impossible. Fan repair was nothing but a can of worms. People always regarded her so hopefully, as though all she had to do was wave a magic wand and a shining new duplicate would spring forth like a phoenix from the forlorn heap of broken sticks they'd handed her with all its sequins and spangles rattling around loose in the bottom of a plastic carrier bag.

But she couldn't afford to ignore even an outside chance of a significant new discovery. So she'd agreed to this interview, though feeling rather put upon in view of how busy she was at the moment with additions to the on-line catalogue behind schedule and the introduction for her projected guide to *The Fans of the Meynell Collection* due in shortly to her editor at the University Press.

The minutes ticked slowly past as she sat twiddling the pencil between impatient fingers. She heard the muffled crash of Edwin Chadwick's office door further down the hall. Off to his two o'clock class, late as usual. That man was so absent-minded that his students often had to come and haul him bodily away to the coin room…

Annoyance soon set in. According to her watch, this boy was now ten minutes late. Perhaps he wasn't coming at all, like so many people without the courtesy to ring and cancel their appointments, who merely failed to turn up. She could've proofread half that introduction by now…

She was about to open her laptop when a hesitant knock sounded on the door.

"Come in," she called, glancing up without much expectation.

The door slowly opened and in slouched a lank, unshaven scarecrow wearing a grubby-looking army surplus overcoat, metal-toed jackboots and tattered jeans which hung loose on his tall, gaunt frame. His sallow skin was sunken beneath high cheekbones, his nose and earlobes were spiked with an off-putting array of sharp metal studs and his long, streaky blond hair straggled down across a khaki canvas rucksack slung carelessly over one shoulder.

Elinor's mouth fell open. Good heavens! Even worse than she'd anticipated...

*

The main wing of the Lydgate Museum had been purpose-built in the mid-nineteenth century to house the university's priceless art bequests and owed a conspicuous debt to classical antecedents.

After jaywalking across Tillington Street through throngs of bicycles streaming into town for afternoon lectures, Jamie paused on the pavement to survey his destination. His gaze travelled slowly up the soaring façade of white Corinthian columns to the stately pediment, where an assembly of stone divinities sat in attitudes of frozen dignity, their heads wreathed in chilly vapours and their eyes fixed eternally on the clouds. Pretty awe-inspiring job location. He turned to mount the broad flight of steps towards the imposing front entrance. The lofty, pillared portico opened into an echoing reception hall, from which a double flight of stairs with dark-veined marble balustrades swept majestically upwards to the sky-lit picture galleries above.

Somewhat subdued by the formal grandeur of his surroundings, Jamie shambled diffidently up to the reception desk, which was manned by a pair of grim-looking attendants. When he revealed that he'd come about a fan, the bluff, bull-necked one threw him such a doubtful glance that for a moment he wondered whether he ought not to have worn some decent trousers and a sweater instead of his scruffy old overcoat and jeans with holes in the knee patches. But the mention of Dr Mitford's name effected a miracle. He soon found himself being ushered with scrupulous politeness through a pair of massive, half-glazed doors, giving access to what he quickly realised must be the conservation and research departments of the museum, normally hidden from public view. Then he and his guide descended some stairs and plunged into a labyrinth of chill, shadowy corridors.

The place was a vast rabbit warren, he thought, wrinkling up his nose at the musty odour of stale, imprisoned air. Imagine coming to work here every day. How'd you ever find your way out again?

Eventually they approached a drab alcove at the end of a long, dim hallway. The only illumination came from the cold, grey light filtering in through a tall window from the well-like shaft of an enclosed inner courtyard.

"Here we are, lad," announced his helpful guide. "That's Dr Mitford's office."

As he spoke, a nearby door flew open and out popped a thin, little man with a high, balding forehead, who wore dark trousers and a tweed jacket smelling strongly of mothballs.

"Good afternoon, sir." Jamie's guide greeted him with a respectful nod.

The little man glanced at him in surprise and, blinking his pink-rimmed eyes nervously, muttered some inaudible excuse about being late as he scurried off down the hall like a harassed White Rabbit, leaving the heavy door to slam shut behind him. The hollow crash echoed eerily through the sepulchral silence.

Jamie stared after the rapidly retreating figure. Had he only dreamed this goblin-like inhabitant of a twilit underworld?

"Young Professor Chadwick, the Curator of the Coin Collection," his guide informed him in a significant whisper.

Young Professor Chadwick? Was the guy kidding? The gnome looked at least fifty, if he was a day.

"Just knock at Dr Mitford's door," his guide advised in a kindly manner. "She'll be expecting you."

He motioned Jamie on ahead, then stumped off back down the corridor, where he was soon swallowed up in the subterranean gloom.

Left alone, Jamie uneasily surveyed the heavy, wood-panelled door with its polished brass knob and nameplate inscribed in forbidding black letters: DR. E. F. MITFORD.

His vision of an exquisite lady of folding rainbows had long vanished in a wisp of smoke. You'd have to be a million years old to work in a mouldering dump like this. It was the sort of place where you could easily lie dead for twenty years before anybody noticed.

Might even walk into her office and find the skeleton of a fossilised old crone stretched out across the desk, draped in a film of cobwebs.

He almost turned back unannounced. What stopped him was the realisation that he'd never be able to reach daylight again without help. And after all, having come so far, what did he stand to lose?

He knocked hesitantly on the door.

"Come in," called a woman's voice, so Jamie walked inside.

At first, all that met his gaze was a sizeable room lined from floor to ceiling with shelves of dreary-looking academic tomes, smelling of beeswax polish and crumbling antiquity. What a holiday camp for earwigs and silverfish! Then he noticed in the centre of the study a massive mahogany desk neatly stacked with filing trays brim-full of paper. Behind this desk sat Dr Mitford herself, exactly the kind of dowdy, middle-aged spinster he'd been expecting. Her mousy hair was scraped back into a severe bun and she wore a drab grey suit and gold-rimmed spectacles perched on her thin, straight nose. She rose briskly at his entrance.

"You must be Jamie Willett," she announced with an air of professional assurance. "Pleased to meet you."

Her tone was dry and clipped. She didn't sound that pleased, to his ears.

"Er... me too," stammered Jamie, lunging awkwardly forward to shake the hand which she'd extended to him in a business-like manner.

"You've come about a fan, I believe. Do you have it with you?"

"What? Oh yeah. It's in here," replied Jamie, pulling off his rucksack and resting it on the hard, brass-studded leather chair which stood directly in front of the monumental desk.

Dr Mitford was observing his movements with such keen attention that it made him fumble clumsily with the broken fastenings. It took him a while to unearth the fan from the litter of plastic bags, headphone cables, torn papers and squashed packets of chewing gum that always seemed to lurk at the bottom of his rucksack. When he finally pulled out the battered red case and tipped the fan into his hand, he thought he heard a sigh escape her.

"It's pretty much falling to bits," he mumbled apologetically, unfurling a few pleats and wondering if he wasn't wasting her time by bringing her this ugly old wreck to examine. From near to, he noticed, she didn't look quite as ancient as he'd first thought –

especially when he caught her eye like that. P'raps more like mid-thirties…

Dr Mitford coloured and drew back at once.

"I'm sorry," she murmured. "It's just that I've never seen a mask fan close to before. I've not made a particular study of them of course, but I do remember a very rare French one with a painted face in the Hermitage collection. It has the same pierced eye slits, but very elaborate silver and gilt guards –" She suddenly stopped. Then, darting a swift glance at his face, she went on, "Please excuse the technical vocabulary. Guards are –"

"Yeah, the slightly wider sticks at each end that guard the fan's safety," interrupted Jamie automatically and then paused as her eyes flicked back to his face in surprise. At least that was what he'd thought. "Aren't they?" Must've made a mistake.

"Well – yes," agreed Dr Mitford quickly. "Er… would you mind if I took a closer look? The leaf seems extraordinarily detailed."

Jamie handed over the fan. She carried it almost with reverence to the long window, beneath which stood a table containing a large wooden bookstand. He trailed after her curiously.

"Opening an antique fan can be very hazardous," she told him, gently coaxing the folds apart. "Often the leaf cracks – old paper can be very brittle – and tends to tear or split along the edges of the pleats. You see... here, and here."

Jamie looked where she was pointing with a pang of remorse. Should've handled it a lot more carefully in the first place.

"What're you doing?" he went on aloud, as she turned the fan over in her deft, slender fingers and examined its border with minute attention.

"Just seeing if there's a name or date of publication on the leaf. When fans were being quickly produced, such details were often cut off the prints to make them fit the mounts. It's always worth checking, but in this case no luck, as you can see for yourself. I suppose there was no card or enclosure inside the case that might help establish a context or provenance for it?"

"Just what you can see."

She clearly knew what she was talking about, Jamie decided with a glimmer of grudging respect.

"A pity. Well, considering its age – and it certainly does appear to date to the eighteenth century – it's not in such bad condition. You don't happen to know if this case is original, do you?"

He shrugged helplessly.

"It's just that it looks as though it's been quite well kept – until recently, at least." Jamie winced self-consciously. "Old fans often pick up a lot of dust and grime from lying neglected in trunks in attic and cellars and so on, but this one's cleaner than some I've seen and none of the sticks are broken either. They'd come up quite respectably with a bit of care and attention."

"I like the ivory carving," Jamie heard himself volunteer, much to his own surprise.

"Yes, it's lovely, isn't it? And the hand-coloured engravings on the leaf are very interesting. Have you taken a good look at them?"

"Well… er… not really."

"I don't think I've ever seen anything like these before. It's absolutely fascinating. Notice the extraordinary detail. I wonder what's going on in that picture." She bent to examine the leaf more closely. "See there, down in the bottom right-hand corner."

Jamie stared hard, frowning with the effort of concentration.

"Looks like a load of fans spread out on a counter," he ventured slowly, since she'd know so much more about fan illustration than he did.

"It must be a fan shop. And that lady standing behind the counter in the pink dress – she'd be the saleswoman. And she's holding up – no, I don't believe it!"

"Believe what?"

Jamie strained his eyes to see.

"Look at that," she urged, pointing excitedly. "She's holding up a mask fan to the customer in yellow. It's self-referential."

Jamie gulped. Self-referential? What the hell was she on about?

Dr Mitford didn't pause to explain, so absorbed was she in the other pictures on the fan leaf. "There's another scene here of a woman standing in a cobbled street. Holding a mask in front of her face, I think. Perhaps she's an actress. And then one of a man and a woman –"

"Looks like she's hitting him with a broom," suggested Jamie, studying the tiny figures more attentively.

"And then what might be a sheet music shop. Four vignettes altogether. There must be some link between them, but I've no idea what it could be. How interesting to try to find out."

"Never realised the pictures might mean something," admitted Jamie thoughtfully.

"Well of course they do. Fans are highly symbolic objects – and they tell us a lot about social history too."

So he'd begun to realise. But right now there was a rather more practical purpose for his visit.

"What do you think're the chances of mending it?" he asked bluntly.

"That depends," she answered, straightening up and looking him in the eye. She was actually quite tall for a woman. Only half a head shorter than himself.

"On what?" he prompted.

"On why you want to mend it. The folds could certainly be repaired to disguise the tears and splits and the rivet removed so the sticks and guards could be cleaned."

Sounded simple enough.

"So it's a possible DIY job?"

"How much patience have you got?" This felt like a challenge.

"It's hard work and very time-consuming," she explained frankly.

"Of course it's possible to undertake repairs at home so long as you

have some simple specialist equipment and are prepared to spend a

lot of time and effort on the job. But with such an old fan you might

be better off bringing it to the museum for proper conservation."

"But wouldn't that cost mega-bucks?" objected Jamie.

"Possibly," she replied, carefully closing up the fan.

"How much?"

"I wouldn't like to name a sum without consulting the other

experts I use in dealing with such matters." She was clearly talking

serious money then. "That's why I said it depends on the reason you

want to mend the fan as to how much you'd consider worth spending

on it."

She politely offered it back to him.

"Now I take it that you actually own this fan?" she asked, as he

reached out his hand to take it.

"It belongs to my family," admitted Jamie, colouring at the

implication of her enquiry. "Really it's my sister, Beatrice's."

"Then I think you need to go home and discuss the matter with her," she advised with what sounded like patronising kindness. "You see, antique fans have various uses. I imagine an elderly relative's given it to her as a keepsake?"

Jamie nodded tersely, insulted by her air of apparent condescension.

"Then she might just want it patched up prettily so she can enjoy looking at it, in which case I could recommend a book that'd help…"

Patched up prettily! What'd she think he was? A child? Or a fool? Who else'd agree to an antique fan being 'patched up prettily?'

"…But if your sister wanted to sell it, then it'd be quite a different matter," she went on more seriously. "In that case she'd really need to consider whether it was worth repairing at all because of the cost involved or whether it wouldn't be better to sell it in its present condition and let a museum or a private purchaser handle the restoration."

"So you think a museum'd be interested in buying it?" asked Jamie quickly.

"Oh definitely. It'd be a valuable addition to any collection. Particularly if that was the original case. I'd love to work on it myself. It's got an interesting history, I can see that. But it's a big responsibility and as such, requires careful consideration. Especially on your sister's part. So I'd suggest that perhaps she, in consultation with your parents, should decide what she'd like to do. And then you could contact me again. I'll give you my card."

She crossed quickly back to the desk and, opening the top drawer, drew out a small, rectangular business card which she handed to him. "If you need any further advice, I'd be pleased to help in any way I can," she concluded brightly. "It's a most intriguing fan, quite apart from its beauty as an art object."

Jamie understood from her tone that their meeting was now at an end. He hastily scooped up the worn red case from where it lay on the table and, slipping the fan inside, bundled it back into his rucksack. Without waiting for any but the briefest of leave-takings, he hurried out of the office, following a short-cut to the side exit which she pointed out to him. The back of his neck burned like fire.

Well of all the insulting hags! "Now I take it that you actually own this fan…" What'd she think he bloody well was? A thief?

"Patched up prettily" indeed! Bet he could do just as good as job on it as her, given time. The visit'd been a total waste of effort and worse than that, she'd made him feel like a mentally backward five-year-old. As for ever contacting her again…!

He glanced down contemptuously at the business card she'd handed him, decorated with a delicate border of pale mauve fans. He'd never sodding well need that again, would he? And he tore it up in a passion of revenge and tossed the tiny pieces into the nearest rubbish bin.

Chapter Eight

The door with the number Elinor was searching for stood sandwiched between a florist's shop and a savoury-smelling Turkish kebab house. Must be right. On the wall hung a large pink sign announcing the Harlequin Dance Studios in bold, black letters. Also it sounded as though a party was in full swing overhead. She rang the bell, looking up at the first-floor windows, which glowed with lights.

Normally she wouldn't accept an invitation like this from anyone but a close friend – especially not one that involved hunting up fancy dress and a mask. But when her flamenco teacher invited the whole class along to her thirtieth birthday party, she decided that if she didn't get out more, she'd end up stifled by life at home with Dad. Besides, it was flattering to be asked to a party by someone like Camilla Quinn.

Camilla radiated glamour and energy. Though only a little older than herself, she'd been a professional for years. Elinor gathered she'd begun her career as a teenager in amateur ballroom dancing competitions and gone on to win a number of prestigious international awards in her early twenties. After appearing in numerous West End shows, on TV and in feature films, she now taught ballroom and flamenco at the leisure centre, as well as running the studio here in Cherry Hinton along with her dance partner and boyfriend, Henry Howard.

Was nobody ever going to answer this door? Elinor stepped back and stared upward at the lighted windows. Probably couldn't hear above the noise of the music... She rang again – more assertively this time.

How chilly it was out here on such a clear, frosty night! Shivering, she pulled her dark woollen coat closer over the red and white flounced skirts and fringed black shawl that she'd borrowed from Camilla's costume store for the occasion. As she did so, she happened to catch sight of her unfamiliar reflection with loosened hair in the glass of the darkened florist's window. Felt a bit of an idiot dressed up like this at her age...

She raised a hand to the red-spangled mask. After struggling for ages to adjust it over her glasses in the Audi's rear view mirror, it'd still bulged so uncomfortably that she'd finally given up and stuffed the glasses into her handbag. She was hopelessly short-sighted, but it was just too bad. Tonight she'd have to make do with peering at the world through a myopic haze…

Clearly no one was coming to answer this door. And if she stood out here any longer, she'd freeze to death. Perhaps she'd just better go home. But then… what a waste of a free Friday night, with Dad busy improving his game of bridge among some retired colleagues. Maybe…

Finding the door yielded to a light touch, she pushed it open and stepped into the welcome warmth of a small entrance lobby at the foot of a steep flight of stairs. Suddenly the music sounded twice as loud.

She rustled awkwardly upstairs, clutching her handbag and the bottle of wine she'd brought as a present for Camilla in one hand and hitching up her long, ruffled skirts with the other. At the top she hesitated on the threshold of an open door. It led into a large, bare-boarded studio, clearly designed for dance lessons since the far wall was lined with mirrors. But instead of reflecting students diligently practising their steps, tonight they prolonged vistas of multi-coloured streamers and strings of shiny tinsel. Beneath a huge cluster of gold and silver balloons glittered a heaving throng of party guests:

cloaked vampires and pirate queens, gold-braided toreadors and court ladies in crinolines flirting lace fans, their ringlets adorned with curling feathers.

"Come in! Come in," cried a hearty voice.

A huge red mouth confronted her, gaping from a stark white face above a yellow and blue polka-dot bow tie. A glass of wine was thrust into her free hand as she strove to focus on the gaudy figure of a circus clown in a frizzy red wig, green-and-white-striped shirt and baggy purple trousers.

"For goodness' sake, Henry," interrupted a bleach-blond houri, shimmering up in a gold bikini top and filmy harem trousers that jingled with gilt spangles, "let the poor girl draw breath before you start plying her with alcohol. Come with me, my dear, and we'll soon sort you out."

Camilla's vibrant blue eyes beamed a welcome over her diaphanous veil as she whisked Elinor off to a little white bedroom where the draped couch was already piled high with coats and wraps.

"For me?" she exclaimed, as Elinor handed her the bottle of wine. "Many thanks. Looks a terribly upmarket label. I'll make sure to save it for a special occasion," tucking it neatly inside a carved teak chest. She paused a moment to run a critical eye over Elinor's costume now that she'd laid aside her coat. "Yes, that'll do very well," she concluded, giving the shawl a final tweak. "Come on, we must have you dancing."

But the instant they returned to the party, Camilla was whirled away by the exuberant circus clown and Elinor found herself adrift in a sea of merry makers.

At first she stood pressed against the wall, feeling self-conscious and out of place in her borrowed finery. Without her glasses, the room was a whirl of flashing lights and blurred outlines. There might be people here from her flamenco class. But in a crowd of masks, how could she be sure? She'd never been any good at small talk and socialising. Paul, with his frank, hazel eyes and hearty handshake, had always instantly broken the ice at dinners and parties, so she'd got used to using him as a shield and following his lead, not going out and making the running herself. She sipped nervously at her glass of white wine, wondering when she could leave.

Soon she noticed a striking couple dancing nearby. The girl had long fair hair and was dressed as an angel with a glittery mask, a tinsel halo and a pair of downy white wings pinned to the back of her gleaming silver gown. The man had a neat, dark beard and looked like a gangster in immaculate white shirt and pale fawn trousers with knife-edged pleats. He wore elegant spats and a slouch hat pulled down low over his brow and he danced with style and verve.

As Camilla and the clown spun past, Elinor saw her tap the gangster imperiously on the shoulder and whisper a quick word in his ear. From the glance he cast in her direction, Elinor guessed that she was the subject of their brief exchange. So she wasn't surprised when a few moments later, the gangster politely excused himself from his partner and made his way over to where she was standing.

"Care to dance, señorita?" he asked in a courteous American twang.

Elinor hesitated. She knew he was under orders. But why not? The beauty of a mask meant that she could behave as she liked and no-one'd know who she was. She squared her shoulders. Tonight she was going to enjoy herself for a change. So she set down her empty glass and allowed him to lead her onto the dance floor.

She soon found she was enjoying herself. It was fun trying to work out what her mysterious partner looked like from the edited highlights of his features that she could glimpse above the silky beard. Certainly he had an expressive mouth, dark, slicked-back hair and bold black eyes, which gleamed through the slits in his velvet mask. But he skilfully evaded all her efforts to discover his name and it was far too noisy to make conversation, so she eventually gave up and devoted her energies to dancing.

*

Jamie was late arriving at Adam's sister's birthday bash. It was the first party he'd attended since being ill and he was planning to enjoy himself that night. Cam's insistence on fancy dress was a bit of a drag, but she always laid in such huge stores of liquor that he didn't mind showing willing. It'd been easy enough to borrow a blue mask off Bea, Mum's straw gardening hat and an old checked shirt and wellington boots from Dad to turn himself out as a rough approximation of a garden scarecrow.

When he poked his head into the studio, the first person he saw was a gangster, unmistakably Adam, dancing with some brunette he'd picked up in a ruffled red and white dress and a lacy black shawl.

Didn't think anything of it. Adam was always getting off with some new skirt or other. But over the top of a beer glass, his eyes studied this one with increasing interest. Looked several notches above Adam's usual prey and she was certainly a mover. Didn't just shuffle dismally from one foot to another. Had a real sense of rhythm and her flounced skirts swung gracefully around her slim-waisted figure. So who was she?

As he stood in the doorway watching, Bea bounced up in a flurry of silver and white angel wings.

"Here you are at last," she hissed. "Good. You can go and ask her to dance."

Jamie reluctantly tore his eyes from the Spanish señorita and turned to survey his sister. Her mouth looked pinched and cross.

"Ask who to dance?" he enquired coolly.

"The woman over there that you've been leering at ever since you turned up. The one dancing with Adam."

Oh ho! So that was how the land lay, was it? Bea'd been eclipsed by the Spanish señorita, and her nose was well and truly out of joint.

"Dunno who she is," he retorted, not planning to let himself be bossed around by his kid sister. "Don't care to dance with a stranger." And he lifted his glass casually to his lips, just to show her who was in charge.

"Her name's Elinor Mitford. Cam told me."

Now where'd he come across that name before? Sounded horribly familiar...

"She works at the Lydgate Museum," added Bea.

Elinor Mitford? From the Lydgate Museum? *Elinor Mitford!* Jamie choked into his beer glass. "You gotta be joking." His eyes veered back towards the Spanish señorita in stunned disbelief.

"She's the one you went to see this afternoon, isn't she?" continued Bea furiously. "Old and ugly, you said. What a liar! Just look at the way she dances. She's not old and ugly at all. This is all the fault of that Spanish fan. I wish I'd never set eyes on it. And as for Adam Quinn," she growled through gritted teeth, "I'm never going to speak to him again in my whole life. Men! You're all the same. Two-timing bastards." And Bea flounced out of the studio in a passion of tears.

Jamie let her go. When she got into a strop, Bea was totally unreasonable. Nothing he could say would do any good.

But he couldn't help glancing back at Adam's partner, doubting the evidence of his own eyes. Straight, dark hair. Long nose. S'pose it could just possibly be her...

He left the room to pour himself another drink.

*

After several dances Elinor needed a rest. At this point she expected the mysterious gangster to murmur some excuse and vanish into the crowd. But instead he asked if she'd like a drink and escorted her gallantly out of the crush into the quieter hallway, where bottles and glasses stood on a silver-draped table laden with party food. There were several incongruous characters milling around the salmon crostini and mushroom paté with drinks in their hands: a monk, a strong man with gigantic, padded biceps and what looked dimly like a country yokel in jeans and a checked shirt.

"Are you sure you wouldn't prefer to be dancing?" Elinor enquired, anxious that her partner shouldn't continue to put himself out for her sake.

"Not if you're going to talk to me instead," he shot back, offering her one of the two glasses of white wine that he'd picked up from the table.

Elinor accepted it gratefully. Interesting how his American accent seemed to have faded…

"Do you know Camilla well?" she asked after they'd both drunk a couple of preliminary mouthfuls, angling for information that might help pinpoint his identity.

"We go back a long way," he remarked evasively.

An ex-boyfriend or dance partner perhaps?

The alcohol flooded her veins with a pleasant warmth and began to loosen her tongue.

"I really don't want to stand in the way of you and your other partner," she remarked, taking another sip from her glass.

"Oh Beatrice's just the sister of an old friend of mine." He dismissed her scruples airily. "I'd rather be here with you."

"Beatrice?" echoed Elinor with interest. "That's an unusual name. And this's the second time I've come across it today."

The gangster threw her a questioning glance.

"I saw someone at work this afternoon whose sister was called Beatrice. She owns a very unusual eighteenth-century mask fan."

Why did the dark eyes behind the black velvet mask suddenly blink?

"Jamie Willett," he exclaimed.

"Yes – how'd you know?" she asked, only realising how close he was standing as she registered the pointed canine teeth gleaming in his arch smile.

"Old acquaintance of mine. He'll probably be here tonight."

"Has he arrived already?" Elinor glanced round vaguely.

"Haven't seen him yet," he said, his eyes fixed on her face. "He's always late anyway. Bit of a lone wolf. But Bea's still here somewhere."

"Really?" Elinor was delighted. "You know, I'd love to have a word with her about that fan – to find out what she plans to do with it. After all, it's she who owns it, isn't it? Not her brother." She turned towards the studio door, hoping to spot the angel among the crowd of swirling figures. The country yokel passed across her line of vision, but she directed her attention impatiently beyond his hazy form. "You can't see her, can you?"

The gangster didn't really bother to look.

"Not at the moment," he replied, "but I can easily introduce you later on. Like another drink?"

"But I haven't finished this one yet," protested Elinor, laughing. She glanced down at her glass. "Oh dear. It's empty. How did that happen?"

"Here. Let me fill it up for you," he offered, holding out a half-empty bottle.

"No, really." She put her hand over the glass. "I'm starting to feel a bit light-headed as it is."

The gangster set the bottle back on the table. The attentive way his bold, dark eyes were riveted on her was flattering, but all the same it made her feel a little uncomfortable.

"So what'd you think of the fan?" he asked.

"It's clearly an antique. Pity the boy doesn't know how to handle such a valuable object."

"The boy?"

"Yes. Jamie – Willett, did you say? You're a friend of his?"

"I know him," he replied, seeming to imply 'not very well'. He looked a fair few years older than Jamie anyway.

"He's so – young," added Elinor with a giggle, emboldened to confide in her companion by the intimacy that'd sprung up between them in their secluded corner. "I mean, the adolescent get-up, those ugly metal piercings. And the effort of keeping up a conversation with him. Not exactly Prince Charming, is he –?"

Alerted by a sudden warning pressure on her bare arm, Elinor stopped speaking. She glanced down at the gangster's well-manicured hand and then swiftly up into his face. A shadow that she couldn't quite read seemed to flicker across the back of his eyes.

"What's wrong?" she cried, instinctively wheeling round in the direction of his gaze.

She didn't have far to look. At the table beside her stood a tall, fair-haired scarecrow in a pale blue mask. So what? But as she stared up into the wide grey eyes, light glittered on the silver rings in his earlobe and she finally understood. That scarecrow was Jamie Willett. And he'd just overheard every word she'd said!

There was a moment's strained silence as Elinor and the scarecrow stood gazing straight at each other with the echo of her careless remarks hanging in the air between them. Then Elinor started forward, jolted to her senses, with an exclamation of regret already forming on her lips. But it was too late. The scarecrow had already flung abruptly away.

"You weren't to know," the gangster stepped in to reassure her. "Didn't recognise him myself or I would've warned you before. Come on, it's too late to do anything about it now. Let's have another dance."

He caught hold of her hand and tried to pull her back towards the studio. But Elinor couldn't help glancing over her shoulder at the scarecrow's receding back. How could she have got so carried away by wine and flirtation as to utter such thoughtless and insensitive words – and to a complete stranger too?

Her pleasure in the evening was entirely destroyed.

*

Jamie swallowed hard and tried to ignore what he'd just heard. But her words persisted in forcing themselves upon his inner ear. Adolescent. Ugly. Not exactly Prince Charming. She made him sound so immature, awkward, uncouth even. And the cool, scornful tone in which she'd spoken. As though he belonged in the wilderness or jungle, not the company of polite society.

He headed for the comparative peace of the kitchen where the serious drinkers always congregated, deliberately planning to get very, very drunk indeed. Nothing else could blunt the stinging sharpness of this pain.

Camilla's tiny kitchen, with its grey granite worktops and designer appliances, was clearly meant for show rather than practical convenience. That evening it was stacked so high with crates of glasses, cans of beer and boxes of bought-in canapés that there was hardly room to move, but this didn't bother those who had gathered there for one purpose only. Jamie settled himself with a tumbler at the breakfast bar amid a forest of bottles and, pushing up the ill-fitting mask, which felt annoyingly hot and prickly, began to swallow blindly whatever he could lay hands on, regardless of the debris of corks, paper plates, torn foil peanut packets and dishes of crisp crumbs piling up around him.

"So this's where you're hiding yourself, Jamie-boy," exclaimed a voice sometime later.

Jamie felt a sudden arm clap him round the shoulders. He raised his head dully and then lowered it again. What'd Adam want with him? Wasn' he too busy chattin' up that old hag from the museum to have time to spare for his bes' mate?

"You're not gonna take what Ellie said to heart, are you?" Adam persisted, planting himself on the cane barstool nearby.

"Oh so she's 'Ellie' now, is she?" growled Jamie, pouring himself another beer.

Adam ignored the jibe.

"She was ever so slightly tipsy back there, you understand, and wasn't to know you could hear every word she said. Come on, man. Get over it. Why don't you make it up with her and have some fun too instead of sitting here drinking yourself into a stupor?"

"With that stuck-up, insulting bitch? No thanks. I'd rather leave her to you."

"Hey, you're ruining my night," Adam resumed in a more serious tone. "She was coming along fine and now she won't dance anymore. She's talking about going home – and it's not even ten o'clock."

"Jus' as well," retorted Jamie thankfully. "You don' want anything to do with a woman like that."

"Oh but I do," came the startling reply. "Can't you see the eyes on her?"

Jamie stared. Was he hearing right?

"What eyes?" he demanded.

"You blind? Haven't you noticed the way she has of fixing you with those beautiful, shy eyes of hers like nothing else in the room exists?"

"Prob'ly short-sighted. She was wearin' glasses this afternoon," pointed out Jamie grumpily.

But Adam ignored him. He went raving on like a mad man about soft brown hair, long dark eyelashes and porcelain smooth skin. When he claimed that he couldn't wait to make out with her, Jamie was utterly revolted.

"Ugh! You must be joking," he exclaimed. "She's ugly and – well... old."

"Old? Bet she's not more than twenty-five."

"But she's done a doctorate, got a job, written a book, travelled the world. You turned into some kind of fuckin' pervert who wants to screw women old enough to be your mother? You're out o' your mind. She's got no style, no boobs. She's not your type..."

"What you mean is: she's not *your* type," retorted Adam succinctly. "We all know your type, don't we, you great, gangling giraffe? Boobs, bum and no brain. I've had enough of that sort of dame. This lady's got class. She's smart, she's literate – and she's got a great little ass."

Jamie plunged his head into his hands.

"I give up! Guess you'll see sense when she tells you to go take a running jump."

"*If* she tells me to take a running jump," observed Adam significantly, springing down from the bar stool and vanishing from the kitchen.

Jamie sank his head morosely into his beer glass. The whole business was unreal. P'raps he'd got so drunk he was starting to hallucinate…

"Adam told me I'd find you here," announced a sudden, quiet voice in his ear.

Was he starting to hear things too?

He jerked up his head and found himself staring unsteadily into a pair of beautiful, shy eyes fringed with long, dark lashes, which were fixed upon him as though nothing else in the room existed. Their expression was unmistakably contrite behind the glittering red mask.

Pulling this off to reveal a tense and rather flushed face beneath, she came straight to the point.

"I'm so sorry for what I said just now. It was thoughtless and unkind. I should never've said it. Please forgive me."

Jamie, who'd made up his mind never to speak to her again, found his resolve rapidly thawing in the warm glow of her repentance.

"Oh don' mention it. Doesn' matter," he replied rather gruffly, unused to having someone beg his pardon with such politeness. He stared at her in dumb silence for a moment, then realised he was behaving just like the social incompetent she'd accused him of being. So he groped hastily around the bar and, with a clumsy attempt at courtesy, offered her the remains of a green plastic bowl of crisps. He dimly remembered being taught manners as a child but had never had much call to use them since.

She accepted a tiny palmful of salty crumbs and then asked, "I was just wondering – have you talked to your sister about the fan yet? – you know, to find out what she'd like to do with it?"

Jamie looked her straight in the eye.

"Yeah. I mean – yes. Had a word with her this afternoon. She said she was happy to do whatever you thought best."

"I see. You know, I've been thinking things over, and it struck me that the most sensible idea might be to find out exactly how much it'd cost to have it professionally repaired."

"D'you think it's worth it?"

"It's always better to deal with facts than uncertainties – and it'd make me feel a lot better about my rudeness tonight if I could help you in some way."

Seemed fair enough.

"So what d'you suggest?" he asked.

"Well, I've an old friend called Peter Mowbray, who lives out in the countryside in Suffolk. He owns a fan workshop and repair business and if anyone could tell us what to do with your sister's fan, it's him."

"You reckon?"

"Why don't I give him a call and ask if we could go out to visit him? Would you be free some time over the weekend – say perhaps on Sunday…?"

Chapter Nine

"But it's only nine o'clock," protested Mum, wide-eyed with surprise.

She glanced up from the breakfast table as Jamie stumbled blearily into the kitchen, pulling on the only unholed jumper he could find in his drawers.

"Yeah – and?" he demanded, smothering a yawn behind one hand. True, he felt pretty rough, but he wasn't planning to let on as much to her.

"I haven't seen you up and dressed so early in years."

Jamie shrugged. Did she have to make him sound like the laziest slob on the planet? He headed to the cupboard and groped along the shelf for a mug.

"Usually get dressed when I'm going out," he retorted tartly, pouring himself a hot coffee from the pot on the bench.

"Going out? At this time of the morning? Where to?"

"A place called *Fantasy* in Little Downing. Somewhere in Suffolk, I think."

Jamie was beginning to perk up. A few swigs of coffee always made him feel a lot more human.

Dad's head emerged with a sudden rustle from the Sunday papers.

"That a theme park or a music festival?" he enquired in a bland voice.

Sarcastic old bastard. He'd fix him.

"Neither," replied Jamie innocently, wiping his mouth on the back of his hand. "It's a fan workshop."

Dad stared.

"A what?"

Jamie repeated the words with as much patience as he could muster at that hour of the morning, but Dad still looked unconvinced.

"So how're you planning to get to this place in – in Suffolk, did you say?"

"Drive of course."

"I need the car to take the boys to football."

"Never asked to borrow it. Elinor's picking me up…"

Jamie deliberately ignored the swift look exchanged by his parents, who were clearly wondering who 'Elinor' was. Let 'em wonder. Good exercise for their ageing brains.

At that moment he glanced at the kitchen clock and uttered a yelp of dismay. "Hell! That the time? She'll be here in five minutes. Gotta get moving."

He cheekily filched the croissant off Mum's plate as he slid past, swerving out of range of her retaliatory slap. At last he was feeling more his old self – better, in fact. With a sudden surge of energy, he swooped along the hallway and burst into the living room on the hunt for the Spanish fan.

At that moment his ears caught the rumble of an unfamiliar car engine outside in the sleepy, Sunday morning street. She was here!

Stuffing the croissant into his mouth whole and trying not to slop the remains of his coffee over the carpet, he rummaged around the low, glass-topped table where he remembered tossing the fan in disgust when he arrived home on Friday afternoon. Seemed like years ago.

Finally unearthing the slim red case from underneath a concert programme of Bea's, he shot back out into the hall to grab his army surplus rucksack, scattering crumbs of butter pastry after him as he went. Tucking the fan case inside his rucksack and shoving one arm into the sleeve of his old overcoat, he leapt to the front door to wrench it open. It refused to budge.

"Key?" enquired Mum, who'd suddenly materialised behind him in her turquoise towelling bathrobe, offering him hers with a superior smile.

"Thanks, Ma," he replied, grinning back as he unlocked the door.

"You planning on carrying that coffee with you to Suffolk?"

Jamie glanced down at the half-empty mug in his left hand. He took one last gulp, then thrust it back at her and raced out the door, tossing her the bunch of keys as he went.

Brrr! It was freezing out here. A quick glance over his shoulder showed him Mum successfully fielding the keys and lingering on the doorstep to wave goodbye, probably hoping to catch a glimpse of Elinor. Too bad the blue Audi'd overshot the house and driven further on down the road.

His breath steamed in the frosty air. Jerking on his other coat sleeve, he summoned an extra spurt of speed and caught up with the car as it was turning at the end of the cul-de-sac. He pulled open the door and instantly recoiled in shock. He was climbing into the wrong car! The driver was a stranger.

With her hair scraped back into a neat bun and wearing a dark woollen coat, this woman bore a strong resemblance to the ageing spinster in the grey suit and glasses whom he'd encountered in the basement of the Lydgate Museum on Friday afternoon. Where was the shy, soft-eyed Spanish señorita with the mass of floating brown hair that he'd danced with at Cam's party on Friday night? – at first for the fun of provoking Adam, he had to admit, but later because he really wanted to. Couldn't recognise her without the mask.

As he hesitated doubtfully, ransacking Dr Mitford's face for traces of the Elinor he'd been looking forward to seeing again, the woman threw him a swift nod of greeting.

"Good morning. Are you going to climb in? You're letting in the cold."

It was certainly her voice. He recognised the clipped, business-like tones at once. Obediently he manoeuvred his long length into the passenger seat, feeling subdued and awkward all over again in her presence.

She threw him a sideways look as he slammed the car door shut, asking, "Am I too early?" with what might've been an ironic arch of one dark eyebrow.

Was she making fun of him? Hard to tell.

He shook his head, abashed. Didn't know what to say to this stranger, so he huddled up inside his coat, staring straight ahead in silence as she turned into Chesterton Road and drove out along the hard, bright, winter streets towards the city bypass.

Perhaps he'd made a mistake in agreeing to this visit, he thought uneasily, shooting a surreptitious glance at her clear profile with eyes focused on the road. Perhaps he'd been drunker than he thought on Friday night. Ringing up some old guy out in the Suffolk marshes and asking to bring him a fan to look at. What could he, Jamie Willett, possibly have in common with a so-called 'Liveryman of the Worshipful Company of Fan Makers' like Peter Mowbray?

"I'm sure you'll really like Peter," remarked the strange woman, as though reading his thoughts. "He's been in the business of repairing and restoring collectors' fans for years. My uncle swears by him – and he's extremely fussy."

"Your uncle?"

"Yes – Uncle Fabian has a fine collection of historic fans, mostly inherited from my grandfather."

"So fans run in your family then?"

"You might say so." She smiled as she neatly negotiated a roundabout, then put her foot on the accelerator, pulling down the screen to shade her eyes from the glare of the low-riding sun. They sped along the slip road and out onto the dual carriageway heading east towards Newmarket. "It's certainly how I got hooked in the first place. When I was a little girl, my mother often used to take me down to visit my grandparents in their big, old house in North London and as a special treat Grandpa'd take me into his study. He was the director of a tea importing company and he used to bring back all kinds of things from his travels. You know: masks, porcelain, old coins, Persian rugs and so on?"

Jamie nodded, looking up in spite of himself.

"I always remember his study with the blinds pulled down against the sun, like a sea-green cave under the water..."

He could see her in his mind's eye: an inquisitive little girl poking around among all those exotic foreign treasures that nestled, half-hidden, in shady corners...

"On one wall there was a big, old wooden cabinet full of shallow drawers. Grandpa'd make me point to one. Then we'd pull it open together and look to see what was inside, lying hidden under tissue paper wrappings. I never knew what would emerge: a feather hand screen from Papua New Guinea or an iron military fan encrusted with gold and silver from Japan; a colourful American art deco leaf advertising champagne or perfume, or a layered lacquer fan from the Maldive Islands. Sometimes it'd be a handful of huge Edwardian ostrich plumes and other times a miniature toy for a tiny doll or a cream lace cockade for a court presentation... I used to sit on his knee and he'd tell me stories about them: where they'd come from, what they'd been used for, the places where he'd bought them. I've never forgotten the spicy perfume of sandalwood sticks and the rustle of embroidered silk and the cool, smooth discs of delicately painted ivory on the Chinese fans of a thousand faces..."

Jamie found himself gradually relaxing as he listened to her talk. He began to adjust to her appearance. Amazingly enough, Elinor and Dr Mitford were one and the same person.

After they left the dual carriageway, they drove for what seemed hours across flat, ice-logged fens, until Elinor suddenly turned down a narrow lane, bordered on either side with high hedgerows and overhung by a network of bare branches, stark against the wintry blue sky. At the far end of the lane stood an open metal gate beside an old oak tree, whose twisted roots sheltered clumps of pale snowdrops, just pushing their gleaming heads above the frosty leaf mould in the hard sunshine. Beyond the gate, a gravelled driveway wound its way across a dank lawn towards a farmhouse backed by several out-buildings: a big, corrugated iron shed and a long stable block ending in a couple of derelict workers' cottages built of moss-covered brick.

As they pulled into the farmyard, a muddy red tractor came chugging up the lane from the still-frozen fields. In it sat someone who waved vigorously in response to Elinor's beep on the horn. The rumble of the engine died away and out of the cab clambered a stout, wind-blown woman wearing faded jeans and a man's checked flannel shirt under a quilted, green waistcoat. Looked like a farmer.

"See, it's Susan," cried Elinor eagerly, turning off the ignition and throwing open the car door.

Susan came striding to meet them in heavy, black wellington boots, holding out welcoming arms to enfold Elinor in a massive bear hug. A tan and white collie dog pelted after her, barking furiously.

"Good to see you again, Ellie," Susan exclaimed in unconcealed pleasure, drawing back to survey her with shrewd hazel eyes. "You're looking thinner than I remember. Sure you're eating properly?" Without waiting for Elinor's reassurance on this point, she launched into enquiries about her father and the situation at home.

Jamie hovered awkwardly in the background, fending off the enthusiasm of the excitable collie dog, until Susan turned to rescue him.

"Down, Bess," she commanded with a warning gesture. Pushing back the straggling hair from her plain, honest face and regarding him with keenly appraising eyes, she shook his hand heartily.

"Hello," she greeted him without further preamble. "You must be Jamie – Ellie's told me about you."

"Er – pleased to meet you," he stammered, reclaiming his hand from her firm grasp and hoping none of his fingers were broken.

"You've brought the fan, haven't you?" she went on, motioning the dog on ahead of them in the direction of the house. "Peter was terribly excited when he heard about it. Mask fans are so rare. He's been looking forward to seeing it ever since Ellie called and told us you were coming. But why am I keeping you out here in this freezing cold? Come in, come in – I'll put the kettle on. I do hope you like gingerbread. I baked a big batch earlier this morning, knowing you'd arrive famished after your long drive. Here – come right this way. Make yourselves at home..."

And she showed them round the side of the house into a big, warm farm kitchen, pausing to tug off her muddy boots and pull on a pair of wooden clogs that clicked busily over the worn quarry tiles as she bustled about putting the kettle on to boil.

Shortly after Elinor and Jamie had settled themselves at the round, scrubbed pine table, the outer door opened again and a tall, thin man entered. He wore wire-framed glasses and the long, white hair and flowing beard of an Old Testament prophet. This turned out to be Susan's husband, Peter, who also hugged and kissed Elinor, now rosy-cheeked and slightly tousled from her buffeting at the hands of the keen easterly wind.

With Bess the collie lying at their feet on the coir mat in front of the old-fashioned kitchen range, they all sat feasting on fresh, buttered gingerbread and strong tea out of a round blue and white spotted pot. Tasted delicious.

At first Jamie felt shy and didn't say much as he listened to Susan chatting good-naturedly away to Elinor about family news. The Mowbrays apparently had three sons, who were now all grown up: one married with two children, another whose wife was expecting their first baby in the spring and the youngest, who'd now left home to join a veterinary practice in the Lake District.

"It's a long way away," observed Susan with a wistful sigh. "Roger and Tom can bring the grandchildren up from London for the weekend, but Sam'll hardly ever be able to get back and we've no-one at home now to keep an eye on the place so we could drive up to Penrith to visit him. And you can be sure he'll be finding a young woman from those parts to settle down with one of these days. How time passes. Doesn't seem so long ago that they were all tramping in from the school bus of an afternoon and wolfing down whatever was in the kitchen almost faster than I could serve it up onto plates. And now not one extra mouth to feed beyond our own two. I still cook far too many potatoes at dinner time. We don't know what to do with all the left-overs…"

"But the pigs are living the life of Riley," put in Peter, his blue eyes twinkling gently behind his spectacles.

"Just a pity none of the pigs is interested in running the business," grumbled Susan. "I thought Tom might take over when we retired – he's always been good with his hands. But no. He off and turns into a cabinet maker instead. Got more work than he can handle down in Greenwich. I've told Peter the business is getting too much for him now his eyesight's not what it used to be. He needs to advertise for an apprentice. But who'd want to come and live out in the wilds of Suffolk to work with fans nowadays…?"

She went on lamenting to Elinor, so Peter tipped Jamie a wink and the pair of them slipped away and left them to it.

Leading Jamie back outside and across the yard to the long, low building opposite, Peter stooped his lofty head under the blue-painted wooden lintel and preceded him into a comfortable, bare-raftered studio with huge, plate-glass windows that caught the sun like a glass conservatory. The workshop smelt seductively of wood, glue and paint. Beside the windows, so the natural light fell on it, stood a large trestle table, while wooden benches ran around the other three walls, stacked with intriguing boxes and chests of tiny drawers, which Jamie's fingers itched to investigate.

Peter sat down at the table and laid the Spanish fan on a sloping white plastic stand. He switched on the beam of a powerful lamp and began to inspect it with the aid of a big, angled magnifying glass, examining every part of the leaf and checking all the sticks meticulously. It took a very long time.

Meanwhile Jamie couldn't help darting interested glances around the studio, at the bright exhibition posters hanging on the roughcast cream walls alongside various fan-shaped frames and the filing cabinets ranged side by side in the neat little office, which he could glimpse through an inner doorway.

"Something the matter?" enquired Peter after a time, clearly noticing the restlessness of his gaze.

"What? Oh – no – not really. Just all looks a lot more organised than I'd expected," admitted Jamie, moved to confide in the old man since he'd begun to feel more at ease in these surroundings.

"Well, it's a business like any other." Peter smiled, as he carefully turned the fan over to study the tears in the leaf. Jamie couldn't help noticing the respect with which he treated the tattered old object, supporting its folds in his big, gentle hands as tenderly as though it was a bird with an injured wing.

"But what call is there these days for a fan-making business?" he blurted out in genuine puzzlement. "Aren't fans just museum pieces? Nobody uses them anymore, do they?"

"Not so much in England perhaps, but we're not the only country in the world…"

Even as he spoke, memories flashed through Jamie's head of stall holders he'd seen during his summer travels in the Philippines, waving away flies amid the noise and bustle of the fruit market with cheap paper hand screens, and of graceful Balinese dancers in ceremonial head dresses hiding their faces with richly gilded leather fans.

"…It's a niche market, I admit," Peter went on, pausing in his work, "but I've a strong international client base of museums and private collectors who keep me busy with restoration and repairs. I build fan cases too – like that pear wood frame over there," directing Jamie's attention to a half-finished project on the other side of the table.

"Who for?"

"This one's a commission for a rich American lady living in Boston, who's been coming to me ever since the first public exhibition I mounted of my work back in 1989. She happened to be over visiting from the States at the time and asked if I could repair a small coming-out ball fan of her grandmother's that she didn't want to throw away for sentimental reasons. An exquisite little carved horn brisé fan with swags of blue forget-me-nots that only needed re-ribboning. Cleaned it for her too and she was so delighted that she told all her friends. I soon found myself inundated with frayed silk parasols, broken mother of pearl clasps and net purses with tiny holes in them. Over the years I've worked out how to repair them all. And then of course there's the other side of the business."

"The other side?"

"Yes. Film and theatre productions."

Jamie threw him a questioning look.

"Think about those lavish costume dramas on TV. They all need period fans. So producers contact me to hire them or even have the most important ones specially made. I can provide a fan from any date between the sixteenth and the twentieth centuries," he declared proudly. "Of course there's lots of research involved, which Susan enjoys helping with – she was originally a graphic designer before she took up farming. In the old days it used to entail frequent train trips down to London to visit the Courtauld or the V & A, but nowadays with the wonders of the internet, we can do much more from the comfort of our own studio-office here," gesturing in the direction of the doorway Jamie had noticed before. "But there's still a limit to the number of new commissions I can undertake for wedding or anniversary fans, simply for lack of time and hands to do the work. It's a highly specialised job and requires a certain type of mind and an unusual skill set… You know, I have to tell you that this is a most fascinating fan. Do you see the words on those speech bubbles coming out of the mouths of the angry couple there?"

Jamie strained his eyes to follow Peter's pointing finger.

"G-U-E-R-A-M-I-N-O," he spelled out. " 'Gueramino. Este enojaris.' Sounds like Spanish to me. But then that stands to reason, doesn't it, if it's a Spanish fan?"

"Any idea what it means?" asked Peter.

Jamie shook his head.

"No. Should do, I guess. Spain's where my mum's side of the family comes from a couple of generations back…"

He hung his head with his usual shrug of inadequacy.

There was a moment's silence, then Peter suddenly suggested, "Why don't you take a wander round the studio and look at anything you like?"

Jamie raised his eyes with a glimmer of interest.

"Really?"

"Really."

And Peter bent back over his work, in which he at once seemed totally absorbed.

At first, despite the open invitation, Jamie felt rather constrained at the idea of rummaging around someone else's business premises. So he strolled up and down with his hands firmly clasped behind his back, peering at an engraving on the wall opposite of an old-fashioned fan factory and then at the workbench, on which stood a tempting array of glass jars neatly labelled 'ivory', 'mother of pearl', 'tortoise shell', 'wire' and so on, full of broken scraps, some so tiny that they surely couldn't ever be any use.

It was a paradise of fascination. In pull-out plastic boxes, he discovered tools like punches and bobbin drills – probably for making holes in bone or ivory – and little pairs of pincers and pliers.

For loosening stubborn screws? And a drawer full of what looked like bathroom toiletries: cotton wool, nail files and babies' toothbrushes. Tweezers with flat ends. Razor blades. A container of cocktail sticks and a basket of wooden clothes pegs. Whatever would you need those for? Emery paper – fair enough – and paint brushes of all sizes. A tape measure, fine sewing needles, pins, countless reels of coloured ribbons stacked tidily one on top of the other…

He was just starting to poke through the vast assortment of tubes of powders and glues when he heard a gentle knock. He glanced up and saw Peter rising to open the door to Elinor.

"Come on, you two. Lunch time," she announced with a smile.

Lunch time? But they'd only just had morning tea. Jamie opened his mouth to protest when he caught sight of the old-fashioned clock on the wall above the door and closed it again in bewilderment. Inexplicably, it was now well after one. Where'd the hour and a half gone?

They all sat down together for Sunday lunch around the kitchen table, now spread with a freshly laundered, blue gingham cloth. Jamie came face to face with the most enormous plateful of roast chicken he'd tackled since falling ill and succeeded in demolishing the lot, even finishing up a second mountain of mouth-melting roast potatoes and crisp green beans which Susan piled relentlessly onto his plate. By the time he'd devoured a huge bowl of sticky chocolate pudding, even he had to beg for mercy. Susan wavered for a moment, but to Jamie's sincere relief, finally pronounced herself satisfied.

While Elinor returned to the studio with Peter after lunch to pick his brains on several problems, Jamie helped with the dishes. It was impossible not to respond to Susan's casual questions over the domestic soap suds and Jamie soon realised that she now knew practically his entire life history. At this point there was nothing to do except cheerfully volunteer to help her re-size some photographs on the computer for the *Fantasy* website and by afternoon teatime he felt as though he'd known these kindly people for years.

After tea the Mowbrays accompanied them out to the car, where Peter shook him warmly by the hand and Susan hesitated for just a fraction of a second before enveloping him in a big, motherly hug. Jamie climbed reluctantly into the car and leaned out of the window to wave as they drove away. After the slope of the driveway hid the

Mowbrays from view, he turned his eyes towards the road ahead, still seeing their smiling faces.

"So what do you think?" asked Elinor, her gaze focused intently on potholes in the bumpy country lane.

"Couldn't hope to raise that amount of cash to restore the fan," Jamie answered, shaking his head sadly because it meant he'd never have an excuse to visit this amazing place again.

Elinor nodded. "I guessed you'd decide that."

There was a short pause.

Then she said, "There's another way, you know. Peter suggested it to me."

Jamie looked across at her quickly. "What d'you mean?"

"What're you like with your hands? You asked me on Friday afternoon if it was a possible DIY job."

Only Friday afternoon? Seemed a lifetime ago.

"Pretty fair, I guess. Haven't done much for a few years, though I did used to build a lot of aeroplane kits," he admitted, rather shamefaced because he'd not so long outgrown this childish hobby. "But I've no experience of repairing antique fans."

"No. But I have. I spent two summer holidays while I was at university working with Peter in the studio. We could have a go at restoring it together."

Jamie stared at her profile.

"You're not serious? What's in it for you?"

"Do you need an excuse to spend time on something you enjoy doing? Besides, I've been researching this fan since I saw you on Friday. There's hardly any information available about it. It'd be an interesting job for me after I've finished the guidebook I'm working on at present – you never know what I might discover."

Jamie's heart leapt up.

"You're suggesting we make this a joint project?"

"That's just what I'm suggesting."

"It's a great idea – but –"

He hesitated awkwardly.

"What?"

"Well, it's no good. You see, it's the middle of term and I'm heading back to university in Exeter tomorrow…"

Chapter Ten

It was early evening. Jamie sat in the wide window of the twilit room, hunched over his laptop computer with earphones on. A pool of light from the desk lamp flooded the sheet of notes that he was checking against information on the lighted screen. Since returning to his shared flat on the Exeter campus more than a week ago, he'd been doing some hard thinking at that worn, beech-veneered desk, staring abstractedly at the blank concrete wall of the accommodation block opposite. But now he was so absorbed that at first he didn't hear what was happening right outside his door.

Finally he raised his head. What was that muffled banging? Hastily closing the computer file, he pulled a pad of paper over his notes just as Lindsay burst in, her honey-gold curls streaming loose over her brightly striped scarf and blue tweed jacket.

"You deaf or something?" she demanded indignantly. "I've been practically hammering this door down. Knew you were in 'cos I saw the light on."

"What're you doing here?" he countered, pulling off his earphones and rising abruptly to meet her. "How'd you get in?"

Lindsay stared, taken aback by this brusque reception, her jaws automatically chewing gum all the while.

"Max lemme in as he was going out. What's up with you anyway? I've been texting like mad and got no reply. Even rang and you didn't pick up. Phone's prob'ly dead or switched off – as usual. What is it with you and mobiles? You're so – so unconnected with the rest of the world."

Jamie automatically glanced down at the desk to check where his phone was. Must be here – somewhere… He rummaged among the loose papers on his desk. But Lindsay's sharp eyes spotted it first under a green cardboard file and she pounced on it eagerly.

"Switched off," she cried in triumph. "What'd I tell you?"

Jamie grabbed it from her and stuffed it into his back jeans' pocket.

"Why don't you keep it turned on like normal people?" she persisted.

"Didn't want to be interrupted."

Lindsay opened her eyes wide.

"I was starting to think something'd happened to you. Hell, it's gloomy in here," reaching for the light switch. "Why sit around in the dark?"

Jamie blinked as brilliance flooded every corner of the square, modern box where he lived during term time. Meanwhile Lindsay's bright blue eyes rapidly scanned the bare walls, spotted with blobs of ancient blu-tac, and at last came to rest on the bin, overflowing with torn and crumpled paper.

"Hey, what's up?" she cried. "Like, you've torn down all your posters. Even your Gothic Ghost Train."

Jamie shrugged impatiently.

"Blank canvas," was his enigmatic response.

Lindsay looked mystified.

Feeling he was sounding weird as well as unwelcoming, Jamie at once changed the subject.

"Thought you were gonna be busy with your essay till six-thirty," he reminded her.

"Got fed up of reading after you left," she replied, her brow creased with a faint frown of distaste. "I hate all this boring Anglo-Saxon stuff, you know. Only applied for History because I wanted, like, to do more work on the Second World War." She by-passed the armchair, which was half-buried under a jumble of dirty clothes and, dumping her striped shoulder bag on the floor, dropped down onto the rumpled bed. "Besides, Fran and Nikki came along, you know. Said they were going for coffee, so I decided, like, to take a break too. Fran was telling us all about her sister's engagement party last weekend. She wore wine-coloured silk with pink pearls."

She paused for a response, but Jamie just shrugged. What did he care about pearls and engagement parties?

"After that it was too late to do any more work," she rattled on regardless. "So we've decided to head downtown for burgers and chips with Mike and Don and then to see a film. That's why I was trying to get hold of you. Now I've had to walk all the way over here to fetch you myself. Anyway, come on. Let's go!"

And she bounced up again, eager to leave.

"But I'm in the middle of something," pointed out Jamie, fiddling uneasily with a ballpoint pen.

"Oh that's OK," she assured him with an impatient toss of her curls. "You can catch up with whatever it is later. Come on – we don't want 'em to go without us, you know."

And she thrust out her hand as encouragement.

Jamie disregarded it.

"But I was banking on at least another half hour," he murmured.

Lindsay pulled a face.

"Look, what's got into you lately? You never used to be so boring before you got ill, you know."

Of all the nerve –! Besides, he'd made a deal with himself to reach the end of this topic before dinner.

"Just gimme half an hour," he suggested, biting back a sharp retort. "I'll be ready then."

"But why not now?"

"Because I'm busy. I already told you."

Why did she never listen to a word he said? He flung himself huffily back onto the hard desk chair.

"Oh come on, Jay-Jay." Lindsay at once adopted a more persuasive tone, snuggling her arms around his neck from behind. "It's Friday night. Everyone's going out. Like, I wanna go too."

"Go on then. Nobody's stopping you," urged Jamie, trying to ignore her caresses. He'd made a stand and wasn't going to back down now. "Tell you what: you head off and I'll be along soon."

"But I can't go by myself. Everyone'd think we'd had a fight. Come on, please, Jamie," she begged, bending her head close to his so that a cascade of curls poured over his shoulder onto the notepad lying on the desk.

Jamie brushed them aside. How coarse and brittle her hair felt, he suddenly noticed – like threads of spun glass. He stared out of the window in stubborn silence.

But Lindsay, who was small but persistent, began nuzzling her face into the soft skin in the hollow of his collar bone, mingling her caresses with some well-directed kisses, which he fended off resolutely.

Finding this line of attack unsuccessful, she suddenly demanded, "Well what're you doing anyway? What's so important that it can't wait till later?"

"Oh – nothing," replied Jamie, rising from the desk to stop her finding out.

Too late. Lindsay had reached across and seized the notepad. Jamie tried to stop her, but she'd already caught sight of the papers underneath.

"What language's that?" she asked, pointing to his notes.

"Spanish," Jamie was reluctantly forced to admit.

"Spanish? What on earth're you learning Spanish for? Like, you don't need it for a Computer Science degree."

"No reason," he muttered, clumsily trying to grab the pages back.

But Lindsay resisted with unexpected firmness. She darted out of reach, casually rifling through the hand-written notes and dislodging a little scrap-paper fan, which fluttered to the floor.

"So why do it?"

What excuse would sound least weird?

"Been thinking about it for a while," he confessed awkwardly. "You see, my grandma and my great aunt came to England after the Civil War in Spain… I - I used to speak Spanish to them when I was little. But I can't remember much now."

"Why bother? They're both dead, aren't they?"

"It's my roots, you know – and…well, perhaps I'll be going to Spain this summer. I wanna talk to people there."

"What for? I've been to Spain tons of times. They all speak English, you know. Anyway, I thought you and I were going inter-railing this summer."

"Yeah, but there's also this drama project I'm doing with an old school friend…"

"Oh grow up, Jamie! You and your stupid play-acting."

Jamie recoiled, stung by her dismissive attitude. It was fine for her, being in only the second year of her degree. She didn't have to grow up yet. It was him who was staring straight into the face of an uncertain future.

"So what d'you suggest?" he asked in all seriousness.

"Coming out with me tonight."

Jamie turned away with a gesture of frustration. She had a one-track mind. All she ever thought about was what she wanted.

"I've told you I'll come –" he began.

"Well then."

"– Later."

"But I wanna go now."

"But I sodding well don't."

And he dropped back down onto the chair.

There was a moment's silence as he bent to scoop up the scrap-paper fan from the teal carpet tiles and retrieve the notes she'd tossed aside. Defiantly he smoothed out the creased pages and leafed through them with an unconcerned air.

Glancing sideways, he could see Lindsay fold her arms underneath her protruding bust. She pouted her peach-glossed lips, which exactly matched the shade of her nail varnish and the skin-tight T-shirt she wore under her blue jacket. Her doggedly chewing jaws, and indeed her whole attitude, gave him to understand that he wasn't going to get away with this.

Next moment she plonked herself squarely down on top of his notes.

"Lindsay," he protested as she thrust a navy-blue leg into his field of vision. Her short, jade green skirt was rucked up so he could quite clearly see the pale flesh of her inner thigh gleaming through the textured ribbing of the dark tights. Then she bent down so low that her cleavage was on a level with his eyeballs.

"Now come on, Jay-Jay," she coaxed with kittenish playfulness. "Don't make me cross with you. You can work later, you know. I promise we'll come back here nice and early. And when I'm through with you, then you can read some silly old Spanish, if that's what you really want," all the time stroking the soft down at the back of his neck so that shivers of pleasure tingled up and down his spine.

"Won't be wanting to study Spanish later this evening," admitted Jamie, swallowing hard. Shutting his eyes only seemed to enhance the allure of her musky perfume ten-fold. He fought for a moment, then buried his face in her lap and inhaled deeply. She smelt of soft needlecord, of the pleasures of snuggling up together in a warm bed on a chilly night…

"Mmm," purred Lindsay, running a fingertip lightly along his collar bone. "I like you better this way. Not like you've been since you came back from Cambridge."

Jamie's eyelids jerked open. He raised his head, arrested in the very act of exploring her curves with relenting hands.

"What d'you mean?" he demanded.

"Dunno really." Lindsay paused to consider the question for a moment. "You've been different like – kinda quiet. Sort of wondered if something'd happened while you were away –"

"So what d'you think happened?" exploded Jamie, thrusting her bodily aside as he sprang up from the chair. "I was in hospital with malaria. Hadn't you sodding well noticed?"

"'Course I noticed. But let's not talk about that anymore. Like, it's all over now, you know. I was so upset all the time you were away. Really I was," soothed Lindsay hastily.

But Jamie wasn't falling for this. He wheeled round to face her.

"So upset that you couldn't even be bothered ringing to find out if I'd fuckin' died or not?"

"Oh come on," she replied. "Wasn't that big a deal. They just had to give you the right drugs and you started getting better – that's what you said."

"Didn't feel so simple at the time. For a while there I thought I was gonna die. You've never had that feeling, have you?"

"No – why should I?"

She was staring at him as though he'd gone mad.

"You could try using a bit of imagination. It's pretty lonely, let me tell you. Sets you thinking about what you've done with your life, what you've made of yourself and who's gonna miss you when you're gone."

"Jamie, really –!"

She surveyed him as though he was showing singularly bad taste in even mentioning the subject. But he wasn't going to let her off the hook that easily.

"You start to wonder why your so-called girlfriend hasn't even bothered calling to find out how you are."

"I texted. And rang – more than once. But your phone's always switched off. Besides, I – I was busy."

"Doing what?"

"You know it was my parents' twenty-fifth wedding anniversary. And the second term's been really heavy for me – all those coursework essays and assignments and the presentation to my tutor group. I was absolutely flat out."

"When've you ever been flat out writing essays and assignments? You can't usually force yourself to finish Chapter One of the first book on the reading list before you give up and head off for coffee with your friends. I practically wrote your last assignment for you."

Lindsay gasped.

"And it was the best mark you got so far this year too," he added, quietly twisting the knife.

Shouldn't have said it, but just couldn't help himself. She'd make

him pay hand over fist for that little outburst of truth-telling.

Lindsay shot him a poisonous glare. She drew herself up to her

full height, which even in high-heeled suede boots barely raised her

to the level of his chest, and narrowing her eyes, spat back furiously,

"I'm not gonna stand for anyone saying that to me – not even you.

You're not such a model student yourself. At least I hand in my

assignments on time. What've you done that's so much cleverer than

me? When I suggested you meet me at the library this afternoon, I

was surprised you even knew where it was. You don't exactly have

to be dragged out at closing time, do you? All you ever do is hang

around the Student Union with your mates, drinking yourself under

the table and playing stupid games of pool. Or you're slumped in

front of TV watching football or darts. Max told me the other day

he'd overheard your course tutor saying he'd never known anyone so

consistently under-performing. You should clean up your own act

before you start in on me."

"Well of all the little –!" spluttered Jamie. "You're absolutely,

bloody –"

He broke off, realising at the very moment he opened his mouth to deny it that she was absolutely, bloody – right. Other people thought he was a waster too, not just his course tutor. His defence collapsed at once and he turned away to shield his self-disgust from her unsympathetic eyes.

He hated her. She was small and mean-minded. Adam's verdict pin-pointed her perfectly: "Boobs, bum and no brain." But what sickened him even more was the realisation that she was all he was ever going to make out with if he kept on the way he was headed.

Lindsay instantly seized her advantage.

"Now come on, Jay-Jay," she cooed. "Give up on the brain-strain for tonight and come out with me instead. It's not as though you've gotta hand in that Spanish assignment tomorrow – or ever. You've been working too hard. Like, you need a bit of a break." She held out her hand and gazed up at him with melting blue eyes.

Jamie cursed his own lack of will-power even as he let her take him by the hand and lead him triumphantly away from his desk.

Chapter Eleven

One overcast Sunday afternoon shortly before Easter, the Willetts' front doorbell rang loudly. Ignoring it with a selective deafness born of long experience, Bea carried on with her flute practice in the dining room. At last count Mum'd been working her way through a huge pile of ironing in the kitchen. She'd be bound to answer it. Two, three, four…

Before long, footsteps clattered out of the kitchen and someone whistled their way cheerfully along the hall. Mum couldn't whistle. Geoff was out. Must be Marc. Who could concentrate on playing with that piercing racket going on? Back to the start of the passage again. Two, three, four…

Next came a muffled exchange of conversation on the doorstep and then Marc's voice bellowing from the foot of the stairs,

"Hey, Mum! There's some weird, black-haired guy at the door for you."

Bea lowered her flute. Marc was utterly hopeless. You'd think he'd've learned by now that, however odd a caller looked, it was rude to describe him as "weird" to his actual face.

"Just coming," called back Mum's voice over the banister railing. "Ask him to wait a moment please."

Bea frowned. Who could it be? The only arrival they were expecting this afternoon was Dad back from Exeter with Jamie and his belongings at the end of term. Oh well, none of her business. And she raised her flute again. Two, three, four...

Footsteps thudded up the hall and then came a loud thump as of some heavy object hitting the ground. A chilly draught whipped through the house, blowing the dining room door open with a crash and spiralling gleefully round Bea's ankles. Honestly! Why did Marc insist on freezing the house out?

Now Mum came clomping downstairs muttering to herself,

"Perhaps it's one of the neighbours complaining about the hedge along the side passage..."

That did it! Bea banged her flute down on the table and raced out into the hall screeching,

"Shut that door, Marc! I've got A-Levels this summer. How can I practise with doors banging, people bawling their heads off and everyone thundering up and down like a herd of elephants?"

She and Mum reached the foot of the stairs at the same moment. There they found Marc leaning innocently up against the newel post. The hall was deserted and the front door shut.

Mum gazed round in consternation.

"You haven't left the poor man standing out in the cold, have you? Remember your manners, Marcus Willett."

Bea peered out through the coloured glass, but there was no shadow on the doorstep.

"It's OK, Mum," Marc reassured her cheerfully. "I showed him straight in."

Mum gasped.

"Marc, what've I told you before about never letting strangers inside the house?" gazing round as if half-expecting to see the intruder making off with the television.

"Where's he gone?" demanded Bea.

"The kitchen. At least that's where he was headed." And Marc grinned, showing no signs of remorse at possibly endangering their very lives by his thoughtlessness.

"The kitchen?" exclaimed Mum in horror. "What's he doing in my kitchen?" and whirling round, she instantly stumbled up against a bulky rucksack lying at the foot of the stairs alongside a couple of big, black plastic bin liners of what looked like dirty washing.

Bea directed a sharp glance at Marc, who was killing himself with laughter. Then she heard the fridge door open and caught sight of the prowler in the kitchen. His head was inside the fridge, so all she could see was a pair of very long legs in scruffy denim jeans. They looked oddly familiar.

"What's going on here?" asked Mum suspiciously.

At the sound of her voice the prowler at once withdrew his head from the fridge.

"Hi, Mum," he announced brightly. "I'm home."

"Jamie," she cried, "it's you!"

Bea blinked. This – Jamie? But he looked so different…

"Marc, you little fiend," exclaimed Mum, turning on him at once. "I should've known you'd be having me on."

"That's one thing I love about you, Mum. You fall for it every time." Marc chuckled, dodging the playful cuff she aimed at his head. "So what's with the weird hair, Jay?" he went on coolly. "I'm so used to you lookin' like a streaky haystack that when I opened the front door, I hardly recognised my own brother. Chemists in Exeter run out o' yellow dye then?"

"Ha, ha," retorted Jamie mirthlessly, returning to the fridge. "I'm starving. There anything to eat in this house?" The next moment a loud cry of disgust escaped him. "What on earth are these revolting things? Why does Geoff have to keep 'em in here? Just kills your appetite seeing them oozing around in their jars."

"They're for the wild-life pond he and your father are digging in the back garden," Mum told him, calmly filling the kettle. "I baked cinnamon biscuits yesterday. The boys might've left you one or two in the blue and white jar. Marc, go and give Dad a hand with the rest of Jamie's stuff. Scoot now."

Marc reluctantly obeyed.

Bea, who'd hung back, struggling to come to terms with the startling alteration in Jamie's appearance, watched him rummaging around the work bench. It wasn't just the different hair colour...

"At last!" cried Jamie in triumph, unearthing the biscuit barrel from behind an electric circuit board and several pamphlets about do-it-yourself pond projects.

"Well, this's a turn up for the books," Mum remarked, eyeing him up and down appreciatively. "I'd forgotten that you're actually not bad looking underneath it all. I never really felt blond suited you – or red and purple either for that matter. What d'you think, Bea?"

"Can't believe my eyes," she replied, advancing to join in the fun. "What a vision of loveliness! Had a fight with a lawn mower then, Jay? Haven't seen the back of your neck for years," walking around him in mock-serious appraisal as if he were a museum exhibit. "You know, it makes you look almost human."

"I can always rely on my family for an ego boost," grumbled Jamie through a mouthful of biscuit crumbs. "I've had to listen to Dad's sarcasm all the way back in the car and now you two start in on me. Makes me sorry I came home at all."

"And you've lost loads of metal too," Bea added, scrutinising his face.

"Oh I give up," exclaimed Jamie, extracting the last biscuit from the jar. "I'm back off to help Dad with the boxes."

"You mean you can still carry heavy boxes?" Bea giggled. "Thought you might be like Samson. When your long locks were shorn off, all your strength vanished with them. So who's playing

Delilah then?" she raised her voice to call after him as he slammed the back door on her taunts.

She and Mum exchanged significant glances.

"I wonder what's brought this about," Mum speculated.

"What – or who," commented Bea enigmatically, heading back to the dining room.

*

She was still practising when Geoff returned half an hour later from his expedition to the river carrying two more plastic jars of wildlife for the new pond. As soon as he set eyes on Jamie, he congratulated him on his conservation-minded abandonment of hair cosmetic companies, which he held responsible for polluting so many of the country's streams with noxious effluences...

By now Jamie was fed up with everyone's witticisms. He flicked off the TV, tossed aside the remote and lounged upstairs. As he unstrapped the rucksack in his bedroom, his eye chanced to fall on his old guitar, which stood propped against the desk. Hadn't played for months.

On impulse he picked it up and examined it, then strummed a tentative chord. Ergh! Horribly out of tune. He sank down on the bed and set about testing the strings and adjusting the pegs. Then he started to play…

"Thought that was you," observed a sudden voice.

Jamie broke off at once. He glanced up and caught sight of Bea's head stuck round the door, presumably attracted by the sound of music. The room was streaked with late afternoon shadows. Must've been playing for a while then…

"What's that piece?" Bea asked. "Sounded quite fun."

"Oh nothing. Just mucking around."

"You used to be quite good when you were at school, didn't you?"

Jamie shrugged his shoulders non-committally.

Bea was usually most approachable after she'd finished her music practice, he remembered, so this might be the moment to mention what he had in mind. But better soften her up with a few general pleasantries first. He enquired how the A-Level revision was going and what gigs she had on at present.

"Oh the usual Easter concerts," she replied, stepping into the room. "And Hugo and I are planning to start up a chamber group."

"Hugo?" Never heard that name before. "Who's he?"

"Hugo Channing-Jones. Didn't Mum tell you we're going out?" Bea boasted casually. "He's the organ scholar at Trinity. I've been playing a lot for them lately. In fact I've just agreed to help out with *Beggar's Opera*, their summer production this June. Hugo'll be playing keyboard of course. He's absolutely phenomenal. You OK yourself? Mum said you'd split up with Lindsay."

"Yeah. Wasn't working out." Jamie promptly changed the subject. "Look, Bea, there's something I wanted to talk to you about."

"Yes?"

"That fan of yours. You remember, the Spanish fan."

A cloud instantly settled over her brow.

"Oh I certainly remember that," she retorted bitterly.

"When I brought it back from Suffolk, what'd you do with it?"

"Dunno. Tossed it in a drawer somewhere. Might've thrown it away."

Jamie sprang up from the bed in dismay.

"Bea, you haven't!"

"Why not? I don't want it. I never got the trip to London that Adam promised me. He hasn't been in touch since the weekend he came up for Cam's party."

Jamie could see the resentment simmering in her eyes.

"You haven't really thrown the fan away, have you?" he asked quickly. Bea was just vindictive enough to do it.

"No. All right, I haven't," she admitted slowly.

Jamie heaved a quiet sigh of relief.

"Why keep on about it anyway?" she snapped. "What's it matter to you?"

Had to tackle this diplomatically. So as not to flutter her into saying no outright.

"Haven't thought any more about what you'd like to do with it, have you?" he enquired soothingly.

"No. Why should I?"

"Then it wouldn't bother you if I had a go at repairing it?"

"Don't see how you can. It's torn right down the middle and falling apart in other places too."

"Yeah, but I'd like to try all the same. I've read up a book or two on mending old fans and I've had an offer of help to work on it."

Bea's eyes narrowed.

"An offer of help? From that woman?"

There was no doubt she meant Elinor. He didn't dare lie.

"Well – yeah. But she knows what she's doing, Bea. No denying it'd be a lot of work. The fan'll have to be dismantled, cleaned and repaired. It'll take several weeks. But I'd like to have a go – if you'll let me."

Only as he heard himself practically begging this favour from her did he realise how much it mattered to him. He was almost trembling as he hung on her reply.

"Oh I don't want the stupid thing," declared Bea pettishly. "Take it, if it'll make you happy."

"And you'll give me your permission to repair it in writing?"

"OK, OK – if I have to. But I don't know why you're making so much fuss about a useless old piece of junk that nobody wants. You're turning into a real crank, you know…"

*

With patient persistence Jamie finally managed to wheedle both fan and written permission out of Bea, without which Elinor Mitford absolutely refused to proceed.

He carried them both in his rucksack next morning down to the Lydgate Museum to keep the appointment he'd made by email the previous week. He also wore a clean pair of jeans without holes in the knees.

Negotiating the labyrinth of corridors to Elinor's office felt slightly less daunting than he remembered and although he took a couple of wrong turns and was forced to retrace his steps, he eventually caught sight of the familiar alcove at the end of the long, dingy hallway. He was approaching the office along a beam of light, which fell on the blue-grey vinyl from a nearby window, when he heard the sound of a side door opening and saw Elinor herself emerge into the passage.

She was dressed in a neat, though rather subdued, plum-coloured suit. But from its lapel shone out a dazzling, gold, fan-shaped brooch studded with tiny rubies and milk-white pearls, which gleamed and glittered in the shaft of spring sunlight. In her hand she held a sheaf of papers.

Jamie was going to say hello, but at the last moment stopped himself. Instead he let her glance travel over him without returning the slightest sign of recognition.

"Good morning," she greeted him in a polite, but neutral tone. "Can I help you? It's not easy finding your way round this place, is it? Are you lost?"

"I don't think so," replied Jamie, struggling to keep a straight face.

"Who're you looking for?"

"Dr Mitford."

She blinked.

"I'm Dr Mitford. But you don't have an appointment, do you? I'm afraid I'm expecting someone else quite soon, you see."

"Yes, I've made an appointment. It's about this fan." He shrugged off his rucksack and pulled out the case.

Elinor stared at it in puzzlement as he lifted the lid and revealed its contents. Then she raised her eyes to search his face. They both burst out laughing.

"Jamie! It's you, isn't it?" she exclaimed. "What d'you mean by teasing me like that?"

"Does it matter how I look?"

"Not really, I suppose. After all, I can recognise you by the fan. So your sister said yes, did she?"

"She did – and I've got it in writing, so you'll know I'm not lying," patting his rucksack with a grin.

"You laugh," she responded soberly, "but one has to be professional about these matters. Come in and we'll take a closer look at it. Now the research for my guidebook on the Meynell Collection's finished, I've really been looking forward to starting a new project…"

She unlocked the door and led Jamie into her office. Together they crossed to the table by the window, where Elinor gently lifted the fan from its case and opened it onto the sloping stand like a book rest, then pulled an expensive-looking phone out of her handbag.

Jamie watched as she worked with experienced precision, photographing both sides of the fan leaf, then measuring its dimensions with a ruler and examining it more closely through a strong magnifying lens, all the while noting down observations on paper in her small, pointed handwriting.

She said they should start by writing a full description of the fan, to ensure that they looked at it properly.

"It's better with two pairs of eyes because we'll both see different things. The detail of the hand-coloured engraving's quite amazing, isn't it? – all those tiny faces on the mask fans in the shop and the cobblestones in the street and the glass panes in those very Georgian-looking windows… Oh, just look here!"

And she pointed to the sheet that the beggar was holding.

"There're some tiny words printed on it, but I can't quite make out what they are. What a shame. Perhaps they'd give us a clue as to the fan's provenance. Looks like 'El' something… Or is it? What do you think? Your eyesight's probably better than mine."

Handing him the magnifying glass, she urged him to transcribe the letters.

"*El Diario de Hoy,*" she read off the paper when he'd finished. "Must be a Spanish fan then."

"My mum did say it'd been given by an actress to a Spanish great-great-great uncle of mine. But I thought only women used fans."

"Not at all. They were common with both sexes in Spain before air-conditioning. Funny though. Spanish fans are usually much more richly coloured and gilded than this one. But *El Diario de Hoy*? Wonder what '*Hoy*' means –"

She reached for her phone, clearly planning to check.

"The Daily Journal," interrupted Jamie in a matter-of-fact tone. "Guess it could be the name of a Spanish newspaper."

He glanced up and met Elinor's quizzical gaze.

"What's wrong?" he asked, wondering what stupid mistake he'd made now.

"You have black hair. You know Spanish. There's more to you than meets the eye, isn't there?" was her comment as she returned to her notes.

Jamie grinned to himself. He'd shown her he was good for something after all.

At that moment there was a loud rap on the door. Elinor's invitation to enter was hardly out of her mouth when the door flew open and in breezed Adam.

Jamie's jaw dropped in astonishment. What was he doing here?

Chapter Twelve

It was all very well for Adam to breeze in claiming he just "happened to be passing" and wanted to know if Elinor would join him and Cam for dinner that night. But from the way the two of them spoke, Jamie soon gathered this wasn't their first meeting since Cam's party in February: Adam seemed to have been taking an unusually close interest in his sister's welfare lately and had met them at least twice – perhaps more often – after flamenco lessons for drinks with Henry at a bar in town.

What was also clear was that Elinor was responsible for the Spanish play venture coming off at all. She made light of her efforts, claiming it was just a bit of research and a well-phrased application to a local arts authority.

"Besides," she told Jamie as they waited together on the platform at Cambridge station the Friday morning after Easter, "I hear that most of the funding's come from Henry's father, whose software company seems to be making more money than it knows what to do with." Then, with a quick change of subject, "So – you're looking forward to starting rehearsals tomorrow?"

Jamie stared back at her. Staying with Adam in London was a cheap means of escaping home for a weekend, but then again, rehearsing was always such bloody hard work…

"Guess so," he mumbled with a non-committal shrug.

"Adam certainly is," she went on in evident approval. "He's been telling me all about his concepts for this production."

Oh he had, had he?

"Adam's full of big ideas," Jamie muttered, his enthusiasm tempered by long experience.

"Yes – and I'm glad of it," she rejoined warmly. "He deserves a lucky break. That long stint he did with the Australian film company in Indonesia after graduating from Central certainly proves he's committed to his profession."

Jamie frowned. The Indonesian episode had been a total fiasco: he certainly wouldn't have called flying all the way round the world to end up as extras in two days' filming for a TV commercial 'a long stint with an Australian film company'. And where'd she got the idea that Adam had already graduated?

"At least he has aspirations," she went on. "So many people just drift aimlessly through life and couldn't care less about anything…"

Had she broken off at that point because a middle-aged businessman waved her on board the train ahead of him? Or had she deliberately fallen silent as it struck her who she was speaking to: the biggest waster, the most aimless drifter of all time? He'd never know…

The crowded train sped on its way to London. Jamie sat idly pretending to read *The Comedy of Errors*, but really he was thinking. Now and then he cast a covert glance at Elinor, who sat on the opposite side of the table behind a pile of papers. She seemed totally absorbed in the proofs she was reading and his eye followed the mesmeric motion of her pencil as it traced occasional marginal corrections. Several times she glanced up, touching the pencil point to her lips in thought. Once she even caught his gaze and smiled absently. But he knew her mind was elsewhere.

He stared out of the rain-flecked window at the stormy black sky and flat fen landscape hurtling past, lulled by the gentle rocking motion of the carriage…

Perhaps it was a waste of time to have agreed to go with her to the Fan Museum in Greenwich, where she'd business to transact with some woman she knew about loans for an exhibition in Spain this coming summer. But she told him that Aurélie Brisson, with whom she'd trained at the V & A Museum, was very knowledgeable and likely to be able to give them some information about the Spanish fan, which they'd taken apart last weekend at Elinor's place.

This was a pretty upmarket Georgian terraced house on the Tillington Road, which looked like a museum with its marble-topped console tables, imposing crystal chandeliers and glass-fronted cabinets of delicately painted porcelain. Elinor had politely overlooked his diffident glances around the black-and-white-tiled entrance hall with its panelled walls, painted soft powder blue and adorned with select engravings of old maps and antique street scenes, and whisked him straight up several flights of stairs to her private attic workroom as though ashamed to be seen in his company.

There they settled down together at an old pine desk near the sloping skylight, laying the Spanish fan on a piece of white flannelette sheeting like a patient on an operating table, to begin the process of dismantling it.

At first the rivet pinning the sticks together had simply refused to unscrew. Both of them fiddled for ages with their fingers and then a set of jeweller's pliers, trying to coax even one of the studs at either end to budge. No luck.

"I warned you it was slow work, didn't I?" said Elinor with a sigh of frustration. "It's probably stiff with corrosion. Here, you hold the fan with the rivet end pointing down while I squeeze some penetrating oil onto it."

Jamie watched her apply a pinprick of oil to the stubborn pin.

"What's the use of a tiny drop like that?" he asked.

"Penetrating oil travels further than you think… No, no, don't lay it down like that! The oil will take the dirt with it and slide up the sticks and stain them and the leaf too. Now wrap the leaf in this plastic bag, so we can see what we're doing. Wait a moment or two, then we'll have another go."

Still no luck.

"Don't think this's working," he announced in the end. "What else can we try?"

"I don't know." He could hear the rising tension in her voice. "I've suggested everything I can think of. Why won't it budge?"

"Here. Let me have a go," he offered quietly.

"All right. But I still don't believe we're going to shift it," as they changed places.

Jamie surveyed the stubborn rivet speculatively. Then he tried easing the little round metal stud back and forth with the pliers and then his fingers. Suddenly he felt an almost imperceptible yielding.

"Look. It's coming. Finally. See here."

And he held out the stud for her inspection, lying in the centre of his upturned palm.

They both stared down at it and Elinor breathed an audible sigh of relief.

What'd she said again?

"Warned you it was slow work, didn't I…? Drifting aimlessly through life… Deserves a lucky break… Rehearsal tomorrow morning… Probably stiff with corrosion. Don't think we're ever going to shift it… Warned you it was slow work, didn't I…?"

The rumbling rhythm of the train wheels throbbed over and over in his head…

"Jamie. Jamie!"

The voice seemed to be calling to him from far away.

He woke with a start, the shreds of his dreams still clinging to his brain like cobwebs, and gazed confusedly around. Where was he? What time was it? The rumbling and rocking had stopped and the train seemed to have juddered to a halt in the oppressive blackness of a tunnel. He jerked upright in his seat.

"It's all right. We're not far out of Liverpool Street," Elinor told him with a smile, apparently amused by his feeble efforts to pretend he'd been awake all the time.

Jamie nodded blearily. He felt stiff and cramped after lying slumped against the hard windowpane.

"I'll get your rucksack down," she offered, tucking the papers she'd been reading away in her handbag and snapping it shut with a business-like click.

Jamie leaned forward to stop her, but she'd already risen to her feet and was reaching down his shapeless old rucksack, which looked so out of place slouched on the table alongside her smart, Italian leather handbag.

Stuffing away his play script, he quickly shouldered his rucksack and scrambled off the train, trailing along behind her through the draughty mainline station towards the underground. After several changes of train, they eventually emerged into the busy brightness of Greenwich High Street. Crossing at the traffic lights, Elinor led the way unhesitatingly through the bustle of shoppers and tourists hunting for bargains in the crowded antiques market until they turned up a nearby side street and left the roar of traffic behind. At last they reached the Fan Museum in a terrace of spacious Georgian town houses built of mellow old bricks and adorned with tall sash windows. A glass fanlight stood above its glossy magenta front door.

Elinor pushed open this door and Jamie found himself stepping over the threshold into a new world. While she exchanged cheerful greetings with an elderly gentleman seated at a bow-legged table in the entrance hall, Jamie's gaze travelled slowly round the elegant apartment, devouring every detail.

A gorgeous paper fan flamed scarlet and gold in the grey marble fireplace, while through the open archway ahead he glimpsed lighted cabinets of glittering jewellery and shelves of brightly coloured books. But what about those painted fan leaves that hung in heavy frames on the primrose yellow walls? Better go and take a closer look.

Seemed pretty old, to judge by the seventeenth century costume of the courtiers, who stood in a semi-circle around a king and queen on their crimson chairs, attended by gentlemen in embroidered coats and heavy, curling wigs and doll-like ladies in lace collars and stiff brocade skirts. A figure in a blue cloak knelt among three winged cherubs, who tumbled among baskets spilling out a wealth of what looked like jewelled stones onto the carpet in front of the king's diamond-buckled shoes. Who exactly were these people and what was the significance of those baskets?

"Ze court of Louis Quartorze, le Roi Soleil, on ze occasion of ze twentiez birthday of ze Grand Dauphin, ze first day of Novembair 1681," announced a cultured female voice, as if in answer to his unspoken query.

Jamie swung round and found himself face to face with the thinly plucked eyebrows and heavily rouged cheeks of a gaunt, brittle woman in a flowing peacock tunic. She wore a cobalt blue scarf bound around her vivid orange curls and her eyes regarded him from beneath hooded lids with an appraisal that was almost rude in its directness.

"You will 'ave noted ze personification of France, who is casting Louis' gift of fifty thousand écus onto a priceless Savonnerie carpet before ze royal family of France," she continued politely, directing his gaze back towards the fan leaf with one scarlet-taloned forefinger. "Ze detail is truly exquisite, hein?"

She smiled, but only with her lips. From the piercing intensity of her ice-blue gaze, he at once understood that his reply was crucial. This was no mere conversational pleasantry, which he could counter with insipid small talk. It was an armed challenge.

He stared blankly at the fan. What intelligent observation could he possibly make? He was hopeless at clever repartee. But an odd detail had struck him about one of the tiny figures. He scanned the semi-circle of courtiers and saw that it was true. Every single fan in the ladies' hands was firmly closed – except one near the centre.

"Why's that woman's fan half open?" he blurted out, glancing back questioningly at the French woman. "What's so special about her?"

Her carmine lips curved imperceptibly upwards and a veiled satisfaction shone out of her shrewd eyes.

"Why zis is Madame in a costume of black chenille flowers embroidered wiz gold," she explained with an almost indiscernible increase of warmth in her tone. "Ze King – 'e 'as clearly not yet given 'is permission for ze fans to be opened, but Madame, as always, takes ze law into 'er own 'ands. Welcome to ze Fan Museum, young man. I am Aurélie Brisson." And with the well-bred formality of a reigning monarch, she graciously extended towards him a lean, blue-veined hand sparkling with diamonds.

Jamie shook it politely and introduced himself in return, aware that he'd somehow passed this test of initiation. Perhaps it was something to do with asking the right sort of question...

He noticed Elinor shoot them a glance of surprise. But she'd no chance to comment since, appearing to forget his presence entirely, Aurélie at once advanced towards her, arms outstretched in theatrical welcome. Her bangles and necklaces clinked and jingled as she embraced her old pupil and kissed her effusively on both cheeks, exclaiming how wonderful it was to see her again and making detailed enquiries about her health and that of her father.

In fact Jamie only realised the immensity of the favour conferred on him as they were following Aurélie at a respectful distance up the staircase hung with Japanese fan prints on a wallpaper of crimson birds and swirling tendrils of foliage.

"You're very privileged," whispered Elinor in his ear. "Whatever did you say to her? She never shakes hands with anyone who isn't a member of the Fan Circle."

Jamie shrugged modestly. But he wasn't sorry he'd managed to impress Elinor just a little, even if he didn't quite understand how.

At the top of the stairs two panelled doors lay invitingly open.

"Our current exhibition, *Masterpieces of ze Fan Museum*," announced Aurélie with a dignified sweep of one well-manicured hand. "Feel free to peruse zeez rooms at your leisure, young man. Zey contain a rare collection of antique beauties, displayed for your delight."

This was less a suggestion than a royal command. From the way she talked, Jamie gathered that Aurélie regarded her fans as so many daughters, to be cherished, protected and exhibited to their best advantage at every opportunity. Refusal to accept her invitation would be an unforgivable insult.

But a single glance into the well-lit room at the front of the house was enough to show that he needed no prompting across this particular threshold. His own instincts drove him eagerly on, tingling with the anticipation of exquisite pleasure.

Not all the fans were beautiful. In the first glass display case he approached lay a simple, brown fibre triangle edged with yellow feathers – from South-East Asia, the label said. He could hardly believe its shared prominence with a magnificent seventeenth century French court fan painted in brilliant gouache, depicting the Judgement of Paris with aristocrats in powdered wigs and satin trains jostling winged cherubs in a graceful woodland setting.

Somewhere behind he could hear Aurélie's voice directing Elinor's attention to a glass-topped case, which apparently contained their latest acquisition.

"A charming Youghal lace fan wiz three blond tortoiseshell guards. So rare. So chic. Gifted by an American donor. Breathtaking, is she not...?"

He felt himself being drawn from case to case, like a greedy child in a sweet shop, agonising whether to spend his precious pocket money on strawberry bonbons or lemon sherbets. Here lay a fan with a tiny timepiece mounted in its flower-shaped pivot, there an ivory fan in the form of a double-barrelled flintlock gun, over there a

Chinese hand screen embroidered with sequins and flowers of shimmering gold…

And then he saw it.

As he turned casually towards the wall-mounted display case near the window, his eye chanced to fall on an open fan in its front corner. He let out a gasp of recognition and drew nearer. Were his eyes playing tricks? No. There it lay, with its smooth, white mask of a face turned eyelessly towards him. The fan had been there all the time, waiting.

He instantly wheeled round to alert Elinor. But his voice stuck in his throat.

As he stood there gaping speechlessly, he saw her hesitate a moment and turn, as if her attention had been attracted by something outside herself. She caught sight of his face and stepped towards him.

"What's the matter?" she cried. "You look as though you've seen a ghost."

Jamie motioned excitedly towards the case.

"Look – look here," he stammered. "Bea's fan. The white mask face and the exact same four scenes: the music shop, the quarrelling couple, the beggar with the news sheet and the fan shop."

He watched her face as she studied it closely.

"Very like," she agreed at last, "though there's something different about the mouth of this mask – can't you see? The chin and jowls are just a little puffier. And look at the monture. These sticks are painted with flowers. And the guards are carved with baroque scrolls, not musical notes and insects and fruit like Bea's."

Jamie looked more closely. She was right.

"So it's not the same fan then?" he cried in disappointment.

"That'd be rare in the eighteenth century, when they were mostly handmade. But they're so similar, it's likely they came from the same workshop – if we can only find out which one. Aurélie, tell us. What do you know about this fan?" turning to the French woman, who had approached to see what was attracting their attention.

"Ah. Ze mask fan from ze Baldwin Collection. She is a bone fan wiz a printed paper leaf of an 'and-coloured etching. Zeez fans are vairy rare. I sink zat I 'ave only ever 'eard of some seven printed and per'aps an 'andful of painted ones. What is your interest in 'er?"

"Remember I emailed you about the Spanish mask fan I'd come across a couple of months ago? Jamie's sister owns it – her great aunt left it to her when she died. I've brought some close-ups to show you in case you can tell us more about it. Here…" pulling her phone out of her bag.

Aurélie studied the photos on the screen briefly through her spectacles, then glanced back at the fan in the wall case. She frowned, as though mentally scrolling through the catalogue entry. "Two shops, two scenes from ze theatre, one showing a London street…"

"A *London* street?" exclaimed Jamie.

"Why yes, I sink zat is so – I will consult ze catalogue, but I am almost certain 'er provenance is mid-eighteenth century Engleesh."

"*English*?" echoed Elinor in disbelief. "But all the words printed on it are Spanish. Are you sure?"

"But ze windows – ze tall, paned windows. You notice, do you not? Zey are windows of Engleesh 'ouses, just like zeez ones 'ere." She pointed to the windows of the room where they were standing with their fine Georgian sashes.

She had soon called up the full entry in the computer catalogue and it turned out to be just as she said: the fan was certainly listed as English – but there was little more recorded about it than they already knew. No indication of what the pictures were on the leaf or how these separate scenes were linked to one another.

Although Elinor's disappointment was somewhat softened by Aurélie's promise to launch an internet enquiry among her contacts abroad, there was clearly nothing more to be done at present. So she disappeared off to the library to begin her research on the items for the Spanish exhibition.

Meanwhile Jamie was treated to a guided tour of Aurélie's finest fans.

After this was over, Aurélie consulted the mother-of-pearl face of a small fan-pendant watch, which hung round her neck on a silver chain, and suggested lunch. Elinor, whom they found immersed in the pages of a massive nineteenth century catalogue, agreed to join them shortly. So Jamie and the older woman descended the stairs together to the museum tearoom.

This was housed in the quiet basement conservatory, lit by wide glass windows overlooking an enclosed garden. As they ordered soup and sandwiches, Jamie couldn't help gazing round at the painted wall murals. Scenic vistas receded into the emerald distance beyond a trompe l'oeil balcony, creating the illusion of an outdoor pavilion with rivers, fields and hills stretching out beyond terrace urns, linked by garlands of glowing fruits and glass-green foliage, and blooming with apricot roses, satin-red peonies and gold-throated lilies.

They sat down together at an elegant, marble-topped table beside the French windows, which commanded an unobstructed view of garden beds shaped like open fan leaves, bordered by neatly clipped box hedges, and planted with wet grey lavender bushes. Raindrops sparkled on every leaf and puddles shone like glass whenever the spring sunshine burst out from behind the clouds, striking dazzling prisms of light from every corner of this walled paradise that lay barely delivered from the frozen grip of winter.

"So why are you 'ere, Jamé?" demanded Aurélie, as she poured fragrant Earl Grey tea into a delicate pink and white flowered cup. It was no idle question.

Jamie drew back defensively behind his coffee mug.

"Well… Just tagging along with Elinor, I s'pose."

"You can deceive uzzer people, but you cannot deceive me," retorted Aurélie, stirring her tea carefully. "Some come 'ere because zey are lovers of beauty, some to 'ave a fan repaired and uzzers because zey search for answers. You 'ave come 'ere to ask questions."

"Yes of course, about my sister's fan," he hedged with downcast eyes.

"Zat is only why you think you 'ave come. Why do you wish to repair your seester's fan?"

"Well... To make it beautiful again, I guess," he confessed with an effort, hesitantly raising his eyes to hers. "I've always liked working with my hands. You know... er... Folding origami birds. Making aeroplane models. Building kites. That sort of stuff. And I like the feel of polished wood and the texture of carved ivory..." He'd begun speaking slowly, groping for the right words, but now he found them simply spilling out of him under the compulsion of her gaze. "I like just sitting, looking at the different pictures painted on the leaves and the patterns of the sticks, thinking about the craftsmanship and care of some long-ago artist painting those strawberries and towers and castanets and butterflies. And I loved taking Bea's fan apart, seeing all the rivets and screws and other tiny components that went into making it –"

There was a sudden thud. Jamie broke off abruptly as the glass door swung open and Elinor burst into the room. Her face was alive with excitement as she flew straight towards them, exclaiming,

"I've just had the most brilliant idea. Aurélie, you said the mask fan from the Baldwin Collection was decorated with theatre scenes, didn't you?"

"Yes. But I 'ave no expertise in eighteenth century English drama."

"No, but I know someone who does. My brother, Nick – you know, at Trinity, who specialises in Augustan literature. He might be able to recognise the play these scenes come from."

Chapter Thirteen

Elinor's eyes ranged over the crowds streaming through the ticket barriers. Possibly a bad idea to have arranged to meet Adam here. The underground was so busy at this time of night. In fact, perhaps she shouldn't' have agreed to go out for dinner at all – just caught a train back to Cambridge so as not to leave Dad alone for the whole evening – again, as he'd just been complaining on the phone. But Adam never took 'no' for an answer… Wait a bit! Was that a hand waving in the crush at the station entrance?

"Adam," she called out, waving back.

Adam started forward to meet them, slightly out of breath.

"Sorry I'm late. Great to see you again," he began. Then, glancing over her shoulder, he recoiled with a face of shocked amazement, "My God, it's not Jamie – is it? I'd never've recognised you," gesturing towards his dark, cropped hair.

Jamie seemed overcome with embarrassment. He mumbled something incoherent but soon fell silent, since Adam's attention had already shifted elsewhere.

"Hey, great outfit," Adam enthused, casting an appreciative eye over her new navy jacket and matching, white-spotted dress.

Elinor raised her eyebrows. A man who actually noticed what you were wearing?

These preliminaries over, Adam glanced in the direction of the exit.

"Come on, you two. We've got places to go and people to see. Tonight it's party time."

"Party time? But I thought we were going out for dinner," objected Elinor.

"Of course," Adam reassured her with unruffled aplomb. "That first. Then on to Alan and Judi's afterwards. Thought you'd like to meet the rest of the company after the help you gave us with that funding application."

"I see…" He sounded so sincere that she didn't like to hurt his feelings by refusing. "Well, just for a bit then. I need to head home…"

Adam led the way out of the station and Elinor automatically fell into step on the other side of Jamie, guessing the two friends would have news to exchange. But for some reason, Jamie soon began to lag behind, leaving her to carry on the conversation with Adam alone. After the way he'd emerged from his shell with Aurélie this afternoon, it was odd how suddenly he shrank back into it now like a snail whose horns had been brushed by a careless finger.

They ate dinner at a new Italian restaurant recommended by Adam under the nearby railway arches. It was fashionable with a young and trendy clientele and the waitresses fell over themselves to fetch Adam anything he wanted, but Elinor found the meal less than restful under the bombardment of blaring music, flashing coloured lights and the constant judder of trains rumbling overhead.

Adam dominated the talk with his lively wit and good humour. He was clearly putting himself out to be charming, as usual, which she wouldn't've minded except for the fact that he almost totally ignored his old friend. As the evening went on and Jamie drank more beer, she made deliberate efforts to involve him in the conversation, but he sank first into a lethargy punctuated by monosyllabic grunts and finally into morose and unresponsive silence.

It was only over coffee that something Adam said inexplicably stirred him out of his taciturn gloom. She'd just passed some casual remark about Adam not knowing how it felt to be by far the baby of the family, unlike herself, since he was so close in age to Cam.

"What'd you say was the gap between you again?" she asked. "Eighteen months?"

Jamie, raising his head, blurted out,

"No, actually more like – OWW!"

He suddenly broke off with a yelp of pain and, shooting a reproachful glance at Adam, bent to rub his ankle.

"Twenty months," Adam informed her quickly, then to Jamie, "Sorry, old man. Foot slipped." Turning to catch the waitress' eye, he loudly announced, "Come on. Time to go. I'll get the bill."

"And I'll just pay a quick visit to the ladies'," Elinor excused herself, fishing a contribution out of her purse and rising hastily from her seat. If she was going to this party of Adam's, at least she'd better freshen up first.

As she was returning a few minutes later, she caught sight of the other two apparently engaged in earnest debate. In fact, she even thought she overheard Jamie heatedly protesting "At least I'm not a liar…" But the moment they caught sight of her, the dispute instantly ceased. She glanced from one to the other: Adam's usually pale cheeks looked decidedly flushed and Jamie appeared indignant, but he at once hung his head, refusing to meet her eye.

Elinor frowned. Why should Adam accuse Jamie of all people of being a liar? He'd many faults to be sure but, if she read his character correctly, deliberate deceit wasn't one of them.

Nor could she even begin to understand his behaviour that evening. Since they'd started working on the fan together, she'd realised that, despite his unpromising exterior, he actually improved on acquaintance. And after all, look how warmly the Mowbrays had taken to him – they'd been on at her for weeks to bring him back to the farm. And how he and Aurélie had hit it off that afternoon, despite the wide difference in age and background.

But tonight it was as though some devil had got into him. No sooner had they walked in through the front door of Alan and Judi's cramped first-floor flat in Islington than he blundered off without a word and was soon lost to sight among the seething crowd of party guests flaunting spiked hair, nose rings and black leather garments loosely held together with safety pins and metal chains. Elinor wrinkled her nose at the strong smell of beer fumes mingled with a thick smoke haze that hung in the stuffy air. It was clear where Jamie was headed: straight off to pour yet more alcohol down his throat. Why did he behave so stupidly?

Adam was too busy hailing acquaintances and being enthusiastically kissed by various girls to notice Jamie's disappearance as he pulled her over to meet his main collaborators in the summer play project. Trying not to mind being hustled through the noisy throng, Elinor shook hands first with Alan, a bald, thickset black man with the commanding air of a Shakespearean duke, then with his short wife, Judi, who was blond, tanned and tough with a bone-crushing handshake. They greeted Elinor with sincere cordiality and thanked her effusively for her help with the project finances, after which Adam insisted on dancing. After all, what other entertainment was on offer? She was a moderate drinker and it was too noisy in this flat to hold a meaningful conversation. Might as well dance away the rest of the half hour she'd mentally allotted to a party where she didn't really feel at ease. After that, she'd politely make her excuses and slip away to the nearest underground station…

But dancing with Adam was fun and before she knew it, the hands of her watch stood at twenty minutes to midnight. High time to leave. She tried mouthing this to Adam, but he just stared blankly back at her. Then she pointed to the door, but partygoers were swirling all around them so they could hardly push their way through the crush. Her temples had begun to throb with the noise and pungent air reeking of cigarette smoke and sickly-sweet incense.

At this point she caught sight of Jamie, being tumbled from hand to hand like an ill-wrapped parcel among a swarm of girls, fingernails painted in rainbow stripes, eyelids glittering with mauve stars and bare shoulders tattooed with rosebuds and tiny red hearts. They were clamouring to clutch at him, dance with him and ply him with yet more liquor, even though he'd already drunk himself legless and was floundering around in a stupor.

She turned her back abruptly. Not her responsibility – thank goodness! Parties really weren't her scene. She and Paul had never seen eye to eye about them either. Why'd she ever agreed to come in the first place?

"Adam," she yelled into his ear as they reached the comparative quiet of the hallway, "I'm heading off now. My last train leaves King's Cross at half past."

"Plenty of time yet," he assured her without even glancing at his watch.

"No. I've really got to go – now!"

She pulled open the front door and, recoiling before a blast of chill night air, glanced down at her thin sleeves.

"My jacket! Where did I leave it?"

"I know," exclaimed Adam, brightening. "Saw it on the sofa in the sitting room."

They turned back to retrieve the jacket. But in the sitting room they found Jamie sprawled all over it, head lolling against a willowy blonde called Maxine, who'd been introduced to her earlier in the evening as the fifth member of the play company.

Pointless asking him to move, given the state he was in. But she could just glimpse a corner of navy fabric protruding from under his left arm, so she caught hold of it and tried to tug the garment free. All that happened was that Jamie toppled sideways over the padded sofa arm, dragging his rucksack and her jacket with him.

Elinor pursed her lips in annoyance.

"Adam, do you think you could lend me a hand with your friend here?" she demanded.

Adam sprang to heave Jamie bodily forward. At that moment Jamie's eyes flickered open and he lurched to his feet.

"Whazzamatter?" he blustered.

"Jamie-boy, you're blind drunk," announced Adam, snorting with laughter.

How could he be even mildly amused by such a revolting spectacle?

Suddenly Jamie stumbled and, reeling sideways, collapsed headfirst into Elinor's arms. She let out a cry, blenching at the foul gust of beery breath that struck her full in her face. He was such a dead-weight that she almost overbalanced, except that Adam sprang to her assistance and with great difficulty the two of them managed to shore him up between them.

"Why didn't you stop him drinking so much?" she exclaimed crossly.

"Can't stop someone who's made up their mind to get stewed," he answered in an oracular tone.

Why would Jamie have purposely made up his mind to get drunk? Meanwhile she was almost suffocating in the rank stench of sweat and body odour that emanated from his clothes like a miasma. She had to escape from this fix somehow.

"How're you going to get him home like this?" she demanded.

Adam looked as though he was about to quell her concern with a dismissive gesture. But suddenly he seemed to change his mind and appealed to her in open consternation.

"He's far too heavy for me to manage on my own. Could you possibly give me a hand?"

"Me? Why not Maxine – or those other girls who've been dancing with him all evening?" with a vague gesture in the direction of Jamie's former playmates.

Adam raised his eyebrows as if to say: what girls?

They'd all vanished like magic.

"But my train home," protested Elinor.

"I'll call a cab. We can drop you at the station on the way."

At least this suggestion offered some hope of escape. Elinor nodded.

"Wait here," ordered Adam. "You keep an eye on him and I'll go and make the call."

He helped her lower Jamie's inert body into the embrace of a plump purple floor cushion. Then he stepped out into the hall. Through the open doorway she could see him talking on his mobile as she sank down beside Jamie, who lay sprawled in a dishevelled heap. How had she ever got into this mess?

"Be here in five minutes," announced Adam on his return. "Shall we haul him out into the street meanwhile? Fresh air might bring him round a bit. D'you think you could heave him up under one arm, if I prop him under the other? – there's always so much of him when he gets like this."

So this wasn't just a one-off occurrence then.

Between them they managed to lug Jamie's unwieldy frame into the hallway and out the front door. Elinor peered up and down the street. But there was no sign of the taxi yet.

Fifteen minutes later they were still waiting.

Elinor shivered miserably. It was starting to spit with rain.

"Operator said they were pretty busy, being Friday night," Adam tried to comfort her, as he perched on the low front wall with Jamie's rucksack beside him, apparently unperturbed.

Elinor glanced at her watch. Nearly five past twelve.

"If it doesn't come soon, I'm going to miss that train," she muttered, biting her bottom lip.

"Relax, Ellie. It's not the end of the world. You could easily stay over at my place. One of my flatmates is away this weekend. You can have Christian's bed."

"Thanks for the offer, but I need to get home," answered Elinor firmly. This was so annoying. With everything she had to do too...

Eventually a red Vauxhall turned the corner of the street and pulled up alongside the kerb. At last! And just in time too. The intermittent drizzle was steadily increasing to a downpour. Elinor leapt to her feet and grabbed her handbag. She caught hold of Jamie's hands and with Adam pushing from behind, they strained to raise his slumped figure from the pavement.

Jamie, who'd been lying motionless all this time, suddenly roused himself and lurched in the opposite direction.

"No, no, Jamie, old man – don't do that," Adam urged, yanking him sharply back. "Ellie, can you hold him while I open the door?"

"Be quick, will you? It's raining," cried Elinor, gazing longingly at the dry rear seat of the taxi. She could feel the cold drops plopping faster and faster onto her head.

"OK. Just balance him there for a moment."

"Adam, help! He's buckling at the knees!"

Jamie slithered out of their grasp, flailing wildly in the air. As he crumpled around her shoulders, his head struck Elinor such a hefty blow across the cheek that tears started to her eyes. Her spectacles were wrenched sideways and clattered onto the wet pavement.

"Not my glasses," she shrieked, rooted to the spot for fear of hearing the sickening crunch of lenses shattering beneath somebody's heel.

"Hold on," exclaimed Adam, stooping to retrieve them.

"Not broken, are they?" she enquired anxiously.

"No. Just a bit bent," he reassured her, poking them back onto her face as well as he could with her head jammed under Jamie's armpit.

"Adam, let's just get him into the taxi," she moaned. Huge, chilly drops of rain were dripping off the ends of her hair and sliding down the back of her neck, as she man-handled Jamie frantically into the back seat.

"I'll get in with him," offered Adam, leaning over the door with chivalrous solicitude.

"No! I'll stay now I'm here. Let's just go."

Adam didn't argue. He slammed the back door of the taxi, grabbed Jamie's rucksack as an afterthought and hastily climbed with it into the front passenger seat.

"Mate had too much to drink?" enquired the driver, a bearded Asian in a black turban glancing into his rear-view mirror. He sounded none too happy to Elinor's ears. "You better hold onto this, miss," he advised, thrusting a plastic bag over the seat back, "or you'll be charged for the cleaning. Where to?"

"King's Cross Station," cried Elinor at once.

"You takin' him on a train like that?"

"No, but..."

The driver turned round. His face showed he meant business.

"Look, I'm doin' the pair of yer a favour by lettin' him into this cab at all. Now we drive him straight where he's goin' or yer all get out and walk. It's more than me upholstery's worth..."

No use arguing. Adam quickly gave him the address, which wasn't far away. The driver grunted and let out the clutch. The taxi pulled away from the kerb.

"Sure you're all right, Ellie?" asked Adam as they bowled along the main road.

"Yes," she snapped back icily.

"Why's he done this to me?" Adam was muttering to himself. "He's gonna have one hell of a hangover in the morning and I was planning to start work early too…"

Meanwhile Elinor crouched in the back of the taxi, seething. This was utterly degrading. To be stuck here, having certainly missed her last train by now, soaked through and crushed flat under Jamie's limp body, holding a plastic bag under his nose, while he snored his head off like a drunken pig! Wouldn't forgive him this in a hurry.

As the taxi slowed down and prepared to stop in the middle of a darkened street, Jamie woke up and began to gurgle and choke. Elinor recoiled in horror. What could possibly cap this disgusting behaviour?

She was soon to find out.

"Oh no," exclaimed Adam. "He's not gonna – Quick! Quick, open the door," he yelled, leaping frenziedly out of the passenger seat and tearing at the handle. In a flash he was dragging Jamie bodily out onto the pavement. Not a moment too soon. Just as Elinor clambered out after them, Jamie began to retch violently and then vomited straight over her shoulder into the streaming gutter.

"– Oh God! That's all we need," cried Adam, bending over his friend, who lay gaping and spluttering in the roadway.

Elinor stood speechless under the pouring rain. Never in her life had she witnessed such a humiliating spectacle! God knows what the taxi driver thought. And what exactly was that vile-smelling warmth that she could feel trickling down the front of her dress?

Adam crouched holding Jamie's head while she paid off the taxi driver, keen to dispatch any witness of this appalling scene. When she turned back, he smiled wanly up at her under the silver light of a nearby streetlamp.

"Well, I suppose at least most of it went into the gutter," he pointed out, as she knelt wearily down beside him and helped pull Jamie to his feet. "Missed you, didn't it?"

"Not exactly," retorted Elinor, very tight-lipped, but unable to let go for fear of Jamie pitching backwards into the lamp post. "Let's just get him inside. I'll deal with it later."

They staggered up the flight of concrete steps and in through a heavy, panelled door. Adam groped for the light, flicking on the switch to reveal the long, shabby hallway of a once gracious Victorian mansion, starkly lit by a single fluorescent strip. Elinor's heart sank even further as her eyes took in the scuffed green walls, dilapidated ceiling and cracked coving.

"Sorry it's not more sightly," Adam apologised, following the direction of her gaze. His voice sounded rather worn.

Elinor pulled herself together and smiled back tremulously. It wasn't his fault, was it? Out-of-work actors couldn't afford any better at London prices.

"Here," she encouraged, "let's get him to bed. Which way?"

They struggled up three flights of stairs. Finally Adam stopped outside an anonymous cream door in an anonymous cream hallway and fumbled in his pocket for the key.

"Here we are," he announced.

He thrust open the door and they hauled Jamie inside by main force, since he was now dragging his feet at every step. In what was clearly the living room stood a large sofa draped with a boldly patterned kilim. They tipped Jamie onto it and he rolled over onto his side and immediately fell asleep. The two of them exchanged glances of relief. Adam tossed the battered rucksack down nearby and they both sank into armchairs on either side of the sofa, listening to his reverberating snores.

Elinor was drenched, filthy and worn out. She glanced round, almost too exhausted to raise her eyes from the drab, grey floorboards.

"Sorry the evening turned out like this," Adam apologised. "I'd never've taken you to that party if I'd realised what was gonna happen."

She shrugged, lacking the energy to make a fuss. Her limbs felt dull and heavy.

"Well, I can't get back to Cambridge tonight now, can I? Especially not completely wet through and smelling like this. I need a shower and somewhere to wash my dress. Do you know if there's a B & B nearby?"

"Look, Ellie, you're tired out. It's too late to try and find a B & B by this time. Why not take a shower here instead? You're welcome to stay the night in Christian's bed. I know conditions're pretty primitive, but I ought to make it up to you somehow for this evening …"

Elinor smothered a yawn. She felt her resolve weakening.

"But what're we going to do with Jamie?"

They both turned their heads towards him as he lay on his back, snorting like a blowing whale. They looked back at each other.

"Why don't we just leave him here to sleep it off?" suggested Adam tentatively.

"I guess it's only for one night," she replied. "Better leave Dad a message…"

Chapter Fourteen

Jamie rolled over and fell with a jarring thump onto the floorboards. His drowsy eyelids sprang open on the grey light of early morning as he found himself struggling among a welter of blankets. There was a dry, woolly taste in his mouth and he ached all over. His temples throbbed and his stomach was churning uneasily. Where was he? What'd happened?

He groped through his memory among the shattered shards of last night. Nothing could blot out the pain of acting gooseberry over dinner, as he listened to Adam trying so hard to impress Elinor, or the sharpness of the kick in the ankle he'd received when he almost gave away Adam's age. After that, things grew hazier. Must've got totally pissed. His mind swirled with a sea of eyes, mouths, naked limbs and floating hair. As he swam among them, he found himself almost colliding with Elinor's blurred face, drifting nearer and then further away. Aware that she was helping haul him out of a car and half-dragging, half-carrying him up some steps, he struggled to free himself from her hands. Deep down inside him something hurt…

He grew dully conscious of the distant splash of water, of a door opening and closing and then of cautious footsteps tiptoeing over creaky floorboards. He stirred feebly.

"Sorry, I was trying not to wake you," Elinor's voice whispered. "How're you feeling?"

He groaned aloud.

After a moment he realised she must be standing beside him. He refused to open his eyes for fear of finding himself gazing straight up into hers.

"Like some water?" she asked quietly.

"No thanks, I'm fine," he croaked, summoning up all his strength and jerking his body upright. A violent wave of nausea washed over him and he sank weakly back against the leather sofa.

"Need a bowl?" He felt her kneel down beside him.

"No, I'm OK." He fended off her supporting hands, keeping his face stubbornly averted. Why waste sympathy on a loser like him?

"At least let me help you back onto the couch."

"The floor's where I belong. Hoped you'd be gone when I woke up, so at least I could've spared you this" – *and myself too*, he thought. A choking lump suddenly swelled in his throat and he threw up a shielding arm to mask his face from her sight.

"Now come on, things aren't as bad as all that," she encouraged. "I'll fetch you a glass of water."

He heard her rise and move away. At least this gave him the chance to pull himself together without feeling her pitying gaze sear his very skin. He swallowed and blinked hard. Then he heaved himself to his feet and groped his way gingerly to the table, where he sank down on one of the black plastic chairs with his groggy head buried in his hands on its worn formica surface. He felt stiff and giddy – and actually rather hot as well.

Light filtered in through the dusty windows above the kitchen sink, but the rest of the curtains were drawn. Must be pretty early still.

"What time is it?" he muttered.

"Seven twenty-two."

He raised his head and steeled himself to glance at her for the first time that morning. She stood running the unfamiliar tap with her back towards him and her dishevelled hair hanging loose over her shoulders. But oh God –! His eyes suddenly widened. She was wrapped in Adam's dark green towelling bath robe! What the hell'd been going on here last night, while he was totally out of it?

"Where's Adam?" he cried, glancing vaguely around.

"Probably still asleep."

So she didn't know for sure?

She turned from the sink and set down a chipped, red-and-white-striped mug of water beside him. He reached out a trembling hand, then, thinking the better of it, slumped back over the tabletop.

"Look, Jamie," she suggested after a moment, "why don't you just climb into Christian's bed and go back to sleep? He's away for the weekend and Maxine isn't arriving for a rehearsal till ten. You'll feel better after you've had more rest."

"No. I'm not tired." He rose and staggered dizzily in the general direction of the bathroom. Had to carry off this humiliating scene somehow...

He examined his bristling jaw and bleary eyes in the clouded mirror above the hand basin, which was square and monumental and cracked with age like the rest of the bathroom fittings. A wash and a shave might help. As he was splashing water over his face, he glimpsed behind his shoulder the reflection of Elinor's navy jacket and white-spotted dress hanging over the antiquated shower rail on the opposite side of the high-ceilinged room. Odd place to leave them overnight.

"What're your clothes doing in there?" he blurted out, returning to the living room on the hunt for his razor.

"Oh – they're still drying," remarked Elinor airily as she rummaged through the kitchen cupboards. "I had to sponge them out last night."

"Drop something on them at the party then?"

"No, not exactly," came her voice from the depths of a cupboard. "They got a bit – splashed."

"Splashed? What with?"

"Er –" She withdrew her head from the cupboard. "Somebody spilt something down me."

"Hope it wasn't red wine. That can be a real bug – nuisance to get out," he remarked, peering around the sofa.

"No, it wasn't red wine. Isn't that lucky? Looking for something?"

"Yeah. My rucksack. Haven't seen it, have you?"

Did that sound casual enough? he wondered – given how stupid he felt at having no idea what'd become of it last night.

Elinor's gaze swerved towards one of the brown, imitation leather armchairs. Beside it sprawled his rucksack, both straps long broken, disgorging its contents over the floorboards: creased play script, toothbrush, razor, old socks with holes in the heels, several pairs of ragged underpants … He met her eye and flushed hotly. Then he dropped to his knees and started clumsily stuffing the pants back into the rucksack. But his consciousness of total exposure to her contempt only caused still more rubbish to tumble out: scrap paper, half-empty packets of chewing gum, loose paper clips and finally even his knife, which hit the floorboards with a dull clunk.

He glanced up and saw Elinor almost killing herself with laughter.

"What's so funny?" he demanded roughly. "What else do I need for a few days in London?"

"Well, a clean T-shirt or two might be useful. And why on earth carry a penknife around?"

"It's not a penknife," he protested. "It's a Swiss Army knife – with scissors and a screw-driver and an attachment for prising stones out of horses' hooves. Never know when it might come in handy."

"Essential equipment for play rehearsals, I suppose."

Jamie grimaced back. Funny how he suddenly felt much better.

"You don't happen to know where they keep the coffee here, do you?" she went on. "Thought we could both do with a cup."

Jamie dropped his rucksack in the armchair and stepped over to show her. As he came closer, he couldn't help noticing the dark smudges under her eyes. And her glasses. Somehow this morning they didn't look level on the bridge of her nose...

"Why don't you sit down?" he suggested, pulling out a chair with unpractised gallantry. "You look a bit done in yourself."

"In a minute. I'll make the coffee first." She peered inside the lid of the kettle.

"Here, let me fill it up," he offered. "That old kettle's quite a weight. You mightn't be able to lift it."

"Oh you'd be surprised," she answered drily, darting him a sideways glance as she opened the fridge and pulled out a carton of milk. "I'm stronger than I look." Sniffing the contents of the carton made her wrinkle her nose, then tip the rancid yoghurt down the sink. "Ugh! Have to make do with it black, I'm afraid."

She spooned some coffee granules into two unmatching mugs and Jamie poured in the boiling water. Then he set the mugs on the table and she sat down in the chair he'd pulled out for her. She looked up as he hesitated.

"Aren't you going to join me?" she asked, curling her fingers round the steaming cup. The aroma of strong coffee tickling his nostrils made him feel almost human again.

"Yeah. But first, I'm gonna sort your glasses for you."

"My glasses?" echoed Elinor, automatically reaching up to touch them.

"They're sitting crooked and it's really bugging me. Give 'em here a minute and I'll see what I can do."

And he reached out one hand for them.

"Oh don't bother," murmured Elinor hastily. "I'll take them to the optician on Monday morning."

"No bother. Come on, hand 'em over. After you've not once let on what a complete arse – er – idiot I made of myself last night, it's the least I can do."

Deftly turning over the fragile wire spectacles between thumbs and index fingers, he held them up to the light and spotted the problem at once. The bridge was slightly twisted. Only take a moment to fix.

He went to fish his Swiss Army knife out of the depths of his rucksack. So much for the scorn she'd poured on it! Then with a cheeky grin, which she returned with interest, he sat down at the table opposite her, whistling softly through his teeth as he straightened the bridge and tightened the screws for good measure.

"What'd you do to 'em last night anyway? Get beaten up in a drunken brawl?"

"How'd you guess?" She smiled over the rim of her green-flowered mug.

"You'll have to learn to keep higher class company, won't you? …There, that's better," examining the spectacles critically.

He rose and moved round the table. At least he could make some impression on her that was a notch above his usual hopeless inadequacy.

She made a move to set down her coffee mug.

"Don't bother," he said. "I'll just slip 'em on for you."

She casually raised her face towards him. He rotated the glasses with neat dexterity, but as he leaned over to fit them on, he suddenly found himself gazing straight into her eyes. They were the colour of deep blue pools. He stood poised on their brink, transfixed by their loveliness.

Elinor lowered her lids at once, setting down her mug and murmuring, "Oh Jamie! You're poking the frames into my ears. Here, let me put them on myself."

As she reached out, her hand grazed his and a lightning tremor shot through his whole body. He stared at her, quivering with surprise.

At that moment they heard footsteps in the hall. They both started as the kitchen door flew open and Adam came breezing in, fully dressed. At the sight of them he stopped short and his eyes flickered from one to the other.

"Well," he declared with a grin, "the Titan awakens. And looking a lot better than I expected him to. Welcome change from last night, isn't it, Ellie? – to see him standing here on his own two feet, rather than knocking your glasses off and puking all down the front of you in a public street."

Elinor had spun round to interrupt him, but it was too late. In a flash Jamie realised that the shame he'd felt on waking was as nothing compared to the humiliation from which she'd been trying to shield him.

*

He instantly fled to the bathroom, while Elinor stared hard at the stained yellow tabletop. How could Adam be so brash and insensitive?

"What's up with him?" asked Adam, flinching as the bathroom door slammed shut and the bolt shot fiercely home.

"I expect he couldn't remember exactly what happened last night," explained Elinor quietly. "Probably feels a bit embarrassed."

"That'd be a first then. Happened often enough before."

"Yes, so you seemed to imply last night." A timely reminder that Jamie was just a waster. No use feeling too much sympathy for him.

"You sleep OK then?" asked Adam, turning to eye her up and down with cool amusement.

Elinor pulled the gaping neck of the dressing gown higher around her throat. Why did his gaze feel so disconcertingly familiar? Of course! It was his dressing gown, wasn't it? Well, she hadn't had much choice but to accept his offer of it last night. And now the only way to restore it to him was to reclaim her clothes from the bathroom. But the savage click of the lock had already warned her that she wouldn't be gaining access there any time soon. So what to do now? Why was it that someone fully dressed always seemed at such an advantage, especially when you were wearing his clothes?

"Like some coffee?" she asked in an effort to distract him. "I've just boiled the kettle."

Adam's eyes flashed upwards to her face.

"I was just thinking how stunning you look in my dressing gown," he joked lightly. "You should wear it more often."

Elinor swallowed hard. So here it was. Up till now she'd managed to parry his probing admiration with a blunted foil. Even when he sat in the armchair last night, watching her emerge from the bathroom after showering and rinsing out her clothes. They hadn't known each other long enough for her to commit to a closer relationship. And instinct held her back. A feeling of something being not quite – right. Something she couldn't exactly put her finger on: a lack of total honesty between them perhaps? Always she seemed to be seeing a mask instead of his actual face, so the true Adam slipped through her fingers like reality vanishing before the wand of a magician. Or maybe the fault lay with herself. After all, Adam was lively, interesting, witty, good-looking. Every woman he met seemed keen to snare his interest. Perhaps she was making excuses, hiding behind memories of Paul. Perhaps she just needed to let go for a change…

She felt herself slowly flushing beneath his ardent gaze and Adam reached out one hand to draw her to him.

Suddenly there was a loud crash. Elinor gave a violent start and both pairs of eyes flew towards the bathroom door.

"What the hell was that?" exclaimed Adam.

"Do you think Jamie's all right in there?"

Next moment a sleepy-eyed girl in plaits and yellow gingham pyjamas shot into the room. One of Adam's flatmates probably, startled out of bed by the noise.

"What was that almighty bang?" she cried.

No one replied. Together, Adam and Elinor leapt towards the bathroom door, yelling Jamie's name. There was no answer from within – only a low moaning sound.

"Jamie. What's going on?" bellowed Adam.

"How're we going to get in?" gasped Elinor. "It's locked – on the inside!"

Adam rattled the door handle, but nothing happened. Then he tried furiously pounding on the wooden panels. Still no response. Finally, setting his shoulder to the lock, he burst open the door with one determined thrust.

"Lucky we've got a pre-war bolt to match the pre-war plumbing," was his only comment as all three of them tumbled into the room.

They found Jamie sprawled in a daze on the bilious green vinyl, still clutching a grey towel in hands that strained like bird claws. At the sound of the opening door, he threw back his head. His face was blanched, his eyes wild, his pupils stark and staring.

"Jamie," cried Adam. "You all right? Passed out, did you?"

"Just f-felt a b-bit l-l-light-h-h-h…" Jamie could hardly stutter out the words.

Elinor had already spotted the empty screw holes in the crumbling wall plaster and the tarnished brass rod lying on the floor near the bath.

"The towel rail must've given way under his weight when he fell against it," she guessed.

She automatically stooped to help him to his feet, but the moment she touched him, she recoiled in shock.

"Adam, he's shivering," she cried. "But his back's covered in sweat and his face is burning hot. Whatever's wrong with him?"

Jamie seemed to be struggling to speak but his teeth were chattering so hard that she couldn't make out what he was saying. Then he made a violent effort to rise, clutching onto her body for support. But at that moment he buckled at the knees and slumped unconscious to the ground.

Chapter Fifteen

It was late on Saturday morning. Bea was home alone, since Mum was at the shop of course and Dad had taken the twins on a trip to the new Space Centre. She was running through a set of pieces before her orchestra rehearsal at Trinity College that afternoon, but just as she started on the final one, the doorbell rang.

People who interrupted music practice were a pain in the butt. Probably selling stuff no one wanted anyway. Perhaps if she ignored them, they'd just go away... She raised her flute dismissively to her lips.

But the doorbell rang again – with an additional thud, as though something had just bumped against the stained-glass panel.

Talk about persistent – But hey! Before Mum left for work, hadn't she mentioned that Geoff expecting an order of microscope parts? Maybe this was the delivery man. Didn't want that package returned to the depot or she'd never hear the end of it. Better go and check.

She set down her flute with a sigh and sped down the hall. Throwing open the door, she fell back in surprise. This certainly wasn't a delivery man.

On the doorstep stood a white-faced woman, whom she dimly recognised, supporting a figure in jeans and a T-shirt, who looked as though he was either fainting or – more probably, in this case – dead drunk.

"Jamie," burst out Bea, aghast. "I thought you were down in London for play rehearsals –"

Jamie seemed to be struggling to raise his head but was clearly still so plastered he couldn't manage to string two coherent words together. Must've been quite a party last night.

"Please, may I bring him inside?" interrupted the woman, who was clearly labouring under his weight. "I've practically carried him from the car and he needs to lie down."

"Of course. Sorry." Bea stood away from the door, then thought better of it and stepped forward to help haul Jamie over the threshold. Wasn't this Elinor Mitford, the fan woman from the Lydgate Museum? What was she doing here with Jamie like this?

Together they struggled to manoeuvre him along the hall, steering him into a chair in the living room, where he lay back, apparently unable to speak but breathing heavily with sweat streaming down his pale, haggard face.

"Wow! Some hangover," remarked Bea, surveying him with crossed arms and a distinct lack of sympathy. "Never seen him this bad before. Why didn't you just leave him wherever he was to sleep it off?"

"That's just it: I'm not sure it *is* a hangover. He passed out earlier this morning."

"Guess it wouldn't be the first time."

"When he came round, he seemed to recover quickly enough. Got his colour back. Ate some breakfast and drank lots of water. Was looking quite normal in fact. But he insisted on coming back to Cambridge with me rather than stay on at Adam's for the play rehearsal –"

"Oh, so you've been at Adam's too, have you?"

Elinor ignored this question, though she coloured self-consciously – looked pretty guilty to Bea. So why'd she been sleeping at Adam's?

"I thought it was probably sensible for him to come home rather than spend the day rehearsing, since he was looking so washed out," Elinor went on, "and he seemed well enough to travel. When we caught the train at King's Cross, he didn't say much. Just sat back in his seat, mostly with his eyes shut. But I was reading, so I wasn't watching too closely. Then a bit out of Royston, I suddenly noticed he was breathing hard, like he is now, and sweating furiously. By the time we arrived in Cambridge, he was clearly far too ill to make his own way home, so I helped him into the car and drove him straight here. But looking at him now, I'm not sure I oughtn't to've taken him to A & E –"

At that moment Bea heard a key in the front door lock. Probably Mum. Faye must've arrived to take over at the shop so she could come home for lunch.

"Mum," Bea called out, "Jamie's just turned up."

"What's he doing back so soon? Isn't he spending the weekend in London?" replied Mum's voice, accompanied by the thud of heavy bags on the hall tiles.

Next minute Mum herself appeared in the living room doorway. She paused on the threshold, regarding the stranger questioningly.

Elinor looked uncomfortable. She'd never met Mum before, had she?

Bea hastened to introduce them, relating how Elinor had just brought Jamie back from London. But even before she'd finished, Mum's eyes slid towards the figure now lying inert in the armchair.

"Whatever's happened?" she cried in alarm, dropping her bulging handbag on the sofa.

"Elinor drew the short straw and got lumbered with carting Jamie home from a party," volunteered Bea. "He's fearfully hung over."

"I'm so sorry to burst in on you like this, Mrs Willett," apologised Elinor, "but he's not been at all well this morning. I thought he'd just had a bit too much to drink last night, but he was keen to come back to Cambridge with me anyway. You don't think he's got some sort of alcohol poisoning, do you?"

Mum had already sprung to the couch and was raking Jamie's face with anxious eyes, laying the back of her hand on his forehead to check his temperature.

"This isn't alcohol poisoning," she declared. "It's malaria. He looks just the way he was in January."

"Malaria?" cried Elinor in bewilderment.

"We'd better get him straight back to hospital. I'll phone for an ambulance."

*

Jamie remembered this. It was like reliving a nightmare that brought you out in a hot sweat when you woke up. Only this hot sweat didn't go away. Not just his head, but even the very marrow of his bones ached and everything wavered before his eyes as though in a heat haze on a sweltering summer day. The floor pitched up and down when he struggled to rise, so in the end he had to give up and lie flat in a bed that rocked like a boat on the waves of the open sea. One moment it was night. Ice froze up his veins and he shivered and shook under the bedcovers till his teeth chattered, unable to get warm. The next moment, light stabbed his eyeballs. Every last hair in his scalp was on fire and his body was burning up, so he threw off all the blankets. Now he heard voices round him, babbling on and on without words. Now he felt an arm under his shoulders, lifting him towards a blurred face that he knew he ought to recognise but somehow couldn't, however hard he strained. It hovered nearer and then further away, swelling larger and larger until he cried out in terror, then shrinking smaller and smaller again until it almost disappeared into nothingness…

Then, what was that strange sound? *Click, click, clickety click* it went, on and on… *Click, click, clickety click…*

At last he lifted his languid lids on bright daylight and found himself staring at a blank cream wall. When he blinked his drowsy eyes, still soft with sleep, the daylight didn't go away and neither did the wall. Gradually he became aware that his head was resting on a fresh-smelling white pillow. Fanning out the fingers of his left hand, he tentatively stroked the patterned texture of the thin blanket and heard the crisp rustle of clean sheets as he stirred and rolled over. Gentle sunlight warmed his face and a deep sense of inner well-being coursed throughout his body, all the way down to the tips of his fingers and toes. Even breathing regularly in and out felt like a miracle. When he stared upwards, he saw the pure blue heavens. Was this death? This blissful sensation of not feeling ill anymore, of absolute tranquillity? Surely not. It smelt so like the world he knew – especially that faint whiff of cooked cabbage lingering in the antiseptic air.

With considerable effort, he managed to turn his head and straightway caught sight of Mum, who sat knitting something pink in the armchair beside the bed. *Click, click, clickety, click* went her knitting needles.

"Where am I?"

The thin, shaky voice seemed to come from somewhere outside himself. It sounded nothing like his own.

The clicking stopped for a moment.

"In hospital, dear," Mum's voice reassured him. "You've been very ill."

"What happened?"

Mum explained that he'd suffered something called a 'recrudescence' of malaria, but that he was a lot better now and would soon be coming home. For the moment, he should close his eyes and rest.

Jamie nodded, perfectly satisfied. Everything must be as it was meant to be. He felt tired, but vividly alive. Not wondering, not worrying about the past or future. Just glad to have this present moment of perfect peace. The comforting click of the knitting needles started up again.

Then he ran his tongue over his lips. They were rough and dry. Eventually it struck him that he felt thirsty. After viewing the problem from every angle, he decided to reach for the water jug that he could see standing on top of the nearby locker. But when he tried to hoist himself up on one elbow, his arm buckled underneath him and something tugged at his wrist.

"No, don't do that, dear," warned Mum, laying a warning hand on his arm. "You don't want to pull the drip out. Lie back and I'll pour you a drink."

Jamie gazed all the way up the clear plastic tube he'd suddenly noticed springing from his bandaged hand. It led to a bottle half full of transparent liquid hooked onto a metal stand.

He tried to help Mum raise him up against the heap of snowy pillows so as to be able to drink more easily from the plastic cup she'd filled for him, but his limbs felt like jelly. Though he strained hard, somehow he couldn't manage to hold the cup himself and she had to lift it to his lips as though he was a baby. Some of it even trickled wetly down the side of his neck. But oh, that water was good! So pure and clean and cool. The best drink he'd ever tasted in his life. He swallowed greedily for a moment, then sank back, exhausted, against the soft pillows.

After some time – didn't know how long – the soothing click of Mum's needles stopped again, so he opened his eyes to see why. She was nodding pleasantly to a harassed-looking Indian woman in a lilac sari, who scuttled past with two children and a plastic bag full of papers in the direction of an elderly man with grey hair and a bushy moustache, who was propped up in bed in the neighbouring bay.

"Mrs Patel," whispered Mum. "Catches a bus up here every afternoon to visit her father-in-law. They run a corner shop on Hills Road and he likes to check over the accounts. It's so hard for her with two little children, having to arrange for a different relative to come each day and mind the shop…"

At least Mum could drive up to the hospital and she didn't have to worry about finding a babysitter for Marc and Geoff in the daytime. But what about her own business?

"Who's minding the shop?" he wondered aloud.

"Oh I've struck a deal with Faye, so if I arrive early and take care of things till lunchtime, she'll do most of the afternoon as long as I go back to lock up at night. Except today, of course, when she's off to her Pilates class. But we've managed to persuade her mum to come and sit for a couple of hours instead. I'm coping."

"Sounds so much trouble," he murmured, at a loss to trace the ins and outs of all these complex organisational details, though he could easily grasp the immense effort she'd made just to come and sit quietly knitting beside him in hospital. "How long've I been here?"

"Three days – counting the afternoon you were admitted."

"Three days! And you've been here every afternoon?"

"Yes, of course."

"Even when I was totally out of it? But why?"

"Because I like to see how you are with my own eyes."

Strangely comforting to think he hadn't been alone in those hours of lost consciousness.

"And Dad's been here too?" he went on, thinking how much had evidently gone on without his knowledge.

"A couple of times. Naturally he can't get away from work in the afternoons, but he's made up for it at night, except yesterday of course when he had to do the weekly shop because I was busy cooking dinner."

"But Bea's been helping with dinner, hasn't she?" The idea that she mightn't've made him feel oddly anxious.

"Of course – when she can. But she's revising for exams and she's got so many rehearsals at the moment – not just *Beggar's Opera*, but chamber music and her usual youth orchestra work. Dad's been running around after her a lot – as usual."

But Bea wasn't the only one his parents needed to run around after, was she?

"So how're Marc and Geoff?"

Mum raised her eyes to the ceiling.

"The washing those two generate! What with the school sports trip to the Lakes and football practice and the pond enhancement scheme. I'm having a hard time talking Geoff into sticking with what he and Dad've already excavated and not digging up the entire back lawn. But you know what he's like… It's enough to make you lie awake at night with worry – if you weren't worried enough already…"

She smothered a yawn with a bright smile and resumed her knitting, while Jamie lay studying her familiar face feature by feature as though he'd never seen it before: dark, wavy hair with a slight tint of bronze in the sunlight flooding in through the great glass window; pearl studded earrings that'd been a gift from Granny when she and Dad got married; high cheek bones, a little worn now with advancing years; warm olive skin, slightly sagging at mouth and throat; dark brows strongly arched above deep-set brown eyes with faint crows' feet at the corners – her laughter lines, Dad liked to call them…

Of course he knew it so well, Mum's face. So well that he hadn't bothered to look at it for years. Would probably have been the first sight he ever saw in his life, wouldn't it? Hanging above him when he was in his cradle or learning to walk, supported by the strength of her hands. He could remember it misting over with pleasure when he presented her with yet another folded origami box for her birthday because he hadn't saved enough pocket money to buy her a real gift from a shop. Or puckering with concentration while she was running through lines with him for the school play or lit up with laughter when he was performing on stage… And what return had he made her for all her love and care of him?

He remained silent, his gaze tracing the pronounced double frown lines between her brows, the criss-cross wrinkles around her tired eyes and lips. How would she have been feeling now if he hadn't come through this?

Sudden sharp tears stung behind his eyes. How stupid he'd been! No one was immortal. After the doctors told him that first time in hospital how lucky he'd been to pull round, still he'd gone on behaving like an idiot anyway. He was nothing but a pain in the arse to the medical staff, his family and probably his friends too. It was a stunning revelation.

He'd got thoroughly and deliberately drunk last Friday night and given Adam such a hard time it'd be a wonder if he ever wanted to see him again. He'd been meant to do blocking rehearsals with him and Maxine on Saturday and with Alan and Judi as well on Sunday and he'd wasted their time and let them all down.

And as for Elinor… The very thought of her made him writhe inside. Adam's words were blistered onto his brain: "knocking her glasses off and puking all down the front of her in a public street." Jamie cringed. One thing for sure: that was never gonna happen again. But how could she ever forgive him for such behaviour? And then having to drag him all the way back to Cambridge and drive him home because he couldn't stand on his own two feet. He wouldn't've got back without her help. Could he ever make it up to her? Worse than that – could he ever face her again? Think how she must despise him…

Suddenly he felt a gentle pressure on his hand.

"What's wrong, love?" asked Mum in a low voice.

"How'd you know anything was wrong?" he managed to quaver out.

"You made a little noise that sounded like a sob."

Jamie gazed up into her eyes, which were dark with concern. At first he didn't reply for fear that all he could utter would be another sob. Finally he swallowed hard and, slipping his hand into hers, pressed it feebly in return.

"Thanks for being here, Mum," was all he said.

Chapter Sixteen

After Jamie returned from hospital, he rapidly gained weight and strength. So it wasn't long before he was able to undertake small jobs around the house like drying dishes and watering seed pots on the back patio. The first time he was well enough to go out, he tottered resolutely down the road to the corner shop to buy a thank you card for the medical staff who'd taken care of him in hospital. He also messaged Adam, offering to spend half of next term's reading week up in London for play rehearsals. But what amends could he make to Elinor?

Mysteriously, while he'd been in hospital, a sort of understanding seemed to have sprung up between her and Mum, which led to her embarrassing habit of referring to Elinor as "a sweet girl", treating her as some sort of family friend and insisting on inviting her over for dinner, despite Bea's chilly reception of the suggestion and his own open horror. Imagine Elinor, who lived in that high-class Georgian mansion on the Tillington Rd, sitting down to eat in their ordinary, overcrowded dining room with his annoying little brothers! Arggh!

But once Mum got an idea in her head, nothing could dislodge it and – worse still! – Elinor had actually accepted the invitation. So he was going to have to face up to her presence in this house for a whole evening – and soon too, since Mum'd asked her over before he could escape back to Exeter for the summer term. At least he ought to be armed for the occasion with some sort of peace-offering. But what?

Flowers? But they were so ordinary. Chocolates? Toiletries? But they were what you bought your girlfriend at the last minute when you'd forgotten her birthday. Something fan-shaped perhaps? But a google search turned up an array of diamond- and sapphire-studded jewellery on the Fan Museum website that was way too expensive and too personal besides. Box files, soaps, hair combs, keyrings? Probably had loads of those already. And he could hardly invite her out for coffee, since she actually had a paying job, unlike himself.

On the grey afternoon before the dinner party he wandered disconsolately for half an hour up and down the gusty streets of the town centre, browsing the gift and bookshop windows for ideas. But it wasn't until he was almost ready to give up and head home that he chanced upon *Sweet Dreams*.

Sweet Dreams stood on the other side of the street from Trinity College in a windswept side-passage opposite the music seller's. A black, wrought-iron gateway framed the entrance to the passage and above the door hung a swinging sign in the shape of a gilt-wrapped parcel with the gift shop's name painted on its pink ribbon bow.

At first sight it looked too upmarket to be promising. His gaze travelled dismissively over the window display of hand-embroidered silk sheets, patchwork quilts and fluffy white towels heaped in studied disarray around lavender scented soaps and long-necked glass bottles of violet bath oil. Clearly all so hideously expensive that they didn't dare expose the price tags to public view. But then again, the situation was desperate. Couldn't go home this afternoon without a peace-offering and he was running out of places to try. But he'd never ventured into a fashionable bed and bath boutique before. Wouldn't he make a total fool of himself...?

At the last moment, struck by sudden stage-fright, he swerved away from the frosted glass door and instead fell to counterfeiting a strong interest in the music shop opposite. But as he was studying the poster for a late-night Spanish guitar gig at the Bell Jar Café this evening, a glittering gold reflection in the dark glass of a mullioned windowpane caught his eye.

Turning his head, he let out a gasp of admiration as he glimpsed a vivid silk square like a dazzling Klimt canvas pegged among a line of scarves in the side window of *Sweet Dreams*. On it, among a riot of lotus blossoms and rainbow-feathered phoenix birds, there floated a young woman in an exotic purple and gold kimono carrying a red and black fan. Perfect! Elinor's wardrobe could do with a bit of a lift. This was gonna be child's play after all.

He drew a deep breath and plunged in through the shop door, which pinged a warning bell as he pushed it open.

*

Ten minutes later, the mocking jingle of the very same bell attended his headlong flight back into All Saints Passage, aflame with confusion and entirely empty-handed. Seen off by a couple of politely helpful shop assistants with posh accents and pink frosted lips, keen to capitalise on his inexperience by sweet-talking him into spending more than he could afford and catching each other's eyes with barely suppressed amusement when he blenched at the price of what turned out to be a pure silk scarf. Worse humiliation followed when he ignorantly stumbled further into the mire over the sizing of a gossamer-thin lemon blouse embroidered with gold butterflies, which they suggested as a substitute for the scarf from the sale basket. Had only narrowly managed to escape their clutches by the skin of his teeth.

Once outside in the grip of a chill breeze, Jamie's glow of agitation soon subsided. Turning into the small, railed garden nearby, he sank despondently down on the wooden bench furthest away from *Sweet Dreams* in a sheltered corner beside a bed of budding yellow primulas. He'd never nerve himself to cross the threshold of that shop again and he had to have that scarf in the window. No matter what it cost, it was right for Elinor. Why hadn't he realised in the first place that if you wanted something classy, you simply had to pay the price on the ticket? And in fact he could even afford it, now he remembered the money he'd recently received from Great Aunt Rosita's will.

Ten minutes later he was still huddled there wondering what to do, with his hands stuffed into the pockets of his black leather jacket and his chin sunk on his chest, when he happened to glance up and catch sight of a figure being blown past among the scrap papers bowling along the footpath. It was Bea carrying her flute case while flurries of wind snatched at her long, fair hair and the ends of her bright red scarf. As she was on the point of crossing the street, she chanced to glimpse him through the black iron palings and paused for a moment.

"Hi there," she called out. "What're you doing here?"

"Thinking," replied Jamie, gloomily returning to his contemplation of the stony cobbles in front of him.

"Don't overdo it, will you? When you're not used to it, the results can be pretty serious," she retorted. But when he made no flippant rejoinder, she went on more soberly, "Hey, anything the matter?" She retraced her steps along the railings and, entering through the arched gateway, came to perch on the bench beside him. "You feeling all right?"

"Yeah." The slight hint of concern in her tone nudged him into confiding his problem to her ears. "It's just that I want to buy something from that shop over there," waving his hand in the direction of *Sweet Dreams*.

Bea glanced at the shop and raised her eyebrows.

"For yourself?" she teased. "Didn't know you were into scented towels and frilly nighties."

"Of course not for myself!" He pulled a face, but her joke did sow the seed of an idea in his mind… Bea looked like she might be into scented towels and frilly nighties. But could he trust her? Well, if he was ever going to get his hands on that scarf, he had no choice, did he? "It's a thank you present for Elinor," he confessed shamefacedly and then, since self-abasement was likely to increase her sympathy, "Should've asked for help from someone who knew what they were doing."

Bea grinned.

"Men never have any idea what women like," she remarked loftily.

"Oh I know exactly what she'd like – it's hanging in the window over there. But I just haven't got the guts to go in and buy it."

"Is that all that's bothering you?" she asked. "Here, give me the money and I'll go and get it for you. But hurry up, 'cos I'm due at rehearsal. We're running through a couple of scenes with the singers today…"

He described to her what he wanted. Then she took the notes he handed her after a quick visit to the nearby cash machine and returned a few minutes later with a parcel wrapped in silver tissue paper and tied with a froth of blue ribbons.

"There you are," she exclaimed, tossing it to him in satisfaction and handing over the change. "What a lovely scarf – such glorious colours. But the price! Don't you think it's a bit steep for a thank you present? She only brought you home from London – not the North Pole."

Jamie shook his head firmly.

"That's the one for Elinor. I knew, as soon as I saw it, that nothing else'd do. Thanks a lot, Bea."

Bea regarded him oddly for a moment, then went on to ask if he was off home now.

"Thought I'd have a browse through the guitar books first," he replied, feeling like celebrating this success. "Might even grab myself a coffee."

"Well, I'll only be rehearsing for an hour. Hugo always has to rush off on Wednesdays for choir practice and I've got lots of revision to do for a mock exam tomorrow. Why not meet me afterwards and we can catch the bus home together?"

Jamie agreed as he stowed Elinor's parcel safely away in his rucksack. He lingered for half an hour in the music shop, trying out some of the guitars, then headed off down the winding old street and sat in a book shop for a while with a mug of coffee. He pictured himself handing Elinor the present and her face of delight as she unwrapped it. But then doubts began to creep in. Would she really like it? After all, he didn't know too much about her taste, but considering her elegant Georgian home, she might think it bright and horribly vulgar. Perhaps he shouldn't've bought it…

At that moment he caught sight of the chrome hands of the moon-faced clock above the coffee bar counter. Hell! If he didn't get a move on, he'd be late picking up Bea. And she was such a tyrant about punctuality too…

He snatched up his rucksack and hurried through the darkening streets to Trinity, breathing a sigh of relief as he heard the mellow notes of a male soloist's voice accompanied by muffled strains of music from behind the closed windows of the concert room. Quietly pushing open the thick oak door, he slipped, a little out of breath, into a red plastic chair at the back of the rehearsal.

A moment later the music broke off in splinters of discord. In the full glare of the lights the stout, hook-nosed conductor was tapping his baton on the metal music stand.

"Tempo's got to speed up there. Chris's leaving you behind. Chris, want to take it again from 'The fly that sips treacle'? And by the way, make it a C there this time."

"Yeah, yeah, I know," replied Chris, who looked beautiful, vain and slightly put out at the correction. "But don't you think I'm too far back on set? After all, Macheath's finally got the stage to himself and I want to make the most of it."

"Yeah, but you need to catch sight of me entering," protested a girl in black with frizzy red hair knotted on top of her head, leaning on the handle of a broom in the corner. "If you're way out there, you'll never see me come on stage."

"I've got a whole soliloquy to deliver. I can make it back in time. What d'you think, Nick?" And Chris turned to address a thick-set man of about thirty with unkempt, straw-coloured hair and a rumpled shirt, seated several rows back in the audience. "Don't you think I need to stand closer to the audience?"

Nick rose and shambled forwards, shirt hanging half out of his trousers and a couple of buttons undone in the middle of his chest. "God knows, you don't need any encouragement to hug the limelight, Chris," he declared good-naturedly, "but I think you're probably right."

"OK," the conductor nodded. "OK, everyone, pick it up again from 'The fly that sips treacle…' We'll run it through to the end of the next number, then call it a day. Places, everyone! Places, please!"

Jamie knew nothing about *The Beggar's Opera* beyond the tunes that he'd heard Bea practising during the Easter holidays between bouts of A-Level revision. He'd no interest at all in where Chris stood on stage, so his eyes strayed from the singer over the members of the orchestra. Should've known things'd overrun and not burst a gasket to get here!

Yeah, there was Bea, waving with an apologetic grin and holding up five fingers to reassure him about the likely delay before returning to the music. And that must be her man of the moment, posed theatrically at the keyboard nearby, looking intense and highly-strung with a single lock of fair hair falling across his high, white forehead. Hadn't expected too much from someone called Hugo Channing-Jones so he wasn't a disappointment. Looked unbearably affected.

Jamie began to feel bored. The air in this room was stale and musty and overbreathed. He slumped back in his seat, since Macheath seemed likely to go on for some time about tasting women and meeting ruin and bewailing the fact that he'd promised to marry this girl, Lucy, who was approaching with her broom to sweep his prison cell…

All of a sudden he sat bolt upright in his seat. What was that girl exclaiming? "You base man, you – how can you look me in the face after what hath passed between us?" as she brandished her broom at Macheath in a stage-fury. It was partly the raised broom that stirred something in his memory, but even more the physical gesture of Macheath's arm lifted to ward off the blow that she pretended to be aiming at his head, as he cringed to avoid it.

Jamie strained forward to catch every syllable in the hope of confirming his flash of intuition. Certainty grew upon him with each passing moment, until by the time the rehearsal broke up he was

quite sure he was right: that scene was one of the four pictures on the

front of Bea's fan!

Chapter Seventeen

Elinor rang the Willetts' bell and stood waiting diffidently on the front step, surveying the rather pretty stained-glass panels, the faded green door paint and the worn, brass threshold. Why had she accepted this dinner invitation? Wasn't she just going to be out of place among people she didn't really know? Of course it was good to make new friends, but there was more to it than that. The desire to eat a home-cooked meal she hadn't prepared herself and spend the evening in a real family for a change? Or perhaps she'd warmed to Marisa Willett's air of motherly kindness. They hadn't spent much time together that Saturday morning a couple of weeks ago, when she'd brought Jamie home from London, but it was obvious that Marisa loved her son and she even envied him for it. No one would've looked so upset if she'd been taken ill herself…

The creak of the opening door made her glance up. On the threshold stood a young teenager with curly brown hair, wearing a green T-shirt with the slogan SAVE OUR RAINFORESTS emblazoned in purple on the front.

"Hello," she said. "You must be one of Jamie's brothers."

"Yes, I'm Geoff," he introduced himself with an awkward air of polite ceremony. "And you must be Elinor. Mum said you'd be here for dinner. Er – do come in."

"You've been digging a wild-life pond in the garden, haven't you?" she ventured to observe, as she followed him down the narrow hallway of the house, which was even more cluttered than she remembered with coats, walking boots and spare bicycle parts. She didn't know much about the younger members of the Willett household, but at least she ought to try being a bit friendly.

"Why – yes," replied Geoff, turning in open surprise.

"Your mum mentioned it to me the other day. We've got quite a big, old pond in our back garden too that I used to love when I was a little girl."

"Would you like to come and see mine then?"

Geoff's abrupt offer seemed so sincerely meant that she could hardly refuse. He guided her straight through the savoury-smelling kitchen, allowing her only the briefest pause to say good evening to Marisa, who was hanging over the pots on the stove with a flushed face.

Outside the back door, the sun was sinking among a rack of clouds on the horizon, sheathing the tips of the fresh green tree leaves in gold. On either side of the curving path of mossy bricks, springing straight and tall from the rich, dark soil that smelt of rain and new life, stood paper-white and scarlet tulips among a wilderness of forget-me-nots, that shone like tiny blue gems in the graceful shadow of a late-flowering pink cherry.

"What a lovely garden," exclaimed Elinor, gazing round in delight.

"Is it?" returned Geoff, following the bright approval of her eyes unmoved. "S'pose so, if you're interested in that sort of thing," unable to disguise a certain dismissive tone at the opinion of a female who probably thought of flowers as house decorations. "It's quite overgrown at the end, which makes it a good habitat for butterflies and beetles. And sometimes from my bedroom window, when it's quiet in the mornings, I see a fox sitting out here on the lawn. I think there must be an earth in the undergrowth just past the back railings."

"Really?"

"Yes – so here we are. The pond's just behind these lilac bushes. Made a pretty good job of it, didn't we?" Geoff grinned, folding his arms and surveying the newly planted pool with undisguised pride and affection.

"It'll certainly be a great place to study wildlife," remarked Elinor politely, doing her best to enter into Geoff's vision for this unpromising oval with its still visible fringe of black lining and muddy earth, sprouting sparse clumps of foliage. At least there was one plant at the water's edge showing a couple of flowers. She fixed on it enthusiastically. "I love those cream and gold saucers – are they some kind of buttercup?"

"From the same genus of ranunculeae, but it's caltha palustris – that's marsh marigold –" he told her, thoughtfully translating the technical term since he seemed to realise she meant well in spite of her pitiful botanical ignorance. "And we've also planted myosotis scorpioides there and some nymph – er… water lilies too in plastic boxes – you can just see the leaves poking up above the surface near those irises."

"Oh and there're some tadpoles wriggling their little legs under the ledge!"

"Yes – and I've got water beetles and a couple of newts as well. I'm planning a colony of water snails and hoping for pond skaters and dragonflies too in the summer…"

"Geoff, did you have to drag Elinor all the way down here?" demanded a voice suddenly from behind. "She's not interested in water snails and dragonflies."

Elinor glanced round and caught sight of Jamie emerging from behind the thorny sprays of a wild, apple-scented rose in a smart pair of navy cords and a fresh, blue-and-white-striped shirt. Those gaunt cheekbones and shadowy grey eyes of his… He was actually not bad looking!

"I was quite happy to come," she protested, resolutely swallowing her surprise. But her intervention came too late. The glow of enthusiasm had already faded from Geoff's face. He shrugged his shoulders and stamped off back to the house without another word.

"Baby brothers," exclaimed Jamie airily. "They think no one cares about anything except what interests them. Now I've got something really exciting to tell you…" He launched into an account of what he'd discovered at the play rehearsal this afternoon. "Couldn't believe it. Aurélie said it was an English theatrical fan and this must be the connection: all the pictures on it have something to do with *The Beggar's Opera*."

"Yes, I know," replied Elinor with perfect composure as they lingered together in the garden.

Jamie started. "What d'you mean: you know?"

"I told you when we were down in London that my brother, Nick, who's a fellow at Trinity, specialises in eighteenth-century English drama. When I saw him the other evening, I asked if he had any ideas about the scenes on the fan."

"Nick? At Trinity?" Jamie frowned. "You don't mean that was your brother I saw this afternoon directing their production of *Beggar's Opera*? Big man with straw-coloured hair? Looks like an inn-keeper from a Restoration comedy?"

Elinor nodded.

"Sounds like Nick. Why're you so surprised?"

"But you don't look a bit alike."

Elinor smiled.

"Neither do you and Bea."

"So I suppose you know all about the fan now?" went on Jamie ruefully now his big scoop had been reduced to yesterday's news.

"No, but it does help that we've got more of a context for it. Nick says the production was first staged in January 1728 and ran for more than sixty performances – it's an old joke that it made the writer Gay rich, and the producer Rich gay. It's full of satire on the politics and musical tastes of the day – and society just loved it. There was a real outburst of Beggarmania: prints of the main characters, playing cards, fire screens, toys and of course – fans. So Bea's fan turns out to be a sort of merchandising spin-off after all."

"But if it's an English fan, why're all the words on it in Spanish? Your brother have any ideas about that?"

"Afraid not. He just told me the play ran at the Lincoln's Inn Fields Theatre in London."

"Jamie," interrupted Marisa, calling from the kitchen window. "Do bring Elinor inside – it must be getting chilly out there."

As they entered the house, a ringtone suddenly shrilled out and Jamie pulled his mobile out of his back pocket to answer it. From the haste with which he excused himself and disappeared from earshot, Elinor gathered it must be a private conversation. But it left her at rather a loose end.

"Can I help at all?" she asked Marisa, who was tasting a bubbling casserole on the kitchen bench.

"Oh no, no, dear! You're the guest. Besides, the chicken's almost done."

"Perhaps I could carry something into the dining room or set the table for you?" Elinor indicated the next-door room, visible through the open hatch.

"Well… if you insist. The cutlery's in the sideboard. I'll call Geoff down to give you a hand. Six places will be fine. We're not planning to wait for Bea – she's out at a concert with Hugo and goodness knows what time they'll be back."

Elinor soon found her way into the dining room and was searching for some cutlery in the battered mahogany sideboard when a voice enquired from the doorway,

"Hey, grub up yet?"

Elinor raised her head and instantly recognised the owner of the curly brown head poking round the door frame. "Oh it's you, Geoff! Yes, I'm just setting the table. Do come and tell me where the glasses are kept. I'm so sorry about what happened in the garden earlier. I was really interested to see your new pond, you know."

Geoff looked momentarily bemused – maybe at a grown-up even bothering to apologise – but then he grinned broadly and told her not to worry.

He'd clearly got over feeling offended then.

"You've changed your T-shirt," she remarked in an effort to promote further conversation. "So you're a football supporter as well as a rainforest conservationist?"

"Err – what?" Geoff glanced down at his red and black shirt. "Oh that! Jus' put on a clean one – guest for dinner, you know."

Astonishingly civilised! Especially for a teenage boy. As she laid the stainless-steel knives and forks on the green cloth patterned with cheerful white daisies, Elinor went on confidentially, thinking back to the way Nick used to tease her when she was little, "Older brothers can be pretty heavy-handed, can't they?"

"You bet! They're so borin' too – 'specially Jamie," volunteered Geoff, turning round one of the dining room chairs and perching on it backwards to supervise proceedings. "Used to be all right – in the old days when he an' Adam were at school together an' played football for the club…"

Odd. She wasn't aware Adam and Jamie had attended the same school. She thought Adam had been educated in London… Still, it wasn't impossible, was it? They'd probably met when Adam was in the sixth form and run some sort of football club for juniors Jamie's age.

"…Pretty ace at building model aeroplanes once too," Geoff was rattling on, "– but now he just likes borin' things like readin' all night long. Mum's really worried about him not doin' well in his exams 'cos of all the stuff he's missed with being ill an' so on. He's headin' back to university on Sunday an' he's got finals soon. Dad says he can't make up for years and years o' doin' nothin' just by workin' hard for a few weeks. But I think it's all to do with girls myself."

"Do you?" prompted Elinor with a smile. She hadn't realised that ultra-serious Geoff had such a funny side to him.

"Yeah – never been any good since he got interested in girls. They're always textin' or ringin' him up – prob'ly talkin' to one right now. How borin' can you get! Know what?"

"What?"

"Reckon he's on with a new one at the moment. Got this parcel in his wardrobe. Saw it when I was lookin' for his ole tennis racket jus' now. All wrapped up in silver paper with fancy ribbons on. Smells awful – all flowery and perfumy. That's how I knew it mus' be for a girl. If he's been out buyin' smelly parcels o' girl's stuff, it mus' be a present. He's usually too mean to buy things for anyone, so it's prob'ly jus' because she's new at the moment. Don't you think so?"

"I expect you're probably right." Elinor nodded, struggling to keep a straight face at the thought of Jamie's likely reaction to these revelations, were he present.

"Marc! Geoff!" they both heard Marisa calling at the bottom of the stairs. "Dad's home. Go and wash your hands!"

Geoff suddenly grinned sheepishly and sprang to his feet.

"Hey! Better jump to it," he declared and instantly vanished from the room.

Elinor stared after him. What kind of boy actually volunteered to go and wash his hands?

Next moment Jamie appeared carrying a trayful of glasses and a jug of iced water.

"Sorry to leave you by yourself," he apologised, setting the tray down on the table.

"Oh but I wasn't," pointed out Elinor. "I've been having a chat with Geoff."

Jamie stared at her.

"No, you can't've been," he contradicted flatly. "Geoff's upstairs."

"Yes, he's just gone up to wash his hands."

"But he's been up there all the time I was on the phone. Lying on his bed reading a book."

Impossible!

"Well I've just been talking to him for several minutes," asserted Elinor in polite annoyance. "He was sitting on that chair over there – you see, the one that's been moved – while I was laying the table."

"Dinner up yet?" demanded Geoff hungrily, bounding in through the door, then stopping short and glancing from one to the other. Elinor at once turned to him and stepped forward in indignant appeal. "Geoff, you'll back me up, won't you?"

"Back you up?" asked Geoff, glancing in mystification from one to the other.

"Yes. I was speaking to you here in this room about five minutes ago, wasn't I?"

Geoff looked blank. "Well… I did talk to you a bit earlier when I was showing you the pond."

"Yes, but later on. You know, when you were telling me about that parcel – the one up in Jamie's wardrobe – remember?"

Jamie flushed bright red and rounded on Geoff, exclaiming, "You little sod! Been poking around in my wardrobe, have you? I've told you to keep out of my room."

"Never went in – honest," protested Geoff in bewilderment. "You've yelled at me before for messing with your stuff. Don't know anything about any parcel."

"But you told me it was wrapped up in silver paper with fancy ribbons," cried Elinor.

"What's she on about?" Geoff appealed to Jamie, whose face of hot rage indicated that he at least had a pretty good idea.

"None of your business," spluttered Jamie, lunging angrily at him. "If I find you've been poking around in my stuff, I'll –"

"You don't have to threaten him just because he's scared to admit he knows about that gift for your girlfriend," interrupted Elinor, stepping between them to intercept the blow.

"It's not for any girlfriend," admitted Jamie, falling back sullenly. "It's for you."

"For me?"

Elinor froze, wide-eyed with embarrassment.

At this point Marisa and Graham appeared in the dining room doorway.

"What *is* all the shouting about?" cried Marisa, gazing from one to the other.

There was a long pause. Jamie fixed his eyes steadily on the ground, clearly seething with humiliation and refusing to speak a word. Elinor was speechless with confusion and Geoff looked as though he thought they had both gone mad.

At that moment they heard footsteps pounding downstairs and a voice yelling out to wait for him. Another Geoff, this time wearing a red and black football shirt, burst into the dining room and stopped short, gazing around them all.

"Hey, what's up?" he demanded. "You all look as though you've just survived a nuclear holocaust."

Elinor gasped. So that explained the change of T-shirt! She stared from one boy in green and purple to the other in red and black and back again, exclaiming,

"Two boys with one face. Jamie, you never told me your brothers were identical twins!"

*

"I'm really sorry about that," Jamie apologised again as he walked Elinor to her car at the end of the evening. "It was all Marc's fault. Deliberately letting you think he was Geoff. One day he'll go too far with these practical jokes of his…"

"Talk about a real-life *Comedy of Errors*." Elinor laughed as she unlocked the car and set her handbag on the back seat along with the gold scarf still half-wrapped in its paper and ribbons. "And thank you so much for the present too," turning back to smile up at him. "You really shouldn't've. It's far too much."

"Just wanted you to know your kindness wasn't totally wasted," Jamie muttered awkwardly.

She didn't like the scarf. He'd realised at once from her expression as she unwrapped it. Too loud and tasteless. She'd duly exclaimed over how vivid and eye-catching its colours were, but that didn't fool him. She was just being polite. He should never've spent all that money on a mere whim…

But he manfully swallowed the lump of disappointment and returned her gaze without flinching.

"Besides, I owed it to you for overlooking my offensive behaviour that evening. Most women would've refused ever to speak to me again, let alone taken me all the way back to Cambridge with them. I just wish we'd had time to do more work on the fan these holidays."

"It'll keep. Perhaps we can arrange another date once your exams are over."

"Pity we haven't had much of a chance to talk this evening either. Our house is like a main-line station with Bea and Hugo and Dad and the harp coming and going all the time."

"Well, it's better than living in a mausoleum," she remarked, and then stopped, clearly realising what she'd just said. "You see, since Mum died, there're only Dad and me in our big, old house and after dinner he usually heads off to work in his study. So there's not exactly a lot of company most evenings. It was fun having Marc and Geoff to talk to."

She sounded quite wistful and – even a bit lonely.

Suddenly Jamie glimpsed his chance. But dare he take it? Wouldn't she just say no straight out? Still, nothing ventured…

"Well, don't go back to the mausoleum yet then," he urged with apparent carelessness. "It's not cold out. Why not come for a walk instead?"

Elinor fingered the miniature brass fan studded with red glass beads that adorned her car keys. Her eyes swerved away from Jamie into the soft, dark night, where the great, silvery face of the full moon sailed high above the treetops, half-masked by veils of Gothic cloud.

"Oh go on," urged Jamie, observing the indecision in her face, "live dangerously for once. We could walk down river as far as the Bell Jar Café. They've got a late-night Spanish guitar gig starting in –" he glanced down at his phone "– in about twenty-five minutes. I'll even buy you a drink if you like."

Why was his heart beating so fast?

"I thought you'd sworn off alcohol for the duration," she shot back.

"I said I'd buy *you* a drink – didn't say anything about myself. Come on, why not push the boat out for once? You're far too hung up about life, you know."

The corners of Elinor's rather serious mouth suddenly lifted. It made her look years younger.

"All right," she agreed, relocking the car.

They set off together down the pathway that led towards the river.

Chapter Eighteen

Elinor sat at her open dressing-table drawer fingering the gold scarf Jamie had so thoughtfully given her the last time she saw him. She'd never have the nerve to wear it. Why choose her something so downright gaudy? And it must've been expensive too, coming from that boutique near All Saints' Garden, as its gift-wrapping proclaimed. Surely he'd known her long enough to realise that she always wore sensible, dark colours these days – ever since Paul had once passed some joking remark about a bright red dress she'd bought making her look like a fire engine – and never noticing how much he'd hurt her feelings. Funny. This was the first time since they parted that she'd thought of him without a pang…

And yet, somehow the scarf was rather eye-catching. And it would go really well with that red dress, which was still hanging in the back of her wardrobe…

She spread out the dazzling square on her dressing table, admiring the way its fabric gleamed in the flood of early evening sunlight that poured in through her window and, with one thoughtful fingertip, caressing the brilliant petals of the lily flowers and the cluster of fiery feathers at the throat of the blue phoenix bird. How suggestively that gold and purple robe slipped from the woman's pale shoulder and how enigmatically she smiled with her red lips, thin, arched brows and almond-shaped eyes. Did Jamie imagine that she in any way resembled this alluring creature? Surely not. She was far too old.

Perhaps if she'd been a few years younger though, she might've worn it this evening. Gathering its silky folds into her hands, she draped it experimentally round her neck. A tug here and a prod there to show off the scarlet fan... In the mirror she surveyed the effect against the collar of her navy blouse. Actually it did make her skin seem to glow –

"Elinor! It's time to leave," Dad's voice called from the bottom of the stairs. A moment later there came a ring on the doorbell. They were here!

She tore off the scarf and stuffed it back into its wrapping paper in the drawer. Better play safe with the grey one she usually wore. Arranging this swiftly in the neckline of her blouse, she glanced into the mirror as she rose. Did she perhaps look just the slightest bit dowdy? Still, no time to change now. She snatched up her handbag and hurried out of the room.

Leaning over the banister, she could see Adam in the hallway below. He was shaking hands with Dad, who was leaning on the walking stick he'd been using since a recent stumble had jolted his confidence. How considerate of Adam to insist on picking them up like this, since the occasion meant so much to Dad.

Both men both raised their eyes as she hurried downstairs and Adam smiled a greeting. Not having seen him for several weeks made her realise how very dull life could be by contrast…

"Ah, there you are, Elinor," exclaimed Dad. "Your friends are waiting in the car. Come along, my dear, or we'll be late."

There was a brief flurry as Elinor gathered up the rug and cushions that she'd left on the hall bench, Adam insisted on carrying them out to the car for her and Dad hesitated over whether to wear his lighter or heavier overcoat.

"But it's a lovely evening," she pointed out, slightly puzzled by his lengthy debate over such a minor decision.

"Perhaps I need a scarf – an old man like me," he quavered pathetically. "I'm sure I'm developing a chill – and you know they always go straight to my chest."

As she helped him into the heavier overcoat, Elinor found herself reassuring him that he'd no need to worry, for all the world as if he was some kind of invalid. True, he'd taken a couple of dizzy turns recently. But the tests the doctors had run showed nothing wrong, apart from the high blood pressure he'd suffered from for years. Why suddenly start behaving this way tonight?

"I can't think why Nicholas is mounting an outdoor production so early in the season," he went on as she handed him back his walking stick.

Elinor stared at him outright.

"But, Dad, it's June – the outdoor play always takes place in June."

"Well, I think it's remarkably chilly for the time of year, don't you, Mr Quint?" He appealed to Adam, who was studying his own reflection rather abstractedly in the gilt-framed wall mirror hanging above the mahogany console table.

Adam jerked to attention.

"Oh…er…"

"Quinn, Dad," Elinor corrected quietly. Odd. He'd known Adam's surname perfectly well at teatime.

"Yes, Quint. Wasn't that what I said? When I first heard the name, I remember it immediately put me in mind of Henry James."

"No – Quinn," repeated Adam, his tone betraying the slightest hint of impatience.

"Oh dear, my mistake," Dad apologised fulsomely. "I'm growing a little hard of hearing these days. I was sure Elinor said 'Quint'. Do forgive me, Mr Quinn."

"Adam. Please call me Adam."

"Very well, Adam then. How delightful to be on such friendly terms so early in our acquaintance. But then there's so much more informality nowadays than there used to be, isn't there? I suppose there's no possibility of your being related to Lord Chief Justice Sir Henry Quinn, an old member of my college…? No? Ah, what a pity. Such a charming and intelligent man…"

Elinor frowned. How very aggravating Dad was being tonight. What was he playing at? All this doddering about and pretending to be hard of hearing, like some senile old man.

Next ensued a major fuss over locking the front door and stowing the key safely away. Elinor glanced across at Adam. He'd clearly resolved to put on a good face despite all provocation and was helping Dad down the front stairs with an air of long-suffering concern. But he was starting to look a trifle worn, like Richard when they went for dinner at Cathy's in Fen Ditton… Like Richard? No, impossible. She'd hardly mentioned Adam before. Dad hadn't the least evidence for believing her relationship with him was serious…

"…And such a charming family of that name that I remember from summer holidays years ago," Dad was rambling on as they reached the foot of the front steps. "But then you've no links with Devon either, I take it, Alex?"

"Adam," corrected Adam, this time with visibly forced politeness.

Elinor's eyes narrowed as she watched the little scene being played out.

So that's what was up, was it? The old fraud! He'd clearly decided Adam posed a threat to the status quo of his household and already opened a campaign to scare him off! She tried to fix him with a warning glare, but he gazed back in bland innocence and she could hardly tell him to stop being so childish in front of Adam. She'd been so looking forward to this evening too. And now…

Outside, the red BMW was parked on double yellow lines that ran along the narrow access lane in front of the terrace. As soon as they reached it, Henry jumped out and politely held the door open for Dad. It turned into quite a performance manoeuvring him into the front passenger seat beside Camilla, who sat at the wheel looking relaxed and summery in elegant pastel peach with a bright aqua scarf. While Dad was enjoying the pleasures of a spacious ride, basking in a miraculous improvement of health and hearing brought on by Cam's lively conversation, Elinor fumed in silence, squeezed tightly between Adam and Henry in the back seat and with the rug and cushions on her lap as well.

It was a warm summer evening with barely a breeze stirring the horse chestnut leaves under a soft, blue sky. As they drove along the backs of the colleges, Elinor drew as deep a breath as possible under the cramped conditions and tried to suppress her forebodings about the evening ahead by concentrating on watching the professional puntsmen in their straw boaters as their craft skimmed expertly along the river past trailing green willows, and on the beauty of King's

College Chapel with its stonework glowing ivory in the mellow golden sunlight.

At Trinity Nick had arranged for them to park inside college so there was only a short distance for Dad to walk through the shady cloisters of the library court, where a make-shift stage was set up in front of the Doric screen outside the Great Hall. The flight of stone steps leading down from the balustraded terrace into the courtyard beneath was bright with boxes of scarlet geraniums, and red-and-white-striped bunting, strung between wrought-iron lamp posts, lent a carnival air to the scene. The semicircle of wooden benches on the cobbled pathway was already filling with audience members, every one of whom annoyingly turned their heads to admire Camilla sauntering past with effortless glamour in her flowing silk dress and high-heeled gold sandals. Elinor felt like even more of an elderly maiden aunt than usual.

"Those benches do look extremely hard," remarked Dad as he lowered himself carefully into the well-padded, low-backed throne that Nick had arranged for him on the middle aisle of the front row. "Are you sure you'll all be comfortable seated there for so long?"

"We'll be fine, Dad," Elinor assured him, bent on occupying the place next door to keep him as far away from Adam as possible. "That's why I brought the cushions, after all."

"I just hope it doesn't rain. Don't you think there's a hint of moisture in the atmosphere?"

"Nonsense, there's not a cloud overhead," she asserted airily. If only the play would begin! Then he'd have to shut up.

"I'm sure I can feel a draught on my back."

"Why not wrap the rug around you? There now... Better? Oh look, Dad, here's Nick."

Her brother provided a welcome diversion as he ambled up to greet them, but it was clear from his manner that he had other matters on his mind and he soon strolled away to his seat at the back of the audience.

Members of the orchestra were by now starting to take their places on the left-hand side of the terrace. Here came Beatrice Willett carrying her flute, in company with a thin, blond youth who headed straight for the keyboard. Perhaps some of Bea's family were here tonight.

Elinor half-turned to scan the audience and soon caught sight of Marisa and Graham seated several rows behind on the other side of the aisle. Marisa smiled and waved a friendly greeting, which Elinor naturally returned.

Adam wrinkled his brow.

"Wasn't aware you knew the Willetts," he commented.

"Of course. I met them the morning I drove Jamie home from the station when he was so ill."

"And didn't you go over there once for dinner?" put in Camilla, gracefully crossing her long, sun-tanned legs on Adam's far side and fanning away a fly with her programme.

"Yes, that was when I met the twins." Elinor gave a short laugh. "What a pair!"

"Twins?" interrupted her father in a querulous tone, leaning forward to catch what they were saying. "Who has twins? What're you all whispering about?"

"I was just talking about the Willett twins," explained Elinor patiently. "You remember, I told you about Marc playing that silly joke on me and pretending he was Geoff?"

"Oh you mean that night you went out for dinner and didn't come home till all hours, leaving me quite alone even though I was prostrate with a migraine?"

Elinor's mouth fell open.

"Dad, you never said –"

"You were out at the Willetts' till all hours?" interrupted Adam in disbelief. "But they're normally in bed by ten."

It felt like a pre-concerted pincer movement.

"It all happened quite by chance," she began defensively. "After dinner Jamie and I walked down to the Bell Jar Café for a Spanish guitar recital. It didn't start till late, so wasn't over till after midnight." She tried to sound casual, but it was annoying to feel herself blushing, as though she had something to hide. It'd been such a pleasant evening too. She couldn't remember being so relaxed in ages, just listening to music in the company of a friend.

"You went out with Jamie Willett?"

This was clearly a major revelation to Adam.

"Yes, while I was lying all alone on a bed of pain," added Dad testily. "You never know when I may be stricken again."

"Isn't that Jamie over there, sitting down by his parents?" demanded Adam suddenly. "I thought he was in Exeter studying for finals."

"They're probably over by now," Elinor remarked, trying to look unconcerned by failing to follow the direction of Adam's gaze, but only succeeding in feeling even more self-conscious.

"What?" exclaimed Camilla, raising her finely plucked eyebrows in astonishment. "You're joking. That's not Jamie Willett. Last time I saw him, he was a blond scarecrow."

"Look again, Cam," advised Adam. "He's undergone quite a transformation since February."

Cam strained her eyes in disbelief, but when Jamie acknowledged Adam's wave, grudgingly had to own herself mistaken.

"I can hardly recognise him, can you, Henry? Haven't seen his natural hair colour for years. And not a single metal stud left anywhere on him. You know, I have to admit, he's scrubbed up pretty handsomely," darting an appraising glance over his distant figure. "A dark horse, that one. Perhaps you'll have to re-introduce me, Adam."

"Now, now, Cam," warned Henry jokingly. "Hands off. He's far too young for you. Just remember he and your kid brother were at school together."

Elinor felt Adam stiffen beside her. There was a sudden awkward pause and an exchange of sharp glances between him and Camilla, who almost imperceptibly shook her head at Henry. His laughing face fell instantly and he cleared his throat in embarrassment.

Elinor at once realised the meaning of this wordless mime. So Adam thought Henry'd just given the game away, did he?

"What's all this about a dark horse?" piped up Dad crossly. "Is there going to be a horse in the play? Do speak up – I can't hear what you're saying."

Henry looked mildly confused but Camilla shrugged her beautiful shoulders and, leaning across them all, explained with a note of exaggerated tolerance in her raised voice, as though speaking to someone mentally impaired, that she'd just been using a figure of speech about Jamie Willett.

At this point Dad turned round and fixed Jamie with a long, hard stare. Then he announced loudly,

"Oh yes. The young man I've seen Elinor smuggling upstairs when she thought I wasn't watching."

All eyes swerved onto Elinor, who flushed hot with confusion.

There were times when she could strangle Dad! He made it sound as though she was having a clandestine affair with Jamie instead of just trying to save him from being ambushed and forced into a long, tedious conversation with her father. And it'd only happened once. It wouldn't've been so bad if Dad hadn't understood what he was saying, but it was quite obvious that he was doing this deliberately.

"We were working on Bea's fan," she began, but at this point Dad loudly hushed her since the orchestra was striking up the overture.

"At least there's nothing wrong with his eyesight," she thought she heard a voice mutter in her right ear, but when she glanced round, Adam was staring straight ahead with folded arms.

The action of the play moved onward at a swift pace. Dad was laughing out loud and clearly enjoying it all mightily, but Elinor sat in a stew of mortification. How had she got into such a mess?

She forced herself to focus on the play, but soon became aware that Adam beside her was shuffling his feet and crossing and uncrossing his legs restively. Seemed like he was enjoying the show as little as she. Not surprising, given his character, that he disliked sitting in the audience watching other people act, but his frequent sideways glances indicated something weightier was pressing on his mind.

The performance was played without an interval so when it finally ended an hour and a half later, Elinor levered herself rather stiffly to her feet, keen to stretch her cramped limbs. Dad had already bounded up, announcing serious reservations about Nick's cavalier disregard of the finer points of the topography of Georgian London, and insisted on hastening over to have the matter out with him.

"I could do with a glass of white wine, Henry," declared Camilla, eyeing the refreshment table. "Come on, everyone, I think we've deserved it."

She grasped Dad's arm with the assurance of a beautiful woman, confident in her powers of persuasion, and they began to move off together with Henry in close attendance. Elinor was on the point of following when she felt a detaining hand on her shoulder. She turned back towards Adam.

"Look," he began, rather red in the face, "what Henry said earlier about Jamie and me being at school together. He's got hold of completely the wrong –"

"No, Adam. Don't," she broke in quickly, keen that he shouldn't entangle himself further. "Isn't it easier just to admit the truth? I've known for some time now that you and Jamie were the same age. When I went to the Willetts' for dinner –"

Adam flushed darkly.

"So you're accusing me of lying to you?" he burst out.

"Not of lying. Perhaps just of not correcting my false assumption. Anyway, what does it matter?"

Adam looked thunderous. Clearly to him it did.

"It's all the fault of that bloody Jamie Willett, isn't it?" he burst out furiously. "He can never keep his sodding mouth shut."

Whatever had made him jump to this conclusion?

"But it's nothing to do with Jamie at all," she protested aloud.

"Ask me to believe that!"

Spitting out these bitter words, Adam flung away and vanished into the milling crowd.

Chapter Nineteen

Jamie had returned home from Exeter the previous day and his mother easily persuaded him to support Bea by attending the opening night of *The Beggar's Opera*. When he caught sight of Adam and Elinor on the front benches alongside Cam and her boyfriend, he instantly guessed that the elderly man seated in state beside them must be Elinor's father.

After the play ended, he saw him rise and head off with Cam and Henry to speak to Elinor's brother, Nick. His own parents were in a hurry to collect Bea and pick up the twins, who were spending the evening with a school friend, so he hastily said goodbye because he wanted to check with Adam about their upcoming play rehearsals in London. But just as he approached, Adam suddenly shot off in the opposite direction. Looked in a bit of a huff too.

"Something wrong with him?" he asked Elinor, indicating his friend's retreating back.

"I think he feels unmasked," she remarked quietly.

Jamie raised his eyebrows but chose to make no comment. She looked in need of cheering up.

"Fancy a glass of wine?" he offered, remembering from their evening out that she didn't like beer. "And maybe we could fix a date for another session on Bea's fan?"

"Why not?" Elinor shrugged and turned to accompany him to the refreshment table, manned by eager student bartenders.

Her father stood with his back towards them, engaged in conversation with his son, but as soon as Camilla set eyes on Jamie, she hailed him enthusiastically, causing the old man to glance round.

"Well, how very extraordinary," he observed to Nick. "A moment ago your sister was in the company of one young man and now all of a sudden he seems to have metamorphosed into another young man of quite a different complexion." He paused a moment and then went on with icy politeness, "I don't believe I have the pleasure of your acquaintance – despite your apparent intimacy with the upper floors of my own home. I am Elinor's father, Professor John Mitford."

Whoa! What was going on here? wondered Jamie. Some sort of family row?

He shot an enquiring glance at Elinor, who hung her head and looked as though she wanted to sink into the ground. Clearly needed time to pull herself together. If he could just draw the enemy fire onto himself…

Endeavouring to appear coolly self-possessed, he held out his hand to her father and introduced himself with courteous formality, adding that he hoped Professor Mitford had enjoyed this evening's show as much as himself.

"Well, well, I suppose it's creditable enough for an amateur production, full of students with nothing better to do after their examinations. It's entirely the responsibility of my son, Nicholas, here." As they shook hands, Professor Mitford's brimming family pride caused him to continue a little less frostily, "And what's your line of work, Mr. Willett? Are you of the thespian persuasion yourself?"

Jamie laughed. Must be confusing him with Adam. But how could he confess that he hadn't the faintest idea what his own line of work was? Better head him off on a tangent.

"Well, I do a bit of amateur acting," he admitted, "but actually I've just sat my Computer Science finals."

"Computer Science? Hmph." There was a marginal increase of warmth in Professor Mitford's tone. "Now that's a field where I really could do with a few pointers. I'd thought of enrolling in one of the university's continuing education courses, but I've had such indifferent health recently that I'm beginning to think I could do with a complete change of scene. Perhaps a holiday in a warmer climate might do the trick… Anyway, I think it's time we were heading home, Elinor. The dampness in the evening air won't do my chest any good at all. Good night, young man. Pleased to make your acquaintance – at last. Elinor, my dear –"

It all happened in a flash. As he turned away, the old man's stick accidentally caught in the cross bar of a nearby bench and he lurched forward. Letting go of the stick, he thrust out one arm to stop himself falling. But this only threw him further off-balance and he began to topple over.

Elinor sprang forward with a cry, along with Henry and Camilla, but the person who was standing nearest was Jamie. He automatically reached out and caught the elderly man in his arms before he crashed to the ground. Then, hauling him upright, he set him down as gently as he could on the nearby bench.

All the colour had suddenly drained from Professor Mitford's face and he was trembling with shock. Elinor at once knelt by her father's side and grasped both his hands.

"Dad, are you all right?" she cried.

The fuss that erupted at this point seemed quite out of proportion to the triviality of the incident, as Jamie saw it. A rug was wrapped round the old man's shoulders. A crowd gathered. One of the cast members ran for a glass of water and there was even talk of an ambulance being sent for.

After he eventually regained his powers of speech, Professor Mitford was so earnest in his exclamations of gratitude that he almost succeeded in convincing Jamie that he'd endangered his own life to achieve a rescue of heroic proportions. When at last he was able to totter feebly to his feet, supported by both his children, it was decreed that he must be driven home at once.

"Yes, I really do think that would be best," he murmured tremulously. "But I thank you most sincerely for the help you've given me this evening, Mr. Willett. I shudder to think what might have happened without your timely assistance. I'm an old man but I won't forget this, you may be sure. Good night. I hope to meet you again under happier circumstances. Come along, Elinor. This chill night air is hardly beneficial to one in my condition. My cold is certainly growing worse."

Elinor and Cam escorted him solicitously away between them with Henry hovering solemn-faced in the rear.

Jamie stood for a moment surveying the now almost deserted courtyard, where the only people left were stagehands stacking orchestra chairs and collecting discarded play props. Then he thrust his hands into his jeans pockets and turned away.

He was strolling thoughtfully through the echoing passageway beside the Great Hall when out of the darkness straight ahead of him stepped Adam.

*

Adam leant casually up against the archway, his arms folded across his chest and his face half-concealed in the shadows cast by the lamplight from the outer courtyard.

"Hi there," Jamie greeted him. "I've been wanting to talk to you."

"Feeling's mutual," retorted Adam with the barest hint of antagonism in his tone.

Hmm… Better play this as though he hadn't noticed. So Jamie went on neutrally, "I thought you'd left already."

"Yeah, so did I. But when I'd walked up and down the Backs for a while and cooled off, I decided I'd behaved pretty stupidly. So I came back again. And what do I find?"

Jamie shrugged. "No idea. What've you found?"

"You – muscling in on my territory."

Jamie stared.

"You crazy? I came over to discuss play rehearsals now that I've nothing else on, only to see you disappearing off into the distance. Elinor's just left with her father and Cam and Henry. You must've seen them go if you've been standing there for more than two minutes."

"Oh I saw them. But I realised it wasn't Ellie I wanted to talk to, it was you."

"Well, you're talking to me. What d'you wanna say?"

"Just this: stop fouling me up with Ellie."

So that's what was eating him.

"Dunno what you mean," Jamie replied. "I've been down in Exeter since Easter. Haven't seen her for ages. And I'm not a friend

of hers on social media. Now if you don't mind, I'm heading home."
He made to push past Adam, who was still leaning up against the
stone archway.

"Not so fast," snarled Adam, stepping forward to lay a hand on
his arm.

Jamie shook it off irritably.

"Look, you can throw your weight around as much as you like
with women, Quinn, but you can keep your fucking hands off me."

"And what's that supposed to mean?" demanded Adam, standing
squarely in his path.

Jamie's hackles rose. Without another thought, he gripped Adam
by both shoulders and shoved him violently aside. Adam wasn't
caught quite off guard, but the unexpected force of the thrust threw
him back against the passage wall and he crashed heavily onto the
flagstones. He picked himself up in an instant and, glaring at Jamie,
launched a furious punch straight at his head.

Jamie ducked and in a moment they were rolling on the ground,
wrestling in serious earnest. Jamie might have had the advantage of
greater height and longer limbs, but Adam wasn't much lighter and
seemed in surprisingly good shape. Besides, his blood was up and

he'd clearly been spoiling for a fight all evening. Looked as though he was even enjoying himself, with his lips drawn back from his gleaming teeth in a savage grimace, as he rained down battering blows on any part of Jamie's body he could reach. Jamie himself wasn't planning to act as anyone's punch bag. He fought back with equal ferocity.

"Now then, now then, what's all this?" a gruff voice bawled out of the blackness above them. "You two young gents oughta be ashamed of yerselves. We don't have no scrapping in Great Court. Break it up this instant or I'll report the pair of you to the Proctors."

Adam gave no sign of even having heard him and Jamie wasn't in the mood to obey anyone. Somebody needed to teach bloody Adam Quinn a lesson…

Next thing he knew, he was being pulled bodily away by a pair of brawny arms.

"You take your sodding hands off me," he yelled, resisting vigorously. "I'm gonna grind his fucking skull into the ground!"

"None o' that foul language round here," barked another deeper voice. "Just because you and your mate've had one too many don't mean you can lay about you like townies. Here, you stop that, you there!" And he swore mightily as he intercepted the full force of the knee that Adam had destined for Jamie's groin.

There was a confused scramble as the second porter, who was built like an ox with massive shoulders, a bullet head and a broken nose, struggled to pinion Adam's flailing arms behind his back. But with his greater agility, Adam eluded his grasp and darted under his outstretched hand to grope for Jamie's throat.

"Oy, Bill! Better get help. Looks like they're bent on doin' damage."

Jamie could feel Adam's fingers squeezing his windpipe, so he kicked him sharply in the shin. Struggling against all efforts to pull them apart, he'd started twisting Adam's arm behind his back when the pair of them suddenly came face to face and caught each other's eye.

There was a long moment of suspense and then all of a sudden Jamie let out a whoop of laughter and clapped Adam heartily round the shoulders.

"You look so stupid – like a pig peering through a shaggy hedge." Adam grinned back in spite of himself.

The pair of them began to rock from side to side in a close embrace, sweaty and breathless and almost splitting their sides with laughter.

The porters looked bewildered.

"Well, are you two fightin' or not then?" asked Bill, apparently a simple soul who liked matters clear cut.

"We *were* fighting," explained Adam between explosions of merriment. "But we seem – we seem to have – to've got over it. D'you know I used to dig holes with him in the sandpit at primary school?"

"Yeah, and I remember when we went on a class trip to a farm and a chicken sat on his head," hooted Jamie.

He and Adam both burst into fresh gales of hilarity.

The two porters exchanged pitying glances. Then Bill, who'd been inspecting their faces closely under the full glare of the lamplight, announced, "You two ain't any of our young gents. What're you doin' here anyway?"

"We've been to see *The Beggar's Opera* – that's a play, you know," gurgled Adam, reaching an arm up around Jamie's neck.

"Well that don't mean you can go round here behaving like bleedin' beggars! Now you just beat it, the pair of you, and think yerselves lucky Ted 'n' me ain't gonna call the coppers. Off with you, you young rough-necks – go on, hop it!"

Jamie and Adam glanced at each other and obediently slunk away. Bill and Ted escorted them as far as the front gate, shaking their heads and muttering, "Right pair of basket cases." Then they began locking up as the bells of the university church chimed the hour through the still night air.

Jamie and Adam found themselves standing outside on the footpath exhausted and dishevelled, surveying one another rather sheepishly through the gloom of the night. Jamie ached all over, especially his left eye, which felt sore and rather swollen. Glancing down, he realised his open-necked linen shirt was several buttons short and Adam had a gaping tear in his smart beige trousers, probably made by the metal toe cap of his own boot. And something dark and wet was dripping down the front of his cream sweater.

Jamie looked up.

"Hey!" he cried. "Your forehead's bleeding."

"Thought I felt something trickling into my eyebrows," returned Adam, raising an exploratory hand to his temple.

"Got anything to mop it up with?"

"Probably some tissues in my jacket pocket… yeah – here they are," fishing one out and dabbing the side of his head with it.

"You're just smearing blood all over the rest of your face. Come on. Give 'em to me. I'll do it," ordered Jamie, impatiently seizing the packet and proceeding to wipe Adam's face with an air of practised efficiency. "Well – you're just as aggressive as you ever were, you little runt, but I don't remember you being this tough before. Been taking boxing lessons or something?"

"No, it's all the warm-up exercises we do in drama class. Hey, that was a pretty good punch I managed to land on you, wasn't it? You're gonna have one hell of a black eye in the morning. Though you didn't do so badly yourself. Not so out of condition as when we were in Indonesia."

"Well I hadn't been playing football for about six months then."

"Thought you were going soft down in Exeter. Would've had second thoughts about taking you on if I'd known you'd started football training again."

"I haven't started football training again. After I was ill at Easter, I decided to work out in the gym instead."

"God! What – weights and all that?"

Jamie nodded.

"Bloody hell! No wonder it felt as though my hand'd just shattered against a boulder," exclaimed Adam, ruefully surveying his bruised knuckles. "I'll know not to pick a fight with you again in a hurry."

Jamie grinned across at him. "Did you see the look on those porters' faces when they realised we weren't trying to kill each other anymore?"

"Must've thought we were certifiable. Why'd you burst out cackling all of a sudden? It's impossible to have a serious fight with a guy who's doubled up with laughter."

"I caught sight of your face. When you get mad, you have this way of pulling your brows down slantwise and sticking out your bottom lip. It's really funny. I've seen you do that dozens of times in the playground at Marston Road Primary when you were even shorter than you are now, picking fights with the older boys. You always were stroppy and pig-headed. Besides, you can't talk – you were the one who started hugging me like I was your long-lost brother."

"It was your hair – sticking up all over the place. Reminded me of that morning – remember in the tent? – when we woke up and you saw that scorpion crawling up your sleeping bag. I've never seen anyone look so stunned."

"I was scared shitless. Jesus, I'd never seen one of those in real life. Gave me nightmares for months afterwards. Not sure I'll ever really care for camping again."

"We go back a long way, don't we?" mused Adam. "I mean, I can't really remember too much of my life when you weren't there too."

"No, that's true."

"We've been best mates for years and you can't turn your back on all that just for the sake of a woman, can you?"

Jamie shook his head.

There was a pause as Adam thrust his hands into his trouser pockets and they picked their way in silence across the cobblestones and sank down, side by side, on a low wall facing the street.

"Things with Ellie haven't worked out the way I thought they would, you know," he admitted wryly. "Believed women were easy game before I met her. A couple of drinks and a dinner date or two and you're away. But all this boring conversation's made me realise that we really don't have much in common. Sometimes when we're talking, she goes quiet and just looks at me. Makes me feel about the size of an ant."

"I know what you mean," agreed Jamie with a grin. "Don't reckon she's interested in either of us, if you ask me."

"She's gonna end up chained to that old man for the rest of his life because he's too selfish to let her go."

"Well that's her look-out, isn't it? Nothing we can do about it. Come on, you heading back to London tonight?"

"Not if I can help it."

"Got somewhere to sleep?"

"Can always go round to Cam's."

"No need for that. How about my floor? Mum won't mind."

"Guess not – after all the times I've slept on it before."

"You can borrow my sleeping bag – the one with the scorpion in it."

"Thanks a lot. We gonna get going then?"

And Adam jumped up and made to turn right along the street.

"Where're you off to?" asked Jamie, not even attempting to follow him.

"Aren't we heading to the bus stop?" Adam paused in surprise.

"Well you could go back on the bus if you liked. But I've gotta drive the car home."

"The car? What car?"

"Mine."

"Hey, didn't know you had a car! How'd you scrape together enough cash to buy it?"

"Used some of the money Great Aunt Rosita left me in her will."

"But they cost to run."

"Yeah, I know. Gotta earn some more in the meantime – till I make up my mind what I really want to do. That's why I've been looking out for a job. Just landed one yesterday."

"A job?"

"Well, there's no need to sound so gob-smacked. I'm not totally unemployable. Programmed for six months before we went abroad on our year out, remember – and every summer break since."

"But you're coming to Spain with us. What about the play? And the holiday afterwards at Henry's father's place?"

"Well I'm coming to Spain for the play. But I won't be staying much longer than a week. Rest of the time I'll be working back at 3-D Imaging in the Science Park. That way I'll be able to afford to run the car and start paying off my student loan."

"Don't believe it. You – planning for the future? What's up?"

"Gotta start doing something with my life. Realised that while I've been ill…"

"So what exactly d'you have in mind? And why d'you need a car anyway? Thought you could just bike to work from where you live?"

But no matter how Adam questioned and wheedled, Jamie refused to elaborate further. His plans were all too vague and unsettled at present. Instead he remarked that it was getting late.

"It's only an old banger, but I don't want it nicked anyway."

"Oh all right. So what make is it, did you say?"

"I didn't actually, but…"

And they strolled off the other way along the street together, deep in friendly discussion.

Chapter Twenty

Jamie held his breath as Elinor rested her paint brush against the saucer of paste and carefully manipulated a strip of nylon gossamer across the last split in the leaf of Bea's fan. Then he took over, pressing his fingers down on the freshly glued fabric to hold it in place. By this time they had teamwork down to a fine art.

Elinor relaxed back in her chair with a sigh.

"Seems a good place to stop for the day," she announced. "Now the whole thing just needs to dry out." She eased her shoulders back and forward and rubbed her neck muscles with her fingertips. "Tense work, isn't it?"

Now she came to mention it, his butt was feeling pretty numb and he had an ache in his lower back. Hadn't noticed it before. But – stop for the day? When they were this close to finishing…

He turned his head, shifting his gaze from his fingers to focus on her face.

"I guess the next step's trimming the fabric then?"

Elinor nodded.

"Yes – and neatening up the edges…"

So little left to do. Why not just keep going? But of course! That was exactly what you had to guard against in this business. Always better to come back to it after a rest. Amazing what imperfections you could spot with fresh eyes.

"After that's all dried and the folds are re-pleated, we'll be able to screw the rivet back in," Elinor added. "Won't be long before we're done. Aren't you pleased?"

Jamie tentatively relaxed his fingers to check that the fabric was sticking to the paper beneath. Hadn't really considered this question.

"Well," he began, "of course I'm pleased Bea will get her fan back looking a lot better than when we started…"

But – pleased that their work together was nearly over? Elinor was clearly under the impression that he was looking forward to finishing the job. Perhaps that's how she felt herself. But how about him?

He wiped the sticky residue off his fingers thoughtfully with a damp towel.

These sessions helping Elinor up in her office and learning about fan repair had been some of the most interesting hours he'd ever spent. What would he do when they came to an end? An almost physical pang pierced him as he imagined being parted from this exacting but exciting task. Taking one of these tattered objects that seemed fit only for the rubbish heap and polishing the sticks, cleaning the leaf, mending the splits until it emerged from your fingers entirely transformed. Painstaking work it certainly was, but so incredibly rewarding…

"Don't know about you, but I could certainly do with a break," Elinor was going on. "How about a cup of coffee and then some fresh air?" She paused, shooting him a swift sideways glance. "That's if you feel like going out of course – with your eye like that. Is it hurting very much? It looks so bruised, it must be terribly painful."

"It's nothing." Jamie shrugged it off.

The look of horror on her face when she'd opened the door and caught sight of him on the front step. It gave him quite a jolt till he remembered how his face must look to an outsider. He'd practically forgotten about last Thursday night by now – except when he caught sight of himself in a mirror – but then women always made such a fuss over a bit of a punch up. Like Mum with her cotton wool and antiseptic lotion.

He'd tried to fob Elinor off by making light of it: "Just another drunken street brawl – you know me." But she seemed so concerned that he'd had to admit the truth – or at least an edited version of it. He could tell it still bothered her though by the way she'd avoided meeting his gaze all afternoon and keeping her downcast eyes fixed firmly on their work. It made him feel uneasy when she refused to look at him. Like he was missing out on half their conversation…

"I can't imagine what you and Adam were thinking of," she observed, checking the rustproof pins that held the fan leaf in place on the blotting paper with unnecessary thoroughness.

"No, probably not. But at least it cleared the air between us. Better than all the bitching and back-biting that Bea goes in for with her girlfriends."

At this point Elinor clearly realised it was no use pressing the point further, so she rose and went to wash up in the tiny bathroom next door. Pretty useful, he'd discovered, since you had to clean your hands after every split you mended so as not to smear excess glue over the rest of the fabric.

When she returned, she started folding the leftover gossamer strips inside the bundle of uncut material.

"So now you've got your degree," she remarked, "I guess you'll be looking for a permanent job. Are 3-D Imaging likely to take you on full time?"

"Could do," he replied, tearing a fresh sheet off the roll of greaseproof paper to cover the fan while it dried. "Hadn't really thought about it."

"You don't sound wildly enthusiastic," she commented quietly, as he replaced the black tissue to shield the fan from light.

"I'm not, if you really want to know," he confessed, handing her the scissors and tin of pins to put back in the top drawer of the desk. "But I've gotta make a living somehow. Might as well do this as anything else."

Her only reply was another silent glance.

Huh! Why couldn't people accept that a job was a job and you just had to get on with doing it? Why did Elinor and Mum always look at him as though they were disappointed that he was likely to earn a decent salary in a useful career? Not everyone could earn a living by following a vocation.

"Where's this go again?" he demanded, holding up the packet of paste granules. She was always so fussy.

"In here."

She pulled open the second drawer down.

As he dropped the packet inside, Jamie's eye fell on something at the back of the drawer that he hadn't noticed before, sitting on top of a couple of wide, flat chocolate boxes that she kept for storing finished fans. It looked like an old, wooden cigar box, edged with green, blue and red stripes.

"Hey, didn't know you smoked Morris and Phillips," he teased, indicating the brand name stamped on the hinged lid.

Elinor screwed up her face.

"So what's inside?" he went on, interested to see what other fan repair equipment she kept stashed away in there.

"A broken fan," she admitted. "To tell you the truth, I've been trying to forget about it. One of my mother's old friends picked it up cheap at a car boot sale and brought it to me a few weeks ago. She wants me to mend it and I didn't have the heart to say no. But I've hardly had a moment to check it over, let alone start on the repairs."

What sort of fan is it? wondered Jamie.

"Can I take a look?" he asked aloud.

"If you like. It's not very rare or valuable and a broken brisé fan's such a sorry sight."

"Even so…"

Elinor raised her eyebrows, but she pulled the shallow wooden box out of the drawer and handed it to him without further protest. Jamie opened the lid eagerly.

Inside sprawled a loose bunch of grimy but intricately carved yellow sticks. Wonder what sort of pattern they would form.

His cautious attempt to spread the leaf left him none the wiser. The fan was little more than a disarticulated skeleton with one or two of the tapering sticks barely connected by fraying shreds of mildewed ribbon. Jamie stared at the wreckage. How much imagination you needed to glimpse even the possibility of beauty in something that had so completely lost its basic structural integrity.

"Bit of a disaster, isn't it?" agreed Elinor. "And you can see how much cleaning it needs too. I'm so busy at present that I think I'm going to have to beg Esther to take it to a professional restorer like Peter Mowbray instead."

True, the ivory was pretty discoloured. And yet…

And yet he instantly realised why Esther had snapped it up at the car boot sale. The delicacy of the perforated patterning, as fine as filigree lace. Once thoroughly cleaned and polished, it'd look pretty impressive.

"See how beautiful these sticks are," he pointed out, gently picking one up to examine it more closely. "That elegant carving and those tiny – are they pink? – rosebuds painted on the shoulder. Isn't this just a cleaning and re-ribboning job?"

"Well… yes," admitted Elinor. "In fact, re-ribboning brisé fans is relatively straightforward, so long as the sticks are all there. But it's the time and patience it'd take to prise the dirt out of all those tiny crevices. I can't bear even to think about it. Come on; let's just pack it away and forget about it. Would you like some coffee?"

He fingered the grubby stick and could only bring himself to surrender it because Elinor indicated that she was waiting to put it away with the rest.

All very well for her to shut the lid and tidy the box back into the drawer, to lead him downstairs to the kitchen for a cup of coffee and then out for a walk along the Backs. But he couldn't forget the sight of those loose sticks, however hard he tried. It bothered him, constantly niggling at the back of his thoughts like a sharp stone in the heel of a shoe. As Elinor stopped to watch the ducks circling the old mill pond or the Queen Anne's Lace foaming white against the dark bushes on the riverbank, it rose before his mind's eye in all its pathetic helplessness. Nothing – not even the pleasure of a walk with Elinor – could come between him and the vision of that broken fan, which only needed time and patience to make it whole again. Bet he could even fix it himself…

While he strolled home along the river through the early evening shadows, it lay in its dark box, forlorn and unloved with all its beauty wasted. Imagine how it must've gleamed when it'd been bought for some young Regency débutante's coming-out ball. Looked the sort of fan that'd suit a shy, young girl in white muslin with pink rosebuds in her ringlets.

Elinor didn't have time to mend it. She was too busy with all the paperwork for the upcoming exhibition in Seville. But if it wasn't too tough a job, why go to all the trouble of taking it to Peter Mowbray? Why not…? No, impossible! Esther'd never agree. But, from what he'd seen of fan repair, the most important thing was endless patience and, with a bit of advice to get him started, why not?

Before second thoughts could give him cold feet, he pulled out his phone right there on the bridge and called Elinor. When she answered, he came straight to the point.

"That broken brisé fan you showed me this afternoon. Since you're too busy to repair it, d'you think Esther'd be willing to let me have a go?" he asked, sounding as casual as he could. Why was his heart racing fit to suffocate him?

There was a short silence on the other end of the phone. Did she think him such a waster he couldn't commit to anything?

"I didn't realise you'd even be interested," she replied.

"I'd really like to do it," he assured her. "You see, since we started work on Bea's fan, I've learned a lot from you. And I also picked up a second-hand copy of that book you recommended on fan repair. Read it through several times. In fact, I was wondering how to start trying out some of the techniques I've been learning about. This'd be a great opportunity."

"But there's no money in it, you know. I mean, Esther's insisting on some sort of payment, but experience should've taught you by now that no one can afford to make the time you need to spend on mending a fan financially worthwhile. You've no choice but to do it basically for love."

What'd she think he was? Only in things for the money? What about the satisfaction that came from doing a great job?

"Yeah, I'm well aware of that," he agreed. "Still, I suppose it's an antique fan, isn't it? If you don't think I could handle it –"

"No, it's not that at all," she broke in. "You're far more patient than me at coaxing dust off soiled fan leaves and likely to do a better job, I know. But why would you want to spend all that time on it?"

That she should ask him that!

"Do you need an excuse to spend time on something you enjoy doing?" he quoted back at her. "Besides, I like old things."

"Sometimes you're so stubborn, aren't you?"

She paused.

He made no reply.

And then, "All right," she conceded at last. "I'll give Esther a ring and see what she says…"

*

After he arrived home, Jamie roamed around the house, unable to settle to anything.

"If you keep on fiddling with that toolbox lid, you're going to break it," warned Dad, who was screwing up a new shelf in the utility room, holding out his hand for another wall plug.

"Get your fingers out of my fish pie," cried Mum, slapping his wrist smartly. "Why don't you make yourself useful for once and set the dinner table?"

"Out o' my way," growled Marc, grabbing back the TV remote. "I always watch *Night Sky* this time on Saturdays."

"You sick or something?" demanded Bea. "Why not go and play your guitar upstairs instead of messing around on the piano when I want to get on with some serious practice…"

And so it went on. Even Geoff scowled at him for losing his place in the book he was reading on the life cycle of earthworms and flounced off with it in a huff.

Finally Jamie got fed up with this continual harassment and shut himself into his bedroom. First he picked up his guitar, as Bea'd suggested, and started tuning it, but he couldn't concentrate on playing, so ended up tossing it aside. Next he began some preparation at his desk for the summer holiday Spanish classes he'd enrolled in at the language centre, but his attention soon shifted onto catching up with old Exeter friends on his phone. Then he flung himself onto his bed and started listening to some music, but after a while pulled out the earphones and lay there staring at the ceiling.

He was starting work at 3-D Imaging next Wednesday. Back to the impersonal, open-plan office and the maple-veneered furniture, the potted palms and the constant tap-tap-tap of computer keys. Was this all life had to offer? Guess he could land a permanent job in a place like that, if money was what he wanted. But was it just money that he wanted? Wasn't it more about working at something he enjoyed doing? But what sort of work *did* he enjoy doing?

His gaze wandered around the room, over the fan repair book on his bedside table, the model planes and origami birds dangling on thin wires from the ceiling, the wall-mounted frame containing the Balinese wooden fan that he'd brought back from his student flat at Exeter.

He sprang up and threw himself back down on his desk chair, staring vacantly at the re-activated laptop screen in front of him. Suddenly he realised he was actually staring at a digital fan. The tiny icon on his browser bar. *Fantasy*. Hadn't checked over Peter and Susan Mowbray's website in weeks. Probably just the same as ever – in need of a really good updating by someone who knew what they were doing…

Yeah – there was the same old photo of Peter with his wire-framed glasses, flowing, patriarchal beard and kindly eyes, just the way he remembered him. His thoughts drifted back to that hard, frosty morning in early spring when Elinor had driven him out to Suffolk to meet the Mowbrays. The workshop that'd so fascinated him. Remember all the tempting glass jars and pull-out plastic boxes. Peter was so lucky to be able to spend his life among them mending fans, making them beautiful and whole again. And he even managed to earn a living doing it. But he was getting old now and none of his sons wanted to take over the business. What'd happen when he and Susan decided to retire? Who'd fix those old fans and inherit that fascinating workshop?

A clear image flashed through his mind of himself hard at work in it.

You must be joking! Buried in the wilds of Suffolk about a million miles from civilisation. Who'd want to live out there?

He checked the online map. Well, Little Downing was only six miles from Bury. And Cambridge wasn't exactly the centre of the universe, was it? Besides, he'd never cared much for company, and someone clearly had to do this job. Who else but he would even be interested?

At that moment the answer to his question struck him in all its perfect beauty. Why shouldn't it be himself? The solution had been staring him in the face all the time and he just hadn't realised.

Suddenly a vision of his whole future spread before him, like the panorama from a high mountain top. Ever since he'd taken a closer look at the ivory sticks of Great Aunt Rosita's fan, he'd been hooked. When he came home from hospital the first time and lay on the sofa wishing he was dead, the thing that had revived his interest in life was his admiration of the craftsmanship and care with which some unknown artist had painted the strawberries and towers and castanets and butterflies on Bea's fan. Then when he'd taken it to Elinor and they started work on it together, he'd begun to appreciate all the separate components that went into making up the beautiful thing that he loved. Working with fans was what he wanted to do more than anything else in the world.

The whole concept was so dazzling, it took his breath away. To be able to do something he really loved – and even make use of his computer skills too. The first thing he'd tackle when he got settled at Little Downing was to liven up this boring website!

But how did you get into a business like fan repair? Would you need a costly Fine Arts qualification before someone like Peter would take you on as his apprentice? Who did you consult?

He paused to rack his brains. His family? His family would only laugh at him and call him a dreamer.

Elinor was the next person that sprang to mind. But her interests were more on the academic side and he wanted to work with his hands – all those little pins and rivets and sequins. That's where his real interest lay. Who had tabs on this sort of information?

Of course! Aurélie Brisson at the Fan Museum in Greenwich. He'd email her at once.

Chapter Twenty-One

"Uncle Fabian," exclaimed Elinor in astonishment, as she entered the upstairs gallery of the Fan Museum the following Tuesday morning. "What're you doing here?"

The tall, thin man, who'd obviously emerged from Aurélie's office, started in surprise and focused his distant gaze on her with some reluctance. He was – as always – immaculately dressed for the warm weather in a well-cut, beige linen jacket and trousers with knife-edged creases and he carried a white straw fedora that he'd taken to wearing in summer ever since his balding crown became undisguisable.

"Elinor, my dear," he greeted her in his highly cultivated drawl. "How delightful to bump into you! Mademoiselle Aurélie told me she was expecting you this morning. But the vigour of your tone," he hinted, a visible tremor quivering through his frame as he raised one languid, white hand to his brow. "I am as yet barely convalescent from the latest onslaught. I feel sure you understand…"

Uncle Fabian's migraines had long assumed legendary proportions in family lore. Elinor at once perceived that her surprise had betrayed her into brash vulgarity and lowered her voice to express sympathy over his recent ill health.

"No worse than usual, my dear," he replied airily, stooping to graze her forehead with a kiss as light as the breath of butterfly wings in gracious acknowledgement of her consideration. "But I always feel so – so wrung out when newly arisen from my bed of suffering. It will pass later in the day. One mustn't complain. So, what news of life on the fenland flats?"

How did he do it? Merely by the subtle modulation of his velvety tones, he managed to convey utter disdain of her existence in a dull, provincial backwater. Of course he was being purposely provocative – after all, he was an Oxford man himself – but he always delivered his witticisms with such theatricality that one was never quite sure whether they were sly snubs or not.

"We're all fine at home," Elinor replied evenly, since it was impossible to be offended with someone who'd never treat her as though she was older than about ten "– though Dad's had one or two dizzy turns lately. The doctor seems to think it stems from a change of blood pressure pills."

"You astound me. John's always enjoyed such a robust and – one might almost say – ox-like constitution, certainly by comparison with myself."

"Yes, well since Mum died –"

"Ah yes, poor Edith," he cut in, thoughtfully stroking his small, neat beard. "She was so delicate, even as a girl. But let us not dwell on such depressing subjects. What brings you to London today, my dear? You've always been so brisk and energetic – trains here, planes there. It's difficult for a mere invalid like myself to keep up with your dizzying programme of activities…"

Elinor smiled. Some people had to earn a living, didn't they? – unlike Uncle Fabian, who'd long maintained a leisured lifestyle on the strength of a nominal company directorship and invested wealth inherited from her grandparents.

"I'm down today on business," she told him. "I'll be taking a number of fans from the museum to an exhibition in Seville next month and I need to complete all the paperwork –"

"Paperwork. How desperately dull! But – Seville, you say? A shame it's so far away or I might just have been tempted over to view the exhibition myself. You must send me a catalogue."

Uncle Fabian leave his rural retreat near Shere and the comforts of British civilisation for the uncertainties of European travel? Elinor struggled to keep a straight face as she replied,

"Why of course. It's being prepared at present by an old friend of mine in Spain."

There was a pause. What else to say? But she so rarely saw her mother's older brother and despite his affectations, she did find him an amusing companion.

"Will you still be here at lunchtime?" she asked. "It's such a lovely day. Perhaps we could take a stroll in the park and eat at the café…?"

His face assumed an expression of perfect horror.

"My dear girl, you can't mean that deplorable public restaurant. I once cast a glance in through its doors out of idle curiosity and retreated as quickly as possible. However, I might be persuaded to take tea and a sandwich with you in the garden here once I've finished viewing the current exhibition. I'm quite panting to behold the Youghal lace fan with three blond tortoiseshell guards that Mademoiselle Aurelie's promised me as its centrepiece."

Elinor could see his gaze, like a greyhound on a leash, already straining in the direction of a nearby glass case and realised that his interest in her, never particularly strong, was rapidly waning by contrast with his attraction to the unusual fan – presumably the reason he'd come up to Greenwich today. So she quickly agreed to meet him in the garden later and watched him stroll away with his characteristically questing posture: head jutting forward like a discerning vulture on the lookout for some rare and exotic titbit. His fan collection, also inherited from her grandfather, was a ruling passion with him. A wife could never have competed with it.

She turned away and knocked softly on the nearby office door.

"Enter," called Aurelie's voice, so she pushed it open.

The director's office at the Fan Museum boasted fine, panelled walls painted a pale shade of mocha and hung with choice historic fan leaves mounted in heavy, protective glass cases. Its wide sash windows, tastefully draped in sapphire watered silk, were thrown open to admit birdsong and gentle breezes from the garden below.

Aurélie was seated at the Georgian mahogany desk near one of the windows, resplendent in black brocade trousers and a Moroccan tunic, stiff with gold embroidery and scarlet beadwork. At Elinor's entrance she glanced up from her papers and, snatching off her spectacles, at once rose and rustled over to embrace her, kissing her with enthusiasm on both cheeks.

"Elinor, ma chérie. Welcome."

Elinor greeted her in return and then, nodding in the direction of the gallery outside, added, "I have to say, I'm astounded. I've just met Uncle Fabian in a state of high anticipation. That Youghal lace fan must be rarer than I thought if he's actually travelled all the way here to see it."

Aurélie gave a short laugh. She and Uncle Fabian were old friends.

"Ah, but zere is uzzer business too. 'E is on 'is way to Christie's zis afternoon, where zere is a vairy rare Louis Quatorze fan on display, depicting ze triumph of Galatée. Members of ze Fan Circle are invited to a private view. I am surprised you 'ave not been made aware."

"Of course! I'd forgotten all about it." Might've known there'd be a possible acquisition at the bottom of it.

"You would care to join us?"

Wouldn't she just! But she did have business here first…

"Perhaps I could see how quickly I finish the papers," she agreed, doubly keen to set to work with the added spur of such an offer. But she'd hardly set her bag down on the desk when Aurélie intervened.

"Before you are beginning, I 'ave an excellent piece of news concerning ze fan zat you make enquiries for."

Elinor looked up at her.

"Oh – you mean –?"

"Ze mask fan – precisely."

"In fact I've discovered myself that one of the scenes on it comes from a play," Elinor told her. "My brother's been producing it in Cambridge. But what else have you learned?"

Aurélie returned to her desk at the window and picked up the papers she'd left lying there when she rose to greet her.

"Zees are arrived by email only yesterday," indicating the sheets she was holding. "I 'ave made contact wiz Ruth at ze Museum of Fine Arts in Boston, which owns anuzzer similar fan. We 'ave exchanged images and details and of course I 'ave become vairy interested when I realise zeez two fans 'ave possibly ze same provenance. Ruth 'as done research on ze Boston fan and sent me several pages of notes. You can see for yourself," offering them to her.

Elinor's eyes rapidly skimmed the information, which told her that the Boston fan had probably come to America with one George Harding, who'd travelled there from London in the 1720s after working as a fan mounter in Cornhill and taken to advertising his wares in the Boston Newsletter of the period.

"You see zat she suggests ze leaf is possibly taken from an engraving by 'Ogarth," Aurélie pointed out.

"Hogarth?" exclaimed Elinor with a fresh spark of interest. "Then I know just the person who'll be able to tell me more. I've reached a bit of a dead end in my research lately, but this'll give me something new to go on." She folded the papers and tucked them neatly away in her bag. "Thanks, Aurélie. Just let me know when I can return the favour, won't you?"

Aurélie looked as though she'd suddenly remembered something.

"Well, now you mention it, I suppose you 'ave no thoughts concerning your uncle's latest project?"

Elinor frowned.

"Project? He didn't say anything to me about it."

"I thought 'e might 'ave mentioned it when 'e saw you just now. 'E is plaguing me wiz emails for over a week, but still I 'ave not an idea of anyone who might be interested."

Elinor had begun rummaging in the depths of her bag for her papers, but she looked up at this.

"Interested in what?"

"Work on ze catalogue of 'is collection. At last 'e decides zat 'e wishes to make zis available online wiz its own dedicated website. But 'e feels 'e does not 'ave ze technical expertise 'imself, so looks for someone to assist 'im."

Elinor nodded. About time too. She'd mentioned this to him before herself.

"Well he's not short of cash. Why not get in touch with one of these firms of professional consultants who'll set the whole thing up for him?"

"Zat 'ave I already suggested. But you know 'ow 'e feels about spending money on what 'e considers inessentials –"

Elinor knew very well. Thousands might be paid over for a Louis Quartorze fan leaf without batting an eyelid, but in other respects Uncle Fabian was an out-and-out miser.

"And 'e also insists ze work must be undertaken by someone wiz an appreciation of fans – no mere ignorant barbarian… Ze ideal of course would be a fine arts student available for summer 'oliday employment, but now zat I am no longer connected wiz ze museum training programme…" Aurélie shrugged her shoulders. "You know of someone at ze Courtauld or maybe in Cambridge 'oo might be persuaded to undertake it?"

Elinor briefly reviewed her contacts at the Courtauld and Lydgate Museums but drew a complete blank there. Of course Jamie was developing an interest in fans and had the requisite computer skills too, but he was about to start a full-time job at 3-D Imaging and she couldn't imagine him and Uncle Fabian ever hitting it off.

"Can't think of anyone – off the top of my head, that is. Suppose I should offer to do it myself, shouldn't I? Trouble is, I've got so much on at the moment." She sighed. "I'll have to think about it. But meanwhile, I really must get started on these forms…"

She busied herself for some time among the files in the library, examining papers and filling in the various documents and declarations. She was so absorbed in her work that, while vaguely conscious of the occasional murmur of voices in Aurélie's office next door, she forgot all about the time until it suddenly struck her how dry-throated she was feeling.

She glanced down at her watch. Heavens! After one and she hadn't had anything to drink all morning. No wonder she felt thirsty. Would Uncle Fabian already have given up on her in despair?

Her eyes flickered towards the window, through which the sun was pouring, illuminating the dust motes floating in the still air. Perhaps he was waiting for her out in the garden. She rose and went to check.

The vantage point of a first-floor window afforded her an excellent view of the fan-shaped parterres below, planted with spiky grey lavender, lily of the valley, sweet-smelling pinks and fragrant old roses. Directly beneath lay the paved patio where on fine summer days, the doors of the conservatory tearoom were usually thrown open to the sunshine. Among the terracotta pots of mauve and cream pansies and scented pink geraniums were scattered marble-topped tables with green, wrought-iron chairs, where visitors might take refreshments.

Because of the large, beige parasols over-shading many of the tables, it was difficult to see their occupants. But that looked like

Uncle Fabian's black-banded fedora resting on a spare chair over there. More intriguingly, beside it she could spy a foot in a rather scruffy trainer. Strange. Not the sort of shoes you'd expect on a person associated with Uncle Fabian…

By craning her neck, she just managed to glimpse a leg in faded denim jeans. Who could Uncle Fabian be talking to? Luckily she'd almost finished up here, so in a moment she could go down and investigate. And while they were having lunch, she'd indicate her willingness to help with the work on his collection. After mulling it over at the back of her mind all morning, it seemed only right to offer, since it'd been her idea in the first place. She'd just have to find the time…

She hurried through the last of the documentation, then slipped downstairs and out through the back door into the garden. But on rounding the corner of the conservatory, she pulled up short.

There indeed was Uncle Fabian, seated with the air of a reigning maharajah under an umbrella in the shelter of the grey brick wall, over which tumbled a cascade of purple clematis on a green, fan-shaped trellis. On the tabletop in front of him stood an elegant, white china tea pot with matching cup and saucer and, as he leant back in his chair, he toyed casually with the teaspoon, a smile of satisfaction overspreading his lean, aristocratic features. But whoever would've expected to see in his company the youth in a faded grey T-shirt and well-worn jeans who occupied the chair opposite?

"Jamie! Whatever're you doing here?" she exclaimed.

"Play rehearsals with Adam," he countered at once. Was it her imagination or did he answer just a little too quickly – like someone who'd thought up an excuse in advance? "I decided I might as well drop in to see Aurélie while I was down in London."

Drop in? You didn't just "drop in" to see Aurélie! You waited till you were invited – or summoned. Was he being entirely up front with her?

"Still, the visit's turned out even more worthwhile than I imagined," Jamie went on cryptically, shooting a sideways glance at Uncle Fabian.

"Elinor, are you planning to seat yourself?" broke in her uncle a trifle testily. He never liked other people hugging centre stage. "After all the banging of doors that heralded your appearance, I'm in no fit state to endure the sight of you bobbing from foot to foot in front of me, bawling like a Billingsgate fishwife. Take pity on my poor head and try to compose your limbs decently on a chair."

Obedient from long habit, Elinor at once pulled out the spare seat. But it was heavier than expected and its cast iron legs inadvertently scraped on the paving stones. Uncle Fabian winced and raised his pale grey eyes heavenward, obviously praying for endurance. To her surprise, Jamie at once sprang to his feet and lifted the chair for her. As Elinor slid into it, feeling like a scolded schoolgirl, he flashed her an encouraging grin. Clearly he already had Uncle Fabian's number.

Meanwhile her uncle had discreetly signed to the waitress to fetch another cup and saucer.

"Well, I think we've happily concluded our business," he resumed, turning back to the table and forgetting his momentary outburst of irritation in renewed satisfaction over some as yet unexplained triumph. "And after successful business, what can be so delightful as sitting out on a shaded terrace partaking of a light luncheon with two such charming young people?"

Elinor stared. What business could Jamie possibly have with Uncle Fabian?

"Do close your mouth, Elinor," Uncle Fabian advised with the superior smile of a cat who'd just drunk a saucerful of stolen cream. "It does give such a bad impression of your quite passable intelligence when you gape like that. For some time now, as you're well aware, I've been looking out for a person with an understanding of information technology, I believe it's called, to mastermind the transference of all the records of my collection into a digital format. You know I pride myself on my unparalleled appreciation of character. So when I encountered this young man in the presence of the Youghal lace fan and we chanced to exchange our impressions of this truly exquisite piece, I instantly realised that, in spite of his not altogether promising exterior –" and he swept a faintly critical glance over Jamie's casual attire and fading facial bruising – "we were entirely in sympathy on matters of importance. Thus, after securing the pleasure of his company this afternoon to view a rare and precious Louis Quartorze fan, whither you might perhaps also care to attend us, I felt he might readily be entrusted with a task demanding such a rare combination of precise knowledge and delicate skill, in addition to computer literacy."

And he beamed upon Jamie with the face of satisfaction that he usually reserved for the acquisition of a new fan.

Elinor glanced from one to the other in astonishment.

So Jamie'd agreed to digitise Uncle Fabian's collection instead!

Chapter Twenty-Two

After finishing work, Elinor liked nothing better than an excuse to drive out to Fen Ditton for a chat with her sister and help give the children their tea. And the following afternoon, she had the perfect excuse.

The large, square kitchen of Yew Tree Croft always felt so welcoming, she thought, as she put her head round its open door, inhaling the mingled odours of freshly toasting bread and savoury garlic and tomato sauce. The house had been a bakery in the days before it and the old farm cottage next door were converted into a single dwelling and since Cathy and Richard moved in, they'd painted its bumpy walls primrose yellow and decorated them with framed etchings, hung blue-and-white-checked curtains at the casement windows and furnished it with a Pembrokeshire oak dresser and reclaimed pine table and chairs.

This afternoon, the table was littered with sodden newspaper, paint-smeared brushes and childish daubs of people and houses in bright primary colours, but the kitchen was deserted. Except of course for her sister, who was busily emptying a jam jar of murky water down the sink.

"Hi, Cathy. Where're Amy and Josh?" Elinor asked, gazing round in disappointment, since when she arrived, they usually came racing to greet her with shrieks of excitement and an avalanche of sticky hugs and kisses.

Cathy turned from the sink at her words. She looked worn out, as usual by this time of day.

"Oh, it's you, Ellie," she exclaimed, pushing untidy wisps of hair out of her eyes. "Well, Amy's playing with her dolls' house upstairs and I've just settled Josh in front of *Wilbur the Wombat,*" nodding in the direction of the living room next door. "That's usually good for a few minutes' peace. Like some tea and toast?"

Elinor readily accepted and while Cathy was putting the kettle on to boil, reached down two mugs from the dresser and cleared space on the table by piling up sheets of newspaper and gingerly stacking wet paint trays on top. Better take advantage of the temporary lull to get straight down to business.

"Here, I've something to show you," she announced as Cathy set the mugs of tea on the table, pulling several enlargements of *The*

Beggar's Opera fan leaf out of her handbag and laying them on the plastic tablecloth for her sister's inspection. "I was down at the Fan Museum yesterday and the moment Aurélie mentioned this might be an engraving by William Hogarth, I instantly thought of you. What's your expert opinion?"

Cathy leant over the table to study the photos.

"Pitty pittures," interrupted a child's eager voice.

A curly, brown head bobbed up in the chair between them and a small hand appeared, tugging at the photos. So much for the delights of *Wilbur the Wombat*!

"Josh," cried Cathy, grabbing his pudgy fist. "Let go. They're Auntie Ellie's." Then, since he looked about to protest, "Now wouldn't you like a slice of hot, buttery toast instead?"

After some spirited resistance, Joshua finally agreed to a peaceable exchange and plonked his denim-clad bottom down on the red quarry tiles to devote his full attention to the toast. Cathy smoothed out the crumpled photos to examine them more closely. After a moment she glanced up at Elinor.

"I'm pretty sure that's a Hogarth engraving. I know he made several different drawings from *The Beggar's Opera*, as well as a couple of paintings. There's a famous one you might've seen before of MacHeath in leg irons and Polly Peachum, the heroine, weeping on the floor of the prison in a white satin gown. Would you like to borrow my catalogue so you can check up the details for yourself?"

Elinor beamed with pleasure.

"Thanks, Cathy. That's just what I was hoping you'd say."

"He actually drew some of the sketches for the painting in Newgate Prison itself," Cathy added. "He has a very precise eye for detail. That monkey for instance."

What monkey? Elinor followed her sister's pointing finger in surprise. Wasn't that a child playing the violin just above the music shop scene? But now she looked more closely, she could just make out the tiny hairy face and body.

"Whatever's a monkey doing there?" she wondered aloud.

"Oh they were all the rage at that period. Hogarth's patroness, the Duchess of Queensbury, kept one as a pet and he often uses them in his boudoir scenes…"

As she spoke, Cathy continued to bustle about, whisking the newspaper and painting gear off the kitchen table and wiping down the bright, sunflower tablecloth. Elinor helped by sponging Josh's sticky mouth and fingers clean of crumbs and butter. Then she heaved him up with a mighty effort, since he was growing fast, and manhandled him into his highchair and plastic bib.

"What've you found out about the rest of the places on the fan?" Cathy enquired over her shoulder, as she popped a pizza into the microwave.

Elinor frowned.

"Didn't think there was anything to find out."

"The building behind that ragged man with the staff, for instance. If you could identify who he represented, it'd give you a clue to his possible location."

"Nick suggested he might be the beggar of the opera's title offering a daily paper to one of the actresses, since she's holding a mask in front of her face. Maybe Lavinia Fenton, who played Polly Peachum in the first production. But the buildings are just generic surely?"

"It's bound to be much more precise than that," replied Cathy, emptying a can of baked beans into a pot and turning on the gas burner. "Hogarth's immensely topographical. Wouldn't surprise me if they're real locations. After all, we know his sisters kept a frock shop in Tottenham Court because we've got surviving records of the trade card he printed for them. You can't tell me they didn't sell his fans along with their dresses. That could even be their business premises," indicating the fan shop. "D'you mind giving Amy a yell for me, sis?"

Elinor nodded thoughtfully.

"But who'd know enough about Tottenham Court in the early eighteenth century to be able to speak with any authority on the buildings in a tiny engraving like this?" she mused, half to herself, as she headed towards the hall and called Amy's name up the stairs.

At that moment the answer struck her. She turned at the kitchen door to catch Cathy's eye and they both exclaimed with one voice,

"DAD!"

Next minute footsteps came racketing down the bare wooden staircase and Amy exploded into the kitchen like a firecracker, auburn pigtails flying wildly on either side of rosy cheeks and green eyes alight as she raced over to throw her arms round Elinor's legs in excited greeting.

"Hello, Auntie Ellie! I didn't know you were here."

Elinor was reaching down Amy's special starry plate and Josh's plastic dish from the glass-fronted wall cupboard, but she abandoned them on the dresser as she bent down to hug her little niece and hear all about what her dolls' house dolls had been doing. Meanwhile Cathy was swiftly spooning baked beans onto the plates.

"Now pick up your plate, Amy, and carry it carefully to the table. Here you are, Josh. Do stop banging that spoon. I can't hear myself think!"

Cathy finally managed to settle Amy on her booster cushion level with the tabletop. After pouring drinks and picking up Joshua's spoon, which he'd already dropped on the floor, and handing him a clean one, she reverted to their idea of consulting Dad about the buildings on the fan.

"I suppose I could," answered Elinor, staring down at the tablecloth.

"What's the matter? He getting you down at the moment?"

Elinor sighed.

"Terribly. I know there's nothing much wrong with him, but it bothers me all the same. When I went to London yesterday, I was on edge the whole time – just in case he felt ill while I was away. And that fan viewing at Christie's that I was telling you about on the phone, remember?" – Cathy nodded in response – "I even left early, so I could make it home before the rush."

"So when you got back, what was he doing?"

"Well… he was upstairs, as it turned out, playing with his new computer. But something could easily've happened –"

"Ellie, if you ask me, you need a change of scene."

"I'm off to Seville soon, you know. Of course I don't plan to stay there any longer than I need to, but what if he's unwell while I'm away?"

"You've got to stop fretting about him. I realise I should take more of the burden off you than I do – but you know what it's like with the children. When he comes here, Josh climbs all over him, or they interrupt him when he's talking and he does so hate that. I think he's just bored, myself. Don't you feel he could do with a new interest? – something to take his mind off his bodily ills. He's had no-one to put him first since Mum died except you, so he just plays on his ill-health to attract sympathy."

Elinor stopped pushing toast crumbs into a little heap on the tablecloth.

"Yes, I know," she admitted, looking up. "But the worst thing is, he's about to retire. I know he'll still drop into college sometimes to eat lunch and use the library, but, Cathy, what'm I going to do? He'll drive me mad if we're cooped up together in that house."

"I've always thought you should've got out before now. You could've married that Australian and moved to Sydney. You were mad to let the opportunity slip through your fingers."

Elinor glanced away. There went Cathy again, adopting that all-wise, older-sister voice of hers. Choices always looked so simple seen through the spectacles of hindsight.

"I couldn't," she murmured defensively. "It wasn't just the way Dad was after Mum died. It was – other things too."

"What other things?"

Elinor drew back. Cathy was always so – so confrontational.

"Well…" How to explain a gut feeling? What excuses could she make? "…things like – like celebrating Christmas Day out in his parents' back garden in the sunshine at a barbecue. It seemed all wrong somehow."

How feeble could you get?

Cathy was clearly not having any of this.

"I should've thought you could cope with a bit of disorientation for the sake of a man you really loved," she pointed out, hitting the nail bang on the head as usual.

"What's 'disorioriation' mean, Mummy?" piped up Amy, pausing with her fork half-way to her lips.

"'Disorientation'… Umm, it's not knowing exactly which direction you should turn in," explained her mother, automatically scooping stray baked beans off the high chair tray with Josh's spoon and tipping them back into his dish.

"Why was Auntie Ellie having disorientitation in Australia?"

"Because she wasn't used to celebrating Christmas in the summertime. Now do eat up, Amy."

"It wasn't just the disorientation," Elinor went on in a bid to recapture her sister's attention. "It was the whole problem of cultural isolation. Sydney's a lovely city – but I was working on European fans in the Hermitage Museum. I simply couldn't give it all up."

"So why not leave home and rent a place in Cambridge like Richard and I did?"

"You were getting married. You had a good excuse."

"You don't need to get married to have an excuse. Or how about moving in with that actor friend of yours down in London?"

"Oh! Are you going to get married to an actor, Auntie Ellie?" interrupted Amy, almost incoherent with rapture. "Can I be your flower girl and wear a shiny pink dress and carry a horseshoe with lace and little roses on it like Charlotte did when her auntie got married?"

Grrr! Why did children always ask such annoying questions?

"No, I'm not getting married," Elinor explained, struggling to be patient.

Amy's face instantly fell.

"Oh. But –" more hopefully, "if you did, I could be your flower girl, couldn't I?"

"Eat up your tea, Amy," urged Cathy, looking big question marks at her sister.

"It all fizzled out," whispered Elinor hastily. "He was too young for me. I knew it all along."

"Well, never mind. Plenty more fish in the sea. Surely you must meet some interesting men in your line of work?"

Professor Chadwick? Dr Hardcastle? Cathy was always coming out with suggestions like that! Elinor pressed her lips firmly together so as not to say something she'd regret.

"Look, Cathy, you've seen my colleagues," she replied aloud. "And I never go anywhere –"

"Trips to London? Conferences in Spain? Amy, your baked beans are getting cold," Cathy prompted, jumping to her feet for a cloth to wipe up spilt orange juice from Josh's overturned plastic beaker.

"Oh – sorry, Mummy," cried Amy, hurriedly gobbling down the baked beans left on her plate in a huge forkful. "Look, they're all gone!"

"All dorn," echoed Josh gleefully, tipping his dish upside down and shaking it so the remaining baked beans splattered against the fridge door and slid down into pools of glutinous orange sauce on the tiles. He stared over the edge of his highchair in amazement at the mess.

"Oh Josh! Yours weren't all gone," cried Cathy.

"What's for dessert, Mummy?" asked Amy. "Can I have some chocolate ice cream?"

"In a minute, dear. I have to clear up this first."

"Here, Amy, I'll get it for you," offered Elinor, rising from the table. Trying to talk seriously with Cathy under such conditions was impossible.

"Hello, everyone, I'm home," announced a deep voice as a tall figure came striding cheerfully through the back door, unbuckling his cycle helmet.

"Daddy," yelled Amy and ran to greet him.

"Rick! You're early," Cathy exclaimed, darting to stir the savoury smelling pot simmering on the stove.

"Mmm, something smells good. I'm hungry as a hunter," exclaimed Richard. "Hi there, Ellie. You staying for dinner?"

Clearly her signal to depart.

"No, I just called in on my way home. Cathy, about that book…"

"Here, Rick, keep an eye on the children for a moment. Get them some ice cream – while I go and fetch a book for Ellie."

"Sure thing. It's been quite a day – got lots to tell you. Shall I serve us up?"

"Wait a bit. I won't be long."

"You're not going out tonight, are you, Mummy?" wailed Amy in alarm, seeing her mother about to leave the room. "You promised to help me learn my spellings."

"I'll be back in a minute. Now you sit down at the table and eat your ice cream. Come on, Ellie."

"So how was ballet today, chicken?" Richard asked in an effort to divert Amy's attention, while Joshua waved his arms and roared to be picked up.

What a relief to leave that ear-splitting din behind, thought Elinor, as she mounted the stairs behind her sister.

Cathy led the way over the creaky, uneven boards of the upstairs hall to her study, a tiny room hardly bigger than a broom cupboard with a drawing board wedged under the window frame and rows of books squeezed into a shelved alcove beside the unplastered chimney breast. She stared blankly at the shelves for a moment and then turned to Elinor and demanded,

"What book am I looking for again?"

"The Hogarth catalogue," prompted Elinor.

"Of course! It's so hard to remember anything in this household." Cathy bent down to scan the line of titles for a moment before picking a large, clothbound hardback off the second-to-bottom shelf and handing it to Elinor. "Here. And there's something else I've been meaning to say to you too. Do you know what?" turning abruptly to face her.

"What?" asked Elinor, glancing up from the book.

"You're just making excuses because you're too frightened to take any chances. Dad's no reason for not getting out and leading your own life."

"But –" Elinor began to protest.

"No, don't interrupt me! People are always interrupting me, so I never manage to finish what I want to say. Why take things so seriously all the time? You're working yourself into the ground. In fact, I reckon you use your job as an excuse to escape from actually living. Now, you're going to Seville next week. Forget about Dad. Nick and I can keep an eye on him. And stop feeling so sorry for yourself. Fly off to Spain. Buy some pretty, new dresses. You always wear such dreary clothes these days. That thing you've got on now makes you look about a hundred years old. And – for goodness' sake! – look around and pick yourself up a handsome new man." She paused with a flushed face, seeming to recollect her own burden of responsibilities. "Now come on, we'd better get back to the bear garden before they send out a search party."

Elinor marched downstairs behind her sister, clutching the heavy Hogarth catalogue to her chest to crush her swelling rage.

Cathy was always handing out advice she didn't need and never paused to listen to her point of view! It was fine for her. She had a husband and a home and a life of her own. But handsome men didn't just grow on trees. Where did you come across them?

Chapter Twenty-Three

It was past five o'clock that stifling Friday afternoon and Fred Baxter had already stuck his ox-like head round Elinor's office door and pointedly asked if she was planning to let herself out the back way tonight. She begged a few minutes more to finish off a catalogue entry, but she could hear him jingling his way inexorably back up the corridor and knew her time was running out.

The nearby offices were silent because everyone else had already gone home for the weekend. Ten minutes ago she'd heard Gerald Hardcastle stump off down the corridor more jauntily than usual since he was making a rare escape with an old school friend for a boating expedition on the Norfolk Broads. And Edwin Chadwick's door had just slammed with a muffled crash. He'd be off to catch the Melbourn bus back to his mother and his birds and his half-finished monograph on Hellenistic coins.

But what was there for her to look forward to? Cathy and Richard were driving up to visit his parents in Lincoln this weekend so she couldn't offer to take Amy swimming in the morning. And Nick and Sandra had called off dinner tomorrow night because Sandra had to stand in for a fellow medic at short notice. She could go out shopping, but she didn't really need anything. And there was that play on at the Arts Theatre, but it'd probably be sold out by now. Suppose she could text Camilla and find out what she and Henry were doing tonight, but she hadn't made it to many flamenco classes lately. At least when Adam was around, life had been a bit more exciting. Now the only prospect ahead of her was of drafting a paper for Seville or having her father ask if she wouldn't like to proofread his latest book chapter. Perhaps Cathy was right after all.

Her head drooped lower and lower. The weight of scholarship and dusty antiquity all around her was smothering her. She could hardly breathe …

At that moment there came a brisk tap on the door. She started in surprise. Must be Fred back again. But Fred wasn't known for the tact of his rapping: he always thundered on the wooden panels. And his keys were still jangling some distance away. Who else could it be at this hour?

"Come in," she gasped out automatically, jerking upright in her seat.

The door opened and a young man entered in neat, navy trousers, a fine blue-and-white-pinstriped shirt and immaculate grey tie. Tall and dark-haired with handsome grey eyes and an air of slightly awkward formality, like a junior officer new to his command. His appearance was so unexpected that for a moment she was almost at a loss to identify him.

She half-rose from her chair and then swiftly sank back down again. No need to look desperate for company.

"Jamie," she exclaimed. "What're you doing here?"

"Hi there, Elinor. Thought you didn't recognise me for a second."

"Oh... I was busy thinking about something else."

"Anyway, glad I caught you before you left for home."

"I was just getting ready to go."

She must look so stupid, staring at him like this. Needed to pull herself together and at least make a show of searching for her bag.

"I've been up in town making a company delivery to the Pure Maths Department," he went on, "so I decided to drop by and see if you were in. Thought I could walk home with you and pick up Esther's fan, now she's agreed to let me try my hand at mending it."

"Why not? So you've started work at 3-D Imaging, have you? You're certainly looking very – smart."

"Oh that." He gestured dismissively. "Everyone at work's been making such a song and dance about it the last few days. I'm just the same person underneath."

"But it's not always easy to see beneath surface appearances, is it?"

There was an awkward pause. Where to go from here?

"Everything well?" she resumed. "With work, I mean."

"It's OK."

"Play rehearsals this weekend?"

"Yeah. Dress rehearsal tomorrow. Probably catch a train to London late tonight. You off to Seville soon?"

"Next week." Why did she feel so awkward in his presence today? "See. I've just had some sample copies of the exhibition flier through this morning. What do you think?" She rummaged through her in-tray for the brown manila envelope and shook out several cards shaped like red and black fans with scalloped edges. She handed him one, accidentally touching his hand with her own as he reached out to take it from her. A disturbing thrill shot through her at the touch of his long, sinewy fingers.

"Looks very Spanish," he commented, turning it over and glancing at the other side. "That map's pretty useful. To anyone planning to visit the exhibition, I mean. What's the Alcazar?"

"The old royal palace in the city centre. I loved the gardens when I was there last summer – so many beautiful pools and fountains and patios scented with jasmine and orange blossom."

"And how about this Apeadero place it mentions here?"

"That's where visitors used to alight from their carriages. At one side there's a staircase leading up to the old armoury, where the exhibition's being held."

"It'll certainly keep you busy putting something like that together," Jamie commented, surveying the front of the leaflet again.

At that moment the approaching rattle of Fred's keys stopped outside the door.

"I'm sorry, we'll have to leave now," Elinor apologised, hastily reaching for her bag. "Fred wants to set the alarm. He's already given me one warning. I'll be in real hot water if he asks whether I'm planning to spend the weekend here."

She smiled rather wryly.

"All right if I just leave these leaflets on your desk?" Jamie asked.

She nodded quickly and turned to switch off the lights without noticing what he did with them.

"It's all right, Fred. We'll let ourselves out the back way," she reassured the custodian, pulling open the door before he even had a chance to knock.

The look on his face as she ushered Jamie out right under his nose! It'd give him something to think about – for a change.

She and Jamie walked up Tillington Street side by side, exchanging casual comments about the fine weather, the approaching summer holidays and the crowd of tourists thronging Cambridge at present. Her drooping spirits began to revive in the fresh air as a cooling breeze from the river fanned her hot cheeks. A pretty girl coming the other way eyed Jamie swiftly up and down and shot her an appraising glance. Envious? Of her companion? Elinor observed him sideways through her lashes. Perhaps he was better looking than she'd once believed...

They soon reached the orderly procession of tall, sash windows and black wrought-iron balconies that formed the façade of Belmont Terrace and Elinor led the way upstairs to the first-floor landing.

"If you'd like to go and sit down," she said, indicating the drawing room door, "I'll just put away my things and fetch the fan for you. Would you like a cup of tea while you're here?"

Jamie nodded.

"Perhaps I'd better see if Dad wants one too," Elinor went on. "He's probably home by now, but I expect he'll be busy in his study playing with his new toy."

She smiled and, as Jamie raised questioning eyebrows, went on to explain.

"The computer he's just bought himself. He's been busy studying the manual for days, but I'm not sure he's got very far with it yet. I think he probably needs to take a course. It's a bit beyond my capabilities."

"Really?" remarked Jamie, as she left him to enter the drawing room alone.

When she returned carrying the box containing Esther's fan, she found him standing over by one of the windows, staring down into the garden far below.

"In fact I've been meaning to email you," she began, laying the box on the bamboo-legged coffee table, "to tell you what I found out about the fan from my sister the other day. I'm convinced that the large building – you remember the one with the dormer windows – is the Lincoln's Inn Fields Theatre where *The Beggar's Opera* was first performed."

"How can you possibly be sure of something so precise as that?"

"I had a chat to Dad about it. He's an expert on the topography of early eighteenth century London – it's his field of research, you know – and he pointed out the engraving of the theatre on one of our table mats downstairs. I've been setting his place with it for years and never looked at it properly before. The theatre stood in an area infested by pickpockets and robbers on Portugal Street, which Dad says was named in honour of Catherine of Braganza after she came to England to marry Charles II. I've gathered enough material now to write a decent-sized article, so I was actually hoping to beg a favour from your sister after we finish work on her fan."

"Which is?" prompted Jamie.

"Her permission to have it photographed at the museum to illustrate my paper."

At that moment the door behind them opened and her father looked into the room.

"Elinor, my dear, home at last," he greeted her. "I thought I heard you come in. And you've brought Jamie Willett with you too. Good evening, young man. I'm pleased to see you again." He held out his hand with unexpected cordiality. Elinor stared. But of course! The incident at Nick's play. Interesting too that he'd experienced no difficulty at all in recalling Jamie's name!

"Jamie's just come over to pick up Esther's old fan so he can re-ribbon it for her," Elinor told him, indicating the box lying on the coffee table. "He's got interested in restoration techniques since we started mending his sister's fan. You remember, the leaf I showed you the other night with the mask face?"

"Ah yes, and the Lincoln's Inn Fields Theatre – I certainly do. Well, don't let me interrupt you, my dear. Just wondering if you'd like a cup of tea."

"Of course, Dad. I was about to put the kettle on myself. I'll bring it to the study if you like."

"Why not sit down, Jamie, and tell me what you're up to at the moment?" invited Dad politely.

Not exactly what she'd had in mind. Why would Jamie want to sit and be bored to death by her father?

But Dad had already offered him a chair and Jamie sat down, looking perfectly at ease. Up to him then! Elinor left them to it and headed downstairs to the kitchen. But she hurried back again with the laden tray. By this time they'd've probably exhausted their entire stock of small talk and be sitting staring at one another in stony silence…

"…Used to collect them myself in jam jars when I was a boy. Well, well, so what's he had in it this summer?" she heard her father ask indulgently, as she elbowed open the door.

As soon as he realised that she was struggling beneath the weight of the large, lacquered Chinese tray, Jamie sprang to lift it out of her hands and set it down on the coffee table. Perhaps he had some manners after all…

While she was pouring out tea from the silver pot into an eggshell thin china cup and handing it to her father, she realised they must be discussing Geoff's wildlife pond, since Jamie went on to mention that although his brother had had some success with mayflies, he was a bit disappointed that so many of his tadpoles had died off.

"He'll just have to be patient," advised her father in a voice of authority. "It takes a while for a pond to become a naturalised haven for wildlife. The planting in ours wasn't well established for a number of years."

"Yes, I saw it in the garden, when I was looking out the window just now."

"It's full of wildlife too: caddis flies, toads, newts galore that'd be bound to appeal to a serious biologist like your brother. He should come over and make some use of it. Lately all I've heard on the subject are Catherine's complaints about the dangers of toddlers falling into it and drowning."

"Kind of you to offer," began Jamie.

Heavens! thought Elinor, sipping her tea. Imagine a twelve-year-old wanting anything to do with Dad!

"I'm sure Geoff has lots of other places to study wildlife," she broke in, to save Jamie thinking up an excuse. "If he's as resourceful as his twin brother, that is."

"You've another brother the same age then?" asked her father.

"Yes, Marcus."

"And what's his particular field?"

"He wants to be an astrophysicist."

"Really? A seriously intellectual household then?"

"I'm not sure I'd say that." Jamie laughed. "– Especially not about Marc. But he and Dad do knock up amateur telescopes together and go out star-gazing some nights when the sky's clear. He's always on about taking a trip to Hawaii or California as soon as he's old enough, where there're really good opportunities to study the sky."

"What a splendid idea! I've always wanted to travel myself, but never really had the opportunity. My wife hated flying and then of course there was the children's education, you know. First Cathy, then Nick, and then we were only just starting to see light at the end of the financial tunnel, so to speak, and along came Elinor, so back we were at square one again. It's been a long slog, but now she's landed a permanent job at the museum, I'm looking forward to a little more freedom in my retirement."

Elinor felt herself flushing.

"Why, Dad, you make me sound such a burden," she cried. He'd never spoken of this before.

"Never a burden, my dear. There's nothing to regret over doing one's duty in life. But your mother was so anxious about your uncertain future when she died. It was all I could do to reassure her that I'd guide you as well as I could, though aware of course that nothing can replace a mother's care. I don't think she'd be displeased with the result. However, one thing that concerns me is that you might find it a trifle lonely here in this big house all by yourself, if ever I should go off travelling. I've always wanted to visit my brother in New Zealand and I don't want to leave it too long or I'll be too decrepit to enjoy the trip. This recent little health scare of mine's made me realise I've no time to lose. It's not easy getting old, you know – useless and played out, health breaking down, brain going soft…"

"Your brain's hardly going soft, Dad," Elinor protested loyally, struggling to blink away the tears stinging behind her eyes at his reference to her mother's care. She cleared her throat, forcing herself to remark in a steady voice, "Why only the other night, when we were looking at that fan together, it took you all of thirty seconds to identify the Lincoln's Inn Fields Theatre."

"Oh that was elementary, my dear. But, you know, I was checking my plans of London that night after you'd gone to bed – I'd forgotten exactly where Portugal Street is, you understand, in relation to Tottenham Court, and bless my soul, if it didn't suddenly occur to me what a useful footnote that'd make in my book."

"Your book?" echoed Jamie.

"Yes. About inter-racial relations in early eighteenth-century London – an absolutely fascinating subject. I've been working on it for years. Of course the reason the area around Lincoln's Inn Fields was notorious for its thieves and beggars was precisely because it was such a hub of the tourist trade – so, one might say, naturally attractive to gentlemen of the road, like MacHeath…"

Jamie frowned thoughtfully and leaned forward.

"What nationality of tourists?" he queried, setting down his cup.

Elinor instantly glimpsed where his train of thought was heading.

"Why, the Spanish visitors who congregated in the streets around the theatre," replied Dad. "Indeed, there was a very well-known coffee house not far from it called *The Spaniard* in their honour –" He glanced in puzzlement from Elinor to Jamie. "What's wrong with the two of you? What've I said?"

"The fan, Dad," exclaimed Elinor. "What we haven't been able to work out all along was why, even though the pictures on the leaf were of English places and people, all the words were in Spanish."

"It must've been printed for the Spanish tourist trade," explained Jamie.

"And you've given us the vital clue to solve the mystery, Dad. Now claim to be useless and played out if you dare!"

"Giving other people ideas is all very well," Dad grumbled, looking more flattered by the compliment than he pretended. "It's having them yourself that's more important. I suppose I'd better get back to the grindstone and see if I can have one or two new thoughts of my own before dinner."

"How's it going in there?" asked Elinor, rising to gather the teacups back onto the tray. "Have you managed to get it to print yet?"

"Yes indeed. I worked that one out this afternoon – though it did take me over an hour. But now I'm getting bogged down over exactly how to manipulate those tabulations. I wish I knew someone more computer literate than you, Elinor, instead of having to waste so much time reading it up in the manual."

"Why not look in the online help?" suggested Jamie. "It's a lot easier than wading through manuals."

"That's all very well, but I'm not sure how one gets to grips with the online help…"

Hmm, mused Elinor. Did he perhaps recall what Jamie did for a living? If he hadn't looked so innocently helpless, she'd've suspected him of fishing for advice…

Before she could change the subject, Jamie rose abruptly to his feet.

"If you like, I could come and show you now," he offered.

"Well… only if you have the time. I thought you and Elinor might be going to do some work on your sister's fan," Dad remarked blandly.

"It won't take a moment. Now exactly what make of computer are we talking about here?"

Elinor stood with the tray in her hands watching Dad sweep Jamie effortlessly off to his study. The old devil! That upward curve at the corners of his mouth told her that, despite all his feigned reluctance, he knew exactly what he was doing. Men! She'd be lucky if she saw either of them again all evening.

Chapter Twenty-Four

The following Monday morning at what still felt like an abnormally early hour, especially after a weekend in London with Adam, Jamie freewheeled into the open gates of the science park, sprang off his bike and locked it onto one of the metal rails with a hasty click. Didn't want to turn up late in only his second week with the company. He strode in through the sliding doors of the open-plan, glass and steel offices of 3-D Imaging, whistling through his teeth and still unbuckling his cycle helmet as he rehearsed the words of Peter Mowbray's encouraging email in his head. Good old Aurélie! Advising him to contact Peter directly had produced an instant invitation to drive out to Little Downing next weekend. And there was also his upcoming trip to Shere to see Fabian Fairley's collection, which he'd been doing quite a bit of work on lately when he wasn't crouched over the sticks of Esther's brisé fan...

"Hi there, handsome," Karishma hailed him from the maple-veneered reception desk, flashing him a flirtatious smile. "Doing anything tonight?"

Jamie threw her a good-humoured grin and a wave of greeting but headed straight to his desk in the usual corner. Couldn't see himself making out with her. Bit unsubtle in her approach – and seriously fishing for a ring, according to office gossip. What a change of attitude, though, in only three days!

Last Wednesday morning he'd showed up for his first day at the hi-tech computer imaging company and the bubbly Indian secretary had just stared at him blankly when told his name and business, then shrieked out that she'd never have recognised him, he looked so different. She'd then persisted in giggling and making a huge joke of his fading bruises every time she set eyes on him until it started to become rather a drag.

But there was someone else besides Karishma who'd been eyeing him up attentively since his arrival and she was a rather more interesting prospect.

Lucinda Smart was the only female analyst in the company who wasn't plain and drably dressed in ashcan grey. Her glossy, chestnut hair was cropped close to her shapely head and her bright blue eyes, outlined boldly in black, snapped and sparkled as she spoke. She always wore short, tight, black skirts with stylish blouses, bright red nail polish and fingers loaded with heavy gold rings. Jamie had madly fancied her the instant he set eyes on her last summer, but she was several years older than him with a live-in boyfriend and hadn't thrown a single glance in his direction. Probably didn't even notice he was alive – until last week.

Once Lucinda made up her mind, she certainly didn't waste time on boring preliminaries. That evening, as he was trying to finish a report before heading home, she planted herself in a business-like manner on the edge of his desk.

"Now then, Jamie Willett," she announced, swinging her long, tanned legs backwards and forwards right under his nose, "you gonna tell me what's happened to you before I go crazy trying to guess?"

Jamie's heart thumped wildly as her brilliant blue eyes beamed straight into his. In with a chance at last? Couldn't believe his luck. Still, better play it cool. Didn't want to mess up his big break.

"Thought you'd've heard the story by now," he replied, manfully maintaining an air of calm indifference as his dazzled gaze slid up her slender thighs and he struggled to stop his hands from doing likewise. "Things don't usually take long to get round this office.

Had a stupid fight with my best mate and my eye got in the way of his fist –"

"No, no, I don't mean the eye," interrupted Lucinda, "though of course that does add a certain something to your manly charms. I mean everything else."

"Everything else?"

"Ever since I've known you, you've slouched around this office in holed jeans and blond hair almost down to your waist. There was so much metal in your head that you practically jangled – and now just look at you!"

The appreciative glance she swept over him from underneath her thick, black lashes practically melted his legs to jelly. Good thing he was sitting down.

"Oh that," he replied offhandedly. "Guess I grew up. So I got a haircut and bought a few new clothes – that's all."

"It's more than that," she maintained, eyeing him speculatively. "It's like you're wearing a whole new personality. I was watching you all last week and you walk taller, you don't mumble any more, you look people straight in the eye when you're speaking to them and you sound as though you know what you're talking about."

"Perhaps I've got more idea of what I'm talking about than I used to."

"Could be. I like it. In fact I like it so much that I'm just about to break my own golden rule and invite you out on a date. How about coming for a drink with me tonight at a little place I know down by the river?"

"What – me? Now?" Jamie gasped. Was he dreaming?

"Yes, you – now." Lucinda smiled playfully. "I like doing things on the spur of the moment. I'm a very impulsive person. Now log off, there's a darling, 'cos I don't like to be kept waiting."

Jamie hesitated. Why the hell hadn't he brought the car to work?

"Come on," urged Lucinda. "You up for it?"

"It's just that…"

How were they gonna get into town?

"Not tied up in a dreary relationship with some tediously earnest girl, are you?"

"No," he replied honestly. Life since Lindsay had been positively monastic in its seclusion. "But –"

"No buts. Out to my car with you at the double. I like to be in the driving seat. You do just as you're told and everything'll be fine."

She patted his hand and flashed him a blinding smile that revealed two rows of perfectly straight, white teeth.

What choice had he? Jamie logged off in the middle of a word. His head was in such a whirl that he remembered – too late! – that he'd failed to save the last five paragraphs. But this was the chance of a lifetime. Wasn't gonna blow it by giving her time to change her mind.

Lucinda's neat, red convertible was parked just outside. Nice one! Looked barely six months old and boasted a digital cockpit screen, climate and cruise controls, parking sensors and probably every other feature known to modern technology. Jamie breathed a sigh of relief. Thank God he'd biked to work after all! Imagine her face if he'd offered to drive her to town his old banger. Everything was gonna be all right after all…

The red convertible roared towards the city centre at breakneck speed until the rush-hour traffic built up. Then Lucinda switched the radio up full bore and drummed her blood-red fingernails impatiently on the steering wheel. Clearly didn't like people getting in her way…

Jamie had never dared set foot before inside the trendy wine bar she drove to. Way beyond his budget. He almost blanched with horror at the price Lucinda paid for their drinks at the bar. How was he ever gonna afford the second round? He'd have to nurse his beer so at least he wouldn't need a refill. Could probably just stretch to another highball for her.

They sat outside at a tiny, round aluminium table tucked away in one corner of the wooden deck overlooking the river, which was jammed with punts and pleasure boats and even the occasional duck, swimming solemnly down by the anchor rings in the jetty. Opposite, the peaked roof gables and square brick chimneys of Magdalene College rose high above walls of weathered stone and the green summer foliage of willow trees. People strolled past from the ice cream parlour next door and traffic buzzed across the nearby, cast-iron bridge.

Lucinda's eyes gleamed like the evening sunlight glinting on the water.

"Now, Jamie-boy," she invited, leaning forward with an air of flattering attention, "tell me all about what you've been doing since last summer." She crossed her slender legs elegantly and, drawing a cigarette packet out of her tiny, gold-spangled purse, offered it to him.

Jamie reached out from force of habit and suddenly remembered he hadn't smoked in months. In fact he didn't really fancy one. He withdrew his hand with a polite refusal.

"But you smoked last year," pointed out Lucinda. "Don't you like this sort?"

"No, it's not that."

"Haven't given up, have you? Been trying to myself. Very nearly succeeded too, but after I split up with Brad – my old boyfriend, you probably remember him from last summer – I thought 'what the hell!' It was all too depressing for words. So what's your magic secret? How'd you kick the habit?" She lit up and blew a leisurely stream of smoke through her scarlet lips.

"Dunno. S'pose I never really enjoyed it. Got used to doing without when I was in Southeast Asia and we were trekking for days on end in the bush. Then I've been in hospital a couple of times this year, so I guess I haven't got back into the habit again."

"You don't look ill."

"No, I'm not anymore. I caught malaria in the tropics, but I've finally been given the all-clear. Got my discharge from hospital last week."

"Great! I always think being ill's so boring, don't you?"

"Er… yes, actually," agreed Jamie.

So what would Lucinda have done if faced, like Elinor, with a situation like that memorable morning in Adam's flat? Doubt he could've expected too much sympathy from her.

Unaccountably, a shiver tingled through him at the memory of Elinor's cool hands on his burning skin as she cradled him in her arms on the floor.

"I'm never ill myself," Lucinda pressed on. "Reckon a lot of it's just diet-related myself – of course malaria's different, but most people's problems are really just the product of bad lifestyle choices. Don't you agree?"

"Ah – probably…"

An image floated through Jamie's mind of the two vertical creases in Elinor's tense, white brow, illuminated by the silver light of a streetlamp, as she helped him up the front steps of Adam's flat. He thought he'd been too drunk even to notice.

"…I work out at the gym three times a week and I find that and a balanced diet are the best preventives against ill-health. Do you eat vegetarian yourself?"

"Not specially."

Elinor's pitying gaze flaying his very skin raw…

"You should consider it. Of course we'll go veggie tonight."

"Will we?"

Her beautiful, shy eyes with their long, dark lashes…

"I'm sure you wouldn't expect me to sit opposite someone devouring a plateful of ghastly red meat dripping with blood, would you?"

"Er – no. Of course not."

She stubbed out her cigarette butt in the metal ashtray and took a sip of her cranberry highball, inquiring,

"Everything OK? You seem a bit distant."

Her reprimand jerked Jamie's wandering wits to attention like a sharp rap over the knuckles. What was he thinking of, drifting off like that in her company?

Lucinda smiled.

"Need to keep your eye on the ball if you want to score a goal, Jamie-boy. Well, drink up. The night's still young and we've got a lot of catching up to do…"

Lucinda obviously had a mental checklist that she ran through with every man she dated and Jamie soon got the uncomfortable feeling that she was ticking off various boxes as she talked to him, rather like the examiner who'd administered his driving test. She quizzed him on what he did in his spare time, exclaimed how she wished she had all those hours to devote to Classical guitar music and grew enthusiastic when he mentioned the play in Spain.

"I can just see you as some tragic romantic hero: who is it? Romeo? Hamlet?"

"No, I'm actually playing Antipholus."

"Anti-who?"

"Antipholus – of Ephesus and of Syracuse. One of two pairs of twins."

"So what tragedy are we talking here?"

"It's a comedy, not a tragedy. I'm not really the tragic hero type."

"I suppose actors are always temperamental. Me now, I prefer films. Less demanding and so much more naturalistic too."

"Well, yes – but what about the words?"

"The words?"

"When you can hear them, they're usually not up to much."

"Who cares about words anyway? I prefer actions – they speak so much more clearly, don't you think?"

"I suppose so – sometimes, but –"

"Now you aren't going to maunder on all night about words, are you? Would've thought you'd have other things on your mind. You ever gonna finish that beer? You can drink as much as you like, you know – after all, I'm driving…"

A razor-sharp vision suddenly flashed across his mind of what sex with Lucinda would be like. She was so efficient and managerial about everything else that he'd never be able to stage a satisfactory performance.

By the time they left the riverside bar, the sun was sinking over Magdalene's rooftops and the shadows of the willow trees were lengthening across the gently lapping water. Jamie felt famished. He'd tried to ease the sharpest pangs of hunger with a packet of crisps, but they were so over-priced that he hadn't bought a second one, and so salty they made him feel even thirstier.

Luckily it was time for dinner. Things'd look up now. The vegetarian restaurants he knew in Cambridge were cheap, so he could afford to make a grand gesture and offer to pay for the meal. Lucinda accepted without hesitation and marched him off at the double to her 'favourite veggie'.

The prices they charged here for glorified celery sticks and cabbage leaves! But what could he do except smile and kiss goodbye to practically half a week's wages? The tofu and bean sprouts almost stuck in his throat. Galling as it was to have to admit it, he was simply not in this league.

Lucinda seemed not to notice. Too busy talking about her summer holiday plans of baking on a white beach in the blazing sun for a fortnight with a blockbuster paperback or two…

How odd that these stark, white brick walls, glossy, lime green vinyl floors and hard, wire-woven chairs should set him thinking about the noisy Italian restaurant under the railway arches in London where Elinor had politely gone thirds with him and Adam on a cheap Italian meal. What had she really thought about it all? He'd no idea.

After dinner, he and Lucinda went dancing. Normally this would've been the highlight of the evening. But Lucinda's pet nightclub boasted doormen in black ties and dinner suits, crystal chandeliers and mirrored walls reflecting corridors of faux marble Venuses. Water jets played in gilded scallop shell fountains. More fistfuls of cash down the drain. A hot sweat broke out on his top lip. In a single night he was blowing what he usually lived on for a month – or even longer…

His chances of featuring as a long-term fixture in Lucinda's life were fading fast, to judge by the tone in which she referred to his 'eccentric' interest in obscure Shakespearean comedies, classical guitar and fans, which he'd mentioned more than once when she seemed under the impression they were talking about computers. But she still appeared keen not to waste the effort she'd already spent on him that evening.

She clearly enjoyed dancing and, as they languidly circled the floor, Jamie gave up all hope of concealing how desperately he was interested in one thing at least. She seemed to find this highly amusing and drew one teasing fingertip down the side of his neck and along his left shoulder blade so he could feel its pressure like a slender pinpoint of flame through the thin fabric of his shirt. His brain reeled as the room spun dizzily around him. His attraction to her was merely skin deep. He couldn't possibly afford to fund a relationship with her on a permanent basis. The whole thing was doomed to disaster, but…

But it'd been months since he and Lindsay split up. It wasn't as though he was doing any harm either – even if it turned out to be no more than a one-night stand. Brad was well and truly out of the picture after transferring to their Edinburgh offices and Lucinda herself was a woman of the world. She knew the score, or she wouldn't've been sparkling up into his eyes and swaying provocatively against his hips like this.

Why fight it? Easier just to play along, he decided, sinking unsteadily back down at the marble-topped table to order one last drink before they drove to Lucinda's flat. Perhaps another beer would shore up his ramshackle courage…

And then a most extraordinary thing happened.

The suave Italian waiter came gliding over with a silver tray bearing his glass of beer and a fancy cocktail for Lucinda and set them down on the tabletop in front of him.

Jamie stared rather hazily at the cocktail, a frothy concoction of lime juice, passion fruit syrup and blood-red grenadine in a tall glass with a sugar-frosted rim, tinkling with ice cubes and decorated with orange slices and a maraschino cherry. On top perched a pleated cockade of fragile, peach-and-white-striped paper.

Lucinda pulled off the miniature fan and tossed it carelessly aside. But Jamie's eyes followed it, as it skittered across the table's smooth, hard surface. After a moment, he leaned over and, picking it up between finger and thumb, stared at it in silent surprise.

Through the mists that fuddled his inner eye, there surfaced a clear image of Elinor's face casually raised to him when he'd fitted her glasses back on that morning in Adam's kitchen. Down his spine shivered a tremor like the one that'd thrilled through him when he accidentally grazed her skin with his hand.

Hadn't thought about it since, but now it shot across his memory like a lightning bolt across the midnight sky, illuminating his present behaviour in all its sordid ugliness.

He gulped, shocked into sudden sobriety.

"I think it's time to go home," Lucinda shouted above the blaring music, as she finished her cocktail.

Jamie started violently.

"Yeah, I think you're probably right," he replied, tucking the peach fan into his breast pocket as he rose from the table. "I'll walk you to the car."

"Aren't you coming with me?" queried Lucinda, clearly disconcerted.

"Only as far as the carpark. It's not much out of my way."

"But I thought –"

"I'm heading home."

"At least let me drop you off."

"No, I prefer the exercise."

Lucinda looked too stunned to argue.

They walked in silence to the car and Lucinda drove off, leaving him to make his way back along the river alone.

It was not yet quite dark and the twilight enveloped him like a grey velvet wrap, soft and shimmering, with a single star, brighter than all the rest, hanging out of reach above the treetops before his dismayed eyes.

At first he strode along at a hot pace, furious with himself for passing up an entirely legitimate chance to score. But little by little he began to walk off his rage. Why couldn't he damned well behave the way he used to? What had stripped him of his manhood and his pride? By the time he drew level with the Bell Jar Café, he knew.

At the footbridge across the river, he paused to lean over the parapet and gaze down into the inky black waters slipping silently past beneath. Almost unconsciously he drew the small, ornamental fan out of his breast pocket and examined it in the lamplight. How beautiful Elinor had looked on that heady, moonlit night when he'd invited her on the spur of the moment to go to the Spanish guitar gig. He smiled to himself.

Of course he'd gone to bed before with girls like Lindsay and Lucinda, because he'd no idea there was anything better. But now he refused to settle for any woman except the one he really wanted.

Yet Elinor was a star quite out of his sphere. Think how much more education and experience she possessed than him. She was a woman, while he was still just a pathetic boy. How could he ever provoke the interest of this lady of unfolding rainbows, this slim-waisted Spanish señorita, this fairy-tale princess in her high ivory tower? She'd never mentioned it, but for all he knew, she might have a man in tow already.

Still, he couldn't give up without trying his luck. Faint heart never won fair lady. For a start, she quite enjoyed his company. She'd said so when they were walking back along the river after the guitar gig. Many men started out from even less. But he couldn't just spin her the usual line: she was far too sophisticated for that. Needed to up his game by quite a way…

He stood for a long time on the bridge, slowly twirling the paper cockade between his fingers and deliberating where to go from here. After all, he did hold a couple of useful, fan-shaped cards in his hand. Last Friday night, after sorting out John's computer problems, he and Elinor had triumphantly screwed the rivet back into Bea's finished fan. But he'd still need to go and pick it up from her after it'd been professionally photographed. And if he slaved every night this week to finish Esther's repair job, then its return would act as the perfect excuse to see Elinor again next weekend before he left for Spain…

Chapter Twenty-Five

Mum had caught one of her periodic spring-cleaning fevers. It didn't happen too often, but while it was raging, anyone with any sense fled, like Dad and Geoff, who'd seized the excuse of a Sunday afternoon lecture on evolution at the Science Centre after dropping Bea off at a rehearsal for her end-of-term concert. To the unlucky ones left behind like Jamie, who'd finally surfaced for lunch from the complex task of re-ribboning the cleaned and polished sticks of Esther's fan, the house had become an obstacle course: stacks of books piled on steps, armchairs blocking the door of the living room and the vacuum cleaner squatting malevolently in the hall, on the alert for its next victim as he returned upstairs to inspect his handiwork…

"OUCH!" he yelled, stumbling against its sharp plastic edge in an effort to avoid the large cardboard box lurking at the foot of the stairs. He stooped to rub his barked shin ruefully. What was this stupid old thing doing here anyway? He aimed a kick at the offending box, but only succeeded in stubbing his toe on the newel post instead.

But hey! Hang on a minute. He examined the box more closely. Wasn't that the one Mum had brought back from Great Aunt Rosita's flat after she died, where they'd found Bea's old fan? Now that reminded him…

Forgetting the pain of his injury, he sank down on the bottom step, pulled open the flaps of the box and began foraging around inside.

There was a clatter of footsteps on the stairs.

"What're you lookin' for?"

Glancing up absently, Jamie caught sight of Marc regarding him with curious eyes.

"Just some old letters I've been meaning to read for ages. I *think* they're somewhere in here."

"Better be careful," retorted Marc smartly. "Your brain might short out."

Jamie pulled a face at him.

At that moment the phone rang.

"Jamie! Marc!" called out Mum's voice from the kitchen. "Can one of you get that, please? I'm up to my elbows in water."

"You do it," Jamie ordered.

"No, you. You're older."

"You're closer…"

The phone kept on ringing. Finally Marc gave in and picked his way towards the sitting room to answer it, grumbling furiously under his breath.

Jamie returned to the contents of the cardboard box. Those old letters of Great Aunt Rosita's would be just the thing to check the progress he was making in reading real Spanish after six improver lessons at the language centre.

Meanwhile Marc's voice drifted to his ears through the open living room door.

"Good afternoon," he heard him say in unusually polite and formal tones. Must be up to something. Well, it was probably a call centre – they deserved everything they got. Marc allowed the person on the other end no time to respond before announcing, "This is Greenwich Royal Observatory. Are you ringing in response to our national survey?"

The unknown caller apparently made the expected reply, disclaiming all knowledge of any national survey. Jamie sniggered to himself. It was always fun hearing Marc spin people a line. How inventive he was!

"Are you sure you're not interested in the survey?" Marc persisted with deliberate obtuseness. "It wouldn't take more than a few minutes of your time to explain the significance of our work…"

The unknown caller seemed to be struggling against the tide of Marc's creativity but was inevitably borne down as Marc launched into a detailed account of the observatory's work. How long would it be before they realised they weren't getting anywhere and rang off?

Jamie began to lose interest. He bent his head back over the box and resumed what he was doing. But as he pulled out handfuls of old photos, he could hear Marc's voice still droning on, asking the caller if they'd be willing to volunteer their house as a viewpoint for the comet which was currently visible in the late-night sky. They must have incredible patience to go on listening to all this garbage. Oh well, none of his business… He returned to the box.

A few moments later, the conversation finally ended and he heard the beep as Marc replaced the handset. Then the living room door opened and footsteps came thumping back along the hall. Jamie automatically shifted aside so Marc could squeeze by.

"Is there really a comet visible in the sky at the moment?" he inquired in passing.

"'Course there is. D'you think I'd go round tellin' lies?'"

"One day you'll get into big trouble with these joke calls of yours," Jamie warned as Marc began scaling the stairs two at a time.

"Rubbish," Marc retorted. "Reckon I ought to be paid for public service, givin' these sad, old people somethin' to think about for a change. That guy I was talkin' to jus' now, for instance."

"You'll probably end up in massive debt," taunted Jamie patronisingly. "Anyway, it's not fair to string call centre operators along when you've no intention of buying whatever they're trying to sell you."

"Why not?" demanded Marc. "Anyway, it wasn't a call centre. It was some dude called John Mitford, askin' to speak to you."

"WHAT!" Jamie shot to his feet. "That's Elinor's dad. What'd he want?"

"How would I know? Didn' give him a chance to say. But he's pretty cool. Really interested in our work at the observatory —"

"You – YOU…!" spluttered Jamie. What a mess! How could he possibly ring back after that and find out why Elinor's dad had really called?

As if in answer to his question, the phone rang again.

Marc turned back downstairs with a gleeful glint in his eye.

What if it was Elinor's dad again?

Jamie elbowed roughly past him. The phone kept on trilling.

"Will you get that, Marc?" roared Mum from the kitchen.

"Sure will," yelled back Marc, shoving Jamie out of the way.

The two of them wrestled furiously to reach the phone first. But Jamie was stronger and prepared to be ruthless, even though Marc, who had tumbled over in the scuffle, was hanging onto one ankle in an effort to trip him up.

"Hello," gasped Jamie breathlessly, snatching up the phone and turning a grin of triumph upon his fallen foe.

"Hello," responded a cultured male voice. John Mitford for sure. "Is this the Willett household?"

"Yes," breathed Jamie, holding the handset as high as he could since Marc was leaping up and down like a puppy trying to wrest a stick out of his grasp.

"This is John Mitford speaking, Elinor's father."

"Yes – of course." Jamie switched the phone to his other hand, clamping his palm over the mouthpiece and hissing at Marc in savage undertones, "Look, I'm gonna throttle you, if you don't stop it!"

"Is there some kind of emergency in your household?" exclaimed John guilelessly.

"No – not at all," pretended Jamie, aiming a casual kick at Marc that sent him hopping down the hall clutching his ankle and yelping in exaggerated pain. "What can I do for you?" Good, he was off to whinge to Mum. That'd keep him out of the way for a minute or two!

"I was just wondering if you could possibly drop round sometime. I'd like to know how to do a spreadsheet."

Just the excuse he was looking for!

"No problem. When're you free?" Jamie asked.

They arranged for him to call round later that evening and John was clearly about to ring off when he suddenly remarked,

"You know, I've just had the most interesting chat."

"Oh really?" queried Jamie, stifling the urge to laugh. Better feign ignorance.

"Yes – I tried ringing you just now, but I clearly reached the wrong number because I ended up speaking to this extraordinary young man at – of all places! – the Royal Observatory in Greenwich. He sounded hardly more than a teenager. Shows just how old I'm getting, doesn't it? Anyway, he was telling me all about this national survey they're conducting at the moment and about people volunteering their houses as viewpoints for some comet that's currently visible in the late-night sky. I suppose your younger brother – Marcus, is it? – wouldn't be interested in taking part, would he?"

Jamie cringed. Suppose he'd better come clean, despite the huge embarrassment.

"Look, I'm terribly sorry," he began. "It actually *was* my younger brother, Marcus, on the phone just now playing one of his stupid jokes. I think he thought you were a call centre."

"Oh – oh, I see." In fact, John sounded more disappointed than angry. "So that means there's no national survey after all?"

"No. I'm so sorry." Jamie winced and pulled a face. "But I do know there's a comet visible in the night sky at present."

What had Marc's stupidity done to his chances of getting in with Elinor's dad? Back to zero – if not negative numbers. He'd murder him for this!

"I suppose Marcus's not still around, is he?" went on John unexpectedly.

"Well… yeah. I think he's out in the kitchen. I could put him on, if you like, so he could apologise in person."

"There's no need for that. You know, it's just occurred to me that Elinor's office window, being four floors up, affords an excellent view of the Cambridge night sky. I know how interested Marcus is in astronomy and I was just wondering if he'd like to come over with you and bring his telescope, so I could take a look at that comet too."

Jamie spotted his chance. Time Marc had a dose of his own medicine. Nice to watch him squirm for a change. And here he was, right on cue, with Mum not far behind, wearing her scolding face.

"He's just coming back up the hall now. I'll put him on."

And Jamie pushed the phone into Marc's reluctant hand with a self-satisfied smirk.

"Now what's this Marc's been telling me –?" began Mum.

"Shh! You can bawl me out in a second, Ma," hissed Jamie in a warning undertone, "but just lemme listen to this first."

He leant up against the newel post in the attitude of one preparing to enjoy the spectacle of well-deserved retribution. Let's hear Marc talk his way out of this one! Or at least trying to wriggle out of entertaining an elderly Cambridge don for an evening.

His face gradually fell. From what he could gather, though hearing only half the conversation, the pair of them were soon chatting away like best mates about astronomy and telescopes and transits of Mercury and Venus. Damn! His plan had completely backfired.

After a while he lost interest in his own discomfiture and turned to Mum, only to find she'd disappeared. Must be in the living room. Carefully avoiding the vacuum cleaner this time, he stuck his head round the door. There she was on her hands and knees, burrowing around like mole beside the sofa.

"Oh, Jamie – it's you," she exclaimed, looking up.

"He deserved it!" Jamie plunged into his own self-defence before she could mount an attack. "And I didn't kick him nearly as hard as he made out."

"Physical chastisement is never justified," retorted Mum sanctimoniously.

"Yeah – in the case of human beings maybe."

"Your little brother's just as human as you are. I'm not prepared to argue this point. Now give me a hand to shift the sofa out from under the window. I want to vacuum round it."

"Sure thing, Ma," he replied, to smooth her ruffled feathers.

"So who's Marc talking to?" she asked as they each took hold of opposite ends of the sofa and lifted it together.

"Elinor's father. He must be desperate for company."

"Don't be so disparaging. Marc has some interesting ideas if you get him on a good day…"

As they tried to lift the sofa away from the wall, it resisted their efforts.

"I think there's something caught round the legs," said Jamie, setting down his end. "Hang on. I'll see what it is."

He crouched down and peered behind it.

"Goodness," exclaimed Mum, looking over the back of the couch. "What's this old blanket doing here? It's covered in dust."

"Must've been there for ages. Last time I remember seeing it was when I first came home from hospital."

Casting his mind back, Jamie recalled Adam picking it up off the sofa and dumping it on the floor to give him room to sit down that evening when they'd found the old fan. Must've ended up under the sofa…

Mum reached over to seize the patchwork blanket and a whole heap of papers slid out onto the floor.

"Great Aunt Rosita's letters," exclaimed Jamie, pouncing on them eagerly. "I've been wondering where they'd got to." Now Esther's fan was finished, he could settle down for a good read.

Mum gave the blanket a thorough shake. Dust rose in a cloud.

"Ugh! Straight into the wash with this."

"What's that?" demanded Jamie suddenly, spotting a slip of paper fluttering to the floor. He reached over to pick it up.

Looked old, to judge by the spidery handwriting and the browned edges. It triggered a sudden replay of memory within him. In his mind's eye, he saw the red fan case splitting apart and falling onto the sofa, while a piece of paper drifted down into the folds of the blanket.

He turned it over wonderingly in his fingers. "It must've fallen out of the fan case."

"What's the writing say?" asked Mum with interest.

Jamie stared at it intently. The handwritten note was in Spanish.

"Something about being a treasured gift from someone called Lav – Is it Lavender F –?"

"No, that's an 'i' – it's Lavinia," broke in Mum, peering over his shoulder. "Perhaps it's connected with the original owner of the fan. Wonder how old it is."

"It'll certainly interest Elinor. I remember her asking when we first met if there was any card enclosed with the fan to help give some idea of its context. Hey, perhaps she'd be interested to see it when I go round to visit her dad this evening –"

"Not much chance of that," interrupted Marc's voice from the doorway.

Jamie turned quickly.

"Why not?" he enquired.

"'Cos he was sayin' she left for Spain this mornin'." Marc smirked and pulled a taunting face. "Hey, c'n I come over with you tonight?" he went on. "Bring my telescope to look through their attic window. Geoff's been round to see their wildlife pond and he's goin' back again too. Don't see why he should have all the fun…"

Chapter Twenty-Six

The late morning sunshine was already baking hot and Jamie's backpack felt a dead weight on his aching shoulders. Runnels of sweat were trickling under his armpits and between his shoulder blades and his damp hair clung clammily to the back of his neck. But he knew where he was going – well, more or less – because of the map on the crumpled, red and black fan-shaped card that he'd pocketed on the spur of the moment in Elinor's office the other day and which he now held in one hand with his phone in the other.

He glanced ahead at the fantasy of stone pinnacles and spiked turrets piercing a cloudless blue sky. Now if this was the cathedral, then that tall tower must be La Giralda. So the Alcazar would clearly lie in the opposite direction…

Turning round, he found himself face to face with towering walls of solid stone, fortified by impregnable defence towers and topped with rugged castellations. The only entrance appeared to be through that red archway over there, which was guarded by a painted lion fiercely trampling a blue and green flag beneath his shaggy paws.

But a line of bored-looking tourists in shorts and sun hats straggled desultorily away from the gate over the entire length of the hot, paved courtyard. It'd be well after lunch by the time he even reached the entrance. Jamie shaded his eyes to consult the fan card in more detail. By the look of this, the exhibition was taking place at the rear of the Alcazar, so perhaps he should ask if there was a back entrance.

He approached the patient-looking guard, who stood checking tickets, and mustered his best accent to ask the way to the fan exhibition. The guard pointed in the opposite direction. So back he trudged the way he'd come and round the forbidding walls beneath the pitiless rays of the blazing sun. Had this been such a good idea after all?

The knowledge that Elinor had left the country instantly lit a burning fever in him to see her again. He lay awake at night aching to feast his eyes on her face, throw himself at her feet and pour out all the passion that was surging around inside him. It'd all seemed simple enough at home when he'd been checking distances and train timetables on his phone and realised that Seville was just a couple of hours further down the line from where he was heading to the play festival at Almagro.

But now it felt very different. All that time spent working out how to reach the Alcazar on unfamiliar bus routes, being jolted along amidst a babble of foreign languages and jostled by crowds of indifferent Sevillans busy with their daily lives…

Finally he caught sight of another gateway in the massive curtain wall and emerged through it into a dazzling square of white-washed façades, which enclosed a sandy courtyard planted with rows of ornamental orange trees. Squinting beyond the reflections in his phone screen, he realised that the golden-yellow building directly opposite must be the Apeadero. Dusty, thirsty and exhausted, he plunged into its welcoming shade.

After draining his water bottle dry, he drew one sweaty forearm over his damp lips and peered around. By now his eyes had adjusted to the interior gloom and he soon spotted a teenager in black with spiky blue hair and a row of silver ear studs loitering among the arcades of double pillars, idly handing out leaflets to tourists leaving the palace. As he picked his way over the patterned cobblestones, he recognised these as black and red fan cards identical to the one he carried. Must be approaching his goal.

The bored student noticed the card in his hand and waved him in the direction of a nearby entrance.

Finally reaching the top of the stairs, Jamie glanced inside the open door. Ahead of him lay a dim room of shining glass cases filled with fans spreading their lace and gauze pleats wide beneath the lights. The exhibition had opened at the beginning of the week and was packed with tourists visiting the Alcazar. But there was no sign of Elinor.

Jamie's heart sank. After all this effort! But then, he reasoned harshly with himself, since she didn't know he was coming, he couldn't very well expect her to be waiting at the door to greet him, could he? He gazed around.

At this point a shapely young woman in a blue sheath dress approached him with a purposeful light in her dark eyes. Her smooth black hair was parted in the centre and pinned into a high bun with a red carnation.

"May I be of assistance to you?" she asked – or, at least, he thought she asked – in Spanish with the utmost politeness, light gleaming on the diamond droplets in her ears as she raised her hand to gesture behind him.

Jamie glanced round. There was nobody there.

"Your backpack," she persisted with a courteous but determined smile. "Would you care to leave it at the desk before you enter the exhibition, sir?"

"What? Oh – that," stammered Jamie, suddenly reminded of its bulky weight. "Actually I haven't come to see the exhibition," he went on, "but a friend. Her name's Elinor Mitford."

Her face lit up. She clearly recognised the name.

"Ah yees. Dr Elinor," she cried in English that was even less fluent than his Spanish. "Thees way please."

Jamie's spirits leapt. So she was here! Next minute, he'd actually see her. His heart thumped wildly in his chest – so loudly that his guide must surely hear it.

But the young woman continued to lead him, unmoved, towards a tall, wooden door in a side passage, then stood aside, leaving him to make his own way inside.

As he knocked, Jamie glanced through the open door into a cool, high-ceilinged room, hoping to catch sight of Elinor at last. Instead he met the enquiring gaze of a pair of intelligent black eyes belonging to a handsome Spaniard seated at the desk inside the door. He was in – say – his early to mid-thirties with a tanned, olive complexion, dark hair springing from a high forehead and neatly clipped moustache and beard. Dressed in an open-necked red shirt and elegantly tailored beige trousers, he radiated an air of unmistakable sophistication and self-assurance.

Jamie enquired in his best Spanish if he knew where Elinor was.

The man replied that she wasn't there.

What a let-down! Naïvely, he'd just assumed she'd be somewhere around the building. Should've texted to check instead of showing up out of the blue to surprise her like this. What was he going to do now?

"Excuse me, please, a moment," continued the man in well-spoken, formal English, rising from his chair. "Are you perhaps a friend of Elinor's, visiting from Great Britain?"

Turning back to survey the deep-voiced stranger more hopefully, Jamie nodded.

"Although at present she is not here, she will return."

Jamie's hopes rekindled.

"Soon?" he asked.

"She is gone to deliver a talk on the exhibition to a group of our colleagues more than an hour ago. She will be back –" he glanced at his gold watch "– in not too long a time, I think."

"Really? Oh well, I'll wait for her then – if that's OK?"

"By all means. Set down your heavy backpack – just by the desk here will be well. Come, let me help you," rising hospitably to help him shrug off the straps, an action that wafted a subtle scent of designer aftershave to Jamie's nostrils. Jamie saw him cast a dubious glance at the battered, old, red rucksack, which had been inter-railing several times around Europe with him as well as all the way to Southeast Asia last year and had clearly seen better days, covered as it was with a thick layer of grimy dust. For the first time he felt embarrassed to realise how many of the grubby badges stuck all over it were torn or half-hanging off and how clumsily that broken strap had been fastened on with a safety pin.

The older man must have felt that he was staring impolitely so he shifted his gaze to Jamie's face.

"And now will you permit me to introduce myself?" he offered. "My name is Andrés de Ceballos."

"Pleased to meet you," replied Jamie, shaking Andrés' lean, well-manicured hand and introducing himself in return. They regarded each other in silence for a moment and then Andrés went on courteously,

"You are perhaps one of the family of Elinor, who travels through Spain on holiday?"

"More of a friend really. I live in Cambridge too."

"Ah yes, Cambridge! I am visiting there myself on several occasions. It is very charming – the colleges, the King's Chapel, the river… the – the Backs – is not that how you call them?"

"Yeah, that's right."

"Are you perhaps studying at the university?"

"No – Cambridge is where I live."

"I see. Oh please, do sit down."

"Just here?" enquired Jamie, indicating the only vacant chair in the room beside the second desk.

"Yes, that is well." Andrés nodded.

Jamie's eyes strayed over the desk, on which rested a neat pile of square, mauve cards. In front of the plastic desk tidy lay a pencil adorned with fans that exactly matched the cylindrical pen holder on

Elinor's desk in the Lydgate Museum. If only he dared pick up the object that her hand must've touched. But with Andrés looking on, shyness prevented him.

"It is the desk of Elinor," Andrés went on with a light of unmistakable respect in his eyes. "I must tell you what an honour it is to have this close relationship with such a scholarly young woman."

Jamie's eyes narrowed. So exactly what kind of 'close relationship' was he referring to here?

"And it has also been my privilege to escort her to many formal dinners and other entertainments during her stay here in Sevilla. You must understand that she and I are old friends. We have known each other well when I lived in London and studied for a higher degree at the Courtauld Institute. And she came also to stay with me when she was in Spain last summer, making various arrangements for this exhibition."

"I remember her mentioning it."

"I have visited briefly with her and her father too in March when I last attended a conference in Cambridge. They have a delightful house so near the city centre."

"Yeah, it's pretty fancy."

So he knew her well enough to stay at the Mitfords' own home...

"I myself prefer to live mostly at an old family property out in the countryside where there is more room to breathe fresh air," Andrés went on.

"Must be a pain commuting in every day," suggested Jamie, thinking of the heavy Cambridge traffic.

A slight frown of perplexity appeared between Andrés' dark brows until he realised what Jamie meant.

"Ah, certainly it would be, but fortunately I also keep an apartment here in Sevilla where I stay during the week time."

Two residences. And one of them sounded practically like a country estate. Must be pretty well off then.

"Do you work here in the Alcazar?" asked Jamie, clearing his throat, which had suddenly grown tight and uncomfortable.

"Yes, from time to time. It is my great privilege to be in charge of mounting temporary exhibitions here in the Réal Alcazar, but also I am lecturing on the History of Art in the Faculty of Geography and History at the university."

"I see," murmured Jamie.

Pretty important-sounding academic position too.

"So you can now understand why I have been working so closely with Elinor. It is much labour mounting an exhibition, even one of this comparatively small size. It has involved numerous communications and we have spent many hours arranging everything even as far as the wording of the exhibit labels. Elinor is very thorough, as well as being personally so charming."

Jamie agreed with a rather sickly smile. It was pretty obvious what this Andrés guy was trying to tell him – ever so politely of course.

"Do you have some interest in fans yourself, señor?" Andrés enquired.

"A bit," Jamie confessed, lowering his eyes so as not to meet Andrés' pitying gaze. Not that he could boast much knowledge compared with this expert company.

"Then perhaps you might like to look through our exhibition while you wait for Elinor to return. It is full of fans of the greatest beauty of eighteenth and nineteenth century Spain."

"Yeah, perhaps I will," agreed Jamie, toying with the pile of mauve cards on the desk to occupy himself somehow.

At that moment the young woman, who had shown Jamie in, put her head around the door.

"Andrés…"

"Si?" Andrés looked up.

As they spoke together, Jamie realised that someone had arrived to see Andrés.

"Si, si… Excuse me." He turned back to Jamie. "I must leave you now for a time. Please to make yourself at home. I am sure that Elinor will return at any moment." He rose and left the room.

But Elinor did not return at any moment.

Jamie despatched a quick text in case he could locate her that way and settled down to wait for the reply. Might take a while, since she was unlikely to respond if she was in the middle of a talk.

At first his eyes strayed around the rough, ochre walls examining bold coloured posters of previous exhibitions: of glazed blue and yellow maiolica, fine lace mantillas and stately nineteenth century court dress.

Then he picked up one of the thin mauve cards from the desk and idly scanned its contents. A cursory glance showed that it was a flyer for the series of talks and activities accompanying the exhibition.

The other side, which was lime green, carried an advert for the exhibition catalogue. After a minute or two he fell to amusing himself by pleating its mauve side into a fan shape. Hmm… reminded him of something he used to fold out of origami paper as a kid. Hadn't made one for years. It was quite complex too. Could he remember how it went? You had to be absolutely precise about getting all the folds even or else the whole thing looked lop-sided.…

As he sat folding the lime green side of a second flyer into a bird base, he was thinking hard.

Why had he come here? It'd seemed a brilliant idea on the spur of the moment, after realising that he had half a day in hand before being due to meet Adam and the rest of the crowd at Almagro. He had entertained visions of breezing into the exhibition, catching Elinor totally by surprise, sweeping her off for lunch at a white-clothed table in one of those patio restaurants he'd glimpsed from the bus, overshaded by myrtle and twining, white jasmine. While a carved stone fountain splashed water droplets over blue and yellow painted floor tiles, he'd have dazzled her with the newly discovered note, plied her with a glass or two of wine to soften her up and then sprung on her an invitation to the play that she wouldn't have the heart to turn down. But his whole plan had misfired. Elinor wasn't here and nobody seemed sure when she'd be back. So what was he gonna do?

By now he'd finished the bird base, so he neatly slipped the doubled fan into it to form the tail and perched the resulting green and mauve peacock on top of the pile of cards. No response to his text message yet. Guess he might as well fill in some waiting time by taking a look at the fans out there.

He left his rucksack propped against Elinor's desk and headed out to make a circuit of the exhibition. Pacing the stone-paved floor with his hands plunged deep in his jeans pockets, he peered over other people's shoulders into the lighted glass cases. In one he caught sight of a fan brightly painted with a fiesta of striped tents and fluttering flags, horses in coloured trappings, soldiers in braided jackets and high boots, women in mantillas and fringed shawls and even a matador in gold and scarlet puffing out his chest with pride. Nearby glowed a golden Isabelino fan with carved and decorated sticks. Here lay a grisaille leaf delicately engraved with galloping horses and there one painted in gouache with an impressive baroque palace and mounted on gleaming mother-of-pearl sticks… But – was that

Elinor over there, just entering behind that wrinkled old man with a stick? He strained his eyes to check, but then his tensed shoulders slumped. No. Just a woman who looked a bit like her.

His gaze roved over the cases and suddenly he realised he was taking none of this in. Ordinarily he would've been excited by this chance to cram his senses with so many spectacular fans of ivory, lace, tortoiseshell, wood, chicken skin. But it was difficult to concentrate on their shimmering beauty when he was so on edge and every moment glancing up to see if Elinor had arrived yet. What was he gonna say to her anyway? Perhaps she'd already returned while he was busy studying the fans. Better go back to the office to check.

But the office was still empty and there'd been no reply to his text. She might've gone anywhere after her talk and he could end up waiting around the entire afternoon without getting to see her. She mightn't even come back today, despite what Andrés had said.

By now he'd begun to feel a hollow void in the pit of his stomach. It was getting late and he needed something to eat. Better leave a note telling her where he'd gone, in case she showed up before he got back.

He seized the pencil lying on her desk and rifled through one of the drawers for a spare sheet of paper. Sitting down on her chair, he began scrawling a note to say he'd called by in passing to show her something interesting he'd found and ask her to the play festival at Almagro but –

All of a sudden he stopped writing.

Who was he kidding? Why not just admit what a stupid idea this'd been. He knew the score. Andrés looked like the handsome hero of a romantic movie. He had a doctoral degree, a settled academic career, a designer wardrobe and at least two residences.

He himself turned up lacking a permanent address or any form of job stability, with holes in his jeans and a tatty T-shirt stinking of sweat, covered in stubble like a tramp after sleeping rough on trains for a couple of days and even last night in the station at Madrid. Why wouldn't she be more horrified than pleased to see him? It'd all been a big mistake. Should've known better than to waste so much time and effort.

Savagely he screwed up his unfinished note and pitched it into the wastepaper bin beside the desk.

What time was it? He checked his phone. Almost three o'clock. Might as well head back to the station, where he could pick up something to eat and catch the next train heading north to Ciudad Real.

Rising decisively, he hoisted the heavy rucksack onto his shoulders and strode out of the office without a backward glance.

Chapter Twenty-Seven

Elinor arrived back at the Alcazar shortly after three o'clock. The talk had gone off well enough: mostly elderly women, keen to fill up long days of retirement, and earnest young university students, pressured into attending a foreign paper by their professors in a bid to improve their English language skills. But the lunch afterwards had been interminable and she'd only just managed to escape.

Hot and sticky despite the air-conditioned taxi ride, she took a shortcut up the back stairs, pulling off her sunglasses and the gold Klimt scarf Jamie had given her months ago. On impulse she'd brought it with her to Seville and worn it today for the first time with her red dress in an effort to brighten herself up. Might as well not have bothered. The museum might've changed location and the people spoken a different language, but basically it was just the same old routine. Earnest university academics, rich, elderly businessmen desperate to be charmed into sponsoring arts events, a promising young barrister, the top of whose head reached about the level of her shoulder… So much for Cathy urging her to start living and find a new man!

When she walked back into the exhibition office, it was empty. But what was that smell? She wrinkled up her nose at the faint whiff of sweat and dust that hung in the still, close air. Odd. Quite unlike Andrés' clean, pine-fragranced aftershave. Who'd been in this room?

She dropped her handbag and folder of notes unceremoniously on the chair and was just tossing her sunglasses onto the desk when something caught her eye. Upside down, as if hastily knocked off the pile of flyers that she'd left out to deal with on her return, lay a mauve and green paper peacock. The scarf slid unheeded from her fingers as she picked up the peacock to examine it more closely.

Its head, body and spindly legs had been skilfully fashioned out of the lime green side of one of the flyers and the spreading tail by doubling a mauve concertina into the shape of a fan. She regarded it in puzzlement. Who could've left it? Andrés? Most unlikely. He wasn't into origami, so far as she knew. So how had it got there? Someone other than Andrés had clearly been at this desk.

"Elinor! At last," exclaimed a man's voice from the doorway.

Elinor jerked up her head. It was Andrés.

"How late you are returned," he observed, entering the office. "I am wondering what has become of you after so long."

"Oh I stayed for lunch," she replied, fingering the peacock thoughtfully. "They wouldn't hear of me leaving before."

"And how was your paper received? I truly regret that my meeting here prevented me from attending the talk."

Elinor replied briefly. Then she held up the paper peacock and asked if he knew anything about it.

At first Andrés regarded it blankly, but after a moment it seemed to prompt his memory.

"Of course! It must be left by the young man from England who is wanting to see you. Naturally I told him where you were gone and he was waiting here for your return. He came from Cambridge, he said."

"A young man from Cambridge – to see me?"

Elinor raised her eyebrows. What young man from Cambridge did she know who'd be in Spain, smelling of sweat and folding paper peacocks?

"Jamie," she guessed aloud.

"Yes, that was his name," confirmed Andrés.

"Whatever's he doing here?" Seville was a long way south of the play festival at Almagro.

"He said nothing of his purpose to me. Perhaps you should enquire it of him yourself."

"Do you know where he is?"

Andrés shook his head, adding,

"However, I did suggest he might like to view the exhibition. Is he not still there?"

Sounded a likely place to find a fan fancier like Jamie. True, she hadn't noticed him when she was passing by a minute ago, but then she'd come in the back way, hadn't she?

"About how long ago was this?" she asked.

"Hmm..." Andrés consulted his watch. "Maybe an hour. Maybe longer."

"Thanks, Andrés. I'll go and see if he's still out there."

Elinor perched the paper peacock on top of the pile of flyers and set off to look for Jamie. How good to see a familiar face from home! She'd met a lot of strangers over the last ten days since arriving in Seville. But why had he come all the way here? Some emergency with Dad? Still in that case, surely she'd've had a call from Cathy or Nick. Had he made some discovery connected with Bea's fan? Then why not text or email? Funny him just turning up out of the blue like this...

She searched among the lighted exhibition cases for Jamie's tall, rangy figure in the milling crowds. No luck. Perhaps he'd got hungry, as usual, and headed off for a bite to eat.

So she made her way along the café terrace overlooking the formal gardens of clipped hedges and tall, feathery palm trees, that throbbed with a chorus of cicadas in the burning heat of mid-afternoon. But he wasn't lounging at a table in the colonnades with a can of beer or a tray of tapas. Could've gone for a wander round the palace instead.

Turning down a sandy path, she passed through the carved Gothic gatehouse under the watchful eyes of a pair of wild stone men, their maces, shields and shaggy faces eroded by time, scanning the high, vaulted halls hung with vast, faded tapestries or tiled with orange monsters, white seahorses, blue birds and green foliage. But he wasn't there either. Where could he have got to?

By now she'd reached the old Moorish part of the palace, a maze of interconnecting patios and apartments. Suddenly through the long vista of horseshoe arches she glimpsed his familiar figure among the crowds of strangers thronging the Courtyard of the Dolls.

She stole closer, bent on taking him by surprise. Yes, that was him all right, absorbed in studying the elaborate stucco mouldings among the black, white and pink pillars. Those tatty old jeans, torn at the knees, and the loose T-shirt with a hole in one shoulder. Elinor smiled. The best thing about Jamie was that he never pretended to be anything he wasn't.

But just as she was reaching out to tap him on the shoulder, the young man turned enquiringly. Elinor recoiled in shock. Not him after all!

She tried to feign a keen interest in the stucco mouldings, then fled as quickly as she could. How embarrassing! She couldn't go round accosting strange young men on the off chance that they might be Jamie. Maybe he'd returned to the office meanwhile…

She was just on her way back through the exhibition when she caught sight of Andrés' wife, Maria. Her area of research expertise was the Spanish Civil War but she'd been helping out on the ticket desk that day, since she happened to be up in town. How did she manage to look so glamorous in that simple blue sheath dress?

Despite now being the mother of three young children, her figure was almost as slender as when she used to visit Andrés in London during her undergraduate days, while he was studying at the Courtauld.

"Ah, Elinor," Maria greeted her, light gleaming on the diamond droplets in her ears. "A young man – errr – has asked for you – thees afternoon."

"Yes, Andrés told me. Said he was looking at the exhibition – but I can't seem to find him anywhere."

"No. He has been here, but about – umm – fifteen minutes ago maybe, I see him to leave with his big bag. He go down these stairs." Maria pointed towards the exit.

Must've left the palace then. Still, no need to give up on him altogether. She could ring and see where he'd got to.

Quickening her pace, Elinor returned to the office, where she'd left her handbag, and discovered a text from Jamie on her phone. But it was a good couple of hours old by now and only told her that he was waiting for her in the office. She rang, but there was no response. Phone was probably switched off or dead, as usual.

"I suppose Jamie didn't tell you what he wanted?" she enquired of Andrés, who was regarding her with eyes of self-reproach.

"No. And I did not even think to ask, since he seemed intending to wait for you. I must apologise deeply, Elinor. I should have asked him to come to lunch with me…"

"Don't worry, Andrés. It doesn't matter – "

But even as the echo of her words still hung in the air, she was surprised to realise that, for some reason, it did. By now her curiosity was thoroughly piqued. She hated not getting to the bottom of little mysteries like this. Why had Jamie come looking for her? The time had come to apply logic to this business.

She cleared the folder, handbag and scarf off her chair and, seating herself at the desk, picked up the little mauve and green peacock. It was a sort of messenger – if only it could speak! She twirled it pensively in her fingers. As she did so, her eyes ranged over the orderly desktop in front of her: the bare metal in-tray, the darkened computer monitor, the black plastic desk tidy, the pile of mauve and green leaflets thrust aside, obviously to clear space to construct the peacock, her fan pencil… Her fan pencil!

Before leaving this morning, she'd set it down after making one or two corrections to her talk. But it was not where she'd left it, lying neatly in front of the desk tidy. It'd clearly been tossed aside in haste and rolled to the edge of the table, almost off into the wastepaper bin below. Who'd been using it? If Jamie had been sitting at her desk here, why would he have picked up a pencil? Probably to write something down. She looked round, but there was no sign of any note propped on the desk.

Then she noticed that the top drawer of the desk wasn't properly shut. If he'd opened that drawer, what had he been looking for?

She pulled open the drawer and gazed inside at the pile of scrap paper she'd accumulated since her arrival. It had clearly been disturbed. So that's where the paper had come from. But what had happened to the note? That he'd meant to write one was obvious. That he'd finished writing it was unlikely, since otherwise it would've been on the desk where she could easily find it. So if he hadn't completed it – or if he'd changed his mind and decided not to leave it after all, what would he have done with it? Taken it with him? Unlikely. Why bother carrying rubbish with you when there was a wastepaper bin right beside the desk?

Her eyes flew to the bin. It was emptied every morning. The only thing inside it now was a screwed up piece of paper. She fished it out and smoothed it down on the surface of the desk.

"Hi, Elinor," she read in Jamie's scrawling script. "Was passing through on the way to Almagro and thought I'd just drop by to take a look at the exhibition. Got something really interesting to show you. Are you coming to the play festival – ?"

That was all. At this point he'd clearly changed his mind about leaving a message, thrown down the pencil, screwed up the note and tossed it into the bin. Why? What was this 'something really interesting' he had to show her? Of course she had a complimentary ticket to *The Comedy of Errors* at the play festival in Almagro, but it had rather slipped her mind in the round of academic dinners, sight-seeing expeditions, museum visits and family celebrations with Andrés and Maria, their children, parents, aunts and various cousins at the country house up near El Pedroso. But this business about 'passing through'. You didn't 'pass through' Seville on the way from England to Almagro. The town was hours north of here, much closer to Madrid. Jamie had clearly made a special trip to visit her. Why? Just to see the fan exhibition?

She glanced across at Andrés' profile. He was busily occupied with his computer screen. No use bothering him. He'd told her all he knew. So she picked up Jamie's crumpled note along with her phone. Needed to think this through in private.

"I'm just going out into the garden for some fresh air," she murmured as she left the office.

She headed out the back way and downstairs into a small, paved courtyard with a scalloped marble fountain bowl at its centre. White roses and pale blue plumbago cascaded down the high walls, scenting the hot air till it was heady with their mingled perfumes.

Sitting down on an old stone bench in the shade of the colonnade, she switched on her phone. Still no message from Jamie. So where exactly was Almagro? Bit of a hike, she decided, consulting the web map. Two trains. Strictly speaking, she'd more than enough to keep her busy here in Seville. And where would she stay? If this was an international festival with a huge programme of plays, seminars and meetings in a smallish town, all the local hotels would probably be full to bursting.

She idly keyed Saturday's date into the search engine and scanned the results. 'Your date is very popular' flicked up in red on the screen. Nothing available with three stars. One or two beds at the youth hostel – didn't fancy that option! – and some at the parador of course. But that was a lot of money to spend for just one night at a play festival.

Of course she'd helped a bit with the grant application for *The Comedy of Errors* and met all the members of the cast, which did give her some personal connection with the company – but did she really want to throw herself in Adam's way? He might imagine she regretted what'd happened and was trying to stir up embers that'd never succeeded in igniting into a convincing blaze.

But then, even if she attended the play, would she necessarily encounter him in person? She'd just be one in a sea of audience – invisible to the actors on stage. And it'd be a chance to go and experience the whole festival, not just a single play. She could make a weekend of it and treat herself to a bit of fun for a change. But was it going to be fun all by herself?

Well, you had to start somewhere. She hadn't been at a festival since – well, since she and Paul went to that street party in Elizabeth Bay. What a ghastly afternoon that'd been. He and his Aussie mates with their girlfriends knocking back beers like troopers at long wooden trestle tables out in the sunny streets under strings of coloured flags, and herself sitting there trying to ignore the nauseating reek of bitter hops and pretend not to be a wet blanket, despite being the only one drinking lemonade.

Like a lightning flash, it had struck her mid-evening that she couldn't possibly spend the rest of her life in this country. To be sure, there was sun and sea and endless beach afternoons down at the marina while Paul, his shirtless dad and his freckled younger brother messed around refitting their ancient yacht. Fun for a holiday – but even the main museum in Sydney possessed only a single, tiny case of fans. Studying high resolution images on a computer screen just wasn't the same as being able to sit at a table, pull on a pair of white gloves and actually examine the tangible object set straight in front of you. Dad had been right all along.

She and Paul got on well enough together in London while she was studying at the Courtauld and he'd been training with an architectural firm in Fitzrovia. He'd been keen to try out new experiences – he was always easy-going and gregarious – so he'd fallen in readily enough with a life spent in a round of exhibitions, films, plays and visits to museums with Andrés, who was young and still a bachelor, and Ruth and her American college professor husband, over on sabbatical from Harvard. But looking back on it, Paul had never really cared for art or history or any of the things she loved with such a passion that she simply couldn't surrender them and still remain herself. Yet, as Cathy had pointed out, she would've tried harder to engineer a compromise for the sake of a man she really loved, wouldn't she? Life with Paul would never have worked out, even if she hadn't had to fly back home to be with Mum. Maybe she'd just been using Mum's illness as an excuse to escape all along… So perhaps now it was actually time, as Cathy advised, to bury her regrets for the past, stop wallowing in self-pity and start living for a change.

Jamie's unexpected visit held out the chance of a fresh start. One small step – but you never knew where it might lead.

She searched the parador website and booked herself a room for the coming weekend.

Chapter Twenty-Eight

The parador at Almagro stood near the centre of town in a restored sixteenth century monastery. In front of its ivy-clad, brick façade lay a cobbled courtyard with a rectangular water basin, while behind the main gate extended a labyrinth of cloisters and palm-shaded gardens.

After a delayed Friday morning train journey from Seville, Elinor wearily pushed open one of the heavy doors leading off a patio gallery to find herself standing in a large, shady room with a handsome beamed ceiling and cool terracotta floor tiles. Her eyes travelled gratefully around pale walls, adorned with a few tasteful prints and several pieces of fine antique furniture: a massive teak wardrobe, a pair of carved wooden chests and a great bed with a blue and yellow tiled head. What a treat to have such an elegant apartment all to herself for two whole nights! She at once set about bathing her flushed face and dusty hands in cold water and tidying her hair and scarf in the dressing table mirror.

By now it was nearly two o'clock. Definitely time for lunch.

Refreshed by deep lungfuls of delicious, orange-scented air floating up from the peaceful courtyard below, she headed back down the wide wooden staircase to the street outside and soon reached Plaza Mayor, the great main square of the town, which was thronged with bustling crowds. Bordered by colonnades of green windowed galleries and hung with bright flags and streaming pink festival banners, it looked a perfect stage-set in itself. Easy to imagine troupes of touring actors in the seventeenth century dismounting here to play in the taverns. Several posters caught her eye, advertising the *Noches Flamencas* that took place almost every night. Pity she didn't have anyone to go dancing with.

Seating herself at a café table in the welcome shade of a sun umbrella, she amused herself by surveying the passing tourists while waiting for lunch to appear. A family with a baby buggy and a tiny brown and white spaniel pup on a lead. A girl in a green striped T-shirt pausing to snap a photo of an elderly woman – her grandma? – with a flower-decked, floppy-brimmed hat. A tall young man in sunglasses, a pale pink shirt and beige chinos. Looked English with a straw boater tipped back on his head like that. Accompanying him was a leggy blonde in a stylish, white and turquoise-spotted sundress and a younger girl with a long, fair ponytail, wearing white, cut-off jeans and a hot pink crop top. Elinor idly watched them approach the table where she sat. The man with his easy stride and graceful gait reminded her a bit of Henry.

At that moment he raised his sunglasses and stared straight at her. She opened her eyes wide. Actually it *was* Henry!

"Hey there, Elinor," he called across to her. "What're you doing here?"

On closer inspection, the two girls with him turned out to be Cam and Bea, both flourishing brightly coloured fans. Elinor waved back and they all came strolling over to say hello. So much for maintaining a low profile in Almagro.

"Elinor! What a surprise," exclaimed Cam. "May we join you? I'm absolutely dying for a cool drink."

"Please do," Elinor said, politely indicating the metal chair opposite.

Henry and Bea dragged over two more from the table next door.

"Thought you were in Seville," went on Cam as she seated herself comfortably in the shade of the umbrella. "Wasn't that where you said you were going at our last dance lesson?"

"Yes, but now the fan exhibition's up and running, it seemed a shame not to do some sight-seeing while I'm in Spain. This festival here's so famous that I decided to travel up for the weekend to see for myself."

"Are you coming to the play this evening?" asked Bea, who was seated on her left, flirting her fan so conspicuously that it was clear she wished to draw attention to it. "It's opening night. We're all going to watch."

"Oh yes, you must, Elinor," urged Cam, languidly fanning herself with a showy red hand screen that perfectly matched the scarlet border on the flounces of her sundress. "Why not come along with us? I'm sure Henry can book another ticket."

"No need," replied Elinor with a smile. "I've got one already."

"Well, isn't it great meeting up like this? We simply must spend the afternoon together before going to the play tonight."

"So where're the others?" she asked, glancing round quickly. "Aren't they with you?"

"No fear." Cam laughed. "Too busy sleeping off yesterday's late-night dress rehearsal." Well that was a relief anyway! "They'll be heading straight to the theatre this evening for all those warmups and vocal exercises that actors engage in before a show. Then after it's over, we're planning to eat tapas at one of the restaurants round here and party till dawn. I've been meaning to say, what a beautiful scarf you're wearing. Is it new?"

"Not exactly," replied Elinor. How thrilling to possess an accessory admired by Camilla Quinn! "I've just been waiting for the right dress to wear it with."

She noticed Bea's eyes fixed upon it too. Had she seen it before?

"Certainly goes well with that red dress you're wearing," Cam commented. "Where'd you pick it up?"

"It was a present – from someone in England," murmured Elinor evasively. This was a bit awkward. Bea might even know who that someone was.

"In fact I'm really pleased we've bumped into you, Elinor," broke in Bea, gazing up into her face with a thoughtful smile. "There's something I've been wanting to say to you – about Great Aunt Rosita's fan."

"Yes?" prompted Elinor curiously.

"Well, first of all I wanted to thank you for all the time you've spent on repairing it. Jamie says it looks practically as good as new."

"It was nothing. Really. I was glad to do it. It has the most interesting history, besides being such a beautiful object in its own right."

Bea looked rather less convinced of its beauty than herself, but she went on anyway,

"I realise it's not just an ordinary fan. It's so fragile and it'd be such a shame if it got torn again, so I was wondering if the Lydgate might like to keep it."

"But it's a family heirloom," protested Elinor. "Surely you don't want to give it away?" She certainly wouldn't, if it'd belonged to her!

Bea looked concerned.

"Oh, I don't want you to think I'm not grateful for all the effort you've put into restoring it. But it just seems to me that it's so old, it might be better off in a museum, where it could be properly looked after and everyone could enjoy it. I feel sure Great Aunt Rosita would like that."

"That's very generous of you. Have you spoken to your parents about this?"

"Yes. In fact it was Mum who suggested it in the first place. But if you don't think the museum would want it…"

"It's not that at all! It'd be a really interesting and valuable addition to our collection of European fans."

"Then that's settled. Mum said she was sure you could advise me about how to donate it."

"Yes of course. Once I'm back in Cambridge, I can make the arrangements. Thank you so much – if you're absolutely sure that's what you want."

"Oh yes – quite sure. I've thought it over and what else could I do with it? Besides, Adam bought me a new one in a fan shop here yesterday." She held it out for Elinor to admire with a gesture of proprietorial satisfaction. So that's what all the fanning and flapping was about!

Bea's new fan had a black leaf edged with lace and bore a delicately painted scene of an old-fashioned garden with a gentleman in knee breeches and a long turquoise coat kneeling at the feet of a pale lady in a powdered wig and pink, hooped skirt.

"Isn't it lovely?" went on Bea happily. "I adored it the moment I set eyes on it."

"I'd always thought of them as dance accessories before," added Cam, "but in this heat, they're really quite useful, aren't they?"

Elinor nodded as she examined Bea's fan attentively and made a diplomatic comment about how pretty and carefully painted it was.

"There's this wonderful shop just round the corner," Bea enthused, clearly encouraged by her interest. "You might like to go and take a look inside, since I know how keen you are on fans. I can show you where it is."

Elinor thanked her non-committally. She didn't really care for modern tourist fans herself, but if Bea insisted, she could hardly refuse an offer so kindly meant.

Certain darting movements of Bea's eyes gave her the feeling that she was debating whether to say something else or not, but at this point Henry interrupted with observations about the lunch menu, so the topic of conversation suddenly turned to food. How disappointing! She'd been hoping Bea might allude to the mysterious surprise that Jamie apparently had for her. But she didn't like to ask straight out in front of the others. Perhaps she could manoeuvre the conversation back to the subject later…

They whiled away the blazingly hot afternoon in the shade of the restaurant umbrella, draining pitchers of iced water and fruity sangria and nibbling plates of tasty pinchos that Henry ordered with expert judgement. So many amusing stories were told about the house party at his father's golfing retreat near Alcazar de San Juan and the fun they'd all been having at the festival and in the swimming pool that Elinor felt almost envious.

It wasn't until the shadows were lengthening and the shops had re-opened that they all rose and made their leisurely way through the hot streets to the old theatre.

The translucent canvas awning, stretched across the open air courtyard to shade the early evening performance from the sun's scorching rays, was being drawn back as they arrived. Cam lamented that Elinor wasn't sitting with them down in the courtyard, but Elinor secretly preferred her perch on a hard wooden chair in the crowded upper gallery with its bird's eye view of the shallow red and white stage. It felt like stepping back in time into a real Shakespearean theatre among an audience restless with the buzz of conversation and the flutter of cooling fans.

The Comedy of Errors had been so long in preparation that Elinor could hardly remember the details of the funding application she'd help to draft and was keen to see the finished production. She expected Adam's performance to be proficient, since he was formally trained, but what about Jamie? He'd never struck her as a natural actor. Would he be any good? And did it matter if he wasn't?

Yet right from the moment of his first entrance, she could hardly take her eyes off him. Much as Adam made her laugh that evening, rocketing around the stage with astonishing vitality, it was Jamie's skill that delighted her more since it was so unexpected. Stunning to realise what an accomplished physical comedian he was – in fact, what a superb double act he and Adam made together. Their timing was impeccable. But where they found the energy to carry off both pairs of rôles she had no idea. As for remembering which part they were playing in which scene – how did they keep it all straight in their heads? She thought she would die laughing in the final scene when the double set of twins finally came together and the whole plot unravelled.

She clapped her palms sore at the end of the performance. Such a triumph for the tiny company to have managed to convey that complex plot of mistaken identities to an audience, many of whom couldn't even speak English. But the whole crowd was alive with laughter and the walls of the theatre rang with loud applause.

From her gallery seat, Elinor could see Bea on her feet, cheering wildly, her eyes riveted so intently upon Adam that it didn't take genius to work out that Hugo Channing-Jones had recently been superseded in her affections – or who'd taken his place. No wonder she'd been making such a play with the fan Adam had bought her earlier on that afternoon!

"Come on," urged Henry, materialising at the foot of the gallery steps with Cam and Bea to meet her when the show was over and the crowd beginning to disperse. "Weren't they just terrific? Let's go round and get them to sign our programmes!"

But Elinor felt shy. Bea, Henry and Cam were all justly proud of their family and friends: they had a right to share in the evening's success. But she wasn't anyone's sister or girlfriend. Just an outsider, who'd no real place in this celebration. She ought to slip off so as not to be in everyone's way in case she made matters awkward for Adam. But how to achieve this with least fuss?

Henry came unwittingly to her assistance when he suggested that what they most lacked at that point was champagne.

"You go on ahead," he urged the girls. "I'll just nip round the corner for a couple of celebratory bottles."

Here was her chance. It'd be much easier to make her excuses to guileless Henry, who wasn't entirely sober after all he'd drunk that afternoon, than Cam and Bea. So she offered to help carry the bottles. Up ahead, Bea and Cam were too busy exclaiming over the play's success to do more than cast a casual glance behind as they pressed forward to the stage door.

After Elinor had steered Henry safely back to the theatre, while he was striding confidently ahead with a bottle under each arm, she murmured something about being rather tired and needing an early night. Then she gradually allowed herself to fall behind until she was swallowed up among the swirling crowds…

*

Over the past two days, Jamie had been successfully postponing any form of rational thought because he was so involved in last minute dress rehearsals and various nail-biting emergencies, such as when Judi woke up this morning with a sore throat and almost lost her voice and Maxine's gown went missing after her suitcase failed to arrive at Madrid airport. But Judi gargled with lemon and honey, sucked eucalyptus throat lozenges and nursed her voice carefully all day long, while Maxine's suitcase showed up in a van at Alcazar de San Juan a full two hours ahead of the time for setting off to the theatre. Partying till dawn at Henry's father's holiday villa, as well as yesterday's late-night dress rehearsal in Almagro ensured that the pain of his futile trip to Seville was entirely dulled by alcohol consumption and sheer exhaustion.

But as he stood in the wings awaiting his first entrance that afternoon, suddenly it all seemed to catch up with him. He leant against a backstage beam hearing the familiar words of the opening scene and wondering what the hell he was doing here, decked out in this ridiculously hot and heavy costume of breeches and jerkin, preparing to act a double rôle in a five-hundred-year-old play written in barely comprehensible English to an international audience in Spain, who spoke God knew how many languages other than his own. Worse even than this, he'd been dreaming of dazzling Elinor with a masterly comic performance and she wasn't even here!

His gaze turned upon Adam standing at his elbow, his brow furrowed in earnest concentration and fidgeting fingers settling the leather money belt more snugly onto his hips, with his whole attention focused upon the job in hand. The smell of rope and wood and hot canvas was stifling and heat waves danced before Jamie's reeling eyes. Salty sweat beaded his top lip as Aegaeon's speech rose towards the well-known climax that heralded his first appearance. Any moment now, he'd be out on that stage…

Suddenly the gold of a woman's bright scarf flashed out from the gallery, momentarily illumined by a ray of the sinking sun. With an almost superhuman leap of inspiration, his dazzled mind grasped that it belonged to Elinor. She was seated out in that audience, wearing the Klimt scarf he'd given her! What did it mean?

At that moment Adam glanced up at him and must've noticed the agitation fermenting in his eyes, for without a moment's hesitation he hissed,

"Pull yourself together, Jamie-boy. It's your cue. Now get out there and act!"

In a split second Jamie knew the moment had come. With Adam right behind him, there was no choice. His mind strained taut as a bowstring as he launched himself onto the stage…

*

"Jesus, you had me worried for a moment there," Adam exclaimed when they were alone in the dressing room after it was all over. "Thought you were gonna keel over in a faint."

"You weren't the only one," admitted Jamie honestly, wiping the back of his sweaty neck with a damp towel. "Sorry to scare the hell out of you. All of a sudden everything seemed about to cave in on top of me like some sort of cosmic implosion."

"What a time to choose! Anyway, thank God you snapped out of it in time. Have to hand it to you, though – you certainly pulled it out of the bag tonight. I know I've said this to you before, but I really feel you've trained for the wrong profession with that Computer Science degree."

"Yeah, I've been having a few thoughts about that myself lately."

"Why not pack it all in and come to London? I'll be busy for the next couple of months touring with a children's theatre group, but after that I've got stacks of plans, including the Edinburgh Fringe next summer with the rest of the company…"

At this point they heard a racket of voices approaching the door and Cam and Bea came crowding into the room. But no sign of Elinor. Hadn't she been there after all?

"Great performance," exclaimed Cam, embracing her brother enthusiastically. "And Jamie – what a gift of comic timing! Congratulations both!"

"Oh Adam," cried Bea, her face alight with joy, flinging her arms round his neck. "I'm so proud."

Jamie turned aside. Didn't care to see them so happy together.

"Hurry up, Adam," Camilla broke in. "We all need a drink. It's been so hot out there despite bottles and bottles of water."

"Yes, and we want to get started on this evening's fun," added Bea.

"This evening's fun?" gasped Adam.

"Oh the play was just the beginning," went on Bea, her eyes bright with purpose. "Now you're coming out with us and after a drink or two, we're going to have dinner and then dance until dawn.

While you were asleep this morning, I was sussing out the trendiest bars and Flamenco clubs. I know just where I want to go."

"La belle dame sans merci," quoted Adam, twining his arms around her waist and dropping an indulgent kiss on her forehead.

At that moment Alan returned to the room in high spirits, flaunting Judi on one arm and Maxine on the other in their brightly coloured sundresses, chattering together like exotic parakeets. Congratulations broke out afresh. Maxine, who'd played opposite Jamie as Luciana, his wife, seemed to assume that he'd be tagging along with her this evening as usual.

But Jamie felt restless and expectant. He turned away his head from the din of voices. Where was Elinor? If she'd really been in the audience, surely she would've come backstage with the others, wouldn't she?

"What's happened to Henry?" he heard Adam ask, glancing round for him.

"Oh, he and Elinor just headed off for some champagne to toast your success," remarked Cam casually.

Jamie jerked up his head. So she wasn't just a figment of his longing. She really had been here after all! His sinking spirits suddenly revived. But wait on –

"She with anyone?" he demanded, not planning to make a prize fool of himself again.

"Not that I could see," Bea assured him with a shrug of unconcern. "She was wearing that scarf you gave her though." She turned instantly back to Adam and the general conversation.

Hope flashed up in Jamie's breast. He was half-suffocating – despite telling himself it meant nothing – even the scarf was not a sure sign. But he might see her at any moment. He turned to hide his face from public view and immersed himself shakily in makeup removal of the most exhaustive thoroughness. How should he act when she appeared? What had brought her to Almagro, apart from the strength of his longing to see her here?

There was a stir in the doorway. Jamie stared into the mirror straight in front of him. There stood the image of Henry with a bottle tucked snugly under either arm. Jamie half-started up from his seat.

"Henry," cried Camilla, advancing to greet him. "I was beginning to think I'd have to send out a search party. What took you so long?"

She approached to relieve him of the bottles and, as she did so, pulled him further into the dressing room. Jamie strained his eyes towards the reflected door frame, expecting Elinor to follow. But the door frame remained empty.

Cam noticed too, despite being busy commandeering all the plastic cups and chipped coffee mugs the dressing room could furnish.

"Hey – what's happened to Elinor?"

Henry scratched his forehead. "Search me, sweetheart. It's the darnedest thing. One moment she was at my elbow, saying something about being a bit tired. Then when I turned round, she'd vanished without trace. Scoured the nearby streets – that's why it took me so long to get here. Perhaps she's opted for an early night and headed off back to the parador…"

Chapter Twenty-Nine

Jamie sank back down on his chair, unnoticed amid the uproar of celebration. He retrieved the makeup wipe that'd dropped from his hand onto the wooden floorboards and went back to cleaning off his eyeshadow, all the time thinking hard, his heartbeat pounding in his ears.

Had Elinor gone home to bed, as Henry seemed to believe? Or was there some ulterior motive for her disappearance? Didn't seem as though anyone was with her, so was there someone she wanted to avoid?

"Come on, Jamie-boy," cried Adam, clapping him on the shoulder with a mug of champagne in his other hand. "It's party time. Why're you so slow tonight?"

Jamie glanced up. "Oh – no reason. You go on ahead. I'll catch you up later."

Adam studied his face intently for a moment and then turned away without further protest. He caught Bea's hand and pulled her along behind him, drawing after them the rest of the company, who flocked noisily towards the door brandishing their various tumblers of champagne. Jamie heard the echo of their voices and carefree laughter receding down the corridor until they finally died away in silence. So much for the party. Now it was up to him to settle this business once and for all.

He reached into his back pocket for his phone, which he'd finally got round to recharging. Wasn't difficult to locate the local parador. Knowing Elinor, if she was all by herself, he'd be sure to find her there, hiding like a mouse in its hole. She always needed a bomb under her to get her out enjoying herself – even at festival time.

He set off from the deserted theatre at a swift pace.

After reaching the parador gate, he was making his way to the desk to ask her room number when he happened to glance round the spacious hall and instead caught sight of her seated in a high-ceilinged lounge just off the reception area. Looked like she was immersed in reading one of the tourist brochures from the coffee table. AND SHE REALLY WAS WEARING HIS SCARF!

The babble of meaningless conversation around him receded, muffled and distant in his ears. He drew a deep breath and, without announcing himself, slid noiselessly down onto the green damask sofa nearby, his eyes caressing the outline of her form.

"Thought I'd find you here," he observed lightly, leaning back against the firm cushions with his hands thrust deep inside his jeans pockets to stop them trembling.

Elinor raised her head from the magazine with a glance of enquiry from those dark blue eyes of hers that turned his limbs to water.

"Jamie," she exclaimed. "What a surprise! I thought you'd be out partying with your friends."

"Not yet. They said you'd been at the play tonight."

"And I must tell you how much I enjoyed your performance. I'd no idea you were such an accomplished comedian."

Jamie acknowledged the compliment with a brief nod. She loved to laugh, so it was no small thing to have impressed her in that way at least, even if he was hopelessly inadequate in every other. But at present he wasn't much interested in how she felt about his play acting. Did she sound very slightly on edge?

"I've been hoping to catch up with you in Spain – so I could show you this," he went on, drawing the wallet out of his back pocket.

"Ah yes, the mysterious 'something interesting' you've found. I've been so curious about it."

"There was a note enclosed with Bea's fan," he told her, fishing out the piece of yellowed paper and holding it up.

A frown of perplexity creased Elinor's brow as she glanced towards it.

"But I checked the case carefully when you first brought it to me. It was empty," she pointed out.

"Yeah, it was by the time I brought it to you. But the other day Mum was doing some spring-cleaning and we found this under the sofa. I reckon it fell out when Adam and I were fooling around the afternoon I first saw the fan."

"So what does it say?" Elinor eagerly reached for the note.

"Doesn't mean much to me, but I wondered whether it might help you work out who originally owned the fan. There's an old family story my mother told me months ago about how it was presented to one of our ancestors by a famous actress. But all the note says is that it was a treasured gift from someone called Lavinia F."

"Lavinia F?" exclaimed Elinor, her eyes brightening as she scanned the piece of paper.

"Yeah – you know who she was?"

"I'll bet it's Lavinia Fenton! My brother told me all about her. She was the unknown actress who played Polly Peachum in the original cast. She shot to stardom practically overnight till all London was full of prints of her in the rôle. She was mobbed and idolised and courted by all the young men – and at the end of the play's first season she ran off with the Duke of Bolton, who'd attended practically every performance. He's sitting on the stage in one of Hogarth's paintings of the scene. I saw him in Cathy's book. It's a real rags to riches love story, stranger than fiction, since the Duke eventually married her and made her a duchess."

"No kidding? Now you mention it, I remember Mum telling me that the actress ran off with someone who made her a titled lady."

"How wonderful! And what an interesting addition that'll make to my research. Do you mind if I keep this for the present?" indicating the piece of paper.

"No, go ahead. Belongs with the fan anyway."

"So your great-great-great uncle must've brought the fan from London back to Spain with him –"

"And after all those years, it finally travelled back to London again with my great-grandmother, when she emigrated with her

English husband after the Spanish Civil War. He met her while he was fighting with the Republicans."

Elinor breathed a sigh.

"What a strange story it is. I feel as though I've been on a journey through time and history with that fan. There's so much to write about. I can't wait to start my paper as soon as I get home on Monday." She paused a moment, then added, "I guess you'll be heading back yourself when the play's over. Managed to secure a full-time job at 3-D Imaging yet?"

"I'm not looking for a full-time job at 3-D Imaging," announced Jamie firmly, feeling this was the moment to declare his future plans so she knew precisely how matters stood. "I've changed my mind about what I want to do."

Elinor raised her eyebrows.

"Well, that's not exactly a surprise, is it? I never felt your heart was in computer science. I suppose it's the drama festival here in Almagro that's made you reconsider. It's a really heady atmosphere... So – you're planning to throw in your computer mouse for the grease paint and bright lights of the theatre, are you?"

Jamie stared at her blankly for a moment.

"Not at all," he protested, realising her mistake. "Never thought of acting as a profession for myself. It's a risky business. Of course I wouldn't say no to another show like this, but in the long run I'd rather stay strictly amateur at that game."

Elinor looked puzzled.

"Well, what are you planning to do with yourself then?" she enquired at last.

"Learn how to make fans."

"Make fans?" She looked bewildered. "As a career? Jamie, you can't be serious."

Great start! How was he ever going to win her round to seeing him as a potential lover, if he couldn't even manage to convince her of his strength of purpose concerning his chosen vocation?

"Yes I am," he asserted stubbornly.

"And you won't go into acting because it's a risky business! Jamie, be practical for once. You can't earn a living out of making fans these days. The only people who buy them are tourists like Bea and Cam, who flap mass-produced ones for five minutes until they break, then throw them into the bin."

"How about collectors and museums?"

"Yes, but mostly they're not looking for new fans."

"I know. That's why I'm planning to learn all about restoration techniques as well." He had to make her understand that this was not some idle whim: this was where he'd been heading all along. "Look, Elinor, it's been bugging me for years what to do with myself when I grew up, what I was really fitted for. There were a whole lot of hobbies I enjoyed – like making kites and model aeroplanes and origami birds. But it wasn't till my mother tipped that pile of Great Aunt Rosita's junk into my lap and the old fan fell out on the sofa that I started to realise what it all meant. Up till then I'd just played at all kinds of crafts without having any greater sense of purpose. But after looking at the pictures in your book and, even more, when I brought the fan to you and we started work on it together… well, I knew then that this was really what I wanted to do with my life."

Elinor was listening, but she still looked sceptical.

"If you're really going to take a big step like this," she began, "I think you ought to go to the Fan Museum in London and consult Aurélie."

"Yeah, that's what I decided myself. So I went to see her. You remember – the day your Uncle Fabian offered me that job?"

"Of course!"

She looked as though she'd just put two and two together.

"I've been down to Shere a couple of times now," he told her. "There's a bit of restoration work to do on the collection there as well as the digitising, you know. But I'm pretty sure I can dovetail that in with the rest of my plans."

"The rest of your plans?"

"Oh yeah, it's all settled. Aurélie's been absolutely ace! You should see the list of contacts she's compiled and the research she's done on courses and clients' websites."

"She would." Elinor smiled with gentle affection.

"And that's not all. The best thing is that she's put me in back in touch with Peter Mowbray. He's been so kind – and Susan as well."

"They're all the same, these fan people, aren't they? – energetic and incurably enthusiastic. So what's the plan then?"

She was starting to come round. It made him feel more confident about the rest of his schemes.

"Well, Peter and Susan have offered me the use of one of the old worker's cottages on the farm to live in while I'm learning on the job. It needs a bit of renovation – well, more than a bit actually," recalling the damp patches on the walls, the cracked ceilings, antiquated plumbing and limited electricity. "But Dad reckons that with a few weekends' hard work, he and I can make it pretty snug and weatherproof. I'm gonna keep on part-time at 3-D Imaging till I've paid off a good chunk of my student loan and then gradually take over more of the business, so it'll free up Peter and Susan to pay more visits to their sons and grandchildren."

Elinor regarded him seriously for a moment.

"You're really looking forward to this, aren't you?"

"You know, I am – and it's a great feeling," he replied, leaning forward and clasping his two hands firmly in front of him. "Not something I'd ever have imagined even six months ago. A goal makes all the difference: knowing what you want and being in control of your own destiny. So I'd just like to say thanks, Elinor, for helping me change my life. Before I met you, I'd no direction, no motivation, no future – and now I know exactly where I'm going. Because of you, I don't need to hide from things anymore. I've gained the confidence and courage to stop wearing masks. So what you're seeing now is my real face and I'll never forget that you helped me find it."

And he reached out his hands towards her, full of gratitude and love.

Elinor gazed back at him – and there were tears glistening in her eyes! She put her hands into his and replied in a low voice that caught in her throat.

"You give me too much credit, Jamie. I might've helped a little, but this is all your own doing. Honestly I can't believe you're the same person that walked into my office such a short time ago, ill and gaunt as a scarecrow… Oh, it's all too much – I think I'm going to cry…" She bent her head, struggling to master her tears.

Jamie wanted her to look at him. So he raised her chin with a gentle finger so her brimming eyes were level with his.

"Great scarf," he commented drily. "Get it from anyone I know? Suits you, like that red dress you're wearing. Hey, you with anyone tonight?"

Elinor swallowed hard and shook her head, dislodging the warm drops so that they splashed down onto the backs of his hands.

"Andrés not fancy a weekend at the play festival?" he went on, his voice husky inside his dry mouth.

She stared at him in momentary non-comprehension until a fresh light of understanding dawned in her eyes.

"Why no, as it happens," she replied demurely. "He usually spends weekends with his wife and their three small children, his in-laws and an assortment of distant cousins up at their family place in El Pedroso." Was she teasing him? "He wanted to come along for company, but I was sure Maria would need him at home. So I told him he mustn't disarrange their plans for my sake and came all by myself."

So much for Andrés then! Jamie breathed a silent sigh of relief.

"Had dinner yet?" he asked.

Elinor shook her head.

"Me neither. Can't face food before I go on stage, so at the moment I'm starving. But after we've had something to eat, dunno if you noticed, there's one of those *Noches Flamencas* things out in the main square tonight."

"Yes, I saw a poster this morning."

"Fancy coming out dancing with me?"

Elinor's eyes smiled through the traces of her tears.

"I thought you'd never ask," she said.

Chapter Thirty

Marisa opened her eyes suddenly, alerted by a sixth sense to the faint sounds of someone moving around the silent house in the grey dawn light. What time was it? Instinctively she turned her head to check the alarm clock on her bedside table. Shortly before five. She lay for a moment listening to stealthy footsteps in the downstairs hallway and the tell-tale creak of the loose tread as whoever it was began creeping cautiously upstairs.

She sat bolt upright. In the dimness of the drawn curtains she turned towards Graham. Should she wake him? But he was breathing with peaceful regularity, sound asleep in the cocooning warmth of the double bed, his arm curled underneath his head. Hadn't had a text, but could it possibly be – ? Better check for herself.

Swiftly she pushed back the bedclothes and swung her legs to the floor, shuffling on her slippers. Then she rose from the bed and, unhooking her dressing gown from the back of the door and pulling it round her, stole out into the hallway. She waited for a moment, hearing the door at the end of the hall scrape softly closed over the carpet, then tiptoed along the passage and paused outside for a moment before pushing it quickly open.

A dark-haired young man stood with his back to her, bending over a rucksack and pulling the straps undone. He wheeled round in alarm.

"Mum," he exclaimed, falling back in relief at the sight of her. "Why the hell did you creep up on me like that? You almost gave me a heart attack."

"I might say the same to you," returned Marisa, advancing into the room and pushing the door closed so as not to wake the rest of the household. "Why are you home so early? We thought you'd be staying longer in Spain."

"I know. Changed my mind. Decided to come back as soon as the play was finished."

"Been overdoing it at the house party? You're looking rather rough."

"So would you if you'd spent the last couple of nights on trains. Sorry I woke you – I was trying to be as quiet as I could."

"Never mind. It's after five. I was half-awake anyway. Not get much sleep on the journey? Those are pretty impressive bags under your eyes. Why not close the curtains now and climb into bed? The boys' term ended a couple of days ago so they're not rising early and you might be able to catch up on a bit of sleep."

"Sounds great. I feel dead beat. But you'll wake me up in a couple of hours, won't you? – before you head off to work."

"Doesn't matter if you stay in bed all day, does it?"

"Yes it does. I've gotta get into town early."

"Into town? What for?"

"To see Ellie. She left Spain on Monday and I haven't set eyes on her for three whole days."

So that was the reason for his prompt return!

Marisa raised her eyebrows slightly and smiled to herself. So she was 'Ellie' now, was she?

"I see," she remarked shortly. "I suppose I don't get to hear any more about it than that?"

Jamie considered for a moment, then added, "Nothing much to tell. Ellie came to the opening night of the play at Almagro. We went out dancing together afterwards. It's gone on from there."

She met his eye and smiled again – more broadly this time.

"Oh, I see. Just an ordinary old love story. Boring!" The quotation tripped provocatively off her tongue.

"Mum, how can you say that?" he blurted out, then stopped, clearly recollecting his own words on the day he first saw the mask fan. He bit his lip. "Well, there's no need to rub it in. You mothers! All you care about is gossip and match-making."

"It's so hard to be right all the time," she taunted, then, feeling she'd exulted over him enough for the present, "You go to bed, Jamie. I promise to wake you up before I go to work."

"Thanks, Mum," Jamie called after her as she left the room.

Marisa thoughtfully descended the stairs and busied herself with a number of household tasks, but when she duly returned to call him at eight o'clock, his bed was empty and she could hear the shower spurting behind the closed bathroom door. Matters must be serious.

"That Jamie home from Spain?" enquired Graham, as he wandered into the kitchen five minutes later, bleary-eyed and still in his dressing gown with his hair sticking up on end.

"Yes – he arrived back early this morning," Marisa replied, stacking hot toast onto a plate.

"He's not due at work today, is he?" he asked, pouring hot coffee into mugs and staring through the kitchen window as if in search of something.

"No." She glanced up, noting the direction of his gaze. "It's not raining, is it? I've just finished hanging the washing out."

"No. Just wondering if I could see any pigs flying by."

"Pigs?"

"Well, what's with all this leaping out of bed before eight o'clock in the morning and barricading himself into the bathroom?"

"He's off to town," Marisa replied, clicking her tongue in a show of mock petulance as she clattered plates onto the breakfast table.

"Off to town? Before noon? What's in town?"

"Elinor Mitford. They seem to have become an item in Spain."

"An item? You mean, Elinor Mitford – the fan lady? She out of her mind? Isn't she a bit on the intellectual side for our Jamie?"

"I think they're very well suited myself. She's got the academic rigour – he's got the skilled pair of hands. They make a good team."

"Like you and me?"

"Like you and me," smiled Marisa, brushing his lips with an affectionate kiss as he fetched the jam and they both sat down together.

"Hi, Dad," Jamie greeted him, swooping through the kitchen door like a ravening hawk in search of prey and pouncing on the slice of toast that his father had just buttered.

"Hello, Jamie. Good to see you in such high spirits. Any chance of using the bathroom for two minutes during the next half hour?"

"Sure thing! I'm done anyway." Jamie paused long enough to pour himself an orange juice and down it in one gulp. "So long then – dunno when I'll be back tonight. Don't wait up!" He disappeared into the hall like a whirlwind and a moment later they heard the front door bang behind him.

"Don't think museums open this early in the morning," remarked Graham, phlegmatically buttering himself another slice of toast.

"I expect he'll find that out for himself," replied Marisa, picking up her coffee mug and wondering why she all of a sudden felt so bereft.

"One thing I'll say for him, he can certainly put on a bit of speed when he sets his mind to it."

She made no answer. Graham glanced up from his toast and she caught him surveying her face as she sat soberly sipping her coffee.

"It's all right, you know," he reassured her. "He's like the proverbial bad penny. He'll turn up again later on tonight and devour all the dinner left-overs in the fridge."

"I know – it's just that…"

She screwed up her face. It was hard to explain.

"Just that what?" prompted Graham.

"Well, with him going to live part of the week with the Mowbrays in Suffolk soon and all this Elinor business – I feel as though I'm losing him. And then Bea'll be heading off to music college this September. All my little birds are flying the nest."

"Yes, but that's the purpose of having children in the first place, isn't it? To fit them to grow up and take their place in the world." Graham reached out to stroke her hand gently. "Cheer up, you've still got me."

"I know. That's what I'm afraid of!"

All of a sudden there was a loud outcry, then a thunder of feet on the stairs. Geoff shot into the kitchen with Marc right on his tail. They were squabbling at full throttle.

"Hey, Mum! He says he ate the last two Weetabix in the packet yesterday and I was saving them for breakfast this morning."

"Well, I was starvin'. How should I know he wanted them? Didn' have a label on them, did they?"

"Boys, really – !"

"Hey, Dad, that toast looks good." Geoff hung suggestively over his plate, while Marc crowded round behind.

"Mmmm. Thought I could smell that warm bread smell driftin' up the stairs. C'n I've some?"

"Me too?"

Graham slapped both sets of marauding fingers smartly and leant over his plate, snarling like a guard dog.

"I've already lost one piece of toast this morning and I'm prepared to defend this one to the death. Any takers?"

They both drew back warily before his fierce face.

"You'll make us some, won't you, Mum?" Geoff appealed persuasively.

"Got any more of that ace raspberry jam?" demanded Marc, plonking himself down in his seat opposite.

Marisa exchanged an expressive glance with Graham and rose from her chair.

"Looks like I haven't quite outgrown motherhood yet," she commented wryly as she went to slice up the rest of the loaf and switch the toaster back on.

*

When Jamie arrived outside the Lydgate Museum, planning to surprise Ellie with his unexpected return from Spain, he found the great double doors firmly shut. He strode once around the block cheerfully enough, but when he came back, they still hadn't budged. How strange. Hadn't ever seen the place closed in the morning. Maybe he should take a look at the opening hours on that sign fixed to the railings. He studied the information in disbelief. Not open till ten! That was forty minutes from now. What was wrong with these slackers?

He glanced up the road. Perhaps he should nip up to Ellie's place and knock on her front door. He started off, but halted before he'd gone five metres. Imagine sitting at the breakfast table with her dad on the other side! No. Better go and buy himself a coffee at that café over the road instead.

He sat in the window with a hot coffee, devouring a couple of enormous almond croissants for good measure, fingering his phone, which had run out of charge, as usual, and wondering what time Ellie usually showed up for work. Surprising how little he really knew about her life, when he came to think about it. Wanted to know everything: what time she got up on a work day morning, what type of soap she used in the shower, what sort of tea she drank for breakfast... The list went on and on. He was only at the start of a long voyage of discovery.

His mind relived their brief weekend in Almagro. Every detail was stamped into his memory by repeated rehearsal throughout those endless hours on trains speeding homewards through Spain and France. He and Ellie gorging themselves on bowls of spicy patatas bravas, sizzling garlic prawns and salty fried haloumi until they could eat no more. He and Ellie dancing among the jostling crowds in the main square. The flash and swirl of bright flamenco skirts, the clapping hands, the drumming heels, the throbbing strings of a borrowed guitar that he played while Ellie danced in a late night, back street café. How she danced! In such an abandonment of passion and joy. The darkness of the night enveloping them like a soft mantle as they wandered hand in hand through the silent streets. A perfectly round, golden moon sailing serenely in the dark sky above the palms and orange trees, rustling gently in the welcome breeze that sprang up over the panting earth after the heat of the day was past. Himself trembling so violently he could hardly carry her off to bed. Then the slow thrill of realisation on opening his eyes in the morning among strange, soft sheets and smelling the fresh, clean perfume of her tangled hair on the pillow beside him. The piercing agony of saying goodbye at the station when she caught the train back to Seville on Sunday afternoon, terrified he'd never see her again. These were things he could never forget...

All of a sudden he realised beads of hot sweat were standing out on his forehead. He gulped and shook himself, glancing hastily across at the museum. The massive, studded front doors finally stood open and he hadn't even noticed! He hastily gulped down the remainder of his lukewarm coffee, grabbed his battered old rucksack and headed across the road.

Swiftly bounding up the front stairs two at a time, he swung in through the revolving glass door and headed straight for the private entrance to the offices and conservation rooms, whistling to himself.

There he found his way barred by the sturdy, tattooed arm of one of the two burly custodians, who a moment ago had been standing at the foot of the sweeping staircase discussing the recent display of English batting in the test at Lords.

"Just a moment, young man," exclaimed the owner of the blue snake with the beady red eye, Fred Baxter, who was the taller of the two, exchanging a significant glance with his colleague over what lads thought they could get away with nowadays. "Afraid I'll have to trouble you for a glance inside that rucksack."

Jamie stopped in his tracks and returned to the desk, watching Fred rifling through his belongings with some anxiety in case he mishandled the contents.

"Don't believe in keeping things too tidy in there, do you?" Fred joked cheekily. "Who you off to see then?"

"Ellie. Errr – Dr Mitford."

"Got an appointment?"

"Not exactly – but I have something for her."

"Likely you have. Let's hope it's something she wants to see. Been here before then?"

"Yeah. In fact I'm pretty sure it was you who showed me the way to her office the first time."

Fred eyed him up and down.

"Well, I don't recognise you," he concluded bluntly.

"No, you wouldn't – I look completely different."

"Know where you're going then, or need someone to show you the way?"

"No thanks, I know exactly where I'm going," replied Jamie, gathering up his rucksack, his good humour unassailable.

He passed swiftly through the heavy fire doors and down the familiar twilit corridor, whistling under his breath and only breaking off to throw a cheerful "Morning, Professor Chadwick!" in the direction of the coin curator, as he caught sight of him outside the office next to Ellie's in an academic huddle with a stout man sporting a bushy walrus moustache. He knocked so boldly on her door that it raised echoes along the corridor, undoubtedly disturbing the earwigs and silver fish in several bookcases.

Professor Chadwick glanced up in surprise.

"Wh-who's th-that b-boy?" he stammered in an undertone, twitching with alarm.

His companion shrugged his shoulders with his thumbs in the pockets of a capacious, red-and-yellow-flowered waistcoat. "These research students are getting younger and younger – just like policemen." And he chuckled fatly, rubbing his hands together at the sprightliness of this witticism.

Jamie didn't stop to exchange pleasantries before barging into Ellie's office and shutting the door firmly behind him.

But inside the office, he came face to face with Dr Mitford, who was seated writing behind the desk. As soon as she saw him, she sprang to her feet, looking as though she didn't quite believe the evidence of her own eyes.

"Jamie! I didn't expect you till tonight," she cried, a deep blush of confusion reddening her cheeks.

"No. Thought I couldn't get back any quicker either. But as soon as we'd taken the final curtain call, I threw the last odds and ends into my rucksack and, while everyone else was celebrating at the party, headed straight for the station. I managed to catch the last train to Madrid, so I came through France with the night mail. Couldn't wait to see you any longer than I had to."

Her face lit up and she was Ellie again.

"I'd been wondering if it was all just a dream," she cried.

"No, the nightmare's real enough!"

Ellie laughed and flew to welcome him as he sprang to enfold her in his arms.

"But you don't look as though you've come straight from the train station," she murmured a moment later.

"No, I stopped off at home for a shower and a change of clothes. Mmmm, you taste sensational."

"Jamie! What if someone were to come in and see you with your hands up my skirt? Stop it at once, do you hear?"

But he could tell she was only pushing him away half-heartedly.

"Suppose you're right. You usually are," he remarked, desisting for the moment and pulling off his rucksack. "Hey, I've brought you Esther's fan. What d'you think of it?" and he flipped open the rucksack's broken straps, pulled out a carefully wrapped packet and handed it to her with a flourish, like a conjuror producing a rabbit out of a top hat.

Ellie undid the wrappings, opened the box and spread the fan wide. She looked up at him with shining eyes.

"Oh Jamie! It's perfectly beautiful. Just like new. Esther will be so pleased. I'll give her a ring this minute – "

"Hold on a bit," warned Jamie, beaming with pride at her admiration of his skill. "First I've got something for you. A present from Spain. Took me absolute ages to find. I was strolling around between performances on the last night of the play and decided you should have a real Spanish fan. So I went into that shop in the main square – you know, the one where Adam bought Bea hers?"

"Jamie, I hope you didn't spend a lot of money on an expensive fan from there."

"No, that's the best of it. Sifted through practically everything in the shop. But…"

"But what?"

"Well… There were one or two I quite liked – but I really couldn't pay that sort of money for them. And the ones I could afford were so tacky, I couldn't possibly give them to you."

"So you didn't buy one?"

Jamie shook his head.

"I'm so relieved," she murmured. "Bea's fan was very pretty – but it's just a stage prop, not a real fan. Those shops are fine for tourists but –"

"Exactly what I decided. So then I had this brilliant idea. I asked them if there were any junk shops in Almagro."

"And were there?"

"Never found out 'cos they couldn't manage to work out what I was asking. Didn't know the Spanish word for 'junk'. But while I was wandering around near the train station in Madrid searching for something to eat, I came upon this little, old shop in a back alley and right there in the dusty window display, along with the moth-eaten mantillas and cracked mirrors, I saw just what I was looking for."

"I'm intrigued. Exactly what kind of fan is this?"

"Oh it's gloriously beautiful! As soon as I saw it, I knew you had to have it. Sticks are ebony, I'm sure, and the painting's so delicate, and best of all, it was going for an absolute song."

"I think you'd better show it to me."

"Of course – it's right here." Jamie reached into his rucksack and extracted something with the greatest care. It was bundled up in an ordinary brown paper bag. "Afraid it didn't come in an old box like

Great Aunt Rosita's fan, but then you can't expect miracles," he went on, unwrapping it gently and holding it out to her in a glow of enthusiasm.

Ellie took one look at it and burst out laughing. In fact she laughed so uproariously that tears sprang to her eyes and Jamie began to bristle with annoyance.

"Well, if you don't like it, you only need to say. I'm not going to force it on you."

"You idiot, it's magnificent!"

"Then why're you laughing fit to burst?"

"Because it suddenly struck me that only you'd bring home something that looked like that and say it was beautiful."

"Well, it is – what's wrong with it?" demanded Jamie, regarding the fan in genuine puzzlement.

"It's only got a broken guard and a torn leaf and it's filthy dirty and looks like it needs about three months' work on the sticks alone."

"Oh that! That's nothing. I'll fix it up myself."

"Is this a present for me? – or for yourself?"

"Well – both, I suppose," he was reluctantly forced to admit. "Anyway, just look at that carving – it's so fine and precise – and the painting on the front leaf. What d'you think's going on in the picture? Looks like a lake with mountains in the background – but what's that circle of people doing at the front? Do you think they're playing some kind of game?"

"Looks like ring-a-ring o' roses or something."

"Do you think it's some kind of Spanish dance?"

"Well, we ought to try very carefully prising apart those folds that are stuck together and see if there's any date or signature. Besides, just because you bought it in Spain, it doesn't mean it's a Spanish fan. You know what happened last time..."

THE END